AF506932

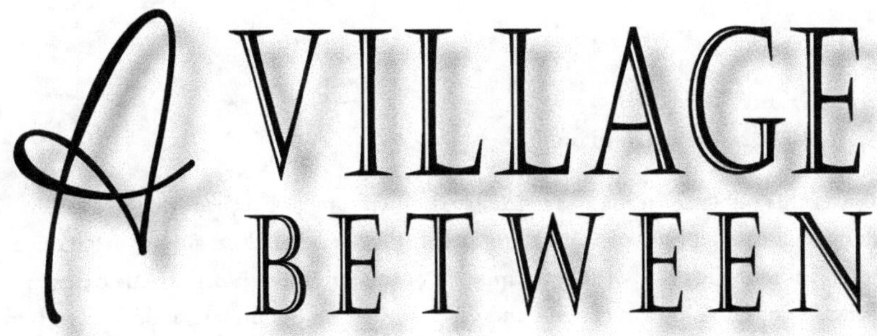

PART ONE

DANA ROTHKOP

NVISION US

CONTENTS

To my parents, who so fortuitously,
brought us here.

PART ONE

CHAPTER 1

Gabe

It's not the sirens that wake me; it's the relentless cawing of ravens. Mustn't have slept more than a couple of hours, but I feel immediately focused anyway, remarkably aware; maybe it's the lack of sleep itself that keeps you from total immersion. I lie silently, the indentation in the mattress beside me already cool to my touch as I slide my hand across Emily's side, flatten out the turned back sheet and check the clock on her bedside table... it's 6:46 and she is up already. I fling off the sheet and blanket which are replaced by a creeping film of anxiety; it sinks into my belly and spreads its uncertainty, tensing muscles and awakening nerve ends while the cool air raises goose bumps on my arms. The siren sound is off in the distance; maybe still on the other side of the lake, can't tell if it's coming or going; sound carries clearly across that stretch of water, but distance and direction get confused. The ravens, they're nearby for sure.

I rise and step into the same stained jeans I'd been wearing last night. They're still damp. My tee shirt and sweat shirt lie at the foot of the bed- still joined- arms aligned, where I'd dropped them. I cover up, pulling them on in one smooth motion. I step over to the window and look out over the trees that obscure the lake off in the near distance to the North. Yeah, the ravens are circling alright, not just here near the house, but off in the distance, above the tracks alongside the lake shore, not just the usual four or six who pick through the compost every day, no, ... must be at least thirty, circling in several groups at different heights, cawing and cackling louder than kids on Christmas morning.

I hear her footsteps on the stairs before her voice. "Gabe… you up?

"Be right there." I say, moving toward the bathroom, then add, "see what? What's all the racket?"

She ignores my questions, whispering loudly, urgently, "Don't wake the boys Gabe. Just come down."

I splash some water over my face, run a toothbrush around in my mouth and scrub some of the dirt out from under my stubby nails.

Downstairs, Emily's got a cup of coffee already waiting. She's in front of her computer at the desk under the stairs between the kitchen and living room, back to me, the slender line of her neck visible under the bundle of auburn hair tied up on her head trying to escape the elastics.

"There's already four updates on the community email, Gabe and it's not even seven a.m. yet. A train has derailed. Pearl called too. She's worried about the bird life."

I pick up my coffee cup from the counter and stare into the steam, sip deeply, then peer over her shoulder at the email headline: "Canadian Pacific Rail disaster." I make out a few sentences beneath.

"Bird life? What…? Whoa… they're really on this. Who's updating at this time of day I wonder? Must be serious."

"Locals. This one's from Ernie, trying to sound official." She answers, she gets up, turning her head to mine for a morning kiss. Then she grabs a sweater from the hooks and pulls it on, head popping out, eyes bright, energized, looking over at me.

"Looks like you need a minute," she smiles. Stepping close, she runs her parted fingers through my tangled hair, pausing to disengage a couple of knots before smoothing it down to my shoulders, squeezing taught, rope-like muscle along my neck then arms until her fingers are wrapped round mine.

Ernie says, "They think it happened sometime after 3:00 a.m. No details. Let's go see, come on. The boys can sleep another hour." She says, bent over by the door lacing up her runners already. "'kay, okay, let me get my boots on." I say, "sounds like the fire department is on the way. Is there a fire?"

"Don't know Gabe, but the first email, the one from Ernie, mentions an ambulance leaving the scene already. Could be that's what we're hearing."

"Oh, shit, people are hurt then." I say, following her.

"I guess." She says, "I think I woke up when the second one came. Ernie mentioned it was an explosive hissing sound that woke him and Sandra, but they live right by the tracks… look… she says, pointing East toward the end of the road as we step out onto the verandah, "looks like steam or smoke still rising."

"Holy shit. What a cloud," I say, "sounds like there's a chopper coming." I look off in the direction where the sound is coming from, West toward Nelson, but I can't see it, just more ravens.

We're met by the brisk spring air as we walk along, fast paced, along the path then down our gravel driveway to the main road below, her long legs easily keeping pace with mine. We can hear a truck or machine driving along before we get to the road and that one is followed by another. They seem to be in a hurry. The chopper has now passed us by and is circling not that high off the ground, in the distance. From the sounds of it the action is not far ahead, just down toward the end of the highway where the asphalt turns to gravel. We see a few parked cars and trucks there. A few people are there already, some walking up to get closer while others stay back, eyes trained skyward toward the rising cloud that Emily had spotted earlier.

"I can smell it." Emily says, glancing over at me for confirmation, wrinkling her nose. "Wonder what that is?"

"Smells chemical to me." I say, "not so much like smoke.

Could be toxic."

As we approach, we see Drake there, standing off to the side of the road, his solid form unmoving like a tree trunk till we step up. He turns to greet us and motions with his arm for us to stand aside as a white pickup pulls in past us and speeds up the road. A firetruck pulls over the hill not far behind him, siren off now, they use a horn blast to alert everyone to stay clear as they move through.

Drake says, "Hey Gabe, Emily, not sure if we should be here. Seems like lots of fumes rising from that spill. That's some nasty stuff flowing out down there."

"Hey Drake." I say, Emily nods to him. A couple more cars show up and stop, pulling over to the shoulder to get out of the way as a red first responder truck comes up too quick, then a green Ministry of Environment truck behind that. They speed up once they pass the congestion and disappear over the small rise ahead. Seems they are stopping not much further up the road. I feel like I need to see for myself what is going on up there, but no one is moving ahead.

I turn to Emily, "Em. Let's get a little closer and have a look." I move off ahead and she follows. Drake says, "Wouldn't go too far up there if I were you. I saw the stuff coming out of those tanker cars and it ain't pretty."

"Okay, Drake… just going to get a quick look." I say over my shoulder. "Be right back."

Two more pickups drive by as we walk along the shoulder– yellow Canadian Pacific trucks this time. A guy has his hand out of the window as they move past as though signaling us to stop, but they don't stop. I follow their lead and don't stop either trying to fit in to the flow and confusion; Emily stays by my side. We move ahead unnoticed.

Just ahead on top of the rise we can see part of the chaos; the tracks are visible alongside the road ahead. We can see along beyond where the road turns and crosses over the tracks, right before a straight stretch in the line, which is now interrupted by a tangled mess of steel, steam, and water. Much of the train is obscured by a curve in the distance. Looks like part of it at least is still on the tracks, but most of the cars we can see in the foreground are turned over and are either toppled onto their side, or in the case of the engine in front, turned almost completely upside down. The engine is mostly submersed in a murky pool of water, steam still rising slowly from its center, a row of massive steel wheels pointing up toward the sky, still, mutilated, like an eviscerated animal.

Several box cars and tanker cars lie overturned behind it, entangled, dug into the mud, brush and toppled trees of the upper bank. And in the ominous space between us and them, like a macabre scene from a horror movie, a spotted fawn drags himself away, along what is left of the rail line, pulling his paralyzed rear legs behind him, desperately forcing his front legs to put distance between him and the men moving through the wreckage.

"Oh. … Oh my God, poor little thing," Emily whispers, her hand through my arm, clenching unconsciously… "and look how many cars, engines… tankers too, like Drake said."

Men are now scattered around the area, some rushing toward the entanglement, others away from it. The way they are moving, glancing around, seems frantic, like they haven't been here long. There are two guys climbing up over the remains of the first engine, looking into gaps.

The air is heavy. The steam seems to have depleted from the original force that must have created the cloud above. Broken rails, bent and suspended, protrude upward from snapped, black, creosote covered ties. Loose gravel and mud, has caved into a gap where the tracks used to be, allowing water which has pooled on the high side of the tracks bank to flow through. We've stopped, back maybe 80 meters from the pool, but we can see the slimy skim on the surface that's flowing out of it; a rainbow film of yellows, blues and tar-black, slowly meandering over the water's surface trailing its way across, snake like, to spill over unimpeded. Someone with a shovel is pushing gravel into the opening trying to dam it, but then doubles over into a coughing fit. Another takes him by the shoulder and pulls him away as he hacks and spits, tripping over loose spikes and splintered ties. The crippled fawn is ignored as he disappears over the bank into tall ferns.

Two men are speed walking toward us waving their arms now. They've got ventilators on and they're motioning us back. I feel eyes boring into me, but I scan the scene and there are no eyes. As they approach, the one on the left, pulls out a roll of red caution tape and begins to unravel it. I'm relieved to be ushered back, wearier of attention than toxic fumes, so when the guys say, "Back folks! Got to stay back. Please, move off." We do. He continues as we turn, "This is not a safe area and we need all the room we can get for emergency crew access." The guy on the right, his voice muffled by the mask, repeats, "yeah, move it on back now." He's grabbing at the loose end of the caution tape that the other one is holding out. He takes it and they move forward to tie off ahead.

"Okay, no problem," says Emily, turning toward the guy in the mask. "Are there toxic fumes coming out of there? What's that smell? Did anyone get hurt? When did…?" She pauses as she stumbles over a loose stone as we move back the way we'd come.

"Please ma'am," The guy with the tape interrupts, "there will be time for questions later. Now be safe and move back. Better if you just go on home at this point. The further away the better." They push us along as the two stretch out the tape between them, one climbing the upper bank of the road, the other dropping down to the lower side, across the tracks which parallel the road. "What about all that water that's flowing over down to the lake?" Emily calls out to the guy on the lower side.

"We're doing our best to control the situation mam." He calls back. "You heard us, please move back."

Once we get back to the junction where the other cars are parked, they tie off the ribbon to form a boundary there to the roadside, then tie a rope across the road as a gate. The guy with the tape stays there to guard the access as more emergency vehicles show up. The place is abuzz with action now. A small crowd has formed behind the line; more cars plug the shoulders; the chopper overhead continues circling; the ravens hang back, lower, avoiding it. You can hear their wings flapping as they pass. "Probably picking up dead fish," Drake says, noticing my gaze, as we sidle up beside him again. "I seen a lot of them chemicals seeping out of those tankers. Must be in the lake by now." He shakes his head.

"You were down there earlier?" I ask him.

"Yep, was out at first light… fishing off the point. Must have been the first one there after the first responders I guess, bout 5:45 I figure. They'd already pulled two guys out of a rail inspection truck that crashed down the bank, took 'em off by ambulance. Then the CP guys showed up and told me to get out of there 'cause of the fumes. Guess they don't want anyone looking in on this any closer." He nods toward the site.

"Anyone killed?" I ask Drake, Emily's expectant eyes following mine, awaiting.

"Can't say, but I guess the two guys they took out of the truck were alive… didn't see 'em though… wouldn't take 'em out dead, would they?"

"And the engineers? What happened to the guys in the engine?" I ask him. "Did it light on fire?"

"Don't know Gabe. Hope they're not still in there, or in that pool… that pool the engine fell into ain't pretty," he says, adding, "probably time to get us some fresh air away from here folks. I'm feeling a little dizzy."

I look over at him then, more closely. His eyes seem filmy, lids half closed, he's leaning on the hood of a car, trying to remain steady, but looks wobbly.

"You okay Drake? Emily says, concerned, reaching for his arm.

"I'll be fine. Think I got too close is all." He says. "headin' home."

He turns and walks slowly away, unsteady. "See you folks." "Maybe you need a ride, eh?" I say as he moves away, feeling like I'd rather be further away too.

"No, Gabe. Just need to get home, that's all. Thanks."

"I'm not feeling great either Em, maybe we should get out of here." I say, shaken, the magnitude of the scene in front of us, the injuries, the uncertainty… all stirring in my gut.

"What if the trainmen have been killed Em?" I say, my eyes far away, not realizing right away that I'm speaking aloud, mumbling, "Why did that inspections truck get tossed right off the tracks? How did it get so serious, so fast? I had no idea…."

"Everyone must evacuate the area." A voice over a megaphone announces, interrupting my train of thought. I glance around me. Emily catches my eye, watching me intently. Others are close, dispersing, voices anxious, talking amongst themselves. Emily takes my arm in a firm grip, turns, pulling me along, but I don't need to be told twice.

The booming voice continues as we walk away. It's a stocky guy with a big mustache, a CP insignia on his jacket. He's not wearing a ventilator like the other ones. He's standing up on the open tailgate of one of the yellow company pickups that's blocking the road. "Please, people, we must clear the area. We will be cordoning off all access within 500 meters for now. Announcements will be forthcoming. Please disperse. "Those who live close to the crash site will be contacted door to door."

In the following days, Procter, the sleepy little village that few know exists is transformed; it's awash in media trucks equipped with camera men, flashing lights and megaphones. This derailment is the biggest disaster ever to affect the Kootenays. Environmentalists have monitors on the ground; so do all levels of government it seems: representatives from the ministry of Environment, both provincially and federally are here, along with Regional District members, the Transportation Safety Board, concerned citizen groups and there's even municipal representation from Nelson - authorities scurrying around everywhere. It looks like an ant hill over there; all involved, inspecting, asking probing questions; a mess of people and action. It's a little unnerving; these bastards have no boundaries. The media seems to have taken hold of this thing and tossed it around between them so much that it's become sensational.

Gotta say though, that the pressure this attention has created, may have been just what CP needed to spur on the job of cleaning up this spill, though, if you ask me, they should have started a lot quicker. We've already lost thousands of fish and wild life of all sorts. The treatment trailer they've set up has processed loons, ducks, geese, grouse, robins, ravens, crows, swallows and sparrows. They even took in a couple of bald eagles, a golden eagle and a heron, some suffering from respiratory problems, others treated for poisoning after ingesting contaminated fish and insects. Many of them died later, some were brought in dead; insects and amphibious life too, mostly frogs and snakes, have been either cleaned up, monitored or incinerated. Sounds like lots of them died in the first hours- a sad sacrifice.

Water, air and soil samples are being taken in an ongoing process. Tons of soil are being excavated from the entire site, removed and incinerated for remediation. The area in the vicinity of the derailment is steep, wet habitat, where the mossy, jagged rock outcrops are usually alive with a constant flow of droplets, forming rivulets, seeping over the vibrant mossy tendrils thriving in growth; they are oblivious to the latest chaos surrounding them; much more oblivious than all those inhabitants who have recently invested hundreds of thousands of dollars in the affluent, nearby, gated community subdivision at Procter's eastern most point. There, elaborate homes have been built just meters from the tracks, just beyond either side of the CPR right of way, all the ones on the lower side are lake front. It's these people that had been forced to evacuate their homes in the early hours, days and weeks following the disaster. Maybe they are thinking twice now about how elite that location is.

Hundreds of thousands of liters of water were pumped up from the site, removed by tankers brought in by rail to be transported to the reclamation center but before they started pumping out the toxic pool by the tracks, a lot of it had overflowed and run down into the lake. Giant chemical sponge mats were used to attempt to absorb any chemicals floating on the lake shore and water surface. Helicopters flew overhead for the first couple days, filming and monitoring. A few motor homes were set up at the end of the road near the site to accommodate media and CP had several sleeper cars and a kitchen car pulled off on a nearby siding to serve emergency crews who worked in shifts around the clock. The village has never seen so much action. Cool spring rains interspersed with warm sunshiny days are usually the recipe for supernatural growth in May, but not now. Maybe I'm imagining it, but it seems to me that spring is on hold right now. A grey mist hangs low, mechanical sounds rumble nonstop, diesel and bleach-like fumes are in the air, riding along the shifting breeze to greet you like the stink of a road worn hitchhiker climbing into your truck cab.

They left the rail line clear so that the intact section could be utilized by the engines towing flat deck cars to access the site. They used these to deliver material and equipment, and later, to remove waste material. It would be three weeks before local evacuees could return to their homes, but even then, many were uneasy about the state of the water and air in the area.

Testing continues to ensure the safety of those living nearby, those that had not been evacuated. The lake is still cordoned off for a three-mile radius around the area below the disaster to create a buffer zone. People, vehicles and boats are not allowed to pass into the disaster area by land or water. The lengths they are going to limit access should alert people to the secrecy of CP's hidden agenda. I've been warning people that this could happen. I hope everyone is paying attention now.

They still haven't even confirmed what the stuff is that is leaching all over the place out there. Probably some kind of acidic compound that will produce two headed frogs and fish with four eyes. The thing is, this is just a minor spill compared to what could happen if a whole train toppled into the lake. This could be the wakeup call people need to warn them of some future catastrophe on a mega scale. It's too bad that fish, birds and insects had to die, but in the scheme of things, maybe this is a measured sacrifice, one that was needed to wake those with influence to the realization that these chemicals need to be transported with restriction and regulation, that these hazardous chemicals, some of them pressurized in tanker cars, can, when spilled, lead to toxic inhalation and mass poisoning. These fuckers that move toxic products through our back yard don't care that the rails are run down, or that the houses and streams are alongside. Their only bloody concern is to get the stuff from A to B at the lowest possible cost to keep the shareholders happy, keep profits flowing in industrial farms, mining and manufacturing, pharmaceuticals too, all the industries that these chemicals feed. I've read that they carry highly volatile, hazardous stuff like white phosphorous, chlorine gas, anhydrous ammonia, chemicals to make fertilizers, for raw materials and fuel additives, any of which, spill, or worse, explode, can wipe out a whole village, lake, or both. Why should we have to live with that kind of threat running through our bloody back yard every day of the week? Why shouldn't those bastards finally be taught a lesson in stewardship? Have they?

I'd been cutting wood late the evening before the derailment, until just before dark. My mind hadn't been on the angle of the undercut as I was taking down the final dead standing larch of the day while dusk approached. The high-pitched whine of my chainsaw motor had engulfed me in that familiar cocoon of sound, my helmet and earmuffs adding a level of comfort to the seclusion, and as my mind wanders, so does my saw cut… too far in. The snag had begun to fall backwards, toward me, pinching my saw blade and knocking off the chain before snapping and kicking off the stump with a loud snap and rolling toward where I stood still clutching at the saw's falling handle as it got spit out. I came to my senses in time to realize I had to let the saw go, and jump back, just before the snag rolled and dropped where I'd stood a split second before, driving itself into the earth at least a foot deep.

Then, as I stumbled back away, the immense weight of the timber forced itself down the bank, peeling open the earth in a jagged scar several meters long before finally slamming into the ground with a sickening thud. It's not the first time something like this has happened while I've been cutting. It always shakes me up. I know I need to focus on the task at hand, but hind sight isn't very useful once you get crushed by a tree. I've been lucky again, but already, my thoughts wander back to where they were - mind cycling, a broken cog reminder - tick, tick tick, each revolution clicking redundantly, building intensity, like a simmering kettle reaching boil.

I'd come home late for dinner… spent. The boys were too engrossed in an episode of Star Trek to notice me come in, Noah barely visible under a blanket on the couch curled up in a ball, and Gavin leaning back on the other end spread eagled taking up most the room. Casey, our black lab is on the rug in front of them; she just turns over on her back and slowly wags her tail along the floor when she sees me, the edge of her mouth drooping in a toothy, comical smile. Emily had been folding some laundry on the counter as she asked me about my day, her hands moving over folds creating creases, piling neat stacks, one for each. I sidle up from behind, hands wandering along her waist pulling her back against me.

"Curried chicken in the toaster oven waiting for you." She says, pressing back against me a moment before clearing the piles away. I quickly devour the plate full of curry, wash it back with a cold beer and get back up on my feet. "Been a long one," I say, "but I got most of what I need for tomorrow's delivery. I'm feeling pretty done but I've still got to run out for a bit anyhow. Great curry."

"Going out." She says, "Why?"

"Uhh, just wanted to see if Randy can take a quick look at my trailer tonight. The hydraulics aren't working right so I can't dump the load. He'll figure it out." I said, draining the last of my beer.

Then I'd just left, without another word, went out again, hadn't come back until she was asleep. She hadn't mentioned it until now… that night, but the CP detectives have started their investigation and she's been interviewed, asked questions about my whereabouts, especially my whereabouts that night.

I guess they'll be asking everyone the same thing… all those who live nearby to the derailment anyway. Emily'd told me that she had reviewed these details in her mind after the CP investigators were at the door questioning her. They had been questioning everyone in the area, but Emily thought that because of my history of bringing attention and opposition to the transport of toxic chemicals through Procter, that CP officials may be taking a special interest in their questioning of her, of us… of me. Plus, she knew that CP and the RCMP had not forgotten about the train blockade just a few years ago. I don't think she seriously suspects that I have been involved in the derailment, but it's obvious that the idea has crossed her mind. She hasn't brought it up with me yet, not directly. I just hope that the investigation leaves her out of it after this. I don't like to see her worry about things, and I don't want to discuss it, not now. The right time will come. Emily understands when to wait.

We're out in the veggie garden late the morning after the investigators had been by; the kids have gone off to school. Emily's asked me to help fix the chicken wire fence that we use as a trellis for the long row of peas to climb. She's pulling a length of the fencing as tight as she can while I tack in a few fencing nails to help straighten out the sag in the middle. She mimics the investigator: 'So ma'am, did you see or hear of anyone or any event that could have played a part in this derailment?' That's what he asked, at first, Gabe. They said they weren't targeting our house, just questioning everyone." I smile to myself, watching her animated description play out on her face, scenes flashing by in her mind's eye, one frame to the next, the expressions vary from stern to curious to condescending, like acts in theater, easy to read.

"And then what did they say? Were they looking for me?" "Well, yeah, they asked where you were now and if you'd been at home that night. They were asking about anything out of the ordinary… sounds, suspicious vehicles, stuff like that. They were asking if I'd heard any rumours. I asked them if they thought someone had deliberately caused the derailment, if that is what they were getting at and he said, not necessarily, that they were just asking people who live nearby the spill if they had seen or heard anything in the hours and days leading up to it. He said they hadn't arrived at any conclusions yet, but that they have reason to believe there could have been intentional interference. He wanted to know if we had both been home at the time… or, … if I'd been home alone." She glances over to meet my eyes, then lets go of the wire as I put the last nail in. She steps back to inspect, accepting my silence, pressing on the now taut fencing, looking down the row. "That's better, careful not to bump the fence now; peas have already popped up," she says, pointing to the intermittent row of sprouts, their vibrant lively tendrils bright against the darkness of the moist, rich soil from which they've sprung. "Got it."

"First day up and already the bloody slugs are eating them." She says, dismay in her voice, bending over to inspect more closely. "Yeah, same as usual, fricking slugs. Drown 'em in beer, like your Mom said," I say, then, trying to get back to where we were… well we were… right? Home, I mean. When they were asking, what did you say?"

"I told them, yes, that you, I and the kids were all here, that we had slept right through it. Right?" she adds, a flicker of doubt in her eye as she glances up at me again, still kneeling over the peas. I focus on my hammer, wait for her to continue. "I asked them if there had been an explosion, something that should have woken us up. And they said, no, no explosion, just a big crash, a lot of grinding steel and shooting steam when it went over. They seemed kind of interested in all the equipment and tools in our yard, not sure why. They kept looking around and taking notes, took some pictures too."

"Pictures." I say, "What's with that? Is it even legal?"

"Not sure. I told them that you cut wood and deliver logs and stuff, do some trenching with the back hoe. Then I kind of got irritated because they had parked practically right on the lawn. I don't like when people park on the lawn. Why can't they just walk a few more steps? What's the big deal? Then they were asking where you were, how to get hold of you, so I told them they could go up to the top of Victor road and try to find you off one of the fork roads. I was kind of hoping they would head up there and get lost, but I don't think they did, just said that they would call you later. I gave them your cell number."

"And so that's it?"

"Well, I guess. For now, anyway. They seemed pretty intent on continuing the investigation, they were hinting that they already had clues and persons of interest. Sounds like they figure someone could have deliberately rolled a boulder into place to clog the culvert. Said they wouldn't be divulging any details, but that we should contact them as soon as we heard anything, that it will be better for people to come clean now, rather than wait."

"Wait? Wait for what?" I say as I bend over to pick up the can of fencing nails, hammer and tape measure I'd brought along.

"I don't know. I guess they mean, it'll be better for the people to turn themselves in than wait till they get caught. They say they are working on leads."

"Sounds to me like just a bunch of speculation… fishing…. I'll talk to them later. Anyway, that boulder they are talking about could have just come loose and rolled down there all by itself."

"Well, yeah, I guess, but that's not what they're thinking." She rises and walks with me back toward the garden gate.

"I figure, they are just trying to avoid blame of this whole mess by trying to make it look like someone could have sabotaged their tracks. Think for a minute about the law suit that could follow if it's shown that the community was put at risk, not to mention all the environmental damage that's been done, was due to their lack of maintenance. They could get shut down, for a while anyway, and pay massive fines." I growl.

"Well, yes, I s'pose." Emily says, then, changing the subject the same hint of suspicion remaining in her eyes, adds, "Gabe, honey, before you take off, will you please try to adjust the latch on the gate and drive a couple more nails into the loose boards on the side of the compost bin? It would be good to keep on it now that the season is in full swing. Comet's been getting into the compost too." She adds, pointing at her, shaking her head.

Comet just starts wagging her tail at the mention of her name. "Haven't you, girl?"

Emily and I have spoken about the issue of transporting dangerous chemicals through the village many times. She has friends too that are opposed, but few, if any, are as vocal as I have been, so she's not that surprised that the detectives may be taking a keener interest in me than others. I've often spurred debate on the issue, especially after the derailment that happened in 2001 not far down the line from where this one was, when several rail cars plunged into the lake, killing two trainmen and spilling thousands of liters of diesel and lead sulfide into the lake.

It's not that she looks at me in an accusing way; it's more like a curious, unspoken question that passes between us, a question she won't ask, one of those silent ones that wait in a bubble, floating around knowing that one day the bubble will pop. I question myself at times too, my own tactics and how I communicate them. It's all related isn't it, when to divulge? The balance between honesty and peace? The intricate rules of a relationship. Do all things need to be spoken or are some things best left unsaid?

CHAPTER 2

Gabe

Back East where I grew up, my folks were great examples of how to leave things 'unsaid.' I remember few family discussions or emotional outbursts in our family home during my time growing up. Not during the primary school years back in Kitchener, nor for that matter, later, during the high school years in Windsor. Our home seemed to run without any major upset, or maybe it was just my own oblivious nature that smoothed out the wrinkles in my own memory. Either way, I have mostly good memories during our time growing up in Ontario. Our parents moved us around from city to city, buying and selling properties as opportunities arose. They were both realtors, still are, but now they just dabble in it more as a past time or to help those closest to them. That's how I ended up with enough cash for a down payment on the property in Windsor. They helped and advised me to get into a small, one- bedroom apartment there when I was just out of high school. I'd been studying mechanical engineering at the University of Western Ontario at the time. The investment part stuck- the studying part, not so much. At the age of twenty-one, I dropped out of the program most of the way through second year, disillusioned with the direction I was going. Fortunately, the apartment had already added a lot of value. This had been a valuable lesson to me, one

I continue to work with today; owning property seems to me, it's the best lever to use, also, the most practical. In the complex world of financial accumulation, property seems like the easiest to understand - it consists of land and structures. You can live on it and grow food from it; a lot more tangible than stock options.

After meeting Emily, the next year, in Nelson, we'd pooled our cash, she had inherited a small cache from her grandfather, and me, I'd sold the Windsor apartment for a profit. Combined we'd had enough to buy the land in Procter. Since then, values have risen and we have added value too with sweat equity upgrades, landscaping, even a pond. We've got lots of water flowing down off the mountain with two creeks on the property. Over the years Emily and I have been able to re- mortgage, drawing enough funds, leveraging our property to purchase other properties, the first being a rental we bought almost fifteen years ago. We'd worked on that one, rented it out and waited another five years, then re-mortgaged it too, and with that cash, bought a third place. Now we are mortgage free in our own home and the other two bring in more rental income than their overall expenses, so we can live a comfortable enough life even when sporadic income streams are a little slow. This gives us both more freedom of choice, allows for more time with the kids when we feel they need it, and best of all, I figure, keeps me from having a boss. Now I'm considering re- mortgaging again to purchase a small mini storage business, just a few kilometers this side of Nelson, out near four-mile. One day, when the properties are all working for me, I figure, I won't have to be cutting wood all the time. How long can a guy cut wood in a life time? I'm not twenty something anymore.

No, we're getting up there now, Emily is forty-four and I'm forty-eight and we've been together most our adult lives, almost twenty-five years. Well except for that trial separation period back in 2003. We moved in together when she was only nineteen, me twenty-three, too young, I guess. We both should have experimented more, or at least, I think I should have. We made it through the first seven years before cracks started to turn into crevices. It was a rough spell, and ultimately led to time on our own, the *sabbatical* we call it. We'd both been with others during that time, but no one that stuck.

She is a local girl, from Nelson and we'd met when I'd come traveling through back in the early winter of 1990. She'd been waitressing at the Taverna, a Greek restaurant in town. I'd come in alone, an unusual sight in that kind of place, she had thought, especially for a young guy. We'd struck up a conversation over my dinner, me pressing her for local information, talking about skiing and live music, where to shop. The place hadn't been too busy, so she'd been able to hang around my table a little longer than necessary. By the time I'd paid my bill, we'd already made a date to go skiing together the next weekend.

Emily had soon abandoned her plan to enroll at the University of Victoria to study in the program for social work and had instead opted to work part time and enroll in the distance education program that they offered locally.

The dating period had been short and intense. Our dreams became fused in images of owning land together, growing food, having yard parties around a bon fire, starting young, living the country life. Within six months we had already moved into the Procter property together, both of us convinced that we had fallen into the future, the fatalistic approach seemed to suit our needs, neither one of us seemed too concerned by the long-term implications of being 'virtually married by common land,' as I referred to our relationship. I figured that once you had shared title to a home that was enough commitment, no need for all the other formalities. The expense, or maybe it was just my fear of speaking in public that led to me dodging the whole marriage thing, the organizing, invitations, pressure to include, feed and appease. No, a wedding was not something I thought particularly important, or for that matter, very meaningful, and Emily had gone along with that train of thought, as she usually did, in her easy laissez faire fashion, seemingly unaffected by, what many, her sister included would consider, after being together a year or two, let alone ten or fifteen, 'long enough to be engaged.'

"Where's the commitment?" Sandy, Emily's younger sister would ask. "What's he afraid of Em? Don't you think that he is trying to leave the door open? Isn't that what lack of commitment implies?"

On only one occasion did Emily repeat any of these concerns to me. I had listened, pondered the statements of her sister as Emily repeated them. Sounded to me like the quotes were used as a tool to pry open the forbidden trunk of trinkets, that it was easier for Emily to borrow the tool, these words, than use her own, to then spread them out as if they were dollar store junk jewelry, not to be taken seriously, to be treated with a smirk and a smile, sarcastically. Yet, the underlying nervous tension that surrounded her carefully placed, overly buoyant, words, appeared to me like a gem mixed into a load of gravel; it was that shiny stone that would at times silently glow, like an ember, in the background of our relationship. I would see Emily sometimes stewing it over, this idea, this 'lack of commitment', like blowing on the coals, but she never blew hard enough to light the fire.

Emily likes to say, playfully, that she has fallen in love, not with me, but with our land. "It's the rich soil that I love Gabe, the vegetables and fruit. They're so satisfying; and they never talk back, kinda like Casey." She is in love with Casey too, our dedicated hound, only three years old now, but already attached to us all like one of the family. Emily is the nurturing type. Her love and energy sink into the soil that produces a freezer full of vegetables and berries and a root cellar full of preserved fruits, jams and juices.

She loves the stream that runs through into the pond behind our house. That pond provides year-round entertainment, it's the one we dunk in in the summer heat or skate on when crisp winter weather allows. Gold fish spawn in its greenish depths producing minnows, who when unwittingly choose to rise too close to the surface, are scooped up by a passing King fisher. He will land and chatter in nearby tree branches in appreciation of his meal. Reeds grow on the pond's bank and a rope swing hangs from the arcing branch of a willow tree. On warm summer days the kids and their friends, run and swing from that rope until the lawn runway, turns into a muddy trough. Casey loves the water too and when the boys are in there tossing a stick, she'll take a running leap and clear three meters or more, diving toward it like a super hero. A few years ago I decided we needed a sauna by the pond so I set out to fix up an old shack that had been on the property when we bought it, out back, behind the house, must have been a tool shed or something, built by the Doukhobors out of logs and chinking. I wanted it to be closer to the pond, so I jacked it up, slid two timbers underneath as skids and strapped it on, then I dragged it about eighty-meters behind my back hoe till it was only twenty meters or so from the pond. I set it up on blocks and it's been sitting there ever since. When days are cold, or after dark in the summer when the day's heat has subsided, we'll sometimes light the wood stove in there, heat up the rocks in the cage on top for a while then toss water on so that we're all drenched in sweat and steam, ready to make the running dive into the pond.

We have a Guatamalan tapestry hanging in our living room, a cabana and garden scene, with wandering vines and crooked fence posts. Emily likens the weave to the life we have created here. "We have subtle seasonal shades like these too," she says, pointing to lines in the fabric, "rich earth tones, we have threads of compost enriched soil, sun bleached cedar siding, and lush lines of mowed lawn." After a couple of glasses of wine, she'll go on, gazing out the window, her eyes seeing more than mine. "One day I'll learn to weave in those accents of the rock garden, the vivid splash of colour for each flower bed. I'll define them with the contrast of white borders of birch bark and snow, with a backdrop of ice and water and sky." I listen. Emily falls in love, slowly at first, with the idea of this fabric she sees us weave. "But ours is just a tiny square in the much larger quilt of the village community tapestry." She says. Over time, especially in the time after the two of us re-united, after the 'sabbatical', I imagine, that Emily pictures herself, the two of us, now, the four of us, as more and more an integral part of this fabric as it grows in complexity, a fabric that cannot be designed, nor restrained, one that becomes interactive, where all you can do is add a thread here and there, wait and watch as it forms in front of you. To me, this weave she talks about seems automated, out of our control, to me it seems that things will happens as they do. But Emily is convinced that we carefully add rows, like terraces. The village between. "And it's only then that you understand, while you are present, standing between the terraces but part of the scene, observing- "it's only then," she says, "that the tapestry becomes much bigger than just your own rows of thread; it's then you can see that everyone adds their own colour and that sometimes the colours can clash and converge. Here," she says, "at least, in this village of ours, which is only a tiny square in the universal fabric, here at least, these contrasting colours can be 'enchanting, even intoxicating." Her eyes flash with this insight. "Maybe I'll weave the whole thing into a blanket, and it will provide a comforting warmth, it'll cocoon you in confidence, and knowledge when you wrap it round.

"Now it's sounding more like a magic carpet." I say.

I love to hear the passion in her voice when she comes home inspired, over flowing with her latest community revelations. I love the passion but when she carries on in that voice with her eyes kind of glazed over in what I like to call, 'a Kootenay Vision', all idealistic, I do begin to wonder if she is floating off into some sphere where ribbons and rainbows obscure her view of the task at hand.

"I wonder how carefully they will be looking into the accounting of our time that night." She says, her fingers busily tugging at chick weed and horsetail that threaten to invade a sprouting row of red lettuce, "not that there is any problem, just that I don't *really* remember what time you got back. I think I was already asleep. 'Course, how can they know anything about that anyway unless they have actual proof or a witness or something, right?"

"Umhmm, right," I say watching her movements, "sounds like all they've got are groundless suspicions."

"I know that they are more interested in you than most, though, Gabe honey," she says, glancing up, "but that's because of your history, of your opposition, but there's no law against being opposed to something. It's not like you have been trying to hide your position. It's no secret, right? I was just talking with my mother on the phone this morning and even she brought it up." I turn back to pick up the cordless drill and wood screws lying in the grass nearby.

"Oh, really, brought what up?" I ask, as I pull loose screws out from the wobbly gate latch.

"Only asking if those letters you wrote to the editor would put you in the focus of the investigation. She's worried about us, you know."

"Right, of course. I get it." I say as I drive a couple of longer screws into the latch and add some more to the loose cedar slats of the compost bin beside the gate. Emily's mom was referring to the most recent letter I had written, some months ago, entitled: 'Dangerous goods in our Midst'. It had listed all kinds of potential hazards and trace contaminants in PCBs: Persistent Organic Pollutants. I had insinuated that the whole lake could be affected by a major spill and or explosion; that ozone depletion, allergic reactions, water, soil and air contamination were just a few of the potential hazards, that many of the chemicals that CP transported to Teck Resources were fatal if inhaled. I went on to explain how Teck Resources was a key contributor to the problem, that they had even been sued and lost their case in court when the Colville Confederated Tribes filed a lawsuit against them claiming that they had dumped: arsenic, cadmium, mercury, lead, copper and zinc into the Columbia River. My letter had been labeled 'inflammatory,' by local politicians, that it could: 'incite untoward action'.

In a follow up letter in response to opposition, I had spurred added controversy after insinuating that a similar tragedy could occur in Procter as did at Lac-Megantic, Quebec in 2013 when forty-seven people were killed by a derailment and explosion that had happened involving millions of liters of crude oil, "only with trains traveling through Procter," I'd pointed out, "the chemicals can be even more hazardous and volatile. For instance, sulphuric acid can not only be fatal if inhaled, it also reacts violently when it comes in contact with water." I'd written, so I'm not so surprised and neither is Emily, that the investigators are now taking a keen interest in me and our place. They probably know or have heard that few people have been more vocal than me in opposition to them transporting dangerous chemicals through the area. I have always had strong opinions about these things, nothing new there, but like Emily says, 'there's no law against being opposed to something.'

There had been some heated debate, especially after the derailment that had happened here in 2001. It had occurred just down the line from where this latest train derailed. Several rail cars had plunged into the lake killing two trainmen and spilling thousands of liters of diesel and lead sulfide into the lake. There had been a lot of reaction to the spill, especially because of the two deaths, but nothing concrete changed because of it. No new environmental controls were put in place, no new enforced maintenance procedures were introduced at CP Rail. The only change they made was to initiate a new requirement for all trains traveling along this stretch of track to be accompanied, in advance, by a patrol vehicle, to scout for problems on the track. They didn't even remove a couple of the train cars that had derailed, from the lake. They're still out there in twenty feet of water. This latest derailment is much bigger and environmentally speaking, more serious, and though there were no fatalities, it really does point out the risks CP runs, and the lack of funding they are willing to invest in basic maintenance. I hope that inspectors expose the poor maintenance levels. I've walked along those tracks dozens of times and there is always ample evidence of neglect: lots of totally rotten ties, loose bolts, spikes that have popped up, rails worn narrow by over use. Maybe CP will be forced to account for their - profit before safety, policies now. Maybe they will be forced to stop carting their chemicals through our village in this way. Maybe the bastards will have to pay.

"Hey Em, this looks solid enough now. I'm going inside to heat up some of that left-over corn chowder you made. Want some?" I say, picking some loose screws from the grass where they'd dropped.

"Sure Gabe, and maybe put a small side salad together too, okay? I'll be in a few minutes. Just want to thin out the carrot sprouts. Looks like I over planted them again. Some things are always predictable." She scans the row of carrot seedlings below, all packed too closely together into an unruly line of shimmering feathery foliage, like a miniature tree farm. She bends back down to begin thinning, folded at the hips, legs wide apart but straight, tight jeans hugging firm curves, a view I can always appreciate, even after all these years together.

Emily didn't have to learn the basics about gardening, she already had that. Her mother had relied on her kids to help out in the backyard garden over the years, especially after her father had died. They'd lost him in a work place accident. He'd been a faller, a skilled one, but miscommunication had resulted in another faller cutting too close to his position, which ended in the tree her father had been cutting getting clipped by the one coming down the slope. It sent his tree back, crushing him. She'd been only fourteen. Emily, her sister and mother are a very close unit now, probably closer due to their loss. I think Emily losing her Dad like that, has given her some anxiety over the possibility of losing me. She can be very possessive. After the first few years of our relationship, that possessiveness, combined with my own inclination to experiment, resulted in a breakdown. I had little patience and in retrospect, can see that I was single minded, full of blame and anger, not solutions. My solution had been to leave. I had taken off, first gone to live in Calgary, for seven months, considered re-starting the engineering program there, but then decided against it, got a job instead as an apprentice brick layer. I dated another woman for a while, but always stayed in touch with Emily, who, for me, despite our differences, despite our contrasting views, was still the one that felt most like home to me.

I continued on in Calgary for almost a year, making good money, soaking up some of those rich Albertan oil profits for myself. I spent many nights in the King Eddy Blues bar, dancing, drinking and partying with guys from work, with a new girlfriend,

Josie, from Quebec, and the local bar crowd. They were a mix of old time Calgarians, transient oil patch workers, immigrant service employees and always a few Newfoundlanders stopping in on their way to Fort Mac for some city excitement. I have some great memories hanging out around beer-stained orange, terry-cloth tables with Newfies, East Indians, Scots, unlikely, but solid party allies. I'd spent many nights, often with foggy endings, tossing back beers and tequila shots, dancing, laughing, doing coke, smoking hash, the memories mostly blurred now, as they were then. I'd had fun, been gregarious, swinging from light stands, tossing beer cans, singing along to "Angie" in one moment and debating the 'environmental disaster' of the tar sands in the next... a lot of chatter, mostly inebriated.

I knew, after a few months that this direction was not the alternative I'd been looking for. I'd felt worn down, hungover, lacking spark. My creative energy had been sapped and the only thing I looked forward to in the day, was the night. That wasn't enough. One night, after returning in a barely coherent state, and waking up once again with the signature headache and furry tongue, turning over to see if Josie was there, Finding the bed empty, I lay there, studying blotchy water stains on the ceiling. I wondered why, after spending so much time in the company of others, that I felt so alone. My eyes followed the uneven watermarks, again and again, until my vision glassed over, and the stain contours blurred. I kept searching the ceiling for direction, as though it were a map with a set of cross streets I just couldn't find. I forced myself to focus, to remain still, to avoid my usual routine for a moment. I slowly began to form ideas on needing to be cleansed, of wiping the moldy grey matter from the surface, of finding clarity, free from the influence of alcohol, drugs, friends and girlfriends, of finding a place where introspection could occur. That morning began a search. I began to consider my future from a less obstructed vantage point.

But where was this place I searched for? How could I pull myself away from the magnetic charm of the local scene that continually drew me in? I felt so weak, too vulnerable, always drawn toward and easily swayed to alter course, toward those things that attracted me. How could I stay away from the women I wanted if they were there; the bottle that sip by sip added charisma, the white line that lent me confidence, gave me an edge, or the smoke that when drawn deep, would spread a veil of calm over the rest. I knew that my own willpower would not be voluntarily restrained; there was no strength in it. I had been cocooned in the working wage cycle, where the forty-hour week supported the apartment, car, bar tab, recreational drugs, groceries, and bills. Nothing more, no family, no cause, or course, classes or creative outlet, a cycle of subsistence. It had been fun at times, some memorable moments had occurred, but those moments weren't enough, and they were too few. I knew it was time to move on. I'd been angry with myself for wasting time.

I'd considered moving to the Yukon, finding a remote job, maybe in a mine, or a mill. Maybe I could learn to pan gold like I'd always wanted to or begin some preparatory online courses for the Hydrology program I'd always been interested in… in my spare time. But I'd heard of the long dark night up there in the North, where people partied through till light finally dawned, and decided that no, I would need a little more distance from my weaknesses right now. I would need more space between me and my addictive traits. I considered working in a remote fishing camp near Thunder Bay. Saw some postings online for that. Canoeing on the weekends, staying fit, breathing fresh northern air, drinking from streams again, just like back home, up in the mountains.

And then it struck me. It struck me that back home, up in the mountains… in the Kootenays, is where I needed to be. Why travel to remote regions when I could find my own personal retreat right back at a place, I called home? I started thinking it through. Living in the bush, alone, for months. I could set up a nice camp, pack in food, even grow some veggies. Maybe I'd do some panning in my spare time. I'd clear my system, clear my head, re-group, let things run through the sieve till only the vital bits would be left in the bottom, like shiny little gold nuggets. Maybe I would be able to form my life plan more clearly by focusing on those, instead of all the peripheral distractions I had created, the sludge that obscured the rest.

To do this I'd have to remove myself. On the one hand, I likened the idea to a form of banishment, to a prisoner sentenced to a life of seclusion on a remote Island, surrounded by shark infested waters. I would serve the sentence, sentenced for wasting time. On the other hand, the idea of this seclusion, this banishment to the bush, intrigued me. The idea became less one of punishment, more of challenge. I wasn't seeking martyrdom. I became excited by the idea. I would have to survive the cool, wet spring, hunt and gather, create shelter, maybe even grow vegetables. I would pan for gold. Maybe I'd find some, come out of the bush in a few months with a pocket full. I'd carry in back country books to study from, on how to cure meat, dry fish, subsist from, berries, roots and various green chutes and flowers. I could learn to construct things using only rudimentary hand tools. It would be a challenge, an adventure. I'd carry in philosophically interesting books too, perspectives to puzzle over, like, On Walden's Pond, Ralph Emerson's, Nature and Selected Essays, Leaves of Grass by Walt

Whitman. I would study their ideas, learn practical survival techniques, become enriched with knowledge, both philosophical and practical, carry in journals and pens to record all this newly attained enlightenment. I would emerge with my psyche in balance, with a new-found clarity of purpose. No more bars and late nights; no more hangovers with vague memories of good times. No more bullshit. I had this clear vision of this new, enlightened me, emerging, months later, from the dark forest, restored, heroic. In retrospect, I can see that there is some redemption in naiveté. If you knew in advance how misguided you were in the present, you would never challenge yourself to attain these goals. You would play safe, never experiencing all those mistakes. Life would be too simple.

I decided to do it. I gave notice at work, gave up my apartment, parted ways with Josie, who was not particularly traumatized by the news, and packed my things. I figured I'd managed to save enough cash from my last two pay cheques and the damage deposit from the rental to buy most the supplies I would need. I took my cash, packed up my car with the things I'd accumulated in Calgary and drove back to our place in Procter.

Emily too, had previously decided to take off for a while, like I had. She took a job as a cook's helper at a mining camp near Tumbler ridge, so our place in Procter had been abandoned temporarily. We'd mutually decided to rent it out till we both knew better what the next move was, so it was easy for me to just drop by, stash my little Mazda in behind the woodshed and leave again; no drama, no emotional complications. I cut my phone, had no bills or rent, canceled my car insurance. I felt like one of those spies you see in movies that are trying to become anonymous, ridding themselves of any possible connection to bureaucratic life. It felt liberating. I was anonymous.

I let my folks know I would be out of touch for a while. I explained the situation to them and though they empathized with the reasoning, my mother was worried I'd just disappear without a trace, leaving them all to search. In the end, I agreed to carry a search beacon as a compromise. "Yes, Mom, I'll be carrying it at all times. It's compact and easy to use. Fits right into my pocket. Thanks so much. I'll feel better having it." I'd told her. She had bought this thing and sent it to me. A simple transmitter, the Global Fix beacon, water and shock proof, that when activated sends an alarm signal to the nearest search and rescue base, who finds your location by triangulating between satellites. It continues to emit the signal for days, even weeks, if necessary, alerting them of your co-ordinates to within a few meters of accuracy- quite a gadget really, if a helicopter rescue is what you're after, that is.

It had been an exhilarating time - the planning, list writing of supplies, co-ordination of access, pack size. I felt like a survivalist, excited and intrigued by the decisions around what was critical and what was not, by which tools, which books to bring, what kind of food supplies would not only keep, but be concentrated in nutrition and energy. And most intriguing, which location would be most suitable. I needed to find a spot not too far as to be too difficult to access, yet far enough to be inaccessible to others, far enough to dissuade me too, from the lure of comfort and transgression.

In the end, after pouring carefully over topographical maps and Google Earth, I chose the Wilson drainage. It's a mid-sized creek which tumbles down steep, east facing slopes from the Selkirk mountains above, ultimately flowing out into Kootenay lake. There are no access roads anywhere near so there wouldn't be hunters or hikers. I'd heard that East Shore pot growers sometimes boated across the lake to plant their crops up in these West Shore drainages, but I figured I was going to hike high enough up the valley to be out of their way too. The Wilson creek valley is only dissected by the CP rail tracks which wind along the lake shore at its outflow; that's the only human artery. The valley is generally steep and densely forested. There are no trails other than those created by deer, elk and the migrating caribou herd, and it's not too far from Procter by boat… a perfect hideaway.

It had taken me weeks to finally organize my departure. The few people I had told of my plan had been curious, yet disbelieving, unsure, hesitant to remark it seemed to me, so I didn't talk about the retreat much, just kept to myself and immersed myself in the organization. Emily had returned to Procter, to catch up with friends and pick up a few things, just a short break from work, which turned out to be at an opportune time in my timetable. So, with her as one of the few who I had confided in as to the details of this venture, I asked her if she would be the one to drop me off by boat for my final departure. Most our discussions prior to that had simply been a plus/minus negotiation as to whether I should bring our dog, Huckleberry, along.

Huckleberry was our devoted Black Lab who had been living with Emily since our separation. In the end we both decided, her more reluctantly than I, that, this could be an exciting adventure for a dog, but more to the point, that she would be good company, the only company, for me during this time. We had shared little more conversation during that time. We had both accumulated too many unspoken grievances over the previous years, harboured too many hidden hopes, resentments, misgivings, to carry on a serious, thoughtful exchange. This was not the time to unleash that potential flood. We had a trust between us that needs no explanation, so few words were necessary.

I won't soon forget the ride out to Wilson, me steering the little Mercury outboard of our old StarCraft 14 foot tinner over the choppy water as we navigated out of the arm and South, around the point into the main lake, the odd wave catching wind and spraying cool droplets of water up over the bow, to roll down over Emily and all the bags of gear piled in front of and between the two bench seats. She, facing forward, still, except for the undulating motion of the boat pounding over the waves, her hair streaming out behind, fluttering in ribbons in the brisk spring air. It was in early April. Days were cloudy, cool, often wet. This day was no exception. No sooner had we pulled the boat up on the pebbles of Wilson beach than the rain had once again begun blowing in, small waves now beginning to cap and froth, lapping at the tilted propeller and transom of the boat now pulled up on the shore.

"You're going to freeze your ass off in this nasty weather." She said, studying the solid cloud bank above.

"Nah, don't worry, I'll be sweatin' it out packing gear up this hill."

The packs and other gear were all in big black garbage bags so things would remain dry. We tossed them all out on the rocks in just a few minutes, then, as if simply parting for the day, like a typical couple, one going to work, the other staying home, we hugged briefly before she hopped into the tinner and I pushed her off back into the choppy water of Kootenay Lake. She dropped the prop in, pulled the cord till the motor sprang to life, then with a single, final wave, she spun the boat round and facing forward, sped off, faster now, weightless and buoyant, bouncing through the choppy waters toward Procter. Leaving me alone in the rain, surrounded by bags of gear on the gray, rocky beach, my elaborate plans culminating in a resounding moment of ominous silence. A silence that would cocoon me in the coming weeks and months, a silence that from that day onward would spread from this epicenter, like tiny curved lines of motion in a comic strip, emanating like a deafening heartbeat that only I could hear.

At first, I had little time to consider my plight. There was cool weather, rain, and a dense, dark, cedar/hemlock forest to penetrate. I had stacks of gear, some three hundred pounds of it, all needing a place to arrive to. First, I made several trips up across the rail tracks to a preliminary stash, where no one from passing boats could see it. Then, I found a spot higher up, just a few hundred meters higher on the slope, where I decided I would create an elevated sling, a place I could leave longer term food supplies that I could come back for later. Why carry all of it up to wherever the top camp would be right now? I'll have time in coming weeks to return. I had brought along a small pulley with this in mind. With that and a 100' rope, I set up a food stash of nuts, flour, grains, seeds, cooking oil, dog food and other supplies. I suspended it all high off the ground in an old hammock. I double garbage-bagged it to keep things dry. The rest of the gear and food I would divvy up and carry in three loads once I figured out the destination. It had been hard enough just hauling it this far, up over rotting dead-fall trees, through the low sweeping limbs of hemlock that would gently brush your face with each passing, sending droplets of moisture down your neck. I'd spent a bit of time slashing the worst of the limbs away with my machete, along the route I'd used to haul things up to the stash, but soon realized that I would not have time to build a proper trail at this point, so I abandoned that idea. Now, I needed to find the best way up to higher elevations, to a remote site, suitable for a long-term camp; a place open enough to be well lit, yet sheltered enough to provide protection and enough trees to be able to secure tie-downs to. It would need to be high enough up the drainage to provide isolation so I could be sure no one could easily find it on foot, especially growers, who can be pretty territorial about their work. I didn't want anyone to be able to spot clues of my location, whether it be from trails, smoke, a dog's bark or gunfire.

It took me two days to find a suitable camp location. The first night, I spent nearby my sling stash, exhausted, no energy and little day light left to continue upward, after moving all my gear up the steep bank, creating the stash and finally cooking up a fast meal. Day two, loaded down with an overloaded pack, carrying all the things that I figured would be most critical to establish my base camp, including my pump action 12-gauge shotgun strapped on in front, I set out to begin the exploration. I was excited to venture into the unknown, seeking my new temporary home. I felt like an explorer sent out to map an uncharted land. I imagined that the early settlers of Canada that I'd read about, may have felt this way in anticipation of finally first setting eyes on the plot of land, promised to them by government land acquisition programs back in the 19th century.

Energy pumped through me, enough to add spring to my step regardless of the weight I carried. The relentless drizzle from above collected on each bow, on each leaf and blade of grass, spilling their contents silently over me, on my rain gear as I forced my way through the undergrowth of the steep drainage, always upward, following the powerful flow of Wilson creek just below me a couple of hundred meters as it tumbled through boulders and over slick washed windfall. Wilson Creek, my constant companion, my guide.

With no trail to follow, I simply chose, step by step, the most open available gap and pushed on, Huckleberry by my side, the two of us climbing over fallen logs, under suspended blow down, through slide chutes overgrown with stinging nettle, thimble berry, cow parsnip, and fern, then back into dense undergrowth again where the dark abundant foliage of cedar and hemlock boughs create shadowed mossy layers, where little undergrowth flourishes.

The droplets flow down over my rain gear, over my boots into the spongy forest floor with each step; the drizzle relentless, a constant breeze, chilling. I spent hours struggling up that slope, rising away from the Lake below, gaining altitude, tramping through foliage slowly changing as I rose one contour at a time. By the time light started to wane, I knew that I was still not far enough along. I'd only had one fifteen-minute break all day, enough time to stuff the last two homemade sandwiches that I'd packed, hungrily down. I kept pressing ahead though, trying to find a decent level spot, big enough to set up my fly sheet at least, a place big enough to lay out my sleeping bag and thermarest mattress, but the slope along the Wilson drainage in that area conceded nothing, no reprieve. I continued pushing through the settling light thinking that just through the next thicket, over the next hump there would be an opening, a level step of some description, but none appeared. and so, in my depleted state, with darkness almost complete, I finally just dropped my pack and collapsed on my soggy mat, jammed along the upward side of a rotten log to keep me from rolling down the slope while I slept. I was covered by only a few lean-to branches and my fly sheet, curled up in my sleeping bag, too tired and wet to try to light a fire, Huckleberry curled up right at my feet, exhausted as well. In the darkness, I could hear the wind toppling branches and weak standing snags onto the forest floor nearby, an unsettling sound. I munched handfulls of almonds and a few slices of cheese before drifting off into shiftless sleep, exhausted, tested, but determined, resolved.

At first light, around 5:00 am, I awoke to find several ants and a small black beetle crawling along my arms and chest, making their way further into my sleeping bag. Huckleberry lay nearby, curled up under some boughs against the trunk of a cedar tree. She wagged her way over to me as soon as she sensed me wake and nuzzled her nose into my hair. Soft, rotting wood and needles stuck to my face as I kicked the bag off and shook myself off, shook the bugs out. The rain had stopped finally but every surface was sponge like. Through narrow gaps in the forest canopy, I could glimpse occasional blue slivers in the mostly grey sky above. I was weary, but hopeful that today I would find my site. It wasn't long, maybe another three hours before I finally began to reach some openings, a few subtle benches now interspersed with patchy snow.

I passed over tributary streams, watched as the predominantly cedar/ hemlock forests began to give way to some higher elevation species, sub alpine spruce and Douglas fir mostly. I dropped my pack into the first real open, level area I'd seen during my first two days of relentless upward motion, relieved not to have the tension of gravity's pull for a few moments. I leaned my shot gun on a nearby log and massaged my shoulders where the straps had been digging in. as Huckleberry darted off, ears alert, into the forest.

I rested a moment before scouting out the area. It was level alright, an unusual feature of late, but the opening was too small to allow much sky light to filter through, too much moisture retention, and the creek was a little too far away. Not a great location to set up, but maybe a decent back-up plan if nothing better lay ahead. As I opened my pack to pull out some nuts to snack on, Huckleberry came bounding down the hill from above, her hackles up, ears down, running away from, not toward the Grizzly bear behind her. I quickly realized that her goal was to seek protection not provide it. The bear was heading straight for me. A medium sized adult, probably female Grizzly. She was loping along maybe ten meters behind

Huckleberry, gaining ground, but all this happened within a few seconds so, difficult to gauge the timing and distance.

I glanced over at my shotgun, maybe three meters away, loaded, ready to use, but three or four steps away, Huckleberry had darted in behind me. I moved one step left, toward the gun, but froze when the bear froze too. It came to an abrupt halt, seeing a human in front, and stopped maybe six meters from my position and immediately stood on her hind legs, head high, sniffing the air, her golden muzzle and mane glistening with moisture, catching light. The hump on her neck defined, chest heaving from the chase, saliva dripping from the quivering black gums below bared teeth. I froze in place, heart pounding, breath held, a coiled spring, set to release, and I remained that way those few seconds as the bear grunted and puffed air, snorting the exhale, shaking her head side to side, before dropping to her four paws once again, turning abruptly. With a final dismissive snort, she bounded off from where she'd come. She left me, grateful to breathe again. Huckleberry slouched sheepishly away, behind me, then started wagging her whole body, bounding around, as if this had been some kind of hilarious prank, not a near death experience. This was my first introduction to the upper Wilson bench, an area and a bear that I would soon become very familiar with.

I did find a good camp location soon afterward, maybe another kilometer further on up the valley, in a partially open meadow, along a small stream that dropped down into Wilson creek a hundred meters below. There was an almost perfect circle of tall, spruce trees, the space within, maybe forty feet in diameter. The circle sat in the center of a small meadow. After a bit of clearing and limbing within, this ring of trees became the walls of my camp, the home base I'd been searching for.

This is where I existed the next three and a half months, where I would string up tarps, a wall tent, build a stone hearth for cooking, the area I would gather eatable plants and collect firewood from. The place I would return to day after day, after hiking, searching, gathering, hunting, exploring in all directions, all elevations, walking, always walking... hundreds of kilometers.

In many ways though, over time, I became disillusioned with my plight, with my endless wandering. I found mountain lakes that few had ever seen, picturesque but, disappointingly devoid of fish. I hunted for deer, initially, hoping to utilize techniques of skinning and p4r0eservation to gain a nutritious supply of protein, but after weeks of failure to even get a clear shot off, I made the mistake of shooting one, hitting it with a slug from my shotgun, then as it staggered off to escape, I released Huckleberry from her leash to help me find the injured, retreating animal. This, I later learned, was an amateur move, one I would regret from that day on. Instead of allowing the animal to think it could stop and try to recover and rest without fear of pursuit, (where generally they simply just lie down and slowly bleed out) we pursued it, which generally can give the animal enough of a fear/adrenalin boost to continue the chase much further. In this case, to well beyond any place I could track it. I lost my temper at that point and punched out at poor, innocent, Huckleberry, who was oblivious to what she'd done wrong. After that she had begun withdrawing from her usual good-natured character, becoming more cautious; wary of my moods.

The only other hunting opportunity I had during my time on the Wilson Bench was to shoot my neighbor, the mid-sized, Grizzly, Arnica, I called her. Usually I would hear, not see her, somewhere near but distant enough, ripping apart rotting cedar logs that were full of ants. or digging into a hill to unearth a trapped ground squirrel. But one day, I managed to come across her on a steep slope not that far from my camp.

She was grazing on some greens, only a couple hundred meters up the hill from me. I had been still and downwind, so she was not aware of my presence. I'd tied Huckleberry up at camp, which is what I'd begun doing whenever I went out carrying my gun in search of meat. I unstrapped my shotgun and moved silently up a few meters and stopped, hidden behind a mossy log. Arnica had not heard me. I continued to inch forward up the slope, stopping every couple of meters to see if she sensed my movement. When I was within maybe fifty or sixty meters, the only range I felt comfortable shooting from with a slug from my twelve-gauge, I sunk myself carefully between two rocks, the gun barrel protruding, and lined her up in my sights. She stopped grazing then, raised her head, her nose twitching, slightly upturned, searching out any perceptible danger. With her head raised and still, above the dense, leafy foliage, I had a clear shot. Then with my finger pressed tight on the trigger, my breath barely perceptible, every nerve end sensitized, focused, the world in a vacuum…. I carefully released the pressure and lowered the barrel. I remember hearing my own whisper at that point…. 'leave her alone, you idiot,' saying to myself, 'what are you doing?'

The bear sensed my presence then, maybe it was my barely audible whisper, maybe a slight motion or lull in the down draft allowing scent to momentarily drift toward her. She rose to her hind feet a moment, swung her head around both directions, then lowered back down, facing directly at me for a split second, her black eyes flashing like a penetrating laser, the beams shooting, a warning, not a threat. Then, calmly, she lowered herself onto all four, turned in the opposite direction and strode off effortlessly up the steep embankment disappearing into forest cover. It was then I realized my place on the Wilson Bench, that I could live with, not against. Just be, neither prey or predator. From then on, my shotgun remained hanging, barrel down, from the cut stub of a spruce branch beside my wall tent. Huckleberry remained untied. I became an involuntary vegetarian, hunting and fishing had been eliminated. The seed potatoes I had brought, along with the lettuce, squash and zucchini seed, all of which I'd planted in the soil I'd so painstakingly turned over and removed all the weeds and rocks from just outside my ring of spruce, in the clearing, had all been consumed in a matter of days by marauding field mice. The tofu I had brought, which had kept so well preserved and amazingly undisturbed over several weeks, stored within the icy cool upper bank of Wilson creek, hidden in a small cave, was all gone. I had panned for gold in several seemingly ideal geographical locations, (according to 'the Gold Panner's manual' that is), along the creek, and come up empty. Berries I had counted on eating weren't ripe yet. My days became monotonous. Rising, usually running to the outhouse pit to relieve my bowels, which seemed to govern, more each day, what time I should rise. I later reflected that I must have had Giardia, probably from drinking from the small tributary stream by my camp.

With these gaps in my diet, I became better at identifying eatable shoots, mushrooms and roots which, when added to my own supplies, extended the rations quite a ways. I would gather enough miner's lettuce, fern, thimble berry stalk, false Solomon's seal, stinging nettle, and other wild greens from the meadows and slide shoots nearby to steam and add to a small bannock pancake and a few nuts for my breakfast. I was able to sustain myself in this way, with the flour, corn meal, nuts, seeds and beans that I would, from time to time, draw from my stores down at the sling stash below. Some days, I'd shoot a squirrel, but I never really like that meat much. I only ate it because there was no other.

I became thin, streamlined, muscular, like a deer, not a bull. It became effortless to walk quickly, up or down, pack heavy or light, but after the first two months, I tired of simply walking to explore, walking for the sake of walking. I became at times morose, disappointed in myself in my failure to thrive as I had earlier envisioned. I would lie for hours on the split cedar bed I had constructed, writing in my journal, sometimes depressed, listening to the relentless rain patter on the tent top. I would immerse myself in thoughts of Emily, of failing in the relationship, of love and loss. I would consider alternative futures, like raising a family, adding on to the house, cycle these ideas through my mind, write them down, re-read what I had written, realize that it was mostly self-absorbed drivel, then stab at it with the pen, scratching it out, or tear out the page and burn it. I would dream of comfort, warmth and food, of being dry, of being home, in Procter.

I read but did not absorb. "To be awake is to be alive." Thoreau wrote, in Walden, yet I did not feel inspired.

"Not I, nor anyone else can travel that road for you. You must travel it by yourself. It is not far. It is within reach. Perhaps you have been on it since you were born and did not know. Perhaps it is everywhere - on water and land." Whitman had told me. I had considered this, pondered my travels, searched relentlessly for meaning in my plight, but kept feeling inadequate. I tired of my own company, felt sorry for myself. Some days I would have an ongoing dialogue running through my mind, a silent script that seemed pointless. I would swear at my own image in a puddle's reflection, disgusted. I would sing one phrase of a song for days on end, silently at times, then in a whisper or whistle, mumble it aloud, or yell it loud and clear, repeating the fragment for all to hear. Frustrated that I could not remember the next phrase, longing to learn a new song, but bound by this one, the one trapped in my head.

I wrote letters to Emily, to my brother, to family, to friends I had and to friends I wished I had, letters that would never be sent, letters that burned to light my evening fire. I contemplated my own sanity, wondered what the difference was between sane and insane. In my time at Wilson, the spring and early summer brought mostly rain, dark cloudy days and few sunny reprieves, or was it just my dark memories that created that grey reality? I've reflected over many years on that time that I spent alone, there in that ring of spruce, trying to find my way. I've come to decide that I've gained more from reflecting on that period than from the period itself; or is that one and the same thing? It's difficult, I've learned, maybe impossible, to identify the epicenter of significance when you are in it. Usually, unless maybe you are a seer, a guru, a mystic with clairvoyant powers and a third eye - one of those who recognize without the guidance of hindsight those moments where you have planted that tiny seed of wisdom. Unless you are one of those, which unfortunately I am not, you will not recognize that epicenter until you look back at it from a distance.

When I had finally emerged from that experience in isolation, three and a half months later, Emily and I had had a period of rekindling. We both realized that we needed to give ourselves a second chance. We had trampled through mixed emotions that had surfaced. I questioned my past level of commitment. Had I been fearful of expressing my dreams? Had I suppressed emotion as insurance against the fear of failure? Was this suppression the cause of failure? "Why does human emotion need to be so complex?" I asked Emily. "It would be so clear and simple if we could just act and react to what lies in front of us, like a deer does, or a frog. What's my problem?" Sensitive issues were raised between her and I. We discussed frustrations, vented, appeased appetites, commiserated. We seemed to settle into a new sense of security, dropped most of the ego generated energy in favour of compromise and honesty. Things resolved.

I learned to retain journal notes, not burn them; not just journal notes, notes of all kinds, some on scraps torn from a partly used sheet, others on whatever was available at the time, a newspaper margin, a box flap, a torn open envelope, quotes, ideas, a new plan. Sometimes I still glance through them and see that they are much more detailed than I remember taking them. Even though they are kind of scrambled and out of order, they provide fuel for my thought process. Now, I've begun to compile them and try to create a kind of order, chronologically at least. When

I scan them, they are disjointed but maybe one day I can create some flow from the turmoil. Emily encourages me to; thinks I can produce something worth reading one day.

We became comfortable, accustomed to one another again, Emily and I, clear on the past, on our intention for the future. Those addictive cravings of mine still rear up from time to time, like the gregarious friend who drops by in a drunken state, the one who everyone criticizes yet we all secretly miss their spontaneous, unpredictable attention. Even though those attractions, their mystery and unpredictability, tug and pull, I can use them to remind me that I'm just another guy, Emily just another woman, that we can keep them at bay, remain steadfast in the cumulative strength of our bond. Now we are a couple that has formed this irreplaceable connection, one that won't easily be broken. The colourful threads of our history are woven in erratic patterns, the fabric stronger, less vulnerable to tearing due to the irregularity of the weave. Well, that's the way Emily would describe it anyway, in the tapestry model.

I've deflected rogue thoughts over the years, filled perceived gaps with alternative interests, consumed time and energy with the myriad complications of life. Has it worked? There have been times when I've still doubted our future together. Times when I've become frustrated with what I would consider, her lack of drive to excel or at least her failure to commit to personal challenges, to improve, reach her potential. Times when I've felt she was too easily deterred from tenacity in favour of the easier, more familiar road. Her tendency to sweep problems under the rug. Sometimes I've felt reigned in, yet, I've grown - we've grown, to cherish the value that only collective years can provide. We've learned that a complex history is irreplaceable, that, layered emotions, familial bonds and friendships are nurtured more by what the couple has become than what the individual could have been. We've learned that these are all key facets to our relationship, that expectations need to be realistic, not idealized.

I've tried to learn to back off some, to take myself less seriously, not to expect more from others than I expect from myself, to relinquish some of what drives me. We have embraced this formation, she even more than I. She has been, strong, supportive, infinitely loyal and loving, and though I often appear to take these things for granted… I don't.

<hr>

I pull my truck in beside our wood shed and hop out. I'm tired and hungry but feeling like I've gotten plenty done this morning. I jump up into the box and pull the push broom out from where it rides upright in the pipe slot by the cab. I sweep the bark out onto the path, absently looking up the road, wondering if those inspectors from the CP investigation, will be coming along.

They want to look more closely at the accounting of my time that night, but hey, how would they be able to? I drop the broom back into its slot, pondering the possibilities, and head in toward the house to find something for lunch. Could be some leftover stew in the fridge. This won't be the first time they have come after me, nothing new here. I have been vocal over the years in opposition to CP who, I'd always said, had not been divulging accurately, the details of what they have been transporting by rail. But, like Emily says,there is no law against being opposed to something, right? There's plenty of documentation of my opposition, lots of letters to the editor on the issues over the years and I've had more than a few discussions with local MPs and MLAs - not only on this issue but others too, like the ferry cutbacks and clear-cut logging, and more recently, the Jumbo Glacier resort development. Emily had thought that I was being too adversarial toward government at the time, well,basically too adversarial to all authority, but I think she has become more convinced lately that the threat is really real, that big business is taking over important policy decision making. We have had many discussions on that. My philosophy is one of promoting personal responsibility. I want less government control, especially while governments are being installed by big money interests who dump massive amounts of cash into political coffers in order to alter election outcomes. I want to see more freedom of expression by individuals, and I'm not afraid to vocalize my thoughts on the subject.

Em has always respected that fact, even when she disagrees with my opinion. She does agree with my opposition to corporate control though, always has. We have had many discussions over the years about how corporations are becoming more and more the controlling entities of the planet, of how it is corporate kingpins that now call the shots more than governments. Really, corporations own government, and now install selected individuals to rule under the guise of democracy. If these fuckers want to keep dropping by to harass me and my family with these questions, let 'em come. I'll deal with them. They've got nothing on me. There are lots of folks opposed to their destructive profiteering ways. I'm not the only one.

We follow, more often I, than Emily, the posts and blogs of other likeminded individuals and groups, on-line. I'm not talking about those that are living in fear, paranoid, conspiracy theorists who pointlessly debate the existence of the Holocaust or the Apollo moon landings or argue that Reptilians are running the world. Just people with good, healthy suspicions about corporate control. There are many folks who commiserate and plan strategy against corporate controllers. One group I have been following more closely lately: the counter corporate control initiative, the C3, as they liked to be known. I think they will be a very useful and anonymous tool in my plight to raise awareness on many fronts.

This I ponder, as I study and stir the mixture in the pot, stirring, slowly stirring, eyes following the swirl of softened corn, onion and diced potato that bob and bubble in the fragrant chowder, its steam rising over my face- the aromas of home and garden, blending with the moist heat. I sit down with my bowl of stew, chewing, thinking about the investigators; they came by our place again the other day, asking all kinds of questions to Emily, and looking for me, again, to ask more. Again, I wasn't home. Still haven't spoken with them, guess I'll have to make contact at some point, just to keep them from coming back to the house. Fucking meddlers. Just need a little more time to consider first, find out what kinds of questions they're asking, exactly.

I was talking to Angus Mowatt down at the mill on Wednesday. He's always got an interesting perspective on things, often quite bleak, kind of doomsday, but I try to take the time to bounce an idea or two off him when I get the chance, or at least have a listen to his latest angle. He's kind of like the mad professor, always with a new theory, one he knows is true, regardless of opposing mainstream belief. He'll tell you all about it if you give him a chance.

I had just dropped off a nice cedar pole that he'd needed for an arbour project he's working on. I'd salvaged it from recent blow down up on the East fork, managed to cut it into ten-foot lengths and roll them onto my truck bed from the high bank of the road. They were really heavy, cumbersome, still a bit green, but I got them rolling down along a couple 4x4 posts sloped like a ramp that I'd perched up between the upper bank of the road and the side wall of my truck box. Those poles just rolled right over and dropped into the box, with a little guidance. Poor old truck shuddered pretty good when they hit the deck. Thought the first one might just roll right over and knock the opposite side wall of the truck box right off onto the ground, but no, tough ol' truck stayed put. I sold the rest of those poles to the mill for a good price too, some nice clear logs there. Cedar is going for better prices these days, especially clear cedar, so I don't mind picking up some extra logs when I spot good ones up on the mountain. The money is better in that than firewood and I've got a timber mark that I can use from pulling some logs off my own property before, so I use a felt marker to jot the number on each log which legitimizes the load. 'Course, you're not supposed to sell logs from crown land like that, but hey, can't see any reason not to, especially when they are already fallen over, so what the hell.

After lunch I load up my saw and axe in case there's time to pick up a load on the way back, but first I've got to drop by the mill again to pick up my cheque for the poles. When I pull in, there's Angus again, just walked in to the office to pay for some lumber he'd loaded into his truck. Says, "Gabe, been up to no good these days?" in his usual sarcastic tone, a thin smile poking through the gray stubble on his chin.

"Yep, I say, "all kinds, and you, what have you been up to, up on the hill there? How's the family?"

Sage, the girl who works in the office doing books and invoices, is sitting at the desk while we wait for her to fill out the paperwork. "Just be a minute guys." She always seems occupied. Sage, busy but cheerful, a good combination. Whenever she runs out of office work, or the guys are shorthanded and a storm is blowing in, you can see her out in the yard stacking wood or covering piles with tarps. Angus and I move on out to the front step to look out over the lumber yard and mill while we wait. I see my friend Seth's wiry form, out there working the saw, and Fred is pulling freshly milled boards and timbers from the rollers on the far end to sort and stack them. Pat is driving the forklift, his shock of jet-black hair like high gloss paint, greased back, pasted to his head against his dark complexion making him look like he's just dropped in from a Bollywood set, the perfectly combed lines, unwavering against his skull despite the jolting mechanical action. He's got a slight build and that big forklift makes him look small, like a stick man. He's loading stacks of rough-cut cedar into the kiln to dry, an unlit cigarette dangling from his mouth. They don't allow him to smoke down there so if he's not sucking on one of those vaporizers, he makes do with an unlit smoke. Always lots of action down at the mill. I like being there, smelling the fresh sawdust in the air, the pungent humidity of bark, soil and wet wood all blended together with dust and diesel. It forms this distinct aroma that I miss when I've been away - somehow makes me feel rooted, like a worm must when it wriggles into the earth, home, secure in its habitat.

Angus sidles up, too close. I can smell last night's whiskey and maybe a hint of garlic on his breath, a sour blend.

"They're all fine I guess," Angus responds, "making their way. The teenagers are as much a pain in the ass as they can be, especially Leif and Ariel, keeping me up at night, worrying, but nothing new there. Goddamn kids," he says, inching closer.

"Right," I say, "Got that stage coming down the line. I'll stay tuned to pick up tips from you." I say, taking a half step back. "Maybe I should keep one of 'em busy helping me stack wood? Could use some help some days." I mention, considering my mounting list of wood orders.

"Well, yeah, that could be good. Not a bad idea, but I think Ariel is going off to Spokane next weekend, might not be around." "Oh well," I say, "I'll check in with him on timing then.

Maybe I could get him to pick up a part for my winch too, if he's heading across the border. I ordered it on ebay. It's waiting for me at the Metalaine Post office, just across the line... could save me a trip."

"I'll mention it to him Gabe...let you know. Got to warn ya though, those boys of mine might know how to work, but getting them to do it is another thing."

"Working at home is different than getting paid to work." I say as he pulls off his glasses to clean them with the tail of his shirt.

"Yeah, I s'pose," he says in a resigned exhale, "I'll keep trying to train 'em, but if I fail, you'll be hearing from me in exile in Mexico or somewhere. Sometimes I wonder, will they outlive me and turn into real human beings, or will we all just end it together under a cloud of carbon."

"Okay guys, Gabe, here's your cheque, and Angus, your invoice." Sage interjects, calling out to us. She's leaning over the desk, passing the papers to the other side. Impossible to miss the deep cleavage pressing against her button up blouse. "Thanks Sage," I say, walking in to pick mine up, scanning it and handing Angus his bill. He pays and I stroll out behind him. At the side of his truck he turns before opening the door and says, "and Gabe, what's this the CP cops are saying 'bout you anyway? They brought your name up when they were interviewing door to door, asking me and the wife if we knew you. Seems kind of intrusive. What is that all about?" He looks at me intently. "They're doing a lot of door to door right now and if they are asking us questions about you then stands to reason they are asking others the same. Not sure I liked their tone," He says disapprovingly, like a professor rebuking an insolent student. "Sounded a little like police state paranoia to me."

"I guess I'm not that surprised," I say, backing away from him as he leans too close again. "They know who I am from me calling in to the CP offices to complain about lack of information as to the type of chemicals they have been transporting through Procter all these years." I say, now standing in a muddy rut by his tail lights. "I've been on their case for a long time, probably think of me as a thorn in their side." I fold the payment slip and stuff it into my back pocket, "So now they've labeled me as a subversive and are trying to make something of it. Far as I'm concerned, they can ask all they want, won't amount to anything."

"Yeah, well they have been out here with investigations before, haven't they? They haven't forgotten that incident where guys blocked the train from passing a few years back, eh Gabe." He says, shuffling closer to close the gap again. "Bet they're figuring they can link the events. What do you think? Can't say as I'm rooting for them. As you know, I don't mind the subversive types so much." He says, spitting out a fragment of wood from the toothpick clenched between his teeth, a sly smile on his face.

"Right, "I know. I think you're one of 'em," I say, grinning over at him as I shuffle back a bit toward my truck, "and yeah, seems they are trying to link those events, but I can't see how. Sherlock they're not, guess we'll have to wait and see."

"Yep, guess we will. Now you keep a low profile, ya hear, Gabe?" He says, finally turning away toward his truck. Then, as he opens the door, turns and looks me straight on, silently, with that penetrating gaze of his. Angus, he's an odd one, introspective, I guess you would say. Kind of an intellectual type with a sharp edge, very critical, of people, government, and opinionated. He has some interesting, thought provoking ideas, so you often see him bending ears. He is a doomsday type though, so his outlook is often kinda depressing, gloomy. I guess he's probably right about this though; I'll have to watch this investigation closely. This pressure has got to stop. These bastards are hitting close to home, insinuating things, unsubstantiated accusations. I'm beginning to feel caught up in the gloom too, like having a low-lying cloud slowly easing into the valley bottom, enveloping you in weighted haze. I wait while Angus pulls out, then hop in my truck, glancing in my rear-view mirror as a mix of bark, mud and sawdust spin up off my rear tires as I accelerate too quickly, heading for home. "Fucking Sherlock." I say under my breath.

By the time I pull up into my parking spot at home, my fuse is lit, anger burning. I turn off the motor and sit there listening to it tick as heat escapes the engine block; a fly buzzes my head and lands on the inside of the windshield. I crush it with the back of my hand, its yellowish insides smear across the glass. Fucking inspectors invading our space, trying to influence friends and neighbours with hints and assumptions. 'Next one shows up here, I'll bury in the back yard with my bloody back hoe.' I say out loud to the smeared fly. I slam the truck door behind me, then the door of the house as I enter, and without taking off my boots, head straight for the drawer where the phone book is, look up the number for the CPR detachment and call the number from our land line.

A too cheerful voice, female, answers. "Canadian Pacific. Good afternoon. Can I connect you to another extension?"

"I need to speak to someone in investigations." I say. "Oh, and in which jurisdiction sir?"

"I'm in B.C. The Kootenays. It's about the derailment." "Right. Okay sir. I will connect you. Your name please."

I give her my name and she rings me through to another line, where another polite voice picks up. My fingers are drumming on the counter, thoughts jumbling around in my mind. I should have jotted down some points first. Got too many questions, need to emphasize the lack of evidence, the bullying, counter atta…, then I quickly hang up before a new voice breaks the silence. Need to prepare, get my head in order. I look around, stare back at the silent phone, then scan the room again, knowing the house is empty, but checking anyway, feeling self-conscious, unsure how to proceed. I pick up a scrap paper and a pencil, and stare at it a moment as though it were an etch-a-sketch, that would magically begin to fill itself in, like Harold would do in the Purple Crayon books that my father used to read to me as a child. Maybe I'll just draw my own reality… a CP cop car being buried by a back hoe… or, no, got to focus, what to say….

I reach for the coffee grinder to prepare a cup, then change my mind and put the kettle on instead to make tea… too jittery for more coffee. I sit down on a bar stool at the counter while it heats, the bubbling sound somehow soothing. As I stir honey in around the bag of Earl Grey, I begin making point form notes, and the tension recedes. I'm feeling ready, vindicated. I'm innocent until proven guilty. I'm being harassed, targeted groundlessly. Isn't it slander to insinuate to others that a person is guilty of a crime if you have little or nothing to back up the claims? Maybe I can sue them. Got to be on the offensive… Fuckers. Got to think. The electric clock on the wall is ticking away… loud, annoying. I yank the cord out of the wall, cursing it. I scribble down some more notes.

Finally, I pick up the phone to call them, my notes spilling off the page barely legible. Time to get this done. I don't like postponing the inevitable, it makes a person crazy, tossing ideas around in your head until they're spent like wilted lettuce in a spinner. The house is still. The only sound the hum of the refrigerator, ravens calling from the compost outside, a sprinkler cycling on the flower bed near the front door. The receptionist answers again, "Got disconnected earlier," I say, "will you put me through again? The derailment in Procter…"

"Oh yes, sir, we're sorry about that. Here, let me connect you to the Cranbrook detachment. Mr. Framer, was it?"

"Correct." I say, wondering to myself if I had already told them my name or not.

Another receptionist answers, this time a man. "Good afternoon. Investigations I believe?"

"Yes." I say.

"Just a moment, Mr Framer."

There is a pause, a shuffling sound then dead air as he puts me on hold. I put the phone on speaker and rest the headset on the counter by my cup. I frame in my notes with a line of circular blue swirls, watching as my pen presses harder, indenting slightly into the maple counter beneath. A voice breaks the silence.

"Mr. Framer. Blevin here. Detective Pauwels and I have been trying to track you down."

"So I've heard." I say.

"Right, so, probably it would be best if you just came in for an interview. We have questions that need to be addressed. When would be a good time to arrange that? Tomor…"

"Look," I say, cutting him off, "I can answer any question you may have right now. Here I am. Ask away. If you want to ask me in person, you'll either have to arrest me and bring me in or come on back over to Procter." I say, "and if you do, arrange it first. I don't want you over here dropping in and harassing my wife and family anymore." I say, my voice slowly, steadily, picking up speed and volume, tension", then add, "We all know that you are just picking on me due to my past."

"Okay then," says Blevin, let's do a quick review right now, then arrange the interview." He says, totally ignoring my statement. "Seems we have some links to the derailment that lead us in your direction. Of course, we are well aware of your opposition to our rail traffic passing through that area, but we are not referring to that. We like to stick to evidence and witness testimony, not circumstantial guesswork." He says, pausing, shuffling paper again, "Evidence, like the scent trail our dogs followed toward your house, like the boot imprints that we cast from the site where the boulder was dislodged. Evidence, Mr. Framer, from notes gathered by us in interviews with your neighbours and those in the area prior to the derailment."

A silence lingers over the headset. I don't know how to respond. I wait, eyes wandering over my notes, almost inadvertently. "What did you say your name was?" I ask, stammering a bit, trying to gain composure… "Blevin? How do you spell that?" He spells it out. "Just like it sounds," and I jot down the name along the swirls in the margin of my notes. 'What do they really have, I'm thinking; if they have real evidence why aren't they arresting me? Are they going to arrest me? What can I do?'

"Slander," I blurt out, just the one word, sounding like I've just found the missing word in some kind of game show. "Isn't that the description used for groundless accusations inflicted on a person?" I ask, circling the word 'slander' in my notes, my pen point traveling around the circle until the paper gives way, tearing. "Especially when the accusations are repeated to friends and neighbours? Isn't that the word they use?"

Another pause on the line, this time his, before Blevin says "No slander here Mr Framer. As I said earlier, only evidence and statements. And we will be needing some testimony from you, as to your exact whereabouts the night of the derailment. That, and some discussion around a set of photos and casts we have collected. Seems we have a match for a specific tool and likely a boot print. A couple of other items too that you may find interesting; things, we, at least, find very interesting; things we would like to share with you, Mr. Framer."

Background office sounds fill the gap in time, a printer forcing paper through rollers, a barely audible sip, probably from his coffee cup, paper being stacked. "Our timeli…"

I cut him off again, "I'm not interested in your time line, your dogs and casts and bullshit evidence. I've got wood to cut." My voice is rising again, "and if I see you guys on my property again, unannounced, harassing us, maybe I'll just load your car into the bucket of my hoe and drop it in the ditch off my land where it deserves to be. Come back with a warrant or not at all."

Blevin is explaining how this call is being recorded, when I hang up.

CHAPTER 3

Pearl

I’ve seen Amy when she’s gone off, but she don’t usually cause me no trouble. Usually, we can sit for a while and toss some ideas around without her getting too riled up. And sometimes she is just plain thoughtful. Anyways, I like to stay in touch with all the neighbours so I drop by on her from time to time, less now than before. She likes to serve Bergamot tea and she always spikes it with just a little bit of brandy.

Raving Amy Rutherford, as she is known by the locals, lives just a little west of the village in a small pink coloured house, all faded and weathered, its chipped asbestos shingles loose, and the sagging roof lines showin’ its age, kinda like her; she’s years younger than me, mind, but let’s herself look some haggard some days. The yard is usually pretty wild lookin’, with uncut grass and wild flowers, kinda like mine. Apple and plum trees and some wild rose grow topsy turvy, springing up at all kinds of angles between the road and her house. They haven’t been pruned in years, seems to me, kind of lends a look of abandon to the land but it does hide her house from the passing traffic some, somethin’ I think she likes. The neighbours who own it are now retired. They own a lot of acres, partly farmed. Amy’s place is the caretakers house. She doesn’t seem to be doing a lot of actual farmin’, but still, she tells people that she is the caretaker of the land. She’s been around a long time, some twenty-five years or more. Guess the years just go by and things change like they do… slow. I guess her mental state hasn’t improved over the years, her attention to stuff most of us call practical and logical has fallen off - she has become kind of distracted. She sometimes patrols the property lines, makes sure no 'infiltrators are invadin' the land'. And the owners, Rick and Patsy Shepherd, nice old folks, don't have the heart, maybe the courage now, to put her out, so there she is, year in and year out. She can be very provocative. Folks that have grown up in the area are well aware of this, though they know better than to respond with more than a smile and wave. 'Casionally, when, "she's off her meds," as locals likes to say, you can really get an ear full of venom or worse, simply by being in too close proximity.

There are rumours that she burned down a house once. Nothing was ever proved 'bout that, but the feud between her and the guy whose house had burned was well known. She has often been spotted slinkin' round private property in the night, peerin' in windows or suddenly appearin' from the woods onto the highway, striding out, head up, facing forward, like she is on a mission. Her expression is always so sardonic. I like that word. Maybe they made it up by lookin' at one of them itty bitty fish when it was caught in a net, just lookin' out like it knows something they don't know. Sardonic. like she has a secret challenge, a glint in her eye, just waitin' for the one who isn't wary to ask her why.

I used to visit her more often than I do now. Sometimes now, she doesn't seem to want no one just showing up at her door and she don't ever answer the phone so you can't tell 'er your comin'. I pound on her door and I see just the smallest bit of curtain gets turned back from the inside window while I'm knockin', like she's just hidin' out inside waitin' for me to leave. Back a few years ago

I'd go over there regular. I'd pick her some mint, on the way, from the patch just over the bank from her house and I'd bring her a dozen eggs too, something she always enjoys, 'specially if it's free. Being there this morning, seeing the line of rocks she's put across to block the driveway and hearin' her dog Zacky barkin' from the other side of the door, makes me think, maybe it's time to spend a bit more time with her, not less. I think she has become more reclusive these days, but who knows, maybe it's just a phase. I wait at the door for probably ten minutes 'fore she cracks the door open.

"Oh, it's you." She says, opening it up a bit wider. "Thought there was an intruder out there. Come on in Pearl. I'll put my rifle away." She says, as Zacky pushes the door open the rest of the way with his head. It's quite a head too, big as a pumkin. I think he's part Rotweiller and part Shepherd... plenty heavy. Amy props the rifle up inside a cluttered closet beside the door, turns and says, "can't be too careful…. Tea." She says, not askin', just tellin', like it's mandatory to be carryin' a rifle to tea. She turns and walks down the hall toward the kitchen, her bare legs stickin' out below an old tattered navy-blue robe, her feet shufflin' along in a pair of flat pink slippers. There's just a narrow path open between stacks of newspapers, magazines, Tupperware containers and cardboard boxes all stacked and spillin' over on each side of the hallway.

"Been collecting eh Amy?" I ask her.

"Well, you know, I need to have references." She says, as if I should know better than to ask. "All, good reference articles."

"'Corse." I say. "And what else you been up to these days sides readin' all them articles?" I ask her. She's getting' water in the kettle and settin' it on the stove top. Has to move two pots out of the way to fit it.

"Zacky! Zacky!" she yells down the hall. "You get in here! Goddamn mutt." She shuffles some of the dishes around until she finds a couple of cups and rinses 'em out real quick. "Good ol' Liptons." She pulls two tea bags from an old tin container on the counter. "Gets me goin' every afternoon. So how are you and all your crazy neighbors doin up the hill these days Pearl? You guys been plotting some kind of strategy up there, you and all them subversives?" Zack lumbers in, a long, danglin' drool hangin' from his lip and settles in under the table with a thunk. He's got some weight to him.

"Can't say as we have, Amy. Most plannin' I've done lately is to decide which row to plant my second lettuce crop in. Don't see the neighbors much. How 'bout you, you got yerself a decent garden out there this year?" I say, noddin' toward the back yard. "You always used to grow such good garlic over here, better'n mine ever got. I think you've got the soil for it."

Just then, Zack picks up his head, perks his ears and lets out a series of barks as he runs for the door, jarring the table leg as he passes, the newly poured tea tossing and rolling up over the rim a bit before settling down again.

"Damn dog! Who the hell is that now?" She says moving quickly over to the window behind the kitchen sink that looks out over the driveway. It's all covered over with a thick, dark curtain, behind that, a bent sheet of cardboard is leaning against the glass. She keeps the road side windows covered all the time so the only natural light that can come in is from the window on the far side of the room. She moves the corner of the curtain back a bit and tilts the cardboard aside a little, then leans over to see out the crack, a clump of hair falling in front across her eyes.

Zack is still barking over at the door. "Looks like a couple of goddamn cops." She says, her eyes following some movement toward her door. She moves down the hall toward the door where Zack is barking. "What the hell do they want?" I get over to the sink and pull open the curtain. There's a car parked over at the entrance to her driveway, just the other side of the line of rocks Amy has put across. The men must be on the step already 'cause I can't see 'em. The car isn't marked, but could be a policeman, I guess.

They've been around a lot these days with the big investigation into the CP derailment and all. When that train up and went off the tracks, well, chemicals was flowin' everywhere around there; in the creek, spillin' into the lake, all kinds 'parently, toxic. chemicals that kill life with long names endin' in ide and ic. There have been lots of suspicions. The investigations by CPR police and the RCMP so far have been what they call, 'inconclusive.' But the word is that they figure the rock that caused it, got rolling down the hill with a little help.

The RCMP have a long history of involvement with Amy too, so she's no stranger to them droppin' by. She calls 'em all the time, complains 'bout a neighbour makin' noise or someone aiming a gun at her. She's told me that she's reported 'suspicious movements'. She's called in UFO sightin's and 'guys skulking around tryin' to set fire to her house', so they have become well aware of her special status. She complains that 'those bloody cops just don't take the evidence seriously.' The CPR police have no knowledge of her history nor many leads in the case of the derailment so the investigation continues, and these door to door interviews are bein' conducted. I figure this is probably one of those, but I don't think they have any real notion as to who lives here. "Who the hell is that now?" She asks again, toward the door. I don't say anything. "Tellin' ya," she says, "Looks like a couple cops."

She's peering carefully through the peep hole in her front door now, her face pressed close in; she's tied a blue bandanna round to bundle up her hair that's sticking out in all directions. I can hear the screen door open and they knock. Amy calls out without opening it, "what do you want? Just step back from my door." I move down the hall a bit to have a look. "Hello ma'am." A man says to her, loud enough to be heard through the door. "We are sorry to disturb you, but we are just following up, door to door to try to find information from anyone nearby who could help us with knowledge of the recent derailment, just some routine questions ma'am.

Another voice says, "Identification Ma'am, Blevins and Pauwels." Guess they're holding up their badges to the window 'cause Amy says. "Ha. I knew you were cops. Spot 'em a mile away, city, RC's or CP's, they all look the same." Then she pulls a worn tube of lipstick from her robe pocket, opens it and quickly rubs a smudge across her lips, smacks 'em together and says, "Anyways I knew you were coming, saw it in the way the leaves fell on my driveway this morning."

She opens the door a few inches and peers out, lookin' them up and down. "So, you think I blew up your train then eh?' The two officers are in plain clothes, one with a notebook, the other with a camera hung over his shoulder. They look at one another questioningly, then Blevin says, "No, of course not ma'am. We're just here to see if you have seen or heard anything that could be useful in the days leading up to this event. We are trying to establish the cause."

"Oh, the cause," she blurts, "Of course, someone blew that thing off the tracks. I would have done it myself if I knew how. Bloody government… always meddling in our affairs. Did you know that my father used to be a blaster? Had all kinds of rubber mats around the yard, drills, and boxes full of dynamite and detonators but I never did learn much about that stuff, 'sides, he died thirty-five years ago." She's got the door jammed open between her feet, just enough to see out, keepin' Zack back behind her legs. He's panting hard now, trying to get through.

"Please ma'am, we had no intention of asking you about explosives. There were no explosives involved in this incident," says the officer with the notebook, looking up after jotting down something. "And if there were, we would already have arrested anyone involved, you included. I'm not sure that your attitude toward this incident is very helpful ma'am. Don't you understand the gravity of this situation and the danger that this has put people in, not only the trainmen but also local inhabitants?"

"Danger, yes, I know all about danger." She opens the door fully now, her hand holding onto Zack's collar. She stands facing them, her frayed pink bathrobe tied loosely around her waist, "What about the danger of not having any ferry service at 2:00 in the morning when I'm having a heart attack and can't get to the hospital? How's about that for some danger?

Anyways, those trainmen didn't get killed, not like the last one's you guys killed back a few years."

"This has nothing to do with your ferry service ma'am and that derailment you are referring to was resolved some ten years ago. I'm not sure what it is you are getting at, but you are not being very cooperative, and we will be making note of that, not to mention, your inflammatory remarks."

I can see from the hallway that he's jotting down some more notes. I move a little closer, thinking that maybe I can settle Amy down a bit 'fore she gets herself in trouble. One of them officers notices me there, then he looks up at his partner who continues to be silent, shuffling his feet. He adjusts the weight of the camera that's hangin' round his neck.

"I don't like cops on my land." Amy says, "but when they do come, I'd rather see 'em in uniform, specially the cute ones, but you two don't fit that description anyway. And all I can tell you is that, I've got nothing to tell, so," she pauses, adjusting her grip on Zack who is pulling his weight forward, "I'm telling you that

I want you two goons to get off my property before I let my dog out. And I don't want your buddy there taking any pictures of my place," she nods at the partner, "If he wants some good pictures, maybe he can come back later and we can talk," she says with a suggestive smirk, glancing down at her own drooping cleavage as her partially open robe slips open a bit more.

"We will be reporting in detail on this Ms, Rutherford," says the second officer as they step back from the step at her entry. "You may be required to come into the Nelson detachment to follow up."

"Hah! If you want me in there, you can come and get me. I'm sure you'd enjoy that." She says, shouting behind her, "Come on Zacky, come on boy," she says as he pulls at his collar. The two officers have already turned to leave but look behind as she lets Zacky by. She keeps hold of his collar till they get near the car, then releases him, whispering, "go get 'em boy. Take 'em." He bounds away, toward their car, seeming a little disinterested but ready for some action. They don't take any chances and shut themselves into the car just before he approaches. The second officer holds up his camera and gets a couple shots of the yard, dog and house before they pull out. I can see them all flustered and trying to buckle up their seat belts as they back out onto the road. "Assholes." Amy says, coming back to the table. "Almost flashed them, but they left too quick." She smirks. "That would have got 'em going eh Pearl?"

"Oh, I think you got 'em goin' anyhow, Amy," I said.

While I'm walkin' my way home, I stop to pick up one of them free local papers they leave in the plastic dispensary box by the row of post boxes across from the store. I grab the top copy. The headline reads: "Linked events in Procter?" with a photo of some twisted railway tracks below it. Sure enough, seems like even more rumours are swirlin' round these days, Now, seems like, they are trying to link the 'hold up', that happened 'bout three years ago, to this derailment now. I scans through it to the middle part… it reads:

…in the first incident RCMP said the culprit lit a fire beside the tracks to get the attention of the engineer.

"The fire made them slow down and then this individual had a flashlight or a torch of some type to wave them down," said RCMP Sgt. Jim Raeburn.

The balaclava-clad individual then handed the note to the conductor using a long pole. Once the note was in the hands of the CPR the individual scampered off. Despite calling in the RCMP dog unit the person responsible could not be tracked. Two nights later the train was stopped again when somebody put a lighted flare on a board and set it on the tracks. On the board was a similar note as the first one except this time it was handwritten.

Though no further action has taken place this week, Raeburn said the mischief is a serious concern for police.

"This provides a fear factor because they [CPR] don't know if there has been any further tampering," he said.

That was a statement from the incident three years ago, and then they goes on to try and link the two incidents…

"Tampering, in the present case, would be an understatement. This could be more like sabotage or even terrorism." said C.P. spokesman Gerard (last name?). "If we prove intentional interference in this derailment, serious charges will be laid. Penalties include long term jail sentences."

As I'm wanderin' back home, I'm thinkin': so Procter, the little village that hardly anyone knows is here, is now famous- infamous maybe's the better word, 'specially if they're goin' to be lookin' for terrorists now. It's been a week since the derailment, but there's still media trucks equipped with camera men, flashin' lights and microphones everywhere you look, so can't say it's so peaceful these days. Environmentalists have monitors runnin' round and the government has them official lookin' folks in white coats, technical types from the ministry of Environment, studyin' our air and water, takin' samples. They're provincial and regional politicians too. Seems like everyone wants their picture on the news. Doesn't seem to matter if it's good news or not. I can hear engine noise as I walk, sounds like another locomotive engine comin' through with a tanker car. There's a white, over- sized van parked by the tracks near the road where the highway meets the Irwin road turn-off that heads up to my place. It's got government logos on it. Must be one of them science labs I heard bout. Fish, birds, insects, deer…all been affected, and all them slitherin' creatures too, all bein' monitored. Thousands of dead and dyin' fish and birds have been collected, such a shame. Guess if they can't revive 'em, they study 'em. Tons of soil had to be dug out from the area. They're takin' it out on them train cars and burnin' it, callin' it, 'remediation', whatever that is.

They're sayin' that hundreds of thousands of liters of water was pumped from the site and taken out by them tanker cars. They brought 'em in by rail and took the water away to that 'reclamation center'. Giant chemical sponge mats was used to try and absorb some of them chemicals floatin' on the still water by the tracks and on the shore and on the lake too, at first. Then, later, they floated a huge tube, looks like a giant sausage out on the lake round the whole area. Must be least a mile round, that ring. They say that the tube will suck up them chemicals that's tryin' to float away, all kinds of toxics 'parently, stuff that kills the life outta things, with long names endin' in ide and ic. That tube is yellow and it's sittin' anchored out there preventin' people, and their boats from gettin' into the disaster area by water.

Helicopters was flying overhead for the first couple days too. What a racket. There's a few motor homes set up at the end of the road near the site too, to hold all them media. CP has their own cars set up on the tracks, some of them sleeper cars and a kitchen car, pulled off on a nearby siding so as emergency crews can eat and sleep right there on the job. Them cars are runnin' generators all the time and lights all night, so it seems like you are going downtown every time you walk out the door these days- noise and people everywhere. The main rail line has been left clear so that them CP engines and flat-deck cars can get in there to deliver stuff, material and equipment I guess, and to take out all that waste and spoiled water. It's already been a week and still, them folks who was livin' nearby, can't even go back to their own house. They're sayin' water, air and soil testin' will carry on till they can give the all clear for them folks to come back. Guess that hasn't happened yet.

I've been walkin' 'round the area plenty, every day since the train went over, talking with some of them CP workers sometimes or chattin' with someone from one of them news trailers, but mostly I like visitin' Marney. Guess I'll drop by again now. I met her down at the store the day after they started. She's been cookin' in that CP kitchen car and she'd run outta butter and was buyin' more. Nice young girl, runnin' her tush off down there, cleanin' up and feedin' them hungry guys while at the same time tryin' to keep their hands off her. She has to move in all directions at once, like one of them one-man-bands. Least they put her in her own private room so she can rest when her shift is over. "I got a lock on my door," she told me. I dropped down there to see her on the third day when she was just finishin' up, cleaning up the breakfast mess. She had a few minutes to sit and have coffee on the back platform. She had to reach over and help pull me up to the bottom stair from the track where I was standin'. Her arms are plenty strong for such a little thing and I can feel the rough, dry bumps of callouses on her hand. "I'm not as nimble as I used to be," I tell her.

"Yeah, well you don't need to be Pearl. Only the young and stupid work up on this kitchen car." She smiles, showin' one crooked tooth slopin' out on an angle like it's tryin' to get out over her lip. "How 'bout a fresh cup of coffee?"

"Don't mind if I do. Thanks, Marney. So how you and the crew doin' these days? Goin' to be here much longer?" She pours me a cup and tops up hers before moving inside to sit at the little yellow counter by the window. "Pull up a stool Pearl," she says. "We've been real busy. Got myself some part time help now too so I don't have to do all the dishes, thank God. Good thing, especially now that they've got me feeding some of those government workers too. Yesterday I had more than fifty for dinner: two shifts, and at lunch there was more."

"Sounds a bit overwhelmin'," I nod.

"Yeah, can be, and almost all men too," she adds, lifting her eye brows, "but mostly they're pretty good guys, appreciative you know, so it's okay, mostly. Lots of action out there, apparently. Been listening to the talk at the tables. Seems that after they diverted the clean creek water from entering the contaminated pool on the upper side of the tracks and finished pumping all the contaminated water from the area, the investigators found that big boulder they're all talking about… lodged in the culvert.

Apparently, it was almost three feet around and had it almost totally blocked it off." She shakes her head.

"Hmmm, been wonderin' 'bout that. There's lots of rumours runnin' 'round right now 'bout the cause." I say.

'Yeah, heard some. So, they say that the boulder caused a rise in the water level and that over time, it saturated all the ground along the tracks." She carries on. "They've done some investigation of the area now and say they found a spot about 80 meters above the tracks, up on the bank, where they think the boulder came from. Just down there." She nods her head east down the tracks. "The inspectors that were in here at lunch were saying that they see no sign of erosion around there at all… no other factors that could have caused that rock to roll down. No slides."

"That's sumthin'," I say. She carries on some more. "So, now, who knows what they'll be thinking, but one of the guys that was working the pumps in the pond below that spot told me, it looked to him like someone could a been digging under the low side of where that boulder had been. He was saying that it did look pretty fresh, like shovel marks, not some kind of natural coincidence. Who knows?" Marney says, gettin' up again, lookin' 'round 's though she shouldn't be sittin'.

"Yeah, I read something 'bout that in the paper, but they didn't sound so sure. Guess we'll soon find out eh Marney? They got plenty of them 'nvestigators and news people 'round here to discover almost anythin'. I'm sure we'll be hearin' lots a news reports true and otherwise." I says, sippin' up the last a my coffee. "Guess I'll leave ya to yer choppin' then. Looks like you've got a sack a carrots waitin' for ya there." I say, noddin' over to the row of veggies stacked behind the counter

"Oh yeah, Pearl, always another sack of something to chop up. Hail to the food processor." She says as she bows down to the big ol' machine to her right.

"See ya next time Marney. Thanks for coffee." I say. "I think I can make my way down that step long as I go backwards." I say, as I step over to the hand rails and turn. "You take care now and don't be choppin' anything that's not vegetables ya hear?" I say.

"Okay Pearl. Still got all my fingers now, so you come back and check on them soon." She says holding her hands up, fingers spread. "Looks like we'll be here at least another week or so."

CHAPTER 4

Hailey

I flex my knee and pivot over the log, shovel raised and pointed forward, spear like, poised to stab once again into parched earth ahead. I'm a cave women warrior closing in on her kill. The final shift of planting is finally upon us- with only two days left of tree planting in the season, production speed remains surprisingly high. People are getting pretty burnt out, but now, with the promise of parties, relaxation and a big pay cheque looming ahead, enthusiasm seems to be adding energy to the mix of the crew. I spin round again after kicking the last tree tight with the heel of my boot and raise my spear-shaped shovel, aimed high toward the next plant-able spot ahead. My planting bags swing light against my legs 'cause I'm down to the last couple of bundles. I release the upper straps from my shoulders to dangle loosely at my waist to stop the chaffing for a bit. Were we really designed to carry weight like this all day long? I rub my shoulder as I move ahead. This is my seventh season on the slopes and I often reflect on how my technique has become so much more fluid from season to season. My first season had been brutal. I'd been trying to pay my way through an international studies program at Simon Fraser University. The studies had practically pushed my brain into an explosive state. I'd challenged myself to complete a full course load including an extra class in criminology in the final semester. I guess it was more about finding my way and 'doing the right thing', than anything really grounded in passion or self-direction, because, in the end, all I ended up with, seems to me, was some debt, a pile of essays, and a lot of soul searching, not to mention, a brain with over-strain. I did okay, but never went back. Now here I am, seven years later, a career tree planter? Is there such a thing? If so, I guess I'm well on my way. What used to, at the beginning, be a constant battle between me and the ground ahead, where I had, through pure struggle, force and tenacity, moved from one plantable spot to another, now has become more of a rhythm… less lurching, more confidence. This rhythm accomplishes more at a much faster rate, with less energy. Now, I can go to the next spot, not search for it, move along with a halting flow, exertion, punctuated every two or three meters by stabbing my shovel into mineral soil, eyes reading the ground like a blind man reads Braille, feeling it out in the flash of a glance. Sometimes when I get lost in the groove, I'll plant out a fast 400 from my bag-up, and find myself, right hand in cruise control, searching my right feed bag for the next tree and not finding one there, already planted out to empty without even noticing.

Those are the days where the trees just seem to jump into the ground on their own, the days where you get back to camp with a big day score but feel like you could still do another run. Why can't every day be like that? Those days are far and few between. Usually you just get back to camp, spill yourself out of the crummy and drag yourself toward the cook shack looking about as haggard and dirty as your planting bags. I do seem to have more of an affinity to hard labour than tough studies though. I've always found it easier to challenge my body than my brain. Hopefully this doesn't become a permanent affliction where my brain gets all soft and mushy like the body of some biomedical engineering genius.

"Hey, throw a flag once in a while, will you? Nelly shouts, from back down the slope a couple hundred meters. "Especially when you're puttin' 'em in just the far side of a log. Just planted right beside one of yours, bitch." she says in her chiding tone.

"Watch for the signs girl." I shout back. "Look to the stars.

Feel the tree that is there."

This kind of banter fuels the energy from time to time when we aren't lost in the movement or out of breath or just too wet and miserable to care. These past days have been dry for a change. Spirits are higher. Nelly and I have had more going on in conversation than just the usual wit and rebuttal exchanges. Sometimes when we are nearby one another on a long line with fewer snarb, snag or 'fuck-brush' obstacles to interrupt the flow of conversation, we've gotten into some pretty heavy topics. Earlier we were discussing some philosopher dude she'd studied last semester, at Concordia in Montreal: 'is there such a thing as original thought?' But usually we'd be talking about how some guy was bragging about his sexual prowess or how he was bad mouthing his ex-girlfriend. "Like don't they know, we are all on the same team?" Yesterday, we'd been comparing notes on an 'overlap.' We'd both slept with the same guy at the same camp a month earlier. We were talking about him like we were talking about just having read the same best seller, discussing the details. "What did you think? Was he sweet or what?"

Anyway, all the chatter keeps your mind off the repetitive pounding in of one tree after the other and I'm sure we come up with all kinds of great solutions and insight that can be drawn from in times to come.

The sun is almost overhead now, beating down and rising in waves of heat off the scarred landscape. Slash piles and low-lying brush litter the land, non-marketable logs, mostly hemlock, lay tumbled and scattered at odd angles. Horseflies circle, buzzing and getting tangled in hair; trying to land on their constantly moving targets.

I pry open the earth to slide in another pine plug. There are plenty of good spots with the required mineral soil, but the earth has dried out quickly in the intense heat and most of the planters are discouraged when they occasionally consider the probable futility of planting tiny vulnerable trees on a hot day in parched earth with only more hot, dry weather in the forecast- a recipe for a future replant. So sometimes we say to ourselves, why are we doing this? Most the time we are just too focused on getting the trees in the ground as fast as possible, trying to beat our own pace of yesterday or the pace of the guy right behind you, to be considering the future plight of tree survival. We are opting instead to hit the 400 dollar a day average or in some cases going for the high number of the crew that day. Everyone has a target; accomplishing it is all-consuming. Is it greed that drives us, ego, or something else? There is always a spirited sense of competition amongst the planting crew- all part of the package of toil and camaraderie. Emotional lows and highs storm through the camp, up and down the slope, washing over everyone relentlessly, day after day as boundless energy, then bitter exhaustion in the wake of exertion, scatters debris behind it like a tornado running through a trailer park. By the end, if you survive that long, you are scarred but somehow content, satisfied with accomplishment, with survival, with vivid memories and strong personal connections as calling cards. You don't need to wonder what someone else is thinking. There is no room for neutrality. Opinions and reactions ride close to everyone's emotional surface. When you are under pressure to produce and you're spent with exhaustion, compromise and diplomacy are often left behind and replaced by knee jerk reaction. Reactions incite more reactions, lively arguments, often absurd, spice up camp life, leading to tears, laughter, anger, sexual attraction, jealousy… name the emotion, it's there. Maybe we'll start a new camp game show called, 'Name That Emotion.' It will be more entertaining than The Price is Right.

I pull another plug from my right-hand feed bag and slip it down the back side of my shovel blade forcing the little soil tube to the bottom of the hole before pulling the blade out and kicking the hole closed. My shovel has shrunken from wear, the stainless- steel blade, polished from use, is now only about six inches long, from its original ten. barely longer than the plug of a tree. It's hard to give up your old shovel and replace it. You get attached after planting a couple of hundred thousand trees with a tool. It becomes a comrade and you depend on it to get you through another day. Some of us even get a little superstitious about it like a pro ball player with his favorite bat. I expect it to perform, to miss rocks when I stab it into the ground, thereby avoiding the inevitable 'ping' which sends that reverberating shiver through your wrist and up your arm. I expect it to screef in one clean sweep. I sharpen it. When I'm down and alone on the slope with only my shovel for company, it listens. When I swear at the slash that's tripping me up, curse at the mud that's just landed in the corner of my eye, or at the blister building on my big toe, my shovel listens, she commiserates.

I'm almost bagged out, Nelly", I shout over my shoulder. "How many you got?"

"A bundle and a half." She looks back at me, up the hill. "Won't be long!" I plant out my last few trees, bouncing spot to spot, popping one into a tight little pocket when I see it, triangulating, a kind of forward but diagonal pattern where you can plant more with fewer steps. I put the last one in, spin round, step up onto a nearby stump and scan the ground below. I tie off a blue flag to mark my line and jump off the stump with a shout. Then I thrust myself down the hill through the slash like only a seasoned planter can, dodging and strategically bounding through the entangled snarb of logging debris as gracefully as a rabbit hopping down the road, or so I like to think. I skid to a halt beside Nelly midst a small cloud of dust, reach into her feeder bag and pull out a handful of trees. "Okay, let's get this done then and head back for lunch. I'm starving." I say.

"Thanks Hailey, yeah, I'm ready for a bite." she says glancing at her watch. "Pretty good time - 11:20 am. Earlier bag out than yesterday at lunch. If everyone is moving like this today, we'll be out of here early tomorrow" she says, stopping a moment to button up her loose cuff.

"Yeah, right on. I'm into that. I'm really into that." I say as I pound another tree in. "I'm into a stirred martini in a frosty glass, a soft, freshly made bed in a nice room, with crisp sheets and a hard body lying beside me."

"Ooh yeah, sounding like a realistic fantasy sister." Nelly says as she turns to get around me and continue the line of trees. "Just a day away." We both leap frog each other, planting out the last few on our way back to the skid road below.

Later, as the day wraps up and the dust covered crew cabs pull into camp, the exhausted crew spills out the doors while the dust cloud that follows the trucks settles on them, day packs full of extra gear, tree bags and shovels follow. The usual dirt encrusted attire seems even more degraded lately; the universal garb, stained further by dark, sweaty patches running down backs and underarms; torn sleeves and scratched skin are worn as accessories. We look like a bunch of refugees. There is a sense of accomplishment in the air, an energized vigor brought on by the knowledge that the last day is upon us, that we, those of us left, have survived another season. Many had not. There was quite a long list of casualties - those that had been forced to drop out due to tendinitis in the wrist, back issues and swollen knees, others who'd quit just because they couldn't take it anymore. Then there are always those that are susceptible to the fifteen week flu, a instantly debilitating illness brought on by a person's eligibility to receive employment insurance. We had lost a few of the crew to that phenomena over the past few weeks, something universally unappreciated by both crew and management, especially as we struggle to finish the final trees at the end of the contract.

Despite the exhaustion, the camp feels celebratory. Beer bottles are popping open a little faster than usual, sounding more like champagne corks; smiles are abundant. The crew is milling about, in the shower line, chatting amongst themselves and sorting through misplaced gear or just meandering around camp aimlessly waiting for dinner to be served.

Appetites are always huge in camp, the quality of cooking and ingredients is high caliber and so, from the kitchen, aromas as enticing as any top end restaurant along Commercial Street in Vancouver, float through camp. It's hard to keep hungry planters at bay, but the cook, Ingrid, has little patience for wandering fingers in search of a sample taste so mostly we wait expectantly.

Maurice is just adding up planting scores in the score book when I walk by. He's a foreman, not a planter, not any more anyhow. He used to be but has moved on to a position as crew boss, so now he drives one of the crummies to the block, organizes the planting block and crew and keeps planters from running out of trees and drinking water. The foremen also have to walk across the slope behind the planters to double check on planting quality. They dig up the occasional tree to check for jay roots, or to see if it's planted too shallow, too deep, in the wrong substrate They check spacing79to make sure we aren't putting them in too close or far from one another. We give them a hard time, but at the same time, usually appreciate knowing in advance if the quality is high enough. It's easy to lose track sometimes, especially of spacing, and if you do, and the average quality drops, the results are picked up by the ministry of forests checker, who comes around after we are done an area, lays out a grid of plots, and records all findings within those plots. They have a formula which results in a quality percentile. If we fall below a certain percentage, they call for a replant or fine us. We have pretty good planter quality control on our crew, so we rarely run into replants.

"Hey Mauri, how's production looking today?" I ask, "Figure it'll be a short one tomorrow or will we be doin' overtime? Either way, I'm in it till it's done."

"Hey Hailey, lookin' fresh. Managed to get into the shower ahead of the rush eh? I like that tan. You're gonna look hot like that in your bikini when we get back to the beach. "I'm wearing a sleeveless top. My shoulders are white down to my elbows and my hands are white from wearing gloves, so I have really dark forearms only.

"Yeah, was thinking I'd tape off some stripes on the rest of my body too so that I can have that Zebra look. Think that would look better than the planter tan?"

"Sure, I'll help you out with the tape later."

"You wish", I say, throwing my head back with a smile, and coiling my still wet hair into a pony tail.

"Hey, my score's not on there", I say, glancing at the sheet over his shoulder.

"I put in 1620."

"Okay, got it. Whoa, great production there, girl. Who you been chasing?"

"More like, who's been chasing me, I guess. I was just trying to stay ahead. Had a good day."

"Yeah, looks pretty high. Crew average might be around 1350 today, maybe 1400, from the look of it."

Even if they didn't show it, or ask, most of the crew would want to know where they placed in the 'high baller' grid. I was one of 'them' but never made top score, though I was often top woman planter. We are all after a higher day average, more trees mean more money. Usually the guys have just enough extra power to pick up the top spots, most days anyway.

"Hey Hailey, sauna's hot, or almost there anyway. You in? There's room," Ron says in passing. Ron could always be relied on to get the sauna stoked up after work most days, or to have the morning fire going in the cook shack barrel heater too. I could never figure how he could manage to fit in extra chores to our already full agenda, but he somehow managed it.

"Hey, yeah, sounds like a plan," I say, "sweat off some sweat. Does that actually work or is it like a double negative thing where you end up just back where you started?"

"Yeah, let's see, maybe we'll monitor and report findings, collect soil samples from our skin, maybe create a plant-able spot, report back to Nature of Things or something." Ron says.

"Yeah, maybe we could apply the method to climate change, double change equals no change."

"I'm not gonna change, I'm just gonna strip and jump into the hot box, comin'?"

We make our way over to the dome shaped trailer that houses the sauna, a red-hot stove pipe emits a powerful flow of smoke and sends sparks out above the roof. No one seems too worried about fire hazards. After all, most the forest around camp has already been burnt by wild fire anyhow. The sauna, built on a trailer frame, is a simple wood-framed hut with a couple of windows, cedar benches and wood stove. The arched roof makes it look like a little gypsy wagon. Scratches, dust and dents expose the history of travel and time on its surfaces, worn and weathered like most the vehicles and equipment in camp, people too for that matter. "Change?" someone else quips, "you got change, my meter is running out."

"Okay, that's it," I say, "I'm in, enough of this, let's go cook some dust off our skin."

Once we'd hung our clothes up on the hooks outside the sauna trailer, we go in, naked; there are few secrets in camp, bodies aren't one of them. I open the door to be confronted by that familiar wave of heat and the aroma of cedar as it quickly envelopes us.

"Thought it was hot out there on the slopes today, but nothing like this," says Ron, "maybe after this, it'll feel cooler out there tomorrow…. Whew.", he breathes out and sinks back, leaning into the back wall and taking a long pull off the quickly warming beer condensing in his hand. Dirty, dark droplets run down the ropy veins on his arm as the sweat already starts to bead.

"Doesn't matter about the heat tomorrow," I say, "we'll be pounding 'em in regardless, at high speed just like today 'cause everyone is ready to get 'er done. I'm going to pack up some stuff tonight already, after dinner, just so I'm ready to take off early. Soon as I'm in cell range, I'll be calling in for a reservation at the Lola." The Lola is a resort hotel on the beach front of lake Windermere, where many of us planters like to go to lounge on the day off.

"Yo, sounds sweet Hailey," Ron says, reaching over to touch my knee, which I'm hugging, bent up, pressed over my breasts, "maybe you'll need someone to share that reservation with."

I smile back with a glance, "yes, couldn't let that pristine king size bed be left half made. I'm sure there will be a solution for that problem." I say mopping a back hand of sweat from my forehead. "Time for a bit of a splash there eh hon, cool things down a bit," I say with a wink in his direction, tossing a scoop of water onto the hot rocks of the sauna stove. Just then the door opens and three more planters crowd in shouting through the wall of steam as it bites into their eyes, "jesus! Can't see. Where da bench! Cei boi! Caulice! Tabernac!" Pierre shouts. 'The Quebecers on the crew have the most colourful and exuberant profanity. They really know how to swear and make it sound like they mean it…great to throw a wall of steam at them to fire up that language. I love having them on the crew. There is always at least a third of the crew from Quebec it seems, and they add another layer to the mix, spicing it up with an accent, and attitude and some extra emotion. It also adds to the friction at times, but hey, who doesn't?

Dinner is another elaborate six course ethnic meal, this time Indian. The dishes are spicy and plentiful, a delicious display of abundant sustenance. We planters are accustomed to gourmet meals and by this time in the season we've come to expect to be amazed by some of the dishes provided. Massive stainless- steel baking pans overflowing with veggie and beef curry, dahl, chapatis, tandoor chicken, spinach masala and salads line the serving table. A line of planters immediately files up to begin heaping the delicious steaming array of courses onto plates before settling into one of the four picnic bench tables that comprise the dining area in the cook shack.

After dinner, dishes are done, day scores recorded, then the inevitable lull in energy, the crash, occurs, where that seemingly boundless energy which pervades tree camp, finally falls off the cliff and lands in a pool of quiet exhaustion on the ground.

My muscles ache as usual as I roll over in my sleeping bag the next morning to grab my clock. I squint at it, clearing my eyes of the gummy dust that seems to be emitted on a daily basis, another bodily function these days, the new norm: eye scum. As usual, the alarm clock beside me tells me that it is just a few minutes to alarm time, the natural alarm rhythm pervasive now after months of training. I force my fingers straight, massaging them for a moment to release that claw-like shovel grip which makes its way into my hands each night. Why do the fingers have to remember everything from yesterday? I sit up in my sleeping bag and pull a sweat shirt over my head, careful not to disturb the dew that clings to the sidewalls of my tent.

The crisp morning air is a brisk awakening to the senses. Normally in the mornings, I am fast and efficient, focused on being as prepared each day, as quickly as possible. Every movement and moment count. Focus, if lost means running late and running late means racing to get to the truck before it leaves you behind. Hurrying means not packing enough lunch, missing your morning coffee, forgetting your extra gloves, hat or sun glasses, something to impact your productivity, your edge. Planters are pushed to their physical limit each day, tested, driven by tenacity, ego, greed, responsibility, varying motivating forces. All potentially effected by slight imbalances. The most productive planters are the organized ones. I like to think I'm one of those. I eject from the tent, zip it closed behind me and step just a few paces away to squat and pee before grabbing my day pack, coiling and tying my hair into a quick bun and heading over to the nearby stream to wash. Unless it's pounding rain out, I prefer washing my face and brushing my teeth in the peaceful quiet of the stream each morning. I would rather deal with a few mosquitoes than tackle the chaos of camp sinks littered with oodles of toothbrushes, soap pumps, and grunting people first thing. It's like having your own master bath; that's not asking too much is it? After my tent, it's the only private place I have, somewhere I can put some things in order, come back to them undisturbed, where some flat stones create a shelf, where I've hung a small mirror on a broken tree branch. Maybe if we were staying another month, I'd hang up some pictures and a calendar, laminated ones. Thankfully, I'll be finding my way back home before that happens, back to Procter to my country cabin, all settled into the woods waiting for me to return. My vision of home becomes more idyllic each day; it'll be hard to fulfill, like a mirage. Anticipation can be like that can't it?

I can see as I approach the cook shack that I'm not the only one with a little extra bounce to my step this morning. Realization that the final day is upon us, that the season has gone well, that we will finish in the sun without threat of rain or sleet-soaked gear to burden the mood, all factors adding smiles and positivity to the morning mix.

I am always one of the early risers. I like to arrive to the cook shack just a little before the rush. Ron is always there first though, already having split kindling and lit the barrel heater to take the chill off the cook shack. Ron is generally a very thoughtful and giving character, but I think his morning ritual is as much out of recognition of his own need for that meditative time in the morning as it is to be helpful. I watch his easy fluid motion as he splits kindling off a cedar log, the Stanfield's heavy weight wool shirt stretched over his muscular frame. It looks almost therapeutic, his hands just a blur of motion, automated movement loosening taut muscles, kind of mesmerizing to watch. Within minutes the fire is crackling away under his supervision, beckoning those who enter. Even though the walls of the tent are only canvas, they provide enough insulation for the heat from the stove to take the chill off the crisp morning air that envelopes us at this elevation. June has brought an early summer this year it seems, yet still, at over 4000 feet in elevation, the fluctuation in day/night temperatures is much more extreme than down below. Planters fling the cook shack door open one by one, letting it bang behind them, and after first filling a cup with steaming hot coffee from the urn that Ingrid has already set out, most make their way over to crowd round the wood stove, shuffling feet and staring vacantly while consciousness and caffeine take hold.

When breakfast has been devoured and we've all packed a lunch from the always overflowing spread on the lunch table, it's time to grab our gear one last time, find a spot in one of the crummies and head to the block. Because the production was high yesterday, the forecast is for an early afternoon finish today. Once all the trees of the contract are in the ground, we're done. Everyone is motivated by the promise of time off, of some pampering. Me, I can feel it already, a soft sandy beach, a colourful beach towel, maybe a nail file, an ex-foliating foot rasp and some deep red polish. Or if it clouds over, a spa, where they can just take care of the whole mess while I lay back, eyes closed by the weight of cool cucumber slices.

⁓⦵⁓

I pull off the road at a roadside gas station, my Toyota Tundra 4x4 pickup covered in a thick layer of dust. "Man, I'm not going to want to get close to this thing once I'm clean again," I say to Melvin, who had been the only one who'd packed up his own personal stuff in time to catch a ride out with me this morning. It had taken a little longer to finish all the trees yesterday, so I kyboshed my plan to head into town after work. Besides, it's better to lend a hand in breaking down camp if you can, do your bit, at least for a while. It feels like you are abandoning everyone otherwise. I helped Irene pack all the pots, dishes and food away in bins. We stacked them all up in the back of the bus, jammed 'em in and bungied 'em down so that they wouldn't topple over on the bumpy ride down the logging road later. Others coiled up hoses, loaded propane tanks, coolers and garbage. They dismantled tent structures, tables and plumbing, hooked up trailers to trucks and loaded up the wood stoves, tarps and chairs. By the time I left, there were just odds and ends strewn around the area to wrap up and I figured the managers could handle that part.

"I'm goin' in to grab an ice cream…got a craving. You want?" I ask him, hopping out and watching gravel and clumps of dirt fall from the rocker panels as I slam the door. We'd made it down the long dusty road to the highway, about 80 kilometers worth of potholes and rising dust plumes. It was the first gas station we'd come to and it had a giant ice cream cone painted on a rooftop sign. I stuff the credit card in the gas pump and begin pumping, topping up the tank before going inside.

"I'm coming in too," he says, after rummaging through his day pack for his wallet.

"I'm moving in on a triple scoop with chocolate sauce," I say. I have what I consider a serious addiction to ice cream, and I'd done without for too long; figured I needed the ice cream more than the gas. I have addictions to lots of things. I would be a fat, lazy drunken, drug addict with a hoarding problem if I didn't have the where-with-all to rein in my own bad habits sometimes. There are just so many wonderful things to experiment with out there. Even though in camp, I can get my hands on pretty much any kind of drug, booze, or dessert, mostly I don't partake in a lot of indulgence up there, most don't- just costs too much. After a beer or two at the end of the day, exhaustion so quickly sets in that you feel too comatose to really participate in any kind of partying. "Hey, I've been cooped up for weeks in the back country getting nothing but exercise and good food, so time to get started in on some good old empty calories and general debauchery." I say. "Here's to that," says Melvin, nodding toward me with his coke raised high. The east Indian looking girl behind the counter has just piled a cone high with cappuccino and Cherry Garcia for me.

"Yeah, drench it," I say to her as she begins to squirt black gooey chocolate sauce on to the towering cone, "This is the real shit," I say, "gettin' one?"

"No, got what I need, let's move," he says taking another sip. "Just going to have a quick cig outside before we pull out." He says. He pays cash for his coke and the pack of Player light and moves outside. The girl hands me my cone from the cash counter, "Yeah…. Lunch," I say to her, "thanks." I note the faint aroma of curry or cloves, probably from the girl's reheated lunch. It brings me instantly back to a sidewalk cafe in Madras, India, where I'd spent a few afternoons absorbing the chaos of mass human movement as it unfolded on the street a couple of years earlier while on another winter getaway. Amazing, how a single fragrance can send you off on an ethereal voyage back to India or Tobago, Guatemala or Peru, all those places bottled up and accessible at a moment's notice, all stored conveniently in your olfactory memory, accessible, even from a gas station in B.C. I'm always amazed - how does the human brain work like that?

I step away, licking my cone, savouring it, simultaneously flashing back to the blog I wrote while travelling through all those places. I found it the easiest way to keep up with all my friends and family. Well, except for my parents who couldn't read it because they wouldn't be able to find it online even if I explained the process to them. They are happy not to understand technology. Once a month or so though, I would print the blog and mail it to them. I still record events now sometimes, but I keep most of it on lock down, don't really want to share everything with the whole bloody planet. Sharing is over rated.

Melvin stubs out his cigarette in the gravel and hops in the passenger side as I buckle up, balancing my cone between my knees. I pull out on the highway, feeling the draw of the open road. Sunshine bakes the asphalt, and glances off the water of lake Windermere in the distance, I've got a pocket full of money, time off, and a cone dripping Cherry Garcia down my fingers. Life feels good.

"The rest of the crew shouldn't be too far behind, well some of them anyway," I say, "should be a good beach afternoon in front of the hotel if we can all be there in time."

"Yeah, sounds good to me. The laundry can wait till tomorrow. I'm going to try to book into the resort too, see if they have room, unless you want to share the tab on a bigger room," he says, glancing up at me hopefully.

"Yeah, it's not tourist season yet. I'm sure they'll have room, I'm kinda set on having my own space," I say, deflecting, trying to keep my options open.

"Is it Thursday?" I ask at the check in, trying to fill out the form. "Yes," says the clerk, "Thursday, June twenty-fifth."

"Okay, got it, been a while since I saw a calendar." We check in.

I book a couple more rooms too, one for Nelly and another for Maurice and Irene, his wife. They wanted to be sure to have a room to come to, but it seems there is lots of vacancy. The day has warmed up, clouds are still, off in the distance. I can see the sand on the beach from my room beckoning my body to lay down and relax. I succumb.

Now, the aftermath of a planting season is spread out on the driveway behind my truck in front of me, the Toyota's shiny paint hidden well behind months of layered grime. Soiled tree bags, shovels, the mattress, unfolded tent, clothes and bins full of rain gear, tarps, extra boots and all other necessities of camp survival, all covered in a thick layer of settled dust and laid out in disarray. It had been laying there for a few hours now as I avoided the chore, opting to peruse my place, check out the overgrown lawn and neglected flower garden. A giant black banana slug is finishing off what used to be a tulip in the flower garden out front. Raccoon tracks meander through. I hope they haven't found a way in to the house.

It feels good to be back. A solid place to come back to, familiar and friendly. I've lived here now for over a year, which is a long time for me, so it feels like home now. I look forward to making it my own once more, to cleaning out the cobwebs and stocking the fridge, a bit of mowing and weeding and voila, my own resort. It had taken six hours to drive back from Invermere and I hadn't started early. My head was still foggy from last night's shooters and beer, dancing and sex. A nice fog, the kind of fog I can live with. There must have been at least a dozen of us from the crew at the Station Pub, a local venue with live music where we'd gathered after splurging on steaks and seafood at a lakeside restaurant. We'd shut her down, dancing, spilling drinks, and letting loose till after two a.m. Tree planting stories swirled round, memories fresh, flowing like draft beer from a tap, running rampant, consumed, altered, exaggerated, retold. Spent, athletic bodies flew around the dance floor as if they'd never worked a day. I think it was around 2:30 pm, by the time Ron and I finally made it back to my room. Clothes were quickly shed, anticipation had been building, insinuation strategically placed, promises shared in a glance, in a sensual dance move, now realized, tension broken by our naked bodies finally tumbling together, released. I started gathering all the dirty clothes, chucked them in a pile and stuffed the washer in the back porch as full as I could, a couple of loads to follow lined up on the floor beside it. Stink bugs dive bomb my head and the warm windows, reminding me that this is their space now.

It feels good to be back, to spread out again, put things away, to know I don't have to get up at 5:45 am, even if I do wake up then. To know that I get to sleep off the ground, cook my own breakfast for a change and maybe even eat it alone sometimes, not share my bathroom with mosquitoes, ants and dirt. I put an old Taj Mahal cd in my stereo system opting for some tunes that I don't have on my Ipod, a change. The sound is clear. I crank it up till the floor boards shiver. I can relax now, in solitude, knowing that no one on the crew is going to walk in and change the music, toss out a witty comment, or hang their boots on the back of a chair. "Alone at last", I say to myself.

CHAPTER 5

Ariel

66 I think it's better if we stand," my father said. "Just like this, in a circle facing each other, okay?" Much more an order than a request.

"Why should we?" Leif, my younger brother asks.

"And why not?" Dad answers. "Better than your mother and I talking while you kids are fidgeting on the couch. Everyone is on the same playing field this way, right?" My Dad, Angus is his name, has us gathered, the whole family, standing in the living room, in a circle, to have an 'open and honest discussion', to 'share personal problems or issues that were bothering you'. According to him this is the new age of family communication where nothing is supposed to be kept under wraps. Leif and Luna and I stand awkwardly, Luna with a nervous smile, giggling quietly to herself as we shuffle uncertainly in the circle. "Okay, who wants to start? "He pauses scanning the room through his thick rimmed glasses. He's across from me, by my Mom, a head taller, sleeves rolled up, back straight, like he's ready to go to work. I stand still, staring at the floor trying to be transparent. "Just to get things going, speak up about anything bothering you," he says. "How about you Ariel, got anything to contribute? Anything come to mind?"

I don't move or breathe, just continue watching my feet. I feel the pressure of his eyes but focus instead on the dust trapped between the cracks in the floor boards, at the old woven throw rug, at any other thing, hoping I'll be absorbed by something that my eyes wander over, anything, other than my father's gaze, waiting, hoping that the moment will pass, for him to just let it go. Even though I can hear the birds cheerfully chirping outside, it doesn't alter the somber mood in the room. At this point I would rather have been doing almost anything else, stacking wood, clearing brush in the woods, even weeding the garden. I shuffle my feet and bite a fragment of skin from an already tattered finger nail. My nails are always pared down to the nubs. "Nuthin' is coming to mind", I say, softly, eyes still downcast.

"Well come on Ariel, everything is great then? No problems?

Anybody?" He waits, moving his eyes around from one of us to another.

"No issues at school, no anger, no one is upset with me, with anyone? Something to get out on the table?" Another silence ensues, a prolonged one, agonizingly long. I just want it to end, this awkward, forced confessional. I want to turn and run for it, or crawl through the cracks. My Mom breaks the silence. She seems small beside him, like she wants to be small.

"Well Angus, maybe the kids don't feel comfortable with this forum. Should we leave it to another time or place?" The relief is only momentary.

"No, damn it, we shouldn't leave it to another time.! There is no good time! This isn't about fun and comfort. It's about clearing the bloody air!" His voice elevating with each word. "Not one of you have anything to say?"

There's a brief pause. Mom's fingers interlock, one clasping the other, her loose-fitting work pants ride high up her ankles as she shifts from one foot to the other nervously. She sighs deeply, audibly, shaking her head, glances up at my Dad, catching his eye. "What the hell is the point!" he yells, in her direction. "I can't stand this lack of communication. Am I the only one that knows how to communicate around here?" Volume rising.

"What the hell! Why even try! Jesus H Christ!" His voice has reached full pitch as he turns and stomps off through the doorway into the kitchen and out the door to the back yard. He's swearing as he slams the door so hard on the way out that I wonder if the single pane glass of the old entry will split and shatter onto the floor. It doesn't. There's a silence.

"I'm sorry kids." My mom says. "That just didn't go so well.

Your Dad is feeling a lot of pressure these days."

"Yeah, well I'm sorry too." Leif says. "I'm sorry that he is such a dick." Leif always has a way of clearly expressing himself when he feels like it.

"Leif! Don't talk like that." My Mom says in her stern voice. "I'm not coming to another family talk." Leif says. "This sucks."

I head out the front door to find my bike, feeling the same way but not saying it, hoping not to cross paths with my Dad outside. Leif goes into his bedroom beside the kitchen. My Mom and Luna go into the kitchen. I hear her asking my Mom what the 'H' stands for in Jesus H. Christ. "Is it his middle name?"

Sometimes I wish I could be oblivious like she can be. Sometimes I wish I could say the things like Leif says to my Dad. He's the middle child, three years younger than me, kind of scrawny, only fouteen, but he has no qualms about expressing his frustration regardless of the outcome. He's always been like that. I am usually more diplomatic, or maybe I just have more fear. Leif has been paying the price lately for his outbursts. And even though he is a pain in the ass sometimes, following me and my friends around, or buying the same jeans as me, being a general irritant, I still feel like I need to protect him sometimes, just not sure how.

Last weekend, for example, my Dad was telling Leif and I that the lawn needed cutting around the garden, firewood had to be stacked in the back shed, and mulch put in around the raspberries. "And it had all better be done before you two think you're going anywhere this weekend." He'd said in his calm, ominous way, staring us down, each word shaped like a grenade with a loose pin, "Not like last weekend; got it boys?"

"Yeah, I'll start on the lawn," I say, to Leif, not looking at my Dad. "Meet you outside after."

Leif looks up and says, "I'll move that mulch over now, but I'm going to meet Randy and Chris at eleven down at the bay, so I'll do the rest when I get back." He says, matter-of-factly.

Dad looks up sharply and his calculated words form like icicles, "You'll do no such thing. When the job list is done, you'll go to meet your friends, not before."

"Whatever." Leif says, "then I'd miss out on the weekend. They are leaving in their boat and I'll miss the ride, so I'm going on time. These chores will still be here when I get back." He turns to go outside. I'm still waiting to see what happens, kind of frozen in place. My Dad turns, walks round the kitchen table, and grabs onto Leif's shoulders by the shirt sleeves, bends over to his height, looks him right in the eye and says: "You will be here until the work is done… period. That is that."

"I will be leaving when I finish the mulch and that is that." Leif says back and shrugs off the hands from his shoulders, turning to leave. "So let me go so I can get this stuff done."

My Dad is turning red in the face, the usual temper rising for all to see. He stands up straight, unbuckles his belt and pulls it out of the belt loops fast in one clean sweep. It slips out of his fingers and falls to the floor. "You'll listen, for a change you little bastard." He says, leaning down to grab at the fallen belt, reaching a hand out to grab at Leif at the same time. Leif is moving slowly toward the door, away. My Dad picks up the belt and blocks his exit. I move off toward the living room door, out of the way. Dad swings the belt at Leif. Not sure if he means to or not, but he's picked the belt up by the tip so when he swings it, it's the buckle end that smacks into Leif's back, then into his arm as he tries to shield himself from the second swing. The toque he always wears around the house to keep his hair straightened out falls crooked on his head as he jerks away. "You will listen! You will get your work done! You will not leave this property!" he shouts, each command emphasized by another strike as Leif slowly stumbles toward the back door trying to avoid the blows that are knocking him around on his way.

"Fucking psyco!" He yells, dodging the last strike as he runs out, toque in hand, hair matted into his eyes. The belt buckle slams into the floor.

"I'm not doin' any of it now you fucker. You can do it all yourself!" He shouts back over his shoulder and with that he runs 'round the other side of the house to where his bike is leaning up against the wooden ladder going to the top deck, hops on it and pedals off down toward the trail shortcut to the highway at full speed. I see him pedal by the house, tears of anger and fear stuck to his cheeks, part of his tee shirt is flung up round his torso, a visible welt already rising underneath along his ribs. The laces of his runners are undone and I'm hoping that he doesn't get one caught in his chain before he has a chance to disappear down the trail. Then he is out of sight, disappearing into the tall ferns of the path. My Dad doesn't follow, just stays there in the kitchen, fuming, swearing. "Fucking little ungrateful bastard!" he carries on, swinging his belt at the table now, "rotten, no good, self-centered...." He continues, picking up a chair and throwing it across the room before going out the door, slamming it behind. The chair lands in the corner after knocking over a ceramic potted plant. It's not broken, only cracked. I picked the planter up and scooped some of the soil back in once my Dad had left the room then I put the chair back on its legs before going out the front door. Then I went out to the garden shed. I could see my Dad stomping off into the woods, kicking at things, muttering to himself. I started up the mower, the noise enveloping me, a welcome shield.

Now, again, everyone seems to want to clear out, leave my Dad on his own to stew at home. Mom heads off early to work, saying she needs to drop Luna off at a friend's place. "I'll drop in and say hi to her Mom, haven't seen her in so long." Dad's out in the shop banging things around. There's no one to talk to here; no one except Casey, our black lab. He follows me around the house, nuzzling nervously up against the back of my legs, worried about all the yelling, wondering if he's done something wrong. "It's okay boy," I say. I bend over from the kitchen sink to ruffle the fir on his neck, figure I'd better clean up the dishes before I go out or Dad'll have another fit. Casey forces his head in between my knees throwing me off balance as I try to drop the coffee grounds into the compost pail. I push him off and he starts wrestling my arm back, snarling playfully. I rinse the last pan, then figure it's time to dodge the area, go for a smoke.

I decide to head up Higgins. I bring along my twenty- gauge shotgun just in case I spot a grouse, so I have to leave Casey in the house, all dejected. "Too bad buddy, you just chase 'em all away." I apologize to him on my way out. I have gotten into the habit of carrying the shotgun up there when I go these days 'cause there have been quite a few grouse hanging around and they are an easy target. Usually I go out with friends if I'm hunting grouse, but today, I just want to get away on my own. I've got plans to meet up with friends but not until after dinner. I'm up the road to around the 4-k switch back in about forty minutes, hiking faster than usual, breathing hard, when a grouse spots me coming.

They usually sit right in the middle of the road pecking at things if you see them first. This one flies just off the road into the lower branches of a cedar, down the bank. They aren't the best at hiding, these grouse. I'm only maybe twenty yards off. I raise the shotgun, aim just above his head and fire. He drops off the branch, leaving behind some fluffy down feathers that follow, only suspended momentarily where he'd been, before floating lazily down. He's not a bad size. I flip him over onto his back, pin his wings on either side, one with each foot, and pull the legs up. The breast comes away with one clean pull. I cut the bony legs off, toss the breast in a bag and throw it in my pack. I decide to head back down on the back trail which almost connects to Higgins road at the 4-k switchback, makes for more of an interesting circle walk so you're not covering the same ground twice.

Further down, the path emerges onto another back road- the gravel road that ends at Gabe Framer's place. Pearl lives just a few hundred meters below them before the road goes back to the highway. I don't see anyone as I pass Framer's, but I see Pearl outside her place as I approach. She's whacking down some thistle up by the road by her driveway with a machete. It's pretty warm out but she's got a sweater on over an apron and a long skirt is almost covers her gum boots. Her long gray hair is tangled, loose and falling out of a pony tail. She tries to straighten up a bit when she sees me, but her back never goes all that straight, so that bend combined with the extra pounds she packs in the roll of her belly makes her look a little round.

"Hey Ariel, little one, what you up to?" she says breathing hard, raspy, as I stop in on the path. "Huntin' grouse were ya?"

"Yeah," I say, swinging my shotgun over so it hangs behind on my shoulder by the strap. "Just wandering around up Higgins a bit, getting away. Dad's gone off again."

I've told her before some stories about how my Dad's temper turns him into a time bomb. She's a good listener and never jumps to conclusions about things.

It's not just my Dad's temper that creates tension in the house, it's also his melancholy, emotional, reflections that somehow set me off. I'm not sure which mood I'm more afraid of witnessing 'cause even though the temper tantrums are crazy and kind of violent, they are over fast. But these times of 'soul searching', as he calls them, are slow to unravel and so they can be even more unnerving, especially when they are accompanied by tears, his tears, which they often are.

It sucks when my Mom and Leif and Luna are all away and it's just him and I back at the house, having dinner or watching TV or something and he starts in on the: 'problems between your Mom and I,' the main topic these days. It's usually after he's had a shot or two of his Irish Whiskey. I'm not sure how but I've become the main target for this venting. Maybe it's 'cause I'm the oldest or just the most passive, I'm not sure. I usually just sit and listen, without much comment, waiting for an opening to escape, trying to seem sympathetic, and I am in a sense, but I often find myself thinking that my shoulder shouldn't be the one that my Dad has to cry on... and he does, cry, I mean, and that makes it even more uncomfortable cause I don't know what to say. Sometimes I sit there thinking maybe it would be better if he was just mad again. I've told Pearl about this before. She's a good listener, doesn't talk too much. She doesn't decide who is right or wrong.

"Oh," she says, letting her machete drop to her side. "Well I s'pose goin' up the mountain and shootin' somethin' could be a good thing to do then. Long as you do it careful, not mad… killing something mad makes for bad meat." She pauses, looking me over then says, "How about a cup of tea before you head home?"

"Sure Pearl, sounds great, thanks." I follow her down the short path to her veranda steps. She moves slow but steady over the creaky floor boards into her kitchen. Her place always smells of wood smoke, tobacco and usually something she's just hung up on the wall, like a bunch of garlic or drying bundles of herbs. Today I notice two salted skins, drying, stretched across a board that's leaning up against the wall. Her place is always full of projects and clutter, but she always seems to find what she's looking for.

She fixes us some tea, pushes a full cup across the counter toward me, like a snow plow, pushing seeds and dried beans out of the way. She says: "Sometimes little one, when I'm getting a little overwhelmed by things, in my mind's eye, I just watch my breath. Sounds funny, but you can do it too, just watch it as it turns into a smooth film of water that floods across tidal flats on a white sandy beach, the thin skim rising, flowin' out, risin' again, ocean foam breath."

"Ocean foam breath"- I've heard Pearl speak like this before. At times like this she sounds like she's reading lyrics, kinda calm and mesmerizing, like the guy who hypnotizes groups of people on stage. I wonder how she can change the way she talks, the kinds of words she uses, just like that, from simple to rhythmic. "You can see it with your eyes closed. Try it next time you're home and there is too much goin' on. Just go to yer room, in the quiet, and try to see it, okay?" Then she coughs, stands up and walks toward the veranda door. She flings open the screen door, it's torn screen flapping. She coughs again, a harsh rumbling cough forms from deep in her throat. She walks out on the veranda and spits phlegm over the rail into the weeds below. I can hear it land. "And sometimes," she says re-entering the house, "I can just feel it, so I just gag and spit it out." She smiles, her yellow, stained teeth not at all like 'the white sandy beach' of her vision. Then she sits down and starts rolling up a cigarette from the tobacco pouch by her side. I pull my pack of smokes out from my day pack pocket and light one up too. I don't smoke at home, so it feels good to light one up here, inside, by the counter, relaxed. We sit and watch the blue wisps of smoke rise from the overflowing ashtray between us as we sip our tea.

"Cars are borrowed, and school buses are free," my mother says. That's what it comes down to when commuting back and forth to Nelson to high school these days. If I had my choice I'd be driving in each day. I can drive but don't own a car and rarely did my parents think there is a good enough reason for me to drive to school using their car when there is a 'perfectly good bus that can bring you in'. A couple of the guys own cars. Fin has one, but he's not picking me up today. He has a beat-up black Mustang… 'the Stang cruiser.' I'll catch up with him at school… got to geta refill for my vape pen. He's usually got a good selection.

The only other Procter boy who drives in much is Gunther. He's driving in this morning, but he doesn't offer me a ride, or any of my friends either, for that matter… never does. He is always suspicious of us. He is a cautious guy, always looking behind to see if anyone is following him. He studies a lot and mostly hangs out with his sister and her friends. He earns money doing books for his uncle's company after school and on weekends so he can afford a car and the gas. If Gunther ever shows up at a party, my friends and I follow him around and imitate his habit of keeping his thumb over the opening of his beer bottle. Gunther says that he knows: "One of you guys is going to spike my beer with one of those drugs you use." Now it had become habitual, this thumb plugging thing, and it's become kind of a trademark.

I do ride with Fin sometimes when there is room, not in the mornings so much because he lives a few kilometers down the road, near Harrop, and so he doesn't want to back track to pick me up. Anyway, he isn't always in Harrop. A couple of nights a week he stays at his Mom's place in Six Mile. They've been divorced for a few years now, but he lives with his Dad most of the time. It's not like we have much extra time in the morning to arrange things, or maybe we're just a bunch of super scattered dudes, but we do ride in together when it works; our gang: Mick, Melvin, Fin, Frankie and me; they call me Wifi. Mick says, "Aerials are old school man; they don't even pick up a signal any more. You're one hundred percent Wifi." Guess that makes more sense than Pearl calling me 'Little One.'

I feel lucky to have friends like this. We're all "living in our own teenage time zone" my mother always says. And it's true, especially when it comes to school. We are always right on the edge of making it on time, and though we do make some minimal effort, usually, we just brag to one another about how many 'late slips' we've collected over the course of a semester. You can't enter a class late without one, so you have to have an excuse ready every time, a good enough one to convince the secretary to enter it in the log book along with the time and date, before she gives you a late slip. We would say things like: 'was a target in a hit and run', or 'a dangerous dog cornered me', or 'had to help granny find her teeth'.

One time, Frankie told the secretary, "the weather has been so dry that I had to go up the hill early this morning to water my pot plants or they would have died. Hurried back down but missed the bus." Frankie was always testing the water, checking for reactions. It seems that the secretaries almost look forward to our latest fabrications, although they don't seem to think Frankie is so funny, 'specially after he told them one time that his grandmother had fallen into the pig pen and been eaten by the hogs, that he'd been late pulling her out, "good thing I stayed too," he'd told them, "'cause they only had time to eat one of her legs…got her out just in time." I'm sure our stories liven up their boring old office sometimes, but Frankie can take it a little too far and he says it with such a straight face it can freak you out even though you know it's not true. Doesn't help either that he's kind of rough looking, bulky and tall, looks like he could do some damage if he had to, and with that look in his eye, they probably think he has done, some damage, I mean.

I take the bus home today too, step down off the last step at the last stop. Ours is the final stop of the route. Sour Steve, the driver, turns around at our stop to head back to his place to park for the night. Sour never smiles, hates his job, would rather not see us every morning and afternoon, and if he hears you talking back to him, he'll slam the door shut on you as you step off the bus. It's four thirty; the usual drop time. The drowsiness of the hour-long ride always dulls my senses, especially heading home in the afternoons.

I stroll along the road side toward our place. Two dirt bikes suddenly roar around the corner behind me and speed by, one of them passes only a foot or two from my elbow, too close not to be intentional, I think. I look up and get a glimpse of them as they take off ahead around the next bend, but I don't recognize them or their bikes. I figure they are probably a couple of Albertan kids staying in one of the summer homes along the lake shore down below. I guess they must be out for a school break. They have some different school holidays in Alberta. They come out with all their motor toys, make lots of noise for a few weeks of the year, mostly in July and August, and then go back. Usually if something is stolen or vandalized locally and it's not me and my friends that have done it, and if we don't know who has, we will blame it on, 'the Albertans'. Works for us.

The rumbling of CP engines and machinery in the near distance shakes the ground as I walk along. It's constant these days, all that noise, so you don't think of it much. A giant yellow excavator rushes by along the tracks that parallel the road just 50 meters to my left. Still digging out toxic muck from the spill, I guess.

I veer off the road, right, to go on to the path that goes directly into the bush on our property, up the hill. I like how it appears that there is no entry to the trail. I am in charge of keeping the short cut clear of brush, a job I kind of enjoy; slashing my way down, top to bottom, swinging the sharpened machete back and forth like the bush men of the Amazon do, cutting through all the invading fern and thimble berry bushes. But at the bottom, where the trail meets the road, I always leave it grown in, camouflaged, so that people going by won't know where it is.

My bike has been stolen from the bottom of the trail before. I figured the Albertans had taken it, so since then, I've kept the trail head looking wild and grown over at the entry. I duck under the overhanging alder branch and push the ferns aside. I love the cave-like atmosphere that engulfs you within steps of leaving the open road. The sun in here is filtered, the permanent shade of the cedar canopy above and the groundwater seepage below create a rain forest feel. A fine mist rises from the creek rushing down the hill. The mist settles, feeding the moss and lichen along the path at the bottom of the trail where it curves in a steep banked turn, before straightening out under the old log foot bridge that spans the creek. Further up, nearer the top, the trail opens up more, allowing more foliage to grow in, bracken fern and thimble berry mostly, some devil's club too, especially in the spring.

I press on up the hill to the house. My mother is in the flower garden just outside the back door, weeding in around the yellow ones. She looks up and smiles.

"Hi Ariel, how are you honey. Long day?"

Yeah you know, same old. Looks like the Albertans are out already."

"Yes, I did hear the motor bikes. They're so loud, I can hear them above the train traffic. Don't they have mufflers?"

"Not really. Those bikes aren't street legal. What's to eat?" "I did do some baking. There's bread and cheese and fresh carrots, just picked, so sweet and crunchy," she says, all enthusiastic as if I'm really going to get all excited about carrots and cheese, maybe start jumping up and down clappin' my hands together. I swing open the screen door and let it slam behind me and stride by the counter, picking up a fresh baked cookie off the baking pan on the way by, my day pack still slung over my shoulder.

I climb the ladder to my room in the loft above. We have a couple of ladders at our house, permanent ones, built of solid wood with 2X6 steps. I guess they save space over having a staircase. One goes up to the loft from the living room, where my room is, and the other goes up on the outside to the upper deck, which is outside, just off my bedroom. It's great because I can actually come and go from my loft room through the outside deck exit without going through the house. The loft is my favorite part of the house. I'm grateful to have it - my own private sanctuary. Sure, my brother and sister drop by at times but mostly I have it to myself. I take off the pack, throw it on the floor and pop the rest of the cookie in my mouth. It's another 'healthy treat', as my mother would say. Natural sweeteners, whole oats and carob chips instead of chocolate. I eat them for lack of options, but I do comment about the shortage of real food, in the house, food like other people have. I love to stay over at friends' places where the family feed their kids chocolate brownies and a glass of Pepsi after school. Or they'll have soft, wonder bread sandwiches with Kraft single slices and Miracle Whip for lunch, none of this organic, dried out, whole wheat, seven grain, sprouted bread with tofu-naise.

"You ever tried to spread that stiff, organic peanut butter on crumbly bread?" I'd asked Fin at lunch today. "It just tears it up. Then you have to add some of Mom's homemade jam to it to make it softer, but she doesn't put enough sugar in it, so the whole thing turns sour... wanna trade?"

I tell ya, no one will be trading lunch with me, specially not those solidified sour sandwiches. Casey is usually the one that ends up with those. He can swallow them so fast that you don't even see him chew.

I've seen enough 'natural aged cheddar' and veggie sticks, lettuce wraps and seaweed snacks to last a life time. Those things are the staples in our house. Fortunately, now that I'm making some money, I can get a break from it… buy junk food during school hours from the corner store or go to the A & W for poutine after school when I stay in town for a while. Get a ride home with Fin or someone.

"Hey honey, can you do me a favour and go over to Pearl's place to pick up the milk and butter?" My Mom calls from downstairs.

"Yeah Mom, in a minute. Got a couple things to do." "Okay. Great. Thanks honey."

I sit down up in my loft to sort through my day pack. Got to organize the days transactions before I forget. And anyways, I always like to count cash. I like the feel of it or maybe it's just the feeling it gives me to have it. Some days at school I make some money selling pot. Usually only on Thursday or Friday when kids stock up for the weekend, but today, Tuesday, I'd managed to unload a quarter. I do pretty well some days, now that I have a budget to buy in larger quantities. Last month I'd managed to buy a quarter pound, the most bud I've ever seen. The markup is better when you buy in volume like that, so now I'm making more money on top of creating my own free supply of smoke… a 'fringe benefit', I think they call it, in the Business and Marketing class.

On weekends I smoke quite a bit, more than I really want to, but because my friends know that I always have some, the responsibility to be rolling one up usually seems to fall on me. I kind of like being the one, anyway.

I stash the money inside a slot under my dresser where I keep things from prying eyes, and though it's been piling up faster than before, sometimes I figure I should try to add some honest work to my income stream. Could help me stay in shape too.

I head down the ladder to the living room, through the kitchen and grab a couple of carrots from the sink where they'd been washed before I head out the door.

"Okay Mom, be back in a bit." I say. "When's dinner?" "Oh, a little later than usual 'cause your Dad's in town dealing with the insurance and stuff and won't be back too early, maybe around 7:00 pm."

I stride off, a spring in my step, grab the bike leaning against the shed and swing on. Pearl's place is only a few minutes' walk away, but I usually ride anyhow. If I can't drive, I ride pretty much everywhere. I can strap stuff onto the rack on the back when necessary, if I'm going to pick things up. I pull up to her place, skidding on the gravel and lean my bike up against the fence; it's all shaky and leaning over with gaps in the uneven wire. The gravel road is dusty today, dry. Chickens are circulating through the yard and onto the porch as I walk up, scratching and pecking at crumbs and some wilted celery stalks on the ground. The door isn't quite closed out front, and as I approach a chicken pokes his head out from inside the house, looking out to see who's coming, as if it's up to her to decide if she's going to let me in or not. I can hear Pearl hacking away as I approach. Sometimes she sounds like she'll come apart coughing like that, but then she'll just wipe her eyes and settle out just fine after. Smoking for fifty years probably messes you up pretty good I guess, especially that Drum tobacco she rolls. Her lungs probably look as bad on the inside as her smoke-stained fingers.

I don't knock, just shout in from outside. "Hey Pearl, ya in there?"

"'Corse I'm in here, who else do ya think would be coughing up a lung in my house." She says, "Get on in here little one." I walk in, dodging Suzy, Pearl's little curly haired mutt, as it rolls around on its back on the floor. I step through the confusion of Pearl's house, collections that remind me of the old 'where's Waldo', books where you never knew what you'd find until it's right there in front of you.

Pearl is leaning over the counter in the kitchen munching on salt and vinegar chips, a half empty coke bottle in her other hand. "Coke?" she offers, passing me the bag of chips.

"Yeah, sure. How's it goin' Pearl. Just chillin' out?" I ask. "Thought that maybe if I just stood here long enough eatin' chips while I thought about what to make for dinner, that maybe I'd get filled up and just forget about makin' it." She says, reaching into the bag, "Sometimes I just don't like cookin' for one, 'sides,

I'm running low on supplies. You runnin' errands?" "Yep, Mom said to get butter and milk." I say.

"Just got off the bus didn't cha? Learn something special today, like how to skin a rabbit or did you learn that clouds build up and get darker and get heavier and heavier until the water falls out?"

"Nope." I say. She smiles, crooked yellow teeth poking out. She lights the gas stove burner with a match and sets the kettle on the flame. "Did they teach ya about fire then?"

"No." I say. "Nothing like that, not today anyways."

"You know that a thing lies it's whole life, doesn't matter what it is," she carries on, chewing, watching the bubbles rise in her coke, "it lies it's whole life gathering light. Could be a stick, or a tree, a bird or a cardboard box, or an old mattress, don't matter what, everything's had sunlight on it at one point in time, jus' gathering light." She looks me in the eye to make sure I'm listening, then carries on. "When things was in their original form, they all come from trees and plants and minerals; in one way or another, all things have been in the light, for years and years. Don't matter what, even this coke." She says before taking a big swig, glancing over at me again. I'm just waiting to see what she says. No use in interrupting.

"Then when you set it on fire, all that light escapes and it's shared with the space around it. So, you can measure how long it was in the sun by how much heat and light come out of it. Say, you light a cup of gasoline afire, right?"

"Yeah….?" I say,

"Well, you know what that looks like, how bright and hot, right?"

"And fast" I say.

"Yep, and fast it burns up." She says, "So you know then that gas came from a lot of life, actually from fossils, right, animals and plants and things that had been in the sun for their whole lives and then became super concentrated over time and with pressure, and boom, it just lights up, like it's been waitin' the whole time to get out. See, so nuthin' is really dead. Everythin' has some life in it, some light in it."

"Pearl, I don't think they teach you that in school." I say. I've already finished off the coke and I'm digging into the chip bag for the bits at the bottom.

"Mmm, well," she says, "there's all kinds of schools." She gets up, kicks at a chicken that's pecking at the floor by her feet. It clucks and runs. "Maybe some tea would be better to settle out them toxics we been eatin' eh little one? … or are you in a hurry to get home?" She asks, turning to fill the kettle. I know it sounds funny, but I've never asked her why she calls me 'little one', but she has for as long as I can remember, even though I'm already a full head higher than her now.

"No, it's okay Pearl, got time." I say, "and anyways, today, I never learned any of that stuff. I learned how to sleep in history class while I looked like I was studying." I smile at her. "The trick is to keep your head tilted at the right angle into your hands with your elbows pressed into the desk, like a pivot. If you get the correct angle and balance, then the pressure of each arm keeps the other in check even when you are asleep."

"Ah, so you was studying some engineering in history class then." She chuckles. "…some triangulatin.'"

"Yeah, I guess." I say. She passes the box of different types of teas over to me so I can choose one for my cup.

"It's funny," she says, "you and your friends are 'spected to go to school every day and so you don't want to. It's a chore for youse, … but it's a privilege for others. I've hearda kids in other countries don't get schoolin' 'cause they can't afford it or it's too far from home to walk, or 'cause they're a girl, for whatever reason, they can't go and they all want to go in the worst way. When I was a kid, I wasn't allowed to go half the time either cause of chores had to be done and such, so I always wanted to go to school. 'Sides, I liked them classes where you could learn 'bout words."

"You mean English Lit?" I ask her, while I stir a spoon full of honey into the steamy cup of Chai tea that she's passed me.

"Words." She continues, "just studying words. It seemed like such an easy day if you was only used to guttin' chickens and scrubbin' the insides out- if you could just study words instead. It's all learnin' mind you." she says, jus' different kinds. I always watch people careful who really likes the taste of the words."

"What do you mean, the taste?" I ask.

"You know, the ones that savour each word. They seem to extract flavour from 'em. They tastes the words as they come out of their mouth. Heard a good one today… 'careening'. The guy kinda chewed on it… those kinda people."

I'm never in a hurry to leave Pearl's place, so I usually say yes when she asks if I want tea. A lot of the kids would just pick up the thing they're sent to get, and leave, but Pearl knows I will be around a bit, not in such a hurry, so she always has something for me to eat and drink and I know there will be some kind of crazy story to go along with it. I usually just settle in for a while. I don't even mind the smell of her tobacco anymore or the cloud of smoke that surrounds her and rises off when she's lighting one up. Looks like a slash pile when green boughs catch.

"Careening." she says. "That's kind of a mouth full ain't it? I like that word, ain't sure what it means ezacly, but it sounds like a speedin' roller coaster or a life full of adventure. Maybe I'll be careenin' later on today," she says smiling, "I'm feeling like it. And when I'm done, I'll have careened and then I'll rest for a while and charge up so I can careen some more…. later I'll sti -pu -late" she says, sounding out the word. I like that word too, you know, sounds very proper and accurate, like it ain't makin' a mistake." she says, cradling her cup and taking a sip. Her eyes are real dark, hardly any difference between the pupils and the iris, but if you pay attention you see that they're always catching light, like a passing mention.

"I've got all kinds of words that I like, and I remember lots of 'em." She says.

"You're crazy Pearl." I say, "You don't just use words cause of how they sound. They gotta make sense too." I tell her.

"Cabbage." Pearl says, ignoring me. "If I had a dog, I'd name him cabbage just 'cause I like that word. My dog, Cabbage, would come when I call 'im cause the sound of his name is soft and round. He wouldn't question or wonder why he was bein' called that. He wouldn't be humiliated by his name being a vegetable. He would just like his name and come and sit and not whineat all." "Yeah, well that's different Pearl. Now you're just talking about a dog, not writing, and anyway, you do have a dog and his name isn't Cabbage."

"Well yeah, s'pose that's true, but my next dog will be called Cabbage." she says. "And he'll be all fat and round from eatin' Cheezies, jus' like me," she says grinning, as she swats a fly on the sill with a roll of newspaper. "And if I have a fish, I am going to call him Farley Mowatt." She carries on. "I like that name. I'll train him to lie still on his back and then when you poke at him to see if he's still alive, he'll flip an' swim off like a real tricky fish."

"A tricky fish" I say, shaking my head.

"Yep… and I'll call him Fem for short and then people will think it's one of them mixed gender fish like they talk' bout in the Enquirer, 'n that would confuse everyone and be a good conversation starter when yer bored and havin' tea." She smiles another crooked little smile and looks at me with a mischievous spark in her eye.

"Never going to be bored having tea here if you are going to be talking about cabbage dogs and transvestite fish." I say with a grin, leaning over my steaming tea cup. "I should send the men in white coats over here to check on you Pearl 'cause I think you're getting worse. How much caffeine you had today?" I add.

She ignores me. "And then it could lead to some kind of debate about gay rights and how them113gay people affect fashion and how they wear colourful, plaid, high top runners." She rambles on, mumbling as she rummages through her fridge, then emerges pulling out plastic containers to put on the counter. "There never used to be stuff like that to wear. Did you see them pictures in the Enquirer over there?" she asks, pointing to the pile of newspaper on the floor, spilling out from under the counter, as she closes the fridge behind her with her foot.

"I think you should stop reading that stuff Pearl. You're losing it. Pretty soon you're going to think that stuff is true or that the aliens are going to come down and join you for dinner."

"Now there is an even better idea than just eatin' chips." she says, scratching her chin as if thinking through the meal plan for an alien.

I finish my tea and lean back, tilting the old wooden stool onto its back legs. Pearl turns around and slaps at some more flies by the sink. I step into the living room and sit down on the sunken couch and start flipping through an outdated edition of People's magazine from a stack on the coffee table, looking at pictures, glancing up again when she speaks. Now she's cutting onions and carrots and tossing them into the pot on the stove, adding pinches of different herbs from two different jars and some dried leaves from a branch hanging on a hook on the post beside the kitchen counter.

"Well, guess I'll just wait for them to show up, them men in white coats, I mean," she says, looking up and out the window over the sink, as if to see if they were landing already. "In the meantime, I'll get you yer butter and how much milk? another full gallon or just a two liter?'

"No, just a two liter. You got any of that jerky that tastes like barbecue?"

"Oh, yeah, some. You like that one eh? That's my special recipe and it's from a lean, young deer, don't tell now, I didn't have a ticket for that one. Problem is I never wrote down the ezact amounts of spices I put in that mix so's I'm not sure I can make it the same way next time.

Anyhow, I'll grab you a stick to chew on your way back." she says, reaching up into the cupboard to unwrap a coil of cloth and plastic that cover the jerky.

"Thanks Pearl." I grab the meat stick, clench the end in my mouth and pull the money out of my pocket that my mother had given me to pay with. I put it on the counter and pick up the milk jug and block of butter. "Guess I'll head back now, catch up to you next time eh?" I say through the meat in my teeth.

"Okay, little one," she says, "Hi to your mom for me. You come back soon so I can teach you what you miss when you sleep through class now, ya hear?"

"Okay Pearl, will do…least I stay awake in your class," I say smiling back at her. "see ya."

"Careful on yer way home little one. The forecast is for darkening skies, followed by really dark, then a bunch of hours of night." She says, deepening her voice, trying to sound like a weather man on the radio. She likes to give me that forecast.

"Okay Pearl, you were right about that last time, so I'll watch for it," I say as I turn and walk out through the door, still open. A chicken is there still, pecking away at crumbs on the floor just inside. It scurries out of the way with a cluck. I step over the chicken shit it has left behind on the floor and walk down the steps off the porch, place the milk and butter in the plastic bin strapped on the back of my bike, and swing onto the pedals.

***

At home, I knew I had things to do: an overdue English assignment, math homework and I'd promised my mother I would get the carrot patch weeded and prepped for the second planting, out in the garden. Instead, I find myself curled up in the den, remote in hand, ready to turn off the TV if I hear anyone coming. I'm watching another episode of the Mentalist. I often find myself putting off the inevitable, 'specially when it comes to homework, which mostly just doesn't get done. Sometimes I'll just scratch something out quickly while riding the school bus into town to at least pick up a 50 percent grade for handing in, but more often than not, I show up empty handed. It doesn't really bother me.

If I am going to write, I'd rather just write for myself. I do keep a kind of loose journal. It's not in order, or daily or anything like that, but I do keep it in my stash. Don't really want Leif or Luna getting hold of it, or my Dad for that matter. The pages are usually crowded by graffiti doodling. I get some of my best ideas doodling like that, in the margins, when my mind is kind of absent. Sometimes those ideas will lead to pages of thoughts, like a tangent. I know I'm on one when I scan through and notice pages with no scribbling on the side. Gotta reread those right? Must be serious stuff.

Wish I could get on one of those tangents with learning guitar. I pick it up once in a while, play a few basic notes, try to learn some scales, but soon I get tired of the repetition and the lousy sound and drop the lesson completely. I can always find a good excuse not to continue but then, later, I regret the lack of focus, lack of drive. I guess there's lots of time to learn this stuff later, but it does bug me at times that I usually choose the lazy way out. 'When is later?' I often ask myself.

At least I'm getting my graffiti down. If it's one thing, it's that. My ink-feed pen glides over the cover of my math binder, crazy lettering comes to life in sweeping curves. This is one of the few things I actually like doing these days, honing the message. 'PHALE' it reads. All my notebooks are covered front and back with three dimensional slogans, crazy lettering in creative shapes varying in size. Sometimes I make up words. I figure this one would look good in spray so I drop the binder on my bed and head to the tool shed. Dad doesn't seem to mind if I spray the old plywood that's leaning up against the back wall, so I practice with spray paint on it. I'm trying to figure out how to get less over-spray. I shake up the can as I work, got lots of colour, one fading into the other, adds texture. Sometimes I blend watercolours into the back ground, but I want this one to look smoky for some reason, so I grab a stick of charcoal from my box of pens and smudge some around the outside edge, then spray over it again to make it blend into the back… looks cool. I'm getting more accurate now with the sprays, but I need to find some bigger surfaces to work on. This plywood is just a start. "Jesus, you need some ventilation in here son." I turn as my Dad walks into the shop behind me. "You want to add to your brain damage?"

"Yeah. I'm starting to like the fumes." I say.

"Right, well, you're not going to be sucking that up while I'm around." He says, pushing the door open. He walks to the side and lifts the side slider window up, props it open with board. "Let's get some flow in here.

Oh, and before I forget, Gabe Framer mentioned to me at the mill that he might be looking for some help with wood. Maybe you could make a few bucks over the summer."

"Okay, sounds good." I mumble and grab the can of black and keep spraying.

"And he was asking if you could pick up a package at the post office by the border, at Metallaine, if you guys go down there." He adds. "Some winch part, I think. Save him a trip."

"Right. Okay. I'll call him." I say.

"Whatcha got there?" he asks, looking over my shoulder… "making up words again? Looks like it's on fire." He says, then returns to rummaging through some cans of screws.

"Oh… good." I say, "It's supposed to. Guess I'm getting it then," and spray on, spreading the lines; I weave each end of the 'E' into a creature below. It starts to look like a cyclops but now I'm running out of plywood.

"Looks like you'll need more room than that." Dad says as he moves back toward the door. I glance over. He's carrying two cans of screws and a couple of screw drivers. "Saw some pretty good graffiti on those tanker cars they're moving around down there. You see those?" He asks. "But yours, they're more reminiscent of all those psychedelic sixties rock posters from the Haight Ashbury that I remember." he adds, before heading back to the house.

He's right. Those train cars are a way bigger surface. I've seen some good graffiti go by when the train passes. I figure one day I'll practice on some of those when they are parked down along the siding by the village. 'Course I'll have to wait for all the action to die down first. The tracks are still full of people and machines right now, running back and forth to the spill like infantry. Maybe I'll take some of the old tins of house paint down there, just for practice, later, cause according to Dad, "They're picking through every shovel full of gravel down there trying to pin that mess on someone. Seems to me, they'll be locking someone up soon, and for a long bloody time."

In the meantime, I've been dipping into those tins, trying them out on the inside of my bedroom door, all kinds of wall paints- a variety of blues, grays and whites. I used different sized brushes too, even my fingers. I turned the back of my door into a giant poster with the names and logos of some of my favorite bands, letters weaving in and out, letters behind letters, and another cyclops. I like the cyclops, draw him a lot. He's poking out from behind the text, watches everyone that comes in.

I'm trying to work in some shadow now, spraying gray. I step back to look at my work. It's hard to read, barely legible. Guess I need to work on th1i1s8 some more. Both my Mom and Dad are encouraging when it comes to art and creativity in general, "Follow your creative spirit," my Dad says, "Stay loose and let the forms flow. Just feel it," he says. I used to listen to his ideas more than I do now. Now, his comments always sound like criticism to me, like I'm doing something wrong, or could be doing something better. And who is he to say? He's not a graffiti artist. Anyway, I don't see the graffiti as a real creative thing. It's more of a messaging tool isn't it, a way to show people, anonymously, what you are thinking? Or, maybe sometimes to simply send out a message like, 'fuck you,' but in a creative, colourful way.

These days, I've tried to move past those kinds of statements, 'cause when I see them on the side of a building or something, I think it looks like a waste. I'm thinking that I have to come up with something that's more of a protest. Maybe I'll send a message to all the kids at school who're wearing commercial slogans like Nike, Coke, Vans, DC, for example, all these guys who are basically advertising for corporations. Seems stupid, right? They're actually paying, buying clothes just to advertise for them. So, I've starting using my own slogans, uploading graffiti versions of images I've created onto the computer.

I had one printed onto a white tee shirt at the board shop in Nelson last week. They have a quality shirt printer in the back, and they give me good deals 'cause I'm friends with Jimmy, the owner's son, a buddy from school who lives in Nelson. One of my first shirts said, 'Congo's Fleet master' on it. I never knew why I'd come up with that slogan or what it meant, just liked the sound of it. I tell kids that ask, that it's a great new band. "You gotta hear them. Check it out." Last year I'd printed up a couple more. One said: 'Don't worry, be stupid,' in flowing, overlapping 3D letters- black and red, a really loud combination, and another said, 'Why swim when you can sync,' with navy blue graffiti letters in the form of waves tumbling over a brick wall.

One day when I'd been bored, a few weeks ago, I'd spotted the blank, off white surface, of the side of the desk in Luna's room and had painted, in luminous orange indelible ink: 'funk yer wanker bean' on it in kinda crazy lettering, ornate, overlapping, hard to read. She thinks it's cool, but then again, she thinks almost everything I do is cool, so it doesn't mean much. My Mom had seen it later on in the day and said, "Well, I guess when she gets tired of it, she can always paint it over." But I tell her, "No Mom, cause when I'm famous, she'll be able to cut that off the wall and sell it on eBay for thousands."

Got off the bus in front of the store yesterday 'cause Carlie had come to the village to meet up with Carolyn there. We went wandering along together walking toward Carolyn's house, so I was pointing out the different graffiti styles to her on the cars that we passed by. The cars come and go, only from Nelson these days, none coming from the Creston side cause the tracks are still blocked off in that direction. There are some good quality slogans on the kitchen car and on some of the tankers too, others just have cheap attempts. Some nice lettering wrapping around the headlight of a locomotive says, 'The accidental anarchist.'

"Check that one out on the tanker car," I say, pointing ahead. It has a naked, street-art caricature of a woman who has eyes for nipples. It's tagged: GirlzArt in long flowing letters that overlap in curls, like long hair.

"Nice tits; …they see all." Carlie says. "See, girls are good at graffiti too." She grins.

"Yeah, no shit." I say, "I'm thinking that if the trains are going to be parked down there much longer, I'll go down and add some decals of my own."

"You should." She says, "I don't think anyone'll care. They're too busy with media and machinery to mind you down there with a spray can."120

"Okay, well, I'll give it a shot." I say as she turns up Carolyn's driveway.

"Kay, I'll be lookin' for your signature… or maybe a cyclops." She adds… she's seen my notebooks. "…see ya tomorrow Wifi."

"Yep."

Back at home I mention the anarchist slogan to Dad, figure he'd like that. He says, "… need more of those these days. We're lucky to be alive with the bloody imperialists running rough shod, through our land," he says, making it sound like the CPR was on the attack or something. "… impunity," he says, "They just run their toxic supply chain through our back yards without even taking care of the tracks. They're all part of it:

global domination for profit, son." He says to me as though I'm actually listening, sorry now I said anything, "Don't let them teach you we're living in a democracy when we've got corporations like CP running the show, running rampant, I don't remember voting for CP...." and blah, blah, blah... "carbon footprint, gagging on the air we breathe...haven't got long to live at this rate." I've heard it all before. All his ranting just starts to sound like back ground noise after a while, like what they call white noise. Like when you turn on a fan or hear a chainsaw or mower off in the distance, after a while, you just don't notice the sound any more.

CHAPTER 6

Gabe

mily say's: "I just hope that we don't have more clashes within the community, Gabe, honey. That's my main concern right now, especially with this investigation going on around the derailment." We've both come in, for a late morning tune-up, espresso. I'd been changing the oil on the truck and she's been out mowing grass, trying to keep the vibrant spring growth in check. Her runners are stained green and cuttings are stuck to them.

"You know how rumours start to spread." She says. "I don't want us to return to the days of us against them, like it was with the logging protests." Her brow is still glistening with exertion, her loosely hanging top, revealing as she bends to unscrew the top of the stove-top Bialetti espresso maker. "What if people start rumours of blame?" Emily dislikes the discord within the community that results when issues arise that bring dramatically different views from two sides- often the case with logging, road building and mineral extraction, or the Jumbo Resort proposal, another current bone of contention. There have always been differences in points of view, polarization in the community, but she thinks that people of the community can always find common ground. Emily likes to think that regardless of how you choose to make a living, or who you vote for, what you have studied or not studied, that a community still shares many of the same traits and values: "We buy milk and bread in the same store and bakery; we go to the same post office and drink from the same creek;

we ride together across the same ferry every day", Is how she explains it, preaching her own little sermon.

One thing for sure is that she is much more diplomatic than I am. There are times, I tell myself, when I need to just let the issues rest, like she does, and realize that, like it or not, these communal roots have us all intertwined.

"Yeah, I know Em. I'm laying low these days, don't worry, just doing my deliveries like a good dog," I wink over the table at her, as she looks up through the steam rising from her coffee, sipping, contemplation wrinkled up on her brow, her hair unruly, dancing loosely into her eyes as she shakes her head, doubtfully. "I saw a printed pin up at the Harrop ferry bulletin board," she adds, "in big bold print, with the headline, 'Derailment?' with a question mark after it, a West Kootenay Crime Stoppers posting. They're looking for anonymous tips. It has a 1 800 number." She says, standing by the sink running the hot water to heat up our cups, a nervous expression on her face. "I tore it down when no one was looking. I don't like that kind of thing. It just stirs up speculation."

I walk around, kiss her on the forehead and open the fridge door to grab the milk, "Fucking Crime Stoppers now." I mutter into the hum of the fridge, "What next?" Emily doesn't like the feel of having the community on two sides of another issue. I guess most don't, but obviously, there are some who are actively stirring things up, not willing to just let things ride, … fucking meddlers. Now, they've got her all worked up. Probably Hector posting that bullshit. Glad she ripped it down. I wonder how many more they put up? The stove-top espresso pot starts erupting steam as I pour a bit of milk into the little stainless-steel pot to heat it up for our coffee.

There's no room for that kind of worry in our house right now. Emily has enough to contend with, just balancing the kids' needs, grocery shopping and home maintenance along with her shifts at the store. She's been picking up a few more hours lately. In spring it starts to get busier down there with the first tourists and cottage dwellers arriving. It's not a high wage, but it's so close by and convenient to our schedule that it makes it worthwhile for her to work and subsidize our income. Still, sometimes I wish she had completed her Social Work program so that we could have two full time incomes. The last few years haven't been bad, but before that, when the kids were both babies, it was a struggle for me to keep up on my own. I quickly finish my coffee and head out the back door to tune up my saw as Emily cleans up in the kitchen, says she's going to "spend a bit of time in the reno with my water colours." Says the light is good. She had taken a water colour course a few years ago at Kootenay School of the Arts and she's dabbled in it ever since, but not often. She never completed that course either, lost interest before it was over.

'The reno', is where I've been working on expanding the house over the past couple of years. It's framed and heated now, the addition upstairs, but the third bedroom and second bath are still unfinished with plywood floors, the bathroom still missing fixtures. The stud walls are wired and plumbed but the gyp rock is only partially hung so the rooms are a mix of studs, unfinished gyp rock, vapour barrier and pink insulation. The windows are in, so the light is good from the southern exposure, especially on a clear spring day like this one. Emily sets up her easel in there and occasionally spends time with her water colours. Though mostly, it seems, the easel just takes up space, kind of like that exercise bike she used to have in there. If I ever have a chance to finish that room, it will become Gavin's. Both boys are sharing now, in bunk beds, but at some point, the plan is to give them each a room. I guess I should have added another one at the same time, so we'd have room for a studio or an office.

Noah has half days at school this year, in kindergarten, and Gavin is in Grade Three so both kids head off each morning on the bus to Redfish school. This leaves us more time on our own, a welcome reprieve, but only for a few more weeks, till summer holidays. Hopefully now that they're more independent, Emily will start thinking about her degree again. I've mentioned it a couple of times, but she just agrees that it's a good idea, changes the subject, and then nothing seems to come of it.

Now that the kids aren't babies, she seems more inclined to spend time with her friends than pursuing education. She likes to go out on some weekends with her sister, Sandy, and Sage and Beten, Nipa too, her Indian physiotherapist friend, or other old friends she still has from her high school days in Nelson. A bunch of them are out tonight at the Spirit Bar seeing some band called Five Alarm Funk. I don't expect to see her till late. Noah is making a lego rocket launcher on the throw rug in the living room and Gavin is sitting on the couch nearby flicking through commands on his hand-held Marvel arcade game player, while I put left-over dinner food away.

I've got my music on low but can still overhear Gavin as he loses interest in his game, telling Noah, something about, "the submarine bear." Gavin's always got wild stories he tries to convince Noah of. Noah is the listener, a little timid and being three years younger, is more gullible so he'll often get drawn into Gavin's imagination. "It's so crazy and dangerous, I don't even want to talk about it right now," he tells him, glancing up, then going back to his game. A submarine bear?

It reminds me of a recent outing: the three of us had been out casting for Kokanee in our little fishing boat a couple of weeks earlier and while I'd been busy baiting hooks and tying line,

Gavin had been telling Noah, pointing: "you see… that thing… yeah there, bobbing in the water, just over there?"

"Yeah," Noah says, "it's a beer bottle."

"No," Gavin says, "it looks like a beer bottle, but it's what they call a beer bottle shark." I glanced over to see it. A brown beer or pop bottle was bobbing over small waves maybe ten meters out, just the neck visible. "You see there," Gavin carries on, "that's the top fin, the dorsal, it's shaped like the neck of a bottle, you see, like a deposit bottle, you know, one that people want to pick up for a refund." He says, "Bottle sharks know this and so they just bob around near beaches and boats and wait for someone to swim over or reach down out of a boat to grab at it."

Noah looks hard at the bottle, as it bobs and almost disappears, his brow scrunched up, concentrating. I keep busy, quiet. "When they do," he continues, "the bottle shark just grabs the guy's arm and tears it off and pulls him in and eats him."

"There's no sharks in the lake, is there Dad?" Noah asks worriedly.

"'Course there is." Gavin answers, "one right there. Just grab it then if you don't believe me, dare ya."

"Maybe try using the net, Noah." I say, then you can see for yourself. But as Noah is reaching for the net, the bottle sinks behind the next wave and disappears.

"Oh, see… he heard you. Now he's gone under." Gavin says, pointing at the choppy water.

"Wasn't a shark." Noah says, haltingly, "was it, Dad?" I just smiled to myself, shaking my head, and handed a baited rod to Noah. Something to take his busy mind off the Bottle Shark.

It's usually entertaining to hang out with the boys at home, just the three of us, especially if they aren't fighting. So, when Emily heads off to town to a club for drinks with her friends, it gives me a chance to catch up with them. I do go out too, to join her once in a while, but unless there is some band I really want to hear, I'd rather not go. I'm not one to get out on the dance floor much, so she usually gets her dancing fix with her girlfriends. Last weekend, she called from the bar to tell me she was going to stay at her Mom's place the night. 'Don't want to be driving drunk,' she says, "having too much fun to drive back… sorry honey." Her mother, Trixie, lives in the Uphill section of Nelson and she always keeps a room ready so that Emily and Sandy have a place to drop in to whenever they want. They see a lot of each other.

Trixie is very independent but lonely, always planning lunches and card games with them. She's remained single ever since the loss of her husband even though she'd been only thirty-six at the time. She's dated some over the years, but now seems to be resigned to living alone. I'd met Emily just a few years after her dad had been killed, almost twenty-five years ago now.

We were so young, early twenties then, and it hadn't taken us long to buy our plot of land in Procter together. It had been an impulsive decision, the kind of thing that happens to you, not something you make happen, a thing we've never regretted, not even during 'the sabbatical' year. At that time, our land had only a small cabin on it, not much room, but it was ours and we were proud of it. It was like a pact between us. We had a connection to it, an obligation which strengthened over time and spilled over into our lives. We became more committed to each other as the house and our family grew. It had been a busy time then. We were excited with modifying our new nest, taming the encroaching forest so that light could penetrate the yard and allow sun to warm our pond, and as the time passed, our plans progressed to slowly take shape in the form of two additions to the house and the construction of a woodshed and carport off to the side.

The add-ons to the house came piecemeal when money was available so you'd think it would end up looking kind of disjointed, but it doesn't, not to me anyway. Looks like it was meant to grow that way, like burls on a tree. Though our time was fully occupied, balancing home, kids and improvements with earning a living, Emily and I always seemed to find a bit of time to invest in local issues and events that we've become passionate about. For her, it's usually volunteering for some community event where she'll help with preparing meals for a fund-raising event or helping to organize music or one of the farmers market days. Me, I'm usually more inclined to get into environmental or political issues. Try to make an impact. I'm looking for ways to help organize, energize and empower, especially those on the fringe. I've grown more accustomed to helping make things happen than to waiting around for change to happen on its own.

The dispute around logging permits issued by the forest service near Harrop was probably the first issue that had spurred me on. It had all begun when they had awarded cutting rights to Slocan forest products, and Atco lumber, two local mills, to clear cut various allocated cut blocks slated for logging in the mountains behind Harrop in 1990. Many local villagers were adamant that no logging take place in their watershed or in their view scape. Others thought that it was great to have new roads put in, jobs created. They liked the idea of open clear cuts to guard against wild fires and to attract grazing wildlife for hunting: two totally contrasting perspectives. The conflict pitted neighbors against one another, road builders against 'tree huggers', loggers against protectionists. No middle ground was found despite some attempts by local politicians and Ministry of Forests personnel. There were protests, letter writing campaigns and failed negotiations by those opposed. Things deteriorated further once the Ministry of Forests held their public meeting in the Procter Hall.

It was packed in there, more than 300 people showed up and basically, the forest service told us all that they would be allowing logging in the Lasca area whether we liked it or not. They attempted to sugar coat the message, but it didn't work. It just didn't sit well with most folks in the area and what made it worse was that our local MLA at the time, Howard Dirks found a way to fast track road building approval so that they could start before we had a chance to further mobilize against them. This really helped to antagonize the opposition, of which I was one. There were many voices to add to the chorus of opposition. Some were totally opposed to any amount of logging. Others like me, were not totally opposed to logging in general, but more concerned about protecting the water sources and view-scapes, trying to keep the clear cutters at bay. I figure I can't be opposed to logging 'cause I like to build with wood. I just don't like the giant clear cuts that scar the land and lead to erosion.

No, some logging needs to happen, otherwise we wouldn't have the tongue and groove ceilings and floors in our place. They add character;

wear over the years blends into the groove of the grain and when I crank up the stereo to blast out some old John Hiatt tunes, the soft, irregular surfaces absorb rather than bounce the sound around. Sometimes when no one is around I'll just lay back on the couch with a shot of scotch, listen to music and explore different formations in the wood grain of the ceiling. You can find faces and animals in there and it always changes depending on your angle. Yeah, can't do without the wood.

No, from my point of view, some logging is not the problem necessarily, it's the methods that I disagree with. Why can't they just selectively log? These clear cuts, cutting on steep slopes creating erosion issues, muddy runoff into water sources, and the poor-quality roads which are often built to access remote areas, again, adding to slope destabilization. These are the issues. Several community meetings were held during that time, informational data was distributed by government and industry to try to demonstrate how accountable they were, but the two opposing views, pro and anti-logging continued to collide.

It all came to a head when forest service allowed the logging company to move in and begin road construction. That was another big mistake. Planning had been taking place in the background by those of us opposed, readying for this potential eventuality, while still trying to negotiate for park status. We had steeled ourselves for this though, so on the day the machinery was to be moved in, back in the spring of 1991, we set up a human blockade to stop entry at the access point- Laska road, in Harrop a narrow gravel road on the flats just a few hundred meters up from Kootenay Lake. Some 150 people, mostly locals, blocked the road the first few days, and after that, just a few people would man the blockade in shifts, around the clock to prevent access by machinery. We set up tents, picnic tables and lawn chairs, had a gas camp stove to make coffee and tea and became quite comfortable in maintaining a long-term presence. To us it was a meeting place, to others, 'a shanty town', 'an eye sore.'

During the day there could be vibrant, lively conversation, at times, or alternatively it could be very quiet and feel isolated if just two or three people would be spending long hours there in the dark and rain. I'll always remember Pearl being there, at the camp. I would be there with her from time to time. She would bring a beach umbrella, rain or shine, set it up in its stand in the middle of the road, bring out her lawn chair and her latest knitting project, light up a smoke and just sit there for hours, humming to herself or chatting with anyone within range, like she belonged there, like an old prairie farm wife relaxing on her veranda after a long day in the fields.

Lots of folks made a habit of stopping by, making tea, having a snack or just reading a newspaper. There were confrontations too, accusations shouted from people in passing cars and warnings posted on phone poles, idle threats most thought, but still, unnerving to many. It always pissed me off when there were anonymous threats though. I figure, if someone has an opinion, they should just come out with it, not hide it behind some print out or faceless complaint.

The land owner directly across the gravel road from the blockade had no qualms about his opposition to us being there though. He was a staunchly pro-logging advocate, a chubby retired guy who'd been living there for years. He'd shuffle down to the corner of his land each day and yell insults at us: 'lazy welfare bums,' below. For a few days, early on in the blockade, he thought it would be a good idea to start up his old lawn tractor and run it all day, right across the road from us. It had a broken muffler, and would rattle and spew fumes all day long, or until it ran out of fuel, running away there, idling on high. He would go back to his house where he could sit at his front table and watch the scene with the satisfaction of knowing he had once again been a source of irritation to 'those useless tree huggers,' below. Really though, he was just another part of the entertainment after a while. We'd wave cheerfully at him when he came out. When it was my turn to man the blockade, I'd bring down my ghetto blaster and try to drown out the tractor noise. That way worked pretty good.

The whole situation reached a climax that September, when a legal injunction was launched, which stated that the blockade was illegal and that anyone standing in the way of the road builders accessing the right of way would be arrested. The deadline was set. We were given two weeks to clear out, which gave us two weeks to organize a bigger blockade. Emily and I were part of a committee that were working phones, networking, gathering information, holding meetings and carefully planning the logistics of a mass protest. By the time police, road builders, loggers, the media and all kinds of curious folks showed up that Tuesday morning, there were more than six hundred people spread out along the once quiet back road near the village of Harrop. The helicopter overhead hovered and swooped; his view must have been one of a huge, writhing millipede below.

There was a lot of anticipation on both sides, an odd, almost quiet stalemate, as the two sides awaited the final determination. The Nelson Daily News, reported:

> *"At 8:45 a.m. the RCMP arrived and informed the group that they would enforce the court order," (to have them removed forcibly if necessary.) and "… With silent dignity, young and old were taken by police. Some walked and others were carried. The crowd demonstrated support by applauding each person. "We are frustrated over having to go to such extremes to bring opinions to elected officials," said one spokesperson. The protestors were taken in a waiting school bus to Nelson for arrest processing." (Suzanne Down, NDN vol.76, No.109, Nelson, B.C. wed.Sept.25/1991)*

Few people were shouting or tossing insults anymore, most were just milling about quietly, discussing together what they thought would result. As the overwhelming majority of those at the site were anti-logging proponents, there was a sense of camaraderie. There were cars parked along both sides of the road for miles; the ferry was clogged with traffic, dogs were getting under foot, some people even came on horseback, on bikes and ATVs. Dust rose and fell. Car pools were set up, organized by Angus and Sandy Mowatt, who were driving back and forth all morning dropping people off to help alleviate the congestion. Hailey, a local tree planter from the village had organized a couple of boats to ferry people back and forth closer to the site to save time because the Harrop ferry was so full of cars, people couldn't get over all at once. She'd recruited a bunch of planter friends to come out for the day too to add to the crowd and camaraderie. I noticed Ariel, the Mowatt's son, and his friends, had also gathered in their own little group along the bank by the road, just hanging out and watching the local action. We had all ages. Most of the local kids had shown up, barring those whose parents were pro- logging. If nothing more, those kids just wanted to come cause everyone else had. Petitions were being signed, photos taken and TV interviews were underway. Harrop was, at least, for that day, on the map, maybe for the first time ever, or at least since that big sensational story about all the horses being starved to death decades ago at a nearby stable. Yeah, there was a lot of attention focused on anti-logging campaigns in those days all over the Province, but this one was the biggest in the interior at the time, so we were in the spotlight.

On the blockade, the buses started showing up in the late morning, dissecting the millipede. The RCMP had enlisted three, full sized school buses to haul people away in anticipation of the possibility that many people would be forced to leave, under arrest. A police car escort helped force the buses through the crowd and into a nearby field where there was room for them to turn around and await any possible passengers. Then, the lead officer made his way up onto the highest road side bank overlooking the crowd, and megaphone in hand, announced to everyone: "At this time, it is my duty to read an injunction presented to those who are blocking the road. This is a legal injunction issued by the Crown." He then went on to read the injunction before asking: "Now I must ask you all to step back from the road. Allow the machinery to pass unencumbered. Anyone who does not step back from the road will be arrested and taken into custody at our Nelson detachment. Please now allow the construction crew to pass."

At this point, most people began to slowly shuffle off to each side of the road, grudgingly, but many did not, many of us opted to stay and so began the process of police moving in, questioning each as to their intention. "Are you willing to move from the road?" and when the protester said, "no, I'm not willing," officers would move in, two at a time, one on each arm of the individual and assist them, dragging them off in some cases, which is how they had to remove me. It takes more effort for them to move you off that way, all limp like a noodle. Didn't see any point in making it easier for 'em. They dragged us all away from the road and up to the awaiting buses where we were detained on board by an armed officer until the road was cleared of all those remaining. One of my shoes had fallen off as they dragged me up, but the officer let one of the kids who'd picked it up pass it to me through the open window.

This whole scene made quite a media splash. It seemed to raise a lot of eye brows in Government, locally and Provincially. Sixty-four of us protesters were processed that day in Nelson at the RCMP station. In the end, it was reported, over 600 people had shown up to the blockade and with sixty-four people arrested, a B.C. record for arrests made in one day was set. The local detachment wasn't big enough to fit all of us inside while in custody, so we were all locked up in the police garage beside the detachment, to wait, like cattle in a feed lot. We were finger printed, photographed, then taken one by one to the office where data was recorded on each. A few hours later we were released to await trial. The trial was set to take place in a couple of months.

It ended up being delayed a couple of times and so didn't begin until early in the winter, a few months later. That's when we all gathered again, spilling out the courthouse doors onto the sidewalks and streets in front of the Nelson court house. There was barely enough room for all the defendants in the court room, let alone the press, lawyers and aides, so all the supporters ended up just hanging around waiting outside. The court room was alive with the sound of anxious chatter. Some were worried about getting a criminal record if convicted, others were just angry it had gone this far. Prosecution wanted jail time for the organizers, and fines imposed on all the rest of us to set an example for any future blockaders, while the defense was asking for all of us to be acquitted based on freedom of expression.

Raving Amy was one of the defendants. She never lost her biting, wry smile during the proceedings. I was sitting in the row behind her, kind of relieved not to be beside her. She did not seem intimidated by the threat of jail time, nor of the judicial system in general. "Bunch of assholes," she says, in a hiss, out the side of her mouth, in the direction of Phil, who sat beside her, "Look at this place, bloody police state," she said, spitting out each distasteful word. Not seeming to expect a reply, "I got weeds to pull." As the courtroom proceedings unfolded, most of the defendants waited anxiously, time seemed to drag out. There was a definite lull in motion but because most of us didn't really understand normal court proceeding, time lines and procedures; not a lot of notice was given to the pace.

Eventually, must have been two hours by then, our defense lawyer, Fred Easton, some sharpshooter Eco lawyer from Vancouver who used to work with Green Peace, approached the bench to query the judge as to the timing of proceedings. It was then brought to our attention by the prosecutor's legal assistant, who was responding to questions by the judge, that the lead lawyer for the prosecution was not yet in the courthouse. The judge was not impressed that the prosecution was two hours late. He gave them fifteen minutes to regroup, stood up and left the courtroom.

"So, these clowns can make sixty-four of us just wait around all day like we got nothing better to do?" Amy asks to anyone in the vicinity that would listen, after word got back to us as to the discussion taking place on the bench, her comments echoing thoughts of many of us seated, "Maybe once we start this thing up they can call a little recess while I go and get my tarot cards read or my nails done eh? Think I'll get em painted rainbow. Could take a while." She says, smirking.

No one usually responds to Amy when she starts to go off about things, not the locals that know her anyway. Most folks know better, through their own personal experience, having either witnessed, or been the target of, some pretty angry confrontations with her in the past. All but the newcomers to the area know better than to partake in any conversation that could potentially add steam to Amy's already explosive temper, especially "if she's off her meds."

"Yeah, I got laundry to do," says another, and someone else complained about wanting to go out for a smoke. These wooden benches aren't all that comfy, are they?" says another, a couple of rows down. All of us defendants were grouped together on the wooden rows of benches tiered up to the back on a slope away from the judge's desk. The benches were as antiquated as the courtroom itself, yet somehow the age and heritage of the stone walls and woodwork bring a kind of authenticity to the place. The smell of wood wax and antiseptic cleansers blended with the sweat of congestion. I guess if the place had been all clean and sterile, modern, with glass, plastic and steel, it would have been harder to take seriously.

After fifteen minutes, the judge returned. "All rise," said the clerk. The judge takes his seat, scans the room and, advises the Crown council and our lawyer, Easton, to proceed. But after a few minutes of paper shuffling and sidelong looks from those seated on the side of the prosecution, a lawyer stands to explain: "Your honour, the lead attorney for the Crown Council has not arrived due to a violent storm which has prevented all flights from landing at Castlegar airport today. Due to this act of God, which is beyond our control, we move to adjourn the proceedings to a later date of your choice. We apologize for this inconvenience."

With this statement, an immediate raucous din rose from our crowd. Many angry comments and accusations bounced around the room. We all looked expectantly to Easton, who was concurring with an aide and making a few quick notes. The judge scanned the crowd in front of him as though seeing us all for the first time, then began banging his gavel on the block to quiet the crowd, raising his voice to call for order.

"Defense, how do you respond to this motion?" he asks, eye brows raised.

Easton then rises, note book in one hand, file in the other, pauses glances at the pad then dropping it on the desk with a smack, says, "Your honour, we the defendants do not accept inclement weather as a valid excuse to adjourn. Some eighty people have organized and altered their schedules to be here today, on time, without option of choice. We are here and prepared to see this through today as scheduled by the court." He then pauses a moment, turning to look out over us before continuing to address the judge. "The Castlegar airport, as everyone here knows, cancels flights regularly in winter, every year. This is common knowledge. Therefore, when an important hearing is scheduled, we all know to either drive, take a bus or attempt to fly in a day or two early to ensure arrival. We do not accept responsibility for this lack of planning on behalf of the Crown council and therefore we call for a motion of acquittal. That is all, your honour." And with that he closes his file, returns it to his briefcase, closes it with a decisive snap and returns to his seat to await the response.

Whispers of agreement float through the air as our crowd wonders what is next. The judge calls the defense and acting lawyer for the prosecution to come forward to the bench. They speak together, privately for a moment and return to their seats. The judge makes a few notes, reviews them, then looks up toward all of us in the courtroom. He says, "With reference to the case in front of me, I can sympathize and appreciate that a lot of people have reorganized their schedules and gone out of their way to be here today… on time." With a glance toward the desk of the prosecution. He continues: "I find with the defense that inclement weather and canceled flights cannot be used as a credible defense to delay proceedings. I rule in favour of the motion to acquit."

And with these few decisive words, he hammers the block again with his wooden gavel, says, "Case adjourned," rises and leaves the room. The whole case is over just like that. After a moment's pause, as this reality sinks in, a spontaneous cheer erupted throughout the courtroom. This unpredicted flash ending to what most considered the beginning of a long, complicated process of charges and appeals ended the whole ordeal right then and there. Another momentary silence followed the initial cheers, as if people didn't really know how to follow up or were simply in denial about the simplicity of this opportune moment like someone who has just been told they've won a prize. Soon, people were rising to leave, pounding each other on the back, shaking hands. Smiles, cheers and congratulations greeted us as we met the crowd of supporters just outside as we all streamed out onto the street, victorious.

A break in the clouds sent a flood of warm sun light over the crowd as we emerged; refreshed, enthusiasm in the air. I felt a renewed energy to the cause resulting from this victory and that energy proved not to wane in the months and years to come. That was my introduction to organized protest. Many folks describe feeling empowered by the action we took. I did too; I felt this crack in the wall of government enforcement, a crack of impunity, opening. It reminded me of the Leonard Cohen song: 'There's a crack, a crack in everything. That's how the light gets in.' I began to seeways in. This mind set launched a new framework of rational, lending license to newly formed ideas. I started to envision a place of directed, planned intervention, not just protest, a place where actions taken by corporations in the name of greed, with total disregard for the environment they effected, would be confronted with corresponding response. For every action, there will be a reaction. Isn't that the nature of things?

<hr>

The battle raged on for months after the court case adjournment. Machinery moved in and began road construction. They were blocked again and again. Organized lobby groups continued the fight, slowly gaining ground in the back rooms of government. More arrests were made, and the stalemate continued until eventually government and industry were forced to concede the land and the wilderness area west of Harrop, toward Nelson along Kootenay lake and it became a designated wilderness park: 'The West Arm Provincial Park.' This was another victory celebrated by many, but not all, in our community. The problem then was that the forest directly behind the communities of Harrop and Procter was left out of the park. This became another bone of contention in the following years as forest companies and the ministry of environment eyed up the most easily harvested timber, accessible directly behind our communities.

The momentum created by the opposition to logging and the ultimate creation of the park, led to the formation of the Harrop Procter Watershed Protection Society, (HPWPS). People felt empowered after the wilderness park victory. We took ownership of the destiny and direction of our community, refusing to be led by external power. This group was led by strong and passionate local organizers. They developed an eco-system-based land use plan for the area. They gathered people together and garnered public support for a 'compromise between the economic needs of the community and the environmental ideals of the anti-logging groups. There was overwhelming support for these efforts both locally and from abroad as the community initiative gained more and more attention from people everywhere who were hungry for example alternatives to the confrontational and destructive status quo of logging practices in B.C.

Momentum built, proponents were organized, eloquent speakers left an impact; media paid attention. Eventually, after years of lobbying efforts and organizing, after gaining the support both of government and the Sinixt and Ktunaxa first nations, along with the financial support garnered through grant writing to charitable organizations, the Harrop/Procter community was granted a five-year pilot project designation for our proposal and the community forest became locally controlled. The Community Forest management team went on to prove themselves over the years by providing local jobs and peace of mind in respect to watershed protection. The co-op business branch of the HPWPS, which was in charge of operations, created employment in trail building, forest layout, office work, business planning, public education and outreach. Soon they expected to create local employment in road building and selective forest harvesting, milling and wood sales. They did not want to rely on, nor did they expect, funding from government. By the same turn, they didn't support government with fat donations, not that they could have if they wanted to, and so this too set them apart from big industry logging operations who have always received operating concessions from governments who are beholden to them.

I, like many of us from Procter, have always supported the organization. I even sat on the board a couple of times, but really, I can't claim any credit for the great work they have accomplished. No, I've opted instead to be more of a 'hands on' kind of activist. I figure I can fill a supportive role: in the background. It's always good to have back up.

⸻ ⟡ ⸻

Now, the mill has been in operation for years, logging has taken place selectively and roads have been built without eroding into local streams for a change. Our water supply is protected. Even though I was not one of the key organizers of the community forest, I am proud of what the community has put together here, proud of the people involved. I feel fortunate that we can live in such a small community yet have so much depth of character within it.

In the end, I figure, the result has been a good compromise between water source protection, and logging. That compromise has led to a more peaceful community. The mill that is now operating down in Harrop, has, after almost ten years evolved into an efficient operation, utilizing local contractors and labour, creating good jobs and high-quality lumber products. It's a locally owned, nonprofit business, operating in a sustainable way, logging selectively, perpetually, (unless the forest burns in a wild fire anyway), not a cut and run corporate operation where clear cutting sends short term profit to shareholders on Bay Street.

High quality lumber is being sold, mostly cedar, some even kiln-dried now. The guys running the mill, Seth, Terry, Fred and Pat, give all kinds of advice- even accurate advice sometimes, on building ideas and project estimations, wood quality and strength. People keep coming back, asking for more. I like to question the guys there on building code requirements or dimensional spans, or to figure out how many board feet I'll need for a fencing project or a wood shed. They'll give me an answer whether they know it or not which usually works out pretty good. They have a good reputation now and most folks know that when they buy from our local mill, they are supporting responsible, sustainable, land management which a lot of people seem to respect.

I go there a lot, going to drop by in a few minutes actually; just got to pick up the mail first. When I pull into the post boxes on the way, there is Pat riding upon his Lawn Boy tractor. He pulls up to the boxes too, alongside, while I'm flipping through the junk mail. He drives that lawn mower everywhere, just like it was a regular car, moving just a little faster than I can walk. He shuts it off on the gravel shoulder of the road by the post boxes. He's swearing and lighting a smoke at the same time. He hasn't changed his pasted-back hair style since last time I saw him so it's not moving, all orderly in combed lines. He's wearing a pin striped dinner jacket over some gray polyester shorts… no rhyme or reason. "Hey Gabe, what the hell's goin' on?"

"Just checkin' my junk mail. What's with the wheels?" "Yeah, well I lost my license, right, so this is what I've got.

This fucker hauls ass, and check this out, I've installed a cup holder by the steering wheel for my beer can."

"Yeah, I see that. Quite the cruiser. What you up to, mowin' the right of way?"

"Nah, just getting' some more coffee and maybe a six pack. Gotta wake up, couldn't sleep last night. That mother fucker Gerard, came to my house last night, late, barges his way in, accusing me of taking advantage of this girl who was visiting me earlier. Son of a bitch; how'd he even find out?" He says, grim faced, animated, "Sticking his nose in… came right in without an invite! And she's a friend, none of his business. Felt like using his head as a plunger but I just grabbed that fucker by his shirt and filed him right back out the door. Son of a bitchin' bastard; grabbed him just like this," he grabs hold of the front of my shirt to demonstrate, "and I just hauls him right out the door and tosses him down the steps. Mother fucker, shoulda kicked his ass with a tire iron," he says, kicking his shiny leather boot into the air.

"Holy shit man, then what happened? Did he call the cops or what?" I ask. "You going to get locked up again?" Pat has been in some trouble before, nothing too serious, just a possession charge or two and a couple of drinking driving charges and some claim about reckless endangerment. Doesn't seem to always connect the consequence to the action, not till later on anyhow. Fortunately, he's been pretty harmless so far, hasn't hurt anyone.

"Oh, hell no, that idiot's not going to charge anybody with anything. He just likes to stir things up, so I stirred him a bit, fuckin waste-a-space."

"Okay, then. Glad I don't have to go visiting you in the lock up."

"No… staying clean Gabe, but now I've got to get into town and look for a god damn job. I don't have enough grass cutting jobs. Let me know if you hear of anything eh? Just part time, cause I'm startin' to get more shifts at the mill now, but at this point, I don't even have enough cash for my next six pack. Spent my last pay check on this baby." He says, patting the green hood of his Lawn Boy.

"Yeah. You riding that into town then?" I ask him, smiling, shuffling my mail into a stack.

"Yeah, right. I wish. I'd have to tune 'er up a bit more to get the speed up to eighty. Maybe later if I can find the right parts, you know… maybe bore out the carb. Anyways, could have had a second job already, but missed out cause of all those fuckin' East Indians and Paki's coming to town." he glances up as a car passes by, "Taking all the best jobs, like at Subway and 7-11, couldn't even get on at Walmart. It's bullshit, man, fuckers are taking over. Guess it don't matter so much now, that I've got the part time job down at the mill. They can keep their fuckin' Subway job. I'd rather be driving fork lift than spreading mayonnaise all day long anyhow," He says, then drains the rest of his beer can down his throat, grabs another from behind the seat and pops the tab open with a spurt, plugs it into the holder and guns the idle, as though he's about to go cruisin' off on a Harley. Then he puts it in gear and pulls out without another word, nodding at me as he slips his dark glasses down over his eyes. I watch as he moves away, haltingly, like he's driving a stubborn mule heading down the shoulder of the road.

Yeah, Pat's been working driving fork lift mostly these days. It's good they hired him. Not sure why he's got today off. Guess they only need him part time. He's always got a good story going on, some kind of crazy mix up. I think he gets himself into some tight spots at times with the way he talks and drinks; doesn't seem to have much of a filter. He's prejudiced, (or talks that way anyway), against pretty much every race and religion, even his own: "East Indians, Paki's, A-rabs… takin all the best jobs." He's part Syrian- hates cops, old people, young people, blacks, "'course they're the best at sports, 'cause they got turned into a super human race when the slave trade killed off all the weak ones, doesn't mean they will take over hockey though, we got that one sewn up."

It's a good thing he lives here in the village where we can shut him down from time to time. Who knows where he'd end up if he were in a big city, connected to the wrong influences? Like what if the skin-heads got hold of him. The Aryan Nation or some other fanatical group? Would he even survive in a city, surrounded by the people he so easily insults? It's a funny thing with him, these off the wall statements, like he doesn't really mean them, but needs to gauge the reaction of others, like a toddler who keeps tugging on the hem of a table cloth as you watch and the dishes inch toward the edge. I watch him when he starts up on one of his rants and you can glimpse a hint of this amused expression, an unspoken challenge, the sub plot of his own personal theater, maybe the result of what can occur when one feels secure in his own environment but still needs to gauge the boundaries. They're pretty good about it down at the mill, the guys treat him like a problematic little brother.

I'm there a lot, at the mill, to drop off logs, pick up slabs to deliver to people for firewood, or just to get lumber for my own projects. It's a place of barter and banter where wit will win over logic, and where working hard and playing fair is believed to be more convincing than talking about it. I always spend more time at the mill than I need to. "There's always more bullshit down here than wood," I like to say to the boys, when I drop by. It's best to drop by at coffee time. Usually the guys have a few minutes then to stop and catch up, unless they are pushing to get a big order out. We'll sit round the table in the little staff room, which is barely big enough to fit four chairs, chewing on jerky and cookies, sipping coffee, and discussing current log supply, various custom timber cuts on order, or how deep the mud is in the yard. You never know what you might hear in there. It can be politics, philosophy or some kind of mechanical analysis of a miter cut. The power is always humming through the electrical panels in the cramped little room, feeding supply to the kiln next door, the saw, molder and the dust/chip collection vacuum which never seems to get shut off- all contributing to the back-ground noise that forces voices to always be raised to be heard. The smell of sawdust is always in the air, pungent dry or wet, and though a fair amount of fir, larch, hemlock and pine are also milled here, the aroma of cedar always hangs in the air and dominates. That aroma blends with the steam escaping from the kiln and always reminds me of being in the sauna when someone has just doused the rocks with water. Today, I'm just picking up a few feet of rough-cut cedar, one by fours, for a fencing project I'm helping Pearl with.

As I step into the office, I can overhear Terry, the sawyer… "This latest Mid East invasion is not that dissimilar to the Medieval siege warfare in the 1400s", he says, apparently carrying on a conversation to no one in particular, as he stirs two cubes into his coffee. The other guys don't really seem to be paying attention. "Sure, the technology is different now. We are using drones with smart bombs instead of catapults with boiling oil, but the intent is still to wipe out the enemy without risking our own necks, and really, the issues are probably almost identical. It's interesting isn't it, that history is so repetitive." Terry, the work site historian, usually has some kind of contemplative commentary that sounds like it came from a text book, something he refers to after hearing a radio news bulletin or passing comment. Beat hearing about the weather.

"Yeah, I guess," I say, poking my head into the conversation, "to think that in thousands of years, humans can't evolve beyond finding more efficient ways to kill ourselves. Amazing there's still so many of us."

Seth turns around and looks up. "Hey Gabe, what's up…cup a coffee?"

"Great, love one, sure."

"Speaking of killing ourselves," Seth carries on, "Terry, did you sharpen the chipper this morning, or are we just going to wait till that thing starts sending shrapnel around the mill?" He asks, turning back to the other side of the table. Seth is more or less in charge down here at the mill. Operations manager I suppose you would call him, has his finger on the pulse of the place. One of the first guys I met when I moved here. It's because of him and his entrepreneurial spirit that this mill has become successful, everyone knows that, so, even though there's a healthy camaraderie down here, plenty of sparring, the underlying respect for him is palpable. He gets up, passes me an empty cup from over his shoulder. "Pot's behind you Gabe." I take the cup and reach around

Terry to the coffee maker.

"Yeah, yeah, got that done first thing S man." He says, into the open magazine he's flipping through, "…not to worry man, she's sharper than shrapnel now."

"Shrapnel?" says a high-pitched voice from the other side of the door. "You guys planning something in there?"

Seth looks up, "Hey who's there? Come on in if you can fit." "Just me needin' somethin' to burn." Says Raving Amy. "Burn?" says Seth with a smile, not missing a beat, "What are you burning? You taken up with the Sons of Freedom now Amy?" "Doesn't anyone work around here?" she says, glancing a cursory sideways smirk off Seth but otherwise ignoring him. She opens the door and pokes her head in, stringy hair all trying to escape from a bright bandanna, like a bunch of wilted flowers. Seth turns his back to her a moment, rolling his eyes to me and Terry in the back of the room, then walks past her out the door, not wanting to deal with a customer I guess, or this customer anyway. "Hey Amy, shouldn't be waking us up like that. What do you need? "Terry says, in his relaxed tone, dropping the magazine to look up.

"Very funny," she says. "It is kinda quiet down here though, don't you guys ever work? Not like up near my place, all I ever hear these days is more of that bloody railway equipment. All day and night. Wish they'd just get the hell out." She re wraps the scarf into a tighter knot around her head.

Seth appears in the doorway again behind her, holding a clipboard.

"Seth'll take you out there." Terry says, nodding to him. "Anyways, I just want to know where the best dry slabs are so I can load up enough to keep me going through the spring till it warms up a bit more in the mornings. What do you have?" she says, trying to catch his eye. "Show me the best pile. I don't want any of that heavy, wet stuff that you gave me last time." She warns, stomping off behind.

Seth knew better than to argue when dealing with Raving Amy, though hearing complaints from a customer about the quality of free firewood must be tempting for the witty commentary that usually would accompany his response.

"I'll show you Amy, but how are you calling this weather, cool? Man, we're cookin' down here," he says.

I follow them back around the mill, carrying my coffee, to where all the scrap is piled, most of it bundled into 15-foot-long, oblong stacks about 6 feet thick.

"Can't have too much wood ya know," she says, "always gets burned, if not now, then later."

"There is an open bundle over here that you can pick through.

Take whatever you want." Terry offers.

"'Kay. Got my own saw you know. I'm not asking you to do the work. Wouldn't want to push my luck," she says with her sideways smile.

"Yeah, right, okay. Have at 'er." I'm a few strides back, waiting.

Seth turns back and she watches as we walk away.

"She may be crazy, Gabe," he says, as we step back into the staff shack so he can grab another order sheet off the bulletin board, "but you know, for an older, single, crazy lady, with crude communication skills, she sure can be self-sufficient. More so than many."

The sound of a chainsaw erupts behind us from her direction as we leave the shack again. We turn around to see Raving Amy gunning her little Stihl chainsaw high above her head, as if saluting her own independence, then dropping the spinning chain onto the loose cedar slabs at her feet.

"Glad I'm not in striking distance." Terry says, passing us, heading back to the mill, grinning to himself.

"Okay Gabe, what was it you needed… one by four? Let's go find you some." Seth says, back to business.

CHAPTER 7

Pearl

I thought that it'd be a good day to gather some of them necessary ingredients so the botanical crew could keep makin' their potions down at the ol' school house. They make these tinctures down there to sell at markets, 'medicinal remedies', they call 'em, for digestion and sleepin' and other things. I learned all bout gatherin' wild plants from my Cree grandmother when I was just a girl, so, even though the plants are different here than back east, I've adjusted to it and understand them now. They call it wild crafting. We just called it gatherin'. Sally called last night to let me know that they was runnin' low on chamomile, ginger root and yarrow. Salal and devil's club root too, but I don't think I'll be getting' to those today. Probably I won't go high enough up on the hill to find salal, and the devil's club, well I'll get Ariel to dig that up for me. He's more nimble at dodgin' all them thorns, and he don't seem to mind helpin' out some, that one, more so than most. He's been coming by ever since he was a little one, so now he just fit right in, makin' himself at home. Though now that he's a teenager he'd stop comin' by, but turns out, he comes by more now'n before... seems to me he likes to. Sometimes I watch him close. He'll jus' sit there like a monk in a cave, just starin' out, at nothin', like he jus' needs to be still, waitin' for nothin' to be said.

And other times, we jus' carry on like a couple of chimes in the wind, rattlin' away in all directions but not goin' anywhere. Both ways, he jus' seem like he need a place to go sometimes jus' to get away from troubles at home. Guess we all need that some days.

Anyways, I gotta get out now, move my bones before they get stuck and b'sides, I need a diversion from my dream, so goin' out in the woods'll do me good. Sometimes I wake up with the cloak of a dream kinda draped over me. Meant to be some kinda reminder I s'pose. Sometimes I don't like it, 'specially when you feel that the dream is tellin', then you kind of wait for it to happen. Course, if you're waitin' for it, I guess it reduces the blow when it finally happens 'cause you was already half expectin' it. The s'pression of the dream gets kinda imprinted on the back of my mind, so even if I'de wished for it to fade off, for the layers to wash away the memory, it don't; it just sits there and waits, stuck to your mind like shit on a blanket. So then, I make myself just get out there and face it, like starin' down a bear in the woods, can't run, can't turn away. Sometimes I face my dreams when I'm alone in the bush. I do things better when I'm alone. I pay more 'tention. I always feel at home in the woods, just walkin' and listenin'.

Sometimes I hum the old Cree tunes my grandmother and my mother taught me when I was a kid. It's funny how you remember simple tunes like that forever. Brings back memories to 'company you when you're alone.

I used to go into the woods when I was a kid back East in Asbestos, Quebec. There'd be all kinds of places to explore. My grandfather had a small trap line too, so sometimes I'd follow him along his route. Sometimes he'd bring back a beaver or a mink and skin it. My father taught me to fish in the local streams. He showed me how to cast a reel, to not get snagged; we'd go ice fishin' in Lac Les Trois for walleye and pike. In summers we would just cast from the rocks on shore. My father was a Quebecer and so was my grandfather on his side. My grandmother on my mom's side was Cree, which makes me and my mother Metis. Even though I did learn a lot about the forest and the relationship we had with it, I never did feel like a pure blood Indian. Well, I'm not, only a quarter really, but there is this strength that I get from knowin' I'm part Indian. It don't matter to me, the percentage, or that I'm not a pure blood Cree or Snixt or Haida. I'm more like a Twinkie Indian really, dark on the outside, but all white and soft in the center.

I like to sit at home and watch Coronation Street while I'm eatin' a bag full of Cheezies or nacho chips and dip or have a bath and read the latest news in the Enquirer 'bout the next visit to Canada by the Prince of Wales or a three headed baby being born in Mongolia. That's why I'm fat; from just sittin' round too much, but I'm strong too and can get around better than most my age so I'm not going to worry myself about that. I get plenty a exercise what with all my chores and hobbies. I was lucky to of had the elders live long enough to teach me what they did, to tan a hide, hunt, trap, fish and weave, things most ain't interested in any more. My mother was a great gardener too, back east in Asbestos. Here, there's lots to do in every season. I can't think why folks find the need to exercise, like with weights and machines. You don't get anything done doin' that. You lift the load and it just come back down again. At least if you're stackin' wood, it goes up and stays up there and the pile gets bigger. Or runnin'… them folks that just run, they just run 'round in circles, getting' there and goin' back, without fetchin' or deliverin' anything. They don't come back carryin' a grouse or a satchel of berries or even some mail. Some of 'em even run on a machine like a hamster in a cage. I don't understand it. Even in the winter, you can still work your legs with a snow shovel or with a wheel barrow full of wood. Maybe wouldn't be so bad if they hooked up the runnin' machine to a generator that ran their TV or their toaster or somethin', least then they'd be producin' somethin'.

Here in Procter, getting' round is easier too, than back east I mean, 'specially in the winter. The temperatures are much milder so I git out more than I did there and the bugs aren't near as bad in the summer either. Kenneth used to hate them bugs, always swattin' at 'em, cursin'. He would have loved it here, my Mother woulda too, but now, I've left all their spirits back in Asbestos.

I ain't never studied much, but I always liked to learn new words. I used to speak French with my Father too, so I learned lots of colourful language. A little Cree too. But mostly I spoke English cause my parents put me in English speakin' Catholic schools, like my mother had done. Not sure why they did, cause Mother never made it sound like her schoolin' was much fun either, fact is she never spoke much 'bout it at all. I've heard what happened in those schools, we've all heard, and now we just have to let that demon rest.

My schoolin' wasn't like that. I guess that what I learnt most in schools was language, spellin' and such, not a lot else. Never had that much time for school, what with our farm and all the chores. I had to milk cows every mornin' and after school and then during slaughter times, in the fall, I'd usually have to stay home and help clean chickens or put meat through the grinder, pack and label. I used to like wrappin' up the meat. I thought it was like wrappin' presents, so I'd make 'em all neat with a creased fold and I'd put ribbons round them from the Christmas wrappin' box, just to add some colour. I was always satisfied when I had a whole counter full of them brown paper packets all lined up there. Course I missed a lot of school days and was late a lot. Used to get in trouble, but I never paid much attention to that. Then I would fail… failed two times, so by the time I was fifteen, I was in class with thirteen year olds. The older kids thought i1t5w4 as pretty funny. They'd make fun of me, call me a stupid squaw. It got worse… till I just quit.

When they came after me with the names and throwin' stuff, I'd stand there facin' 'em. I never got scared or backed off. I was always pretty tough, on the outside anyhow. Just stood there like a tree, staring 'em down. A couple of 'em paid the price when they pushed too far, and then I would end up in the Sister's office, with the Headmaster and she would show me the leather strap with the steel studs in it. One time she used it on the back a my hands cause I wouldn't repent. I went home that day and couldn't milk the cows I was so sore, couldn't bend my fingers. After that, I didn't go back to school much. I never did understand too well the repentin' of things. They taught us' bout confession and redemption, but to me it just seem like an endless cycle of sinnin' and sorriness, one enablin' the other. I didn't see the cure in it. So I guess, when I left school behind, I left the religion with it. My parents didn't seem to mind much 'bout either one. Seem to me they was jus' as happy to have me helpin' out round the property. The only part I miss was the writin' part, always liked to hear them long words that I didn't know. Always wondered what they meant and where they came from, why they sounded like that and who'd made 'em up. I'd ask my Mother all kinds a questions 'bout words and other things while we worked together. Usually she wouldn't know the answers so I would look them up later in the old encyclopedia set we had on the shelf. Wasn't so bad missin' school, 'sides, Mother seemed to like the work better if I was there to distract her.

I keep all of her lessons and all the lessons of my grandparents in my mind, so I can use 'em when I'm gatherin' and preparin' plants and meat. Gatherin' from what is offered in the woods is what I like to do. It's so much better than shoppin', 'cept we don't have any Cheezies or pop out there in the woods, so I still need some money.

Today, the clouds are low. Some of the misty ones are still sittin' just above the trees 'bout a third of the way up the mountain, near the bench where I'm headed. The mountain behind my place is all covered in forest and it's north facin' so it keep pretty cool and damp most the time. There's quite a bit of ground water in places, 'specially on the benches where water pools. That bench I usually go to is 'bout a forty-minute walk up the hill, at the speed I goes anyhow. The old path I used to walk went straight up, but a few years ago I made a new one that meanders up with some switch backs so I don't have to struggle to get up there so steep. I can see that no one has been trackin' up my path any time recently, not that there are often tracks, 'cept those of the deer, bear, coyotes and skunks. There's always muddy patches to check tracks, see who's been comin' through.

Up round the bend I cross the creek; it's rushin' down the hill, splashin' drops onto the plank that I've got across it, makin' it slippery. I've got the day pack I usually carry, with a few bags in it, some cloth, others plastic, to keep things separate. I've already cut some yarrow from the field before the path enters the forest on the way up. Along the path here, there's ginger plants, so I stop to dig out a few roots and stuff 'em in. Lots of people tell me they feel confined by the dense forest bein' round, specially prairie folk, feel kind of trapped or claustrophobic, but I like the shadow of the canopy. To me, it's comfortin', a place of calm, where you can stop and be still and watch life jus' drippin' and slitherin' along, where decay and growth are the same thing; you can hear whispers float by, drawin' your attention this way and that.

By the time I'm nearly to the height of the yew grove, the bench, I'm a little winded and I sit on a log for a minute and have a smoke. The yew grove is where I like to come to gather all the moisture lovin' plants. It's got a spongy floor of moss and needles, puddles and pools, b1l5a6ck muddy surfaces. Above there's cedar and hemlock, yew and devil's club. Yew trees have always been mystical to me, like an old sorcerer, always growin' in the darkest parts, bent and gnarly, with soft sweepin' branches of flat green needles all in neat rows, and smooth. The top tip of the yew barely reaches the bottom branches of the cedar and hemlock above, formin' its own under-canopy; it don't care 'bout reachin' for the sun. Its bent body and flakin' bark are like wrinkles, reminds me of my grandfather: aged but solid, rooted, confident, secure in his own self and wise, growin' older, not taller. If the yew could speak, what would he say? These are the kinda questions that run 'round my head when I sit in the grove, while time blends with the breeze around me and I got no one else to talk to 'cept the yew.

I trudge on a little higher, breathin' easier now, and rise round the last bend. Smells like things tryin' to grow. My feet fall soft and wet, slow. There are calm pools ahead where the flats begin, where water gets trapped, providin' a home for tadpoles, water worms and larvae, who live here. I yield to the face of the pool. I know these pools well, been inside, been allowed in, invited. It's hard to explain, but all I can say for sure is that I've lost track of time here, where the span of time between arrivin' and departin' can't be 'counted for; where time and space don't matter. You might think I'm just old and losin' my memory, my marbles, but it's not jus' that; I've been inside the reflection. I've learned to enter it. I've been in between the gills of a mushroom, through strands of moss, along lichen and heather, tasted dew drops from their skin and learnt secrets from their cells. I've learnt that you can go inside the aura, that the spirits there will share the space if you let 'em. It's true that I'm getting' old but some parts never age, like the part that knows how old I am. I settle in for a while.

Later, on the way down, my day pack is packed with roots, leaves, petals and bark. The ladies of the botanical center will be happy. The misty clouds have risen, allowin' filtered rays of sun to warm up the forest floor. I'm just chewin' on jerky I'd packed and hummin' some tune I'd heard on the radio this mornin', one of them ones that gets stuck in your head and no matter how much you try to distract your mind it just keeps poppin' back in there like a jack in the box, just springin' up without any notice. Guess I'll head down to the school house with their plants while it's still light and get one of them sticky cinnamon buns at the bakery while I'm there. Don't think I've had one of them all month so it's 'bout time. Just got to be back in time for kids to be droppin' by like they tend to just before dinner time. That's when most folks pick up their eggs, milk, cheese and things for the next day, so I try to make a point of bein' home. Anyways, I like havin' them kids drop by, or sometimes their parents, other folks too. I've been sellin' more and more these days; I sometimes even run out now. Thing is I don't really want to make more butter, or have more chickens, so I guess I've got enough folks on the list now.

I'm hardly ever lonely here. I've gotten used to livin' on my own, but when those kids drop in, I often think of Kenneth and how he would love to talk to kids of all ages. I do miss him and his playful ways. He added a lot of laughter to our days. I try to picture him in that way, remember him as a playmate, a strong, smilin', hard workin' man, full of energy and opinions. 'Course there's times when his last days haunt me too, when his worn-out body, all drained from the asbestos, was just too weak to move. He would still smile but couldn't laugh much cause his breath was so shallow, the lungs full of fluid and tumors. And I'll always remember that night that he sat up in his hospital bed we had in the livin' room, sat up so he could hug me, and when he kissed me goodnight, it tasted like goodbye. In the mornin' his spirit was gone. I like to think that he passed in his sleep.

I get home, and sure 'nuff, a half hour later, I looks up to find Zoe peerin' into the house from the porch, through the torn screen door. Guess it's time to switch that old aluminum door out, must be from the original trailer, that thing. By now, there's been so many add ons and alterations, you can hardly see the trailer in my house anymore. Zoe don't knock, seems nervous 'bout steppin' in so she stays put, just outside. She's nine years old and lives just a few hundred meters down the hill. Her mother sends 'er over, like lots a parents do, at times, to pick somethin' up from my place. I usually have somethin' they're after, some jerky, eggs, goat milk or cheese, even got butter most the time, things I make myself and people knows the quality will be good and the price right enough, so I never have any shortage of visitors. In the fall I have braids of garlic and onions and sometimes smoked trout if I catch enough extra, but fishin's not so good these days.

"Zoe, what's goin' on with you? Are you pickin' up some eggs today?" I have to call out to her from inside behind my loom. I'm workin' the shuttle and reed back and forth cross the rows of yarn, click, click, clickin'. I'm weavin' one of them geometric designs in a scarf, using terra cotta and burgundy colours. I glance up and see her eyes followin' my hands, the sound, her eyes is fixed, kinda hypnotized as the coloured lines stack up and grow in front of her. "Is your mom doin' some bakin' or are you just here to inspect my screen?"

She moves in a bit closer to open the door, swings it open just enough to step in, and says,

"Yes, momma wants two dozen today if you have 'em," I can carry them back in my new school bag" she says, holding up a bright striped cloth bag that she is lookin' real proud of. She's a chubby little thing, all rosy and bright like a peach.

"Yes, well I s'pose you can. That bag looks sturdy 'nough to carry all kindsa eggs. I'll just finish up now with this fringe here." I tie off some loose ends with a series of overhand knots, "then we'll see what we have for you. I think there's plenty right now. I been collectin' 'em quicker these days as the hens have picked up their layin' with the warmer weather and all.

"Do you know what happens if I don't pick those eggs up out of the nest quick enough every day?"

"No," she says, "what'?

"Well, they eat their own. Can you 'magine, like a mother eatin' her own baby?" I likes to watch when wild pictures cross the face of a little one's imagination. It always shows up in the confused expression and the scrunched up brow.

"First, you forget to collect eggs one night, or maybe two nights in a row, and then when you do pick em up they're all dirty from droppins, and some are cracked from being crowded. When they're cracked, after a while the chickens start peckin' at em. Soon they get a taste for the egg itself and then they begin peckin' at them to break e'm, on purpose, just to eat 'em. A nasty thing." This little one, looks up for a moment, catchin' my eye, while I ties off more rows.

"Once they get a taste for the egg, that chicken won't stop peckin' at 'em and so that bird has to go, otherwise you won't get no more eggs. Yes sir, that one ends up in a stew pot, just like that, so, as you can see, that chicken ends up learnin' a important lesson. She kinda ate herself to death didn't she?" I ask Zoe as she ponders, and shuffles her feet looking round for the answer.

"Too bad she didn't know that", she says finally. "Can we get the eggs now?" The kids that drop by my place to pick things up, usually end up hearin' whatever happens to be on my mind at the time. Some of 'em pay no attention at all, or don't seem to anyhow.

"That's where we're goin' honey," I say, noddin' toward the back porch where there's a second apartment sized fridge. That's where I keep fish 'n eggs and extra butter to sell. "Here you go girl", I hand the two boxes over and help put 'em flat in the bottom of her bright cloth bag. "I guess that'll do it for you then?" "Yep, thanks Pearl. Here is the money my Mom gave me." she says, handing over a fist full of various coins that were stuffed in the bottom of her pocket.

"Okay, perfect. And thank you Zoe. You had better get on back now. I'll see you next time okay? Don't swing that bag too low on the way home now." I throw the coins into a half full jar of change and small bills on the counter.

"'K, thanks Pearl, see ya." She says, in her quiet little voice and walks back out, down the stairs and along the dirt path in front of my house.

She'll probably have most of them eggs broke by the time she gets home. Cute little thing, that Zoe. Probably'll be havin' nightmares now 'bout cannibal chickens. Kenneth would have loved these little kids stopping by all the time. He was always better with 'em than me. Good thing we never had any. I like to see 'em when they just drop by, but it's good too that they just leave again, head home. I can't fathom havin' a kid round for twenty years, like a life sentence. The only one I ever got real close to is Misae, my niece, brother Bernie's kid, still back East, 15 now. We still talk some, her and I, but only on the phone now that I've moved clear across the country. I miss her, she's one that reminds me of me. She's always been real close to me, Kenneth too when she was a baby. He would pick her up and look her in the eye, smilin' like an ape, and she would laugh, all bubbly, from her belly, like a fountain that was sprinklin' smiles all-round the room. It's 'cause of her that I started collectin notes in a scrap book. I figure Misae'll find 'em handy to know one day. I look through it time to time and it makes me smile when I picture her in my mind's eye, readin it. Times when I do come up with somethin' in particular that seems to me a specially good idea, I'll scratch it down in there, or jus' cut it out and send it off to her straight away in the mail. Did that with a recipe bout jam last week. It's not jus' a recipe. Got lots of notes alongside in the margins, bout what I been doin' lately, what I shouldn't a been doin' too. Recipe comments too, like, 'could be any berry', and 'don't worry 'bout the mess', 'if they try to get away, jus squish em.' I been makin' jam outta all kindsa fruit forever. Sometimes I'll come in with a basket fulla berries. Can't be bothered to keep em separate. I jus' dump em on the counter. Once when I did that and they was all scattered round, mixed up, all different sizes, shapes and colours, thimble berries soft and dented, huckleberry's shiny, currents hard, headin' in all directions, I got to thinkin' that they look like cars in a traffic jam. Now I call all the mixed fruit jams, Traffic Jam, so that's the recipe

I cut out and sent to Misae. Left another hole in my scrap book. Kenneth wouldn' approve of that, I was thinkin', cutting that out. He didn't like things left part done or disorganized like that.

Can't believe I still think about him so much, Kenneth, been almost twenty years now since he died, twelve since I've been here in Procter. Too bad I'm not from here 'nstead of Asbestos. If you're from a place with a name like that, you almost expect to be affected by it. Guess it's a good thing that I'm not from Moose Jaw or Horsefly then. Asbestos took my Dad too, not only Kenneth. My family thought it was the best place when we was growin' up there, all full of money and jobs, but once folks started getting' sick, and studies were bein' done, the whole place started dryin' up, just like that. The only thing good came out of it, was the cheque I got when I sold the two houses we had there. The one of my family and the one Kenneth and I owned. Didn't get half what they was worth years earlier though, back in the boom days when asbestos was still the miracle material instead of just a source of contamination. There was studies done in Asbestos and Thetford mines too, showin' that even the air inside the houses and the soil in the yards and gardens was full of them fibers. I had lots a good memories there so there were times I longed for everything to be as it was, but mostly I was relieved to leave.

When Kenneth and I'd visited BC, years earlier, we'd always vowed to return. We'd driven all the way cross, campin' out by lakes and rivers, swimmin' and fishin' long the way. It was the only time I could remember when we'd had that much time to relax together; that by itself was a special thing, but more important was our time in BC. That time became the dream in my mind's eye. The place we would return to, to settle once and for all, where the weather and the water weren't so frozen; where the mountains were steep and wild and the water rushin' down them sparkled. A place where you could breathe deep.

***

Well, I did, make it back - to BC, that is, without Kenneth, sadly, to the mountains and water that me and him had dreamt about, to Procter, the village that was so small you could barely find it, yet big enough to raise a ruckus. I like it 'cause you have to take a boat to get over here, like goin' to an Island, on a road that dead ends so you always get to where you was goin' to, lest yer lost. Ended up buyin' my little house from a young couple,

Gabe and Emily Framer. Got to know them folks pretty good over the years, Noah and Gavin too, their young boys. Gabe, he's a bit of a ruffian, I guess you could say. I like that word, ruffian, sounds like rufflin' feathers or some kinda winter storm. Gabe, he does do some rufflin' of feathers 'round the village too, has plenty of 'pinions bout things. That one is an interestin' mix, like someone threw a logger and a back-to-the-lander in a mixin' bowl and tossed 'em round with a little too much gumption. He always looks a little bit tumbled too, like he coulda just fell outta the bowl, with his long hair and sap-stained clothes mussy and slapdash, kinda like me I s'pose. When he brings me wood or sets his tools up to fix somethin' round the place, he usually comes on time mind you, and don't complain 'bout the chicken shit on the floor like some do. He can work, has some strength. When he puts his shoulder to somethin', it always moves. Emily too, she comes over and helps out some when she's pickin' up butter or somethin', when it's not Noah or Gavin that come.

She's always askin' 'bout flowers or how to keep the onions from rottin' on the vine, likes learnin' and always has a smile. She's a lot taller n' me too, slender like a sunflower, so she can reach up top my cupboards and take down the cannin' pot or the extra clay plant pots I keeps up there. It's good havin' them folks just down the path from my place; I'm glad I bought it from 'em.

It didn't take me long to find it, this place. All I had to do was hang round the bakery with folks and drink lots of coffee every mornin'. I was camped out on a landing at the end of a spur road where nobody seemed to pass by much or pay me any mind. My truck was newer then, ran real good. Now, I gotta roll start 'er all the time and add oil to her motor every couple of weeks. I figured I'd stay up there, on the landing, for as long as it took to find a place of my own, save every dollar I could not payin' rent. Every day I'd start out in the bakery, soakin' up gossip and coffee and eatin' muffins. I looked at a few places that were for sale with one of them realtors, the kind that always has the, 'perfect place for you,' every day, but none of them worked out. Then, one day Gabe had come in on a break, sawdust all stuck to his shirt sleeves. I overheard him talkin' bout the place he was fixin' to sell and so

I asked him 'bout it. Before long we was driving on up there to have a look see, 'fore long it was mine.

My place is just a fifteen-minute walk outside the village, a little east and up on the hill. Gabe had bought it real cheap and rented it out for a couple years but then realized that it needed a lot of work, so he fixed up the old trailer and kind of hid it inside some framed additions, then sold it to me to get his money back. It has enough room round it for me to keep my chickens, a few goats and all my different garden patches. Been almost twelve years ago now, since I bought the place. Now it's got animals all round, chicken wire, piles of soil, manure and compost here and there and stuff growin' all over. Even got some grape vines creepin' up the house along an old mountain ash tree that's leaning up the side. Now the chickens have learned to fly up to the bottom branches and pick grapes off the vines in the fall. Sometimes they even get up onto the roof and peer down over the edge, lookin' like they're waitin' for whoever it is that put them up there to come get them back down. Them chickens got a brain smaller than a marble and just as sharp. I seen one once, bend into a bucket of water for a drink and drown hisself, just forgettin' to stand back up again… well, that's what I tell kids that come over anyhow.

I've got piles of slabs from the mill for burnin' and some old doors leanin' 'gainst the shed up in the driveway by where my old truck is parked, backed in, ready to go. There's a tool shed too, with all kinds of hand tools and wheelbarrow parts and bolts and bits to this and that. I've got what I need here. My place looks like it belongs here, like it's startin' to grow in to the land it sits on, or maybe like it's sinkin' in. Anyhow, I like it lookin' like that, 'stead of trying to tame the grass and keep the gardens behind borders like a lot of folks like, I just let 'em go. I don't have any neat lines with one thing on one side and one on the other, but I know where to look when I need to pick somethin'.

I hop in the truck and shut the door, she still closes with a thud like she should, and when I put the clutch in and put 'er in second, she rolls away just fine, starts up easy like she's just waitin' to go. You might wonder why my truck is a she, cause a lot of folks think trucks should be he, but mine's not, she is more like me, a little bent and wrinkled, soft in the springs, but dependable like an old friend. I call her, 'Bets,' short for Betsy, but now, more like the gamblin' kind, like I'm betting on her to run. It only takes a few minutes to drive to the bakery. I should walk really, but I don't. I like to drive a little every day, roll down the windows and light a smoke, even in the winter. I don't smoke much… or so I says, but somehow, smokin' and drivin' goes together so I do it.

The bakery is at the top of the block, which is good for parkin' on a slope. There's always someone in there to talk to, sometimes even three tables full which really fills it right up. I like it when the talk flows round in there, one conversation runnin' into another, all mixed up- sounds like a yard full of chickens. When I open the door, the sweet smells of baking run right over me as I bring the cool, fresh air from outside in.

"Mornin' Graham," I say. He is at the back counter rollin' out some kinda dough, probably for another batch of them cinnamon buns, somethin' his bakery is famous for. Folks even ride their bikes all the way out from Nelson to get' em, or maybe that is just the reward for ridin' so far. Graham moved in and took over the bakery back a few years, didn't want to be drivin' into town every day to some kind of job, so he made himself one right here. He was a machinist in Winnipeg before he moved here; has himself a glass eye now. You can tell cause both eyes don't line up when they look at you. He told me once, "that eye is the final bonus I got before leaving my job. The best kind of gift, one that keeps on reminding you what you don't want to do."

"Hey Pearl, how's it going today?" he says, glancin' up a moment, adjusting the skull cap he wears when he's bakin'. Guess it's to keep the last few hairs on his head from fallin' into the dough. "Did ya bring in any eggs? We're runnin' low."

"No, don't have lots of extras now, but I could probably drop some off day after tomorrow if that works, 'pendin' on how my birds are feelin'."

"Yep, as many as you can. What can I get you now, don't have much."

"Hey Pearl," says Maggie. She is in the back kitchen, hands busy with something. I can see only her top half through the opening as she moves about readying things for the morning business. They serve a bit of breakfast and some lunch a little later. There's usually not much variety but it's all good. It's not like a regular cafe' in here, where you would sit and get served after readin' the menu. There's no menu. It's more like walkin' into your neighbor's kitchen and hopin' that they'll offer you somethin' to eat- you've gotta hint at it, find out what there is. The chalk board only says:

Menu

Breakfast   Lunch
When we have food.   Prices vary.

"Whatcha choppin' there Maggie?" I ask her. She calls out, back turned, "just prepin' some soup for later. Can I get you something Pearl?" "How 'bout a butter tart, just came out of the oven? Or are you one of those calorie counters? We've got some carrot cake, or I can make an eggwich on an english muffin."

"Calorie counter? Nope, not me. The only calories I ever counted was when I was tryin' to find the best yogurt in the supermarket. If you look hard enough, you can find the one that has the most calories and that is the best one. They don't make it easy though. Those ones are all hid in there with a thousand other yogurts that have zero written all over 'em."

"Yeah, I hear ya Pearl," she says. "Maybe I should make you a burger then," she says, noddin' toward a pile of ground meat thawin' on the counter nearby, the brown waxed butcher paper torn open to expose it, "once it's thawed, that burger looks like it's full of fat."

"Mmhmm" I say, "findin' the fatty one is like playin' hide n seek." I carry on, "I think maybe they should change the supermarket. I want them to have a extra-fat isle, no fat removed, for us folks that want to taste our food."

Two more tables have already filled up with people since I came in, Hector and Sam at one and a couple with those flashy, tight, bikin' clothes on that looks like they got poured into, at the other. They are chattin' away, so I move into the doorway, closer, to talk to Maggie.

"Don'tcha think? A fat isle with full fat butter 'n milk, big, fat eggs, extra fat yogurt, bacon and butter milk. Gum that's full a sugar, full fat ice cream... you know, sometimes I spends half an hour just tryin' to read the small print to figure it out." Maggie jus' looks up from stirrin' her soup, lookin' at me with eyebrows up. "Now, if I forget my glasses like I's prone to, I gotta ask one of them pimply kids that works there after school to look at the labels for me, takes 'em even longer 'cause they can barely read and they looks at me as though I'm some kinda zoo animal just escaped." Maggie's noddin, says, "Maybe Pearl, but I'm not sure too many people will want the fat isle." She smiles, don't think she know what to offer me now.

"Damn straight." says Hector, behind me. "I'll be shoppin' in that fat isle too, Pearl. You get in there and tell 'em how to design their damn store next time you're in, okay?" He says, lookin' up over his coffee cup at me.

Then Graham lifts his head up from where he's still rollin' and cuttin' over at the butcher block counter, says, "Yeah, you would be shopping there, Hector, they could carry that fatty burger that you sold to me. Look at that stuff, more white than red." He smiles, nodding toward the kitchen.

"Hey Hector, mornin' to you." I say, "Yeah, or maybe I'll just open my own fat store out here: 'all the fat all the time.' That'll be my logo.

"I like it," says Sam, "you're always buckin' the trends, aren't ya Pearl?"

"Ahh, I wouldn't know a trend if it bit me in the backside." I say. "What are you two derelicts up to today anyhow? Out causin' trouble?"

"Just having a break with the riff raff, Pearl." Hector says, "Got two trucks hauling gravel this morning. Already done two loads each and it's only ten o clock, so guess we're doin' good. Damn near ran down a couple deer on my first run. Broke so quick that Sam here almost back ended me. I'm tellin' ya, we should have open season on all them goddamn deer - too damn many of 'em for their own good."

"Yeah, good idea, run down a couple," says Graham, "then you could add some lean meat to that crappy burger you sold me eh?" "Nah." Counters Hector, "people will be coming back for more once you get those burgers served… you'll see… if you grill 'em up right that is." He adds with a smirk.

Hector raises beef to sell to locals and people say that when he comes across an old dairy cow or a retired breed bull for cheap, he'll butcher it and grind the whole thing up to sell for burger.

"Yeah," Graham says, back toward Hector, "but if you keep bringing me that geriatric burger, I'll have to start naming it as such, won't I? Just to keep from false advertising? I was thinking I'll call it the 'Hambergeezer.' What do you think Maggie?" he says, smiling over to her, wiping a droplet of sweat from his forehead onto his apron. "Should be a hit eh? We'd be more of a mortuary than a café, we could become known for supporting the assisted suicide movement, the bovine branch." He grins, picking up steam now. "People will be lined up to support the effort, ordering burgers by the bag full." Maggie just raises her eyebrows and smiles to herself, shakin' her head.

"Funny Graham," Hector says dryly. "Well maybe I should add some venison to the mix then. I'll keep the rifle on the passenger seat on the next run. Take out a few."

What a pair, Hector and Sam, like two beans in a pod, always ready runnin' off their mouth 'bout things. Tryin' to get people riled up whenever they can, specially Hector.

"Should just carry guns around, all of us, so we can open fire on 'em whenever we see one on the road. We'd all be safer for it." He says. "Damn right," says Sam, "blast 'em all. Save on car insurance."

The two in the shiny, bikin' suits sittin' at the next table are lookin' up with sideways glances, probably wondering if it's safe to even ride a bike around this area.

"Not sure if everyone carrying a gun would make it any safer on the roads," I say, back to Hector, "My Kenneth used to say we'd all be safer with a gun too. Always had a hand gun under the bed, said, 'can't be too safe.' And I would say to 'im, 'no, 'specially with a loaded gun under the bed.' I figure all of you'se guys shoulda been born back in the wild west, or maybe Texas, would've been more 'preciated then." I say, sidlin' up to the coffee urn to fill my cup. "Maggie, pass me one of them butter tarts will ya? I'll take one with me too, for the road. Gotta head off into town soon."

"Yeah, I figure he had it just about right, Pearl. You too, with the wild west. They had it right back then." Hector says, nodding along with Sam.

"Damn straight." Sam agrees.

I never need much from town these days 'cause I grow and gather so much of what I use just from around here where I live, but still, there are bills to pay. Once a month I go in to the Credit Union to drop off my pension cheque too. I don't partake in any of that online bankin' stuff like so many does these days, don't trust it much, got no use for a computer. Anyhow, I've got to see the doc today, some kind of follow up on tests they took last month. Can't say as I'm too worked up over it though. If'n they hadn't been callin' me, I wouldn't even go. Still not sure I even will, but at least I can get some cash back at the bank so I can buy a pack of them Lucky Strike silvers- they don't sell 'em in Procter and I have a cravin' today. I usually roll my own but sometimes I'll buy a pack. I don't smoke much, but I sure like it when I do and I'm not a quitter.

I don't think I need to quit anything one hundred percent. Why take it that far? Is it just to prove a point? Well, I don't like taking things, anythin' to the extreme. I only smoke a few cigarettes a week, well that's what I tell people anyhow. I drink a little wine every day too, cheap, red wine. I can be a part time vegetarian, but I eat a lot of meat. I exercise most days by walkin' but sometimes, like yesterday, I'll just sit and watch the Oprah Winfrey show instead, put my feet up and eat a whole pack of them Cheezies that turns all your fingers orange. No, I'm not a quitter. I won't just quit anything a hundred percent.

Not feelin' anymore energetic today either and now I don't even need to go out to stock up on things like I thought 'cause Hailey called first thing to confirm that she could come by and learn some willow weavin'. We'd talked 'bout it outside the bakery last week after she'd spotted a half-woven chair leanin' 'gainst my fence when she'd come by to pick up eggs. "That weaving is beautiful and strong." She was tellin' me. "Looks like something I could learn without having lots of tools. Can you teach me how to start Pearl? Can I use the weeping willow branches off the tree in my yard?" Anyhow we'd got to talkin' and now she's comin' over and before she comes she's goin' to stop at the store and pick me up things I'm missin', save me the trip.

She shows up swingin' one of them cloth shoppin' bags by her side, her pony tail swingin' along with it. She's always walkin' like she's got somewhere she got to get to, that one, full of smiles and energy like a half-grown puppy. Solid too, moves like she means it, like one of them women I seen on TV, playin' volley ball in the sand. "You smells like sweet smoke." I says to her when she comes close.

"Oh yeah," she says, "guess I do. I burn palo santo in my bedroom, gets in my clothes."

"Like sweet grass?" I asks her.

"I guess, except it's wood. A soft wood that I got when I was traveling in Pakistan, very aromatic. I love the smell. Hope I can find more when it runs out."

"Yeah, smells good too, not like the sweet grass 'n sage braids we used to smudge with back east, but nice all the same. Reminds me of my grandmother."

"Hmmm. Maybe we can braid some sweetgrass when my Palo Santo runs out then, eh Pearl?" She asks, steppin' up on my porch to bend over and give me a squeeze. "Good to see you again Pearl. Haven't had much chance to catch up since I've been back. Here's your things, had to get you a Bic lighter instead of a box a matches. All out, oh and no Cheezies either, so got you a bag of chips and some red twizzlers." She says, dropping the bag by my feet.

"Thank ya kindly," I say. She stretches up then, arms into the sky, back to the sun beam that has fallen down through some cracks in the cloud. "Needed that," she says, smilin', "had a chill." Right then an old pick up rattles by up on the road, not someone I recognize. It's loud with a bad muffler and one of them dirt bikes is right close behind him, the two stirrin' up lots of dust as they pass. Once they're gone by, I turn back to Hailey, "yes, we should braid us up some nice bundles of sweet grass and we can smudge your place proper. Do it every time you come back from your plantin' trips. Give your place back it's balance, make room for only the good spirits… less, 'corse, ya think the spirits at your place only understands the smoke from them *east* Indians," I say, chucklin' at her but my chuckle turns into coughin' and I got to clear my throat 'n spit. She follows me round back the house, says, "I'll ask 'em Pearl, and get back to you."

"Okay now, here's the stack I been soakin'," I say, pullin' a bundle out from under my back step where I'd stuffed it in a tub of water a while back. "These are wild willow from up on the bench yonder," I say noddin' up the mountain behind us, "where the water pools. We use wild willow, not the weepin' willow.

Doesn't crack, stays strong and supple when it's wet…supple" I repeat slowly, waggin' my head back and forth. "I like that word, rolls around all soft 'n gentle in yer mouth like a marshmallow." "If you say so Pearl," Hailey says, grinning back at me over her shoulder.

"I'll show you one day, where to find it, so you can get more if you need to. Here, we'll start with me addin' some rows to the chair I started before and you can start a new one. Just sit right down there, or maybe we should go back round out front dand wait for the sun to come back out stead of sittin' in the shade of the house." "Yep, sounds better. I'll grab this." She says, heavin' the drippin' bundle of rods under one arm. We walk back 'round and climb up onto the front porch and set down on the bench that's built into the wall there.

Gabe was good enough to include some improvements in the deal we'd made when I bought the place from 'im and this bench was one of his ideas. Fits right into the deck like it grew there, the curve of the slab wood support he'd used givin' it a natural look like the trunk of a tree risin' outta the ground. Hailey and I settle in, her bent over, concentratin' on her first rows, glancin' over at my hands to check as I add rows to the weave. My fingers don't need me to tell 'em how. I move slow but certain, she, fast but wanderin'; my fingers and knuckles are crooked and gnarly like some of the thicker mottled rods that have knots and knobs on 'em. When my eyes blur, I can't tell one from the other, my fingers and hand just weavin' right into the chair like it's part of it. I watch Hailey's work and correct her at first, but she learns quick from watchin' and I can just let my fingers do the work and let my mind wander round. When occasional warm raysland on my body, my fingers slow to a near stop while I let the heat sink in, my eyes close, only the clicking sound of Hailey's switches flickin' between one another breakin' the silence. I guess the weavin' kinda works on yer mind like one of them hypnotists. When the shadow of cloud returns, my eyes open onto the chicken coop to the spot on the outside wall just under the roof overhang where Gabe had run out of shingles, so the tar paper is still showin', flappin' with loose ends where the staples have torn free.

I had seen a lot of Gabe over the first few months of livin' here. He built me the chicken coop and woodshed and fixed up the front entry with this little deck where I sit outside in the mornin' and drink my tea while the sky gets brighter.

He jus' puts his head down and does a job, doesn't say much; gets all absorbed. Sometimes I'd catch 'im mumblin away to himself a little, cursin' some, as he carries on, workin' with his hands while his head is up to somethin' else. Seen 'em get a lot done in one day, picks up steam like a rock rollin' down a landslide.

"Wonder if I'll ever get them shingles finished?" I says, starin' off, Hailey still focused on her fingers, brow scrunched up like a kid with a crayon. I carry on. "'Course, haven't had him around the place for a long time 'cept to drop off some firewood once in a while, Gabe. He's a busy one."

"Yeah and preoccupied too with all the issues" Hailey says, finally stoppin' a moment to look up and straighten out her back. "Not sure if you'll be getting him over to work on one of your projects any time soon." She picks up a new switch from the pile to wind into her work.

She's right. He's becomin' known for his opinions, 'specially now, guess he's really built a reputation for that kinda thing. If he disagrees with something the government does, or some big corporation, he lets 'em know. Everyone knows that he don't like the CP or that Jumbo project either. I've read a couple of his letters to the editor. He knows how to write pretty good and he's not afraid to let 'em know his opinion. I guess if you are lookin' for someone to organize against one of them powers, he could be the one. He doesn't like the CPR movin' their chemicals through our community on their tracks and boy, he got some upset when the government was talkin' 'bout parking the ferry at night and chargin' us a toll to use it; lots a people got upset over that one, not just him.

"Good thing 'bout Gabe is that he can argue with 'em and still make some sense. Doesn't get too riled up the way some do when they're mad." I say. But at the same time, I'm thinkin' I've watched him some, and I can tell you that he's got some kind of anger stewin' round in there, doesn't pop up to the surface much, but it's cookin' away in there like gristle in a crock pot, not getting' any softer. That's what I think anyhow."

"He's been plenty vocal about that Jumbo Glacier Resort plan too." Hailey says, still workin' her switches together, adding a third row. "Gotta say, that I hadn't been paying much attention to it till he did," she adds. "That project stinks you know. He's right. Heard all about it from folks on the other side of the pass where I was working last, near Invermere. They don't like it either, say they have enough ski hills already over there."

Lots of folks have been bandyin' together round that crazy plan, been in the media lots. Them people want to build a resort on top of a glacier that's meltin'. Pretty soon you'd think they'd be skiing on rocks up there, 'stead of snow. Lots of folks are tryin' to stop it. Gabe's done a lot of 'splainin' to folks round town, heard him bring it up often enough myself. He seems to have all the figures in his head bout how many Grizzly bears there are up there, their migration routes, bout the climate change, roads and erosion. He also has all kinds of numbers in his head 'bout the ski hill business- like she says, seems we already have too many in our Province.

"To me, it does seem like a lame brained idea," I say, "this ski resort, all dollars and no sense, but what do I know? One thing for sure is, now, with all the attention round this train crash, there's not too much talk 'bout anything else."

"Yeah, you got that right," Hailey says, "You can barely even walk down the road without running into inspectors and cleanup crews anymore. Too busy for my liking, even in the bakery. Damn! Look Pearl… shit…think I screwed up the fourth row," she says, stopping her work and pushing it over for me to see. I unwind a couple loops and find the problem and hand it back.

"They're poking their nose into everything, taking pictures and recordin' anyone who says anythin' 'bout it," I say, "already had 'em on my door step once and I figure that's enough.

Tiresome and intrusive if you ask me." She mumbles as her concentration turns back to the weave.

"Ya, pretty sure they know what time most folks get up in the morning now, and when they do their laundry." I say. Hailey and I carry on, her learnin' to make the leg of a chair and me, jus' carryin' on with my old chair project as if I really want to get it done. I like havin' her company, much nicer than them inspectors we's talkin' 'bout.

Had two of them CP police inspectors on my door step the other day, askin' all kinda questions, makin' the rounds. It was later in the afternoon and I was snackin' on pretzels, watchin' Ellen Degeneres on TV. Heard 'em from a ways off turnin' round tryin' to back into my muddy driveway. Anyhow, seems they are suspicious that someone plugged up that culvert on purpose and flooded the tracks. They was insinuatin' things that I wasn't too happy 'bout, askin' if I knew Gabe Framer. Told 'em, "Yep, bought my house from him, years ago. They's good people, the Framers," I told em, "good neighbours to have."

"Yes Mam," the CP cop said, the shorter one with the big mustache n' shifty eyes. The other one was too busy watchin' my goats and the gander in the grass who was chasin' 'em when they first came into the yard. Got too close to the nest. "But this Mister Framer, does he work for you sometimes? Does he ever mention the CPR when he is around?" He asked me. I looked the two of 'em up and down like they's a couple Jehovah's Witnesses tryin' to pass off some pamphlets to me 'bout Armageddon.

I pick some stuck pretzel from my teeth, and tell 'em: "Well, he just brings me firewood, doesn't bring up that stuff. "Why you askin' 'bout Gabe anyhow? Seems to me, he can answer just fine for himself, if you ask 'im." I'm getting' a little annoyed with these two already, kinda hopin' they will want to leave soon. "Did you guys get all them spilled chemicals cleaned up down there yet? Seems to me that you should be spending yer energy on that so's we don't have to be breathin' that nasty stuff any longer."

They move in under the porch roof a bit more as the drizzle picks up speed a bit and blows in on an angle. I just stay put in the doorway.

"Yes Mam. We are working on the clean-up twenty-four- seven. Your safety is our priority. We are only here to follow up on questions that have been raised about certain individuals and so your cooperation would be appreciated. If you have any information on anyone or anything that could help in the investigation, we will accept it anonymously at any time. We are only trying to make it safer for all of you here in Procter."

He hands me his card. His partner, the tall, skinny one, finally looks over too, peering into my house over my head, probably wonderin' if the oregano that's hangin' from a nail on my wall is some kind of marijuana I've been smokin'. His head is swivelin' round like a marble in a bowl, takin' in all the facinatin' details. Then he turns to me, smoothin' the last few strands of hair he's got, that's been blowin' around, over the top of his shiny head.

"If you can remember anything that this Framer guy mentioned, anything at all about the CPR please don't hesitate to call. The sooner we get to the bottom of this, the better for everyone who lives out here. Thanks for your time ma'am."

It's startin' to rain proper by now. They step off my porch, lookin' around the yard, drops gathering on their flat-topped caps, drippin' off the front visors. I say, "okay officers, soon's I think a somethin', I'll be callin'," not really soundin' like I means it. "Mind my gander on the way out, he gets real ornery when ya gets too close to the nest."

They'd been lookin' over their shoulders when they left.

Now, Hailey's gone home. Left her first project part done, leanin' up against the wall with mine. I shut the door. It's not cold out, but rain has just started, and I want to keep the sound of it hittin' my metal roof to a minimum, so I can hear my show. I pull up a couple of pillows and get my feet up, try to take the pressure off them varicose veins of mine.

Guess, they have got me wonderin' a little, those investigators. Ol' Gabe seems to have come under the microscope this time for sure. They don't sound like they's interested in anyone else but him. Heard they had a team up there a few days ago that was pouring casts into footprints just like on a TV cop show. Had some dogs up there too back a few weeks ago when they started lookin' round. No one's heard exactly what they've found out yet, but 'course, there's lots of rumours runnin' round. And now with these investigators askin' directly bout Gabe Framer, most of the rumours will be 'bout him. Now, I'm not sure that it's fair of them to be namin' Gabe directly, unless they's got some kinda proof, but say they do? Could be he had a hand in this I s'pose, but to be fair, lots of folks is concerned 'bout the movement of toxic chemicals through our area. We all know that Gabe is the one that's been up against them over the years, warnin' them and raisin a fuss, but there's no harm in that is there? He tells everyone that'll listen.

One time, he was by my place, well before this derailment; he was deliverin' wood to me; he was getting all worked up 'bout this other big rail crash happened in Quebec a couple years ago, carryin' on bout where a bunch of cars carryin' oil blew up and caught fire, killed lots of people. "And we've got the same reckless company carrying chemicals past our door right here in Procter," he told me, "every day, rolling right by, not even telling us what's in those cars. Someone should just blow those tracks right out of there before they blow us all up like those guys in Quebec." He's throwin' wood off his truck onto a pile real hard, like each log is one of them exclamation marks they use for shoutin'. He'd finished unloadin' the wood. Hadn't spoken much after, 'cept right before he left, says, "They already had a derailment just down the tracks from here you know Pearl, not that long ago, back in 2001, killed two guys and took an empty car or two into the lake. If that derailment had spilled millions of liters of chemicals, it would have been a game changer for CP." He says, all serious. Then he shuts the tailgate on his truck, hops in and pulls out, waves at me on his way up the driveway. I guess he meant for me to be left thinkin' bout C.P. derailments, not my next load of wood or the weather. Gabe, he is funny that way, doesn't usually show up empty handed, usually leaves you with a message. 'Course, I figured that message was just for me, so I wasn't 'bout to be sharin' it with them inspectors.

Picked up some mail down at the boxes this mornin'. There's a whole bunch of them green boxes lined up at the gravel pullout cross the road from the Store. Ran into Ravin' Amy down there scannin' people like bar codes at the checkout as they unlocked their mail boxes. You can often times find her off to the side of them mailboxes, next to the wild rose bushes, not hidin' but just kind of on the sideline, half-hidin', observin'. She's got no qualms 'bout just starin' in your direction long as she likes, like Sammy, my Tom-cat does when he's sittin' up on the fridge lookin' down at me. People usually go just after 11:00 am, to pick up 'cause new mail doesn't get dropped off 'till 'bout then. They come and go, walkin' or pullin' in with their cars for a minute to jump out if they're in a hurry. Others just hang round readin' the flyers and chattin' long as the rain's not droppin' on 'em. I guess I must a done somethin' right, cause I'm the only one Amy says hi to. Says it short too, 'siff to say, 'not expectin' a response', so I just nod, as if we'd never even had tea together lotsa times. I've always gotten along okay with Amy, never pays me much mind, but sometimes she can sure have an odd spark in her eye, the kind that could catch fire. 'Takes all kinds of beans to make a good soup', my grandmother used to say, guess she's just one of them beans that didn't soak long enough to soften up right.

I got a official looking letter in my mail. I don't like that kind, usually prefer to throw 'em out, but I've learned that I do have to look through those or they come back at ya later. This one, turns out is from the 'MOH, The Ministry of Health. I've been readin' in the papers 'bout these guys interferin' in farms. No idea how they thought I had a farm, but apparently, they are contactin' all kinds of folks who sells meat and milk from their own places. They want us to buy all our food from a grocery, all vacuum wrapped on styrofoam flats, all processed and sterilized and full of hormones. They want us to drink water from a bottle or put chlorine in it before we drink it from the tap. Most folks in Procter figure they can make their own minds up 'bout that kind of thing, but you do get one once in a while that moves into the area and decides it's time to teach the locals something bout 'bacterial infection' or Giardia, people that likes to show you how to clean better. Seems like folks like that usually don't live round Procter too long, but we have to put up with 'em till they leave. I wouldn't be surprised if one of 'em sent my name in to those people at MOH, just to let 'em know that I could be one of them foolhardy country hicks sellin' dangerous contraband food…food that can jus' jump out atcha and contaminate yer whole place as fast as a house fulla pack rats. I heard that there was a couple, new to town, that had been stirrin' it up lately. They had moved in from Calgary, city folks with lots of money, bringin' city to the country. They was wantin' to get their water supply treated, which is fine so long as it's only theirs, but it's not. They's on a shared system, with folks been drinkin' that same creek water for the past forty years without any problem so their neighbors want nothin' to do with it. It's people like that who needs to stay all safe and sound high up off the street in one of them little condos.

They can stay up there and be sure that there's plenty of chorine in the water and that bears won't be ridin' up the elevator to eat their apples or mess with their compost. They won't even have a compost to worry 'bout. Too bad but seems like some of 'em need to make a detour out to 'the sticks' first, so's they can learn that it's not how they'd hoped it would be after all… save 'em all the trouble of movin' in the first place.

I read through my letter, posted to Ms. P Masson. It's a warnin' bout the penalties for: 'infractions of the food safety act.' Says that they will be, 'coming to your location soon,' just like a new release movie I guess. Seems like they can lock you up for sellin' goat milk these days. 'Corse, I don't have a sign up advertisin' so I don't 'spect to be havin' any of them droppin' by to arrest me any time soon. I'm just glad that I live in a place where most folks aren't afraid to ignore some of them rules. Procter is good that way, lots of folks who will live just the way they see fit, even if it don't happen to fall inside them guidelines. I've done some readin' bout the history here and talked to lots of the old timers too and found that there's been all kinda what many would call, subversive acts, people fightin' the rule makers to live the way they want, not be told how to.

In the seventies there was lots of Procter/Harrop folks who fought the government plan to divert the Kootenay river into the Columbia to make more hydro power: 'The Kootenay Diversion,' it was called. It was stopped. They also helped to organize against clear cuttin' and minin' up at the head of the lake by Fry Creek Canyon and after a couple years of fightin', the 'Purcell Wilderness Conservancy' was carved off, protected on the map, one of the first areas in Canada saved from loggin' by citizen activism. Since then there's been all kinda local protestin' between Procter/Harrop and government, against herbicide sprayin', garbage dumpin', loggin' in the mountains behind, whether it's against puttin' chlorine in the water, cuttin' the ferry service, savin' caribou, wolves or grizzly bears, or takin' over the old school house before it gets knocked down by the district, there always seems to be a battle brewin'.

There's other folks out here who think we can clear cut just fine, and they do it on their own property and seems to me, they do a pretty good job, don't look like a tornado hit the area like some I've seen. Others cut firewood, like Gabe, some hunt deer and elk, grouse, even bear sometimes. Ya hear dirt bikes, quads and gun shots soundin' off up on the hills, 'specially in the fall. Sometimes kids are up there spinnin' through the dirt in their dad's truck just seein' how far the mud will fly. Guess all that stuff's just parta what makes a community tick… adversity… or is it diversity? One of them sity words; I like them words, all proper and neat, endin' all of a sudden like a crack in the ice. Yeah we's jus all different kindsa beans all thrown into the same pot jus' like my Grandma said, bubblin' along happy as can be most days but other days, days when you pick up warnin's from MOH in yer mail for instance, we're more like flies on a glue strip, stuck there whether we like it or not.

I fold up my mail and stuff it into my shoppin' bag and walk toward home. Got chores to do. Filtered sun beams are landin' on the road out between the mail boxes and the store now. Amy has shuffled off in the other direction, makin' her way back home too, stoppin' when any car goes by to turn and watch and see who it is, scowlin'. She inspects every car that drives by as if she's going to discover a wanted man that she can report. Sometimes you see her writing down license numbers.

There's not too many mornings each year in Procter like today, where the air rolls down the mountain in warm waves, and when it does, it picks up the cottonwood fluff and pollen from berry plants, flowers and other trees. Clouds of tiny gnats ride along, swallows chasin' 'em, some of 'em endin' up on the surface of the lake below where the Kokanee and Rainbow can eat 'em. The aromas cross over you real quick, so if yer not payin' attention you miss the drift of honey suckle, cedar, or skunk cabbage, or of a lawn being mowed, maybe fresh cut hay from one of the nearby fields. When I used to ride my bike, those smells would flow by faster and I'd try to name 'em as I peddled. It'd be harder if it was somethin' small like wild strawberry or Juniper, 'specially if you couldn't see it there. Now I just walk, don't want a be fallin' off a bike, so I have more time to 'preciate all of them smells, 'specially now this time of year when the air's warm so you're not in a hurry.

⌘

Couple days later Emily comes by while I'm hangin' up some clothes on the line. She's got Noah, her and Gabe's son with her, still young enough to hold his mom's hand while they walk. He's the youngest, only five so he goes to the kindergarten for half the day. I can usually hear them air brakes as the bus pulls in bringin' em back around mid-day down at the bottom of the hill below where our houses are. Framer's place is only 'bout half a kilometer further up the dirt road from me, us and two other houses are all on the same branch, so I see 'em comin' and goin' quite a bit. Noah is runnin' ahead of her down my path tryin' to catch up to a butterfly that's zigzaggin' all over the yard. He's quick on his feet that one but doesn't say too much. "Hi Noah. Looks like you need a net for catchin' that one," I say, "but then you'd just mess his wings up with a net wouldn'tcha?"

"Yep, wouldn't want to bust his wings off, Pearl." He says, stoppin' to wait for his Mom to catch up. He spots my Siamese cat lookin' down at him from the rafters of my porch, his tail swishin' back and forth like it's fishin' for flies. "Hey Shreddie." He says to him. Then lookin' down at his foot, says, "Smells like chicken poo."

"Well, could be, I say," as Emily walks up, "gotta watch where ya walk round here my boy. I got me lots of obstacles. But right now, I'd say, yer just smellin' my coop. Must be time to clean it out some." Just then, Calvin, my youngest goat kid, starts bleatin' z'iff he's on fire or somethin'. We all look over to see him strugglin' over in the weeds by the wood shed. "Better I go over there and rescue that little trouble maker," I say. I amble on over and untangle him from some farm fencin' that he's managed to get his head trapped in. Comin back, I say, "I swear Emily, if I left these critters here on their own for more n a day, they'd tear it apart like a tornado. How are you two getting' on today anyhow? Just get back from the school bus?

"Yeah Pearl, worked the morning shift at the store," Emily says, "picked Noah up from the bus, so now it's time to head home for lunch. How's it going with you?"

"Calm and quiet, just the way I like it Emily. Hopin' it stays that way." I say, "'Course you never know these days, with all the noise from the cleanup crew on the tracks carryin' on, investigations and such. Did you know that them CP cops was out again? This time they was right here on my porch, just a couple days ago asking questions."

We're just standin' outside my porch now, on the path. Noah is just lookin' round, waitin'. "Noah," I say, mind just pokin' yer head into the chicken house to see if there's an egg or two in one of them nests? Member? Like you did last time?"

"Yep, for sure, Pearl." He says, eyes lit. He takes off. I continue, "Yeah Emily, they was askin' specifically bout Gabe. Seems they think he had somethin' to do with the train crash. I told 'em that if they had questions 'bout Gabe, they should be askin' Gabe stead of fishin' for it round me, lives right up there, I told 'em," I say, pointing on up the hill, Emily watchin' me, "but they was pretty persistant. Can't say I liked the sound of it."

"I know Pearl. They were at our house too, asking me the same questions. Gabe wasn't there. We don't like them publicly sounding like they are putting the blame on Gabe when they don't have any evidence, only suspicion. Course they think of him first cause of all the letters he's written and phone calls he's made to the paper and to CP complaining about the transport of dangerous chemicals through here, but that doesn't give them the right to convict him does it?"

"Well no, not for a second Emily, course can't say I'm much surprised they'd be askin' 'bout him either, what with him carrying on bout the CP all the time like ya say. Anyhow, why don't you come on in for a minute stead of standing out here with the flies buzzin' round."

Noah comes back from the coop holding a single egg in two hands, cradling it as if a live chick is about to hatch out and get away. "Got one", he says, all proud like he had just hunted it down and captured it.

"Okay, that's exactly what we needed then, to make up this dozen," I say, swinging open that squeaky old screen door, complains every time you open it. "Right this way. You two just have a seat at the counter here. You after some milk today too, Emily?"

"Yep, milk n eggs if you got 'em Pearl. You know we love the eggs from you with those bright yellow yolks…oh and a pound of butter too if you've got it."

"Yep, figured, and here's that carton with the missing egg Noah," I hand the box over from where I keep 'em by the back- wash tub, place it on the counter and flip it open. "Is that one you got there clean?" I say to him.

"Yes Pearl, look," he holds up the egg and then pops it in the empty socket. "Now we got a full box." he says, closing it up. "Got it just in time before Shreddie jumped on the roost and scared the chickens off." He says, hoppin' down off the stool and pickin' up my abacus that's sittin' on the coffee table. He starts fiddlin' with the rows.

"Good job. Gotta watch that crazy cat. Well it don't look that clean, but it'll do. A little bit of clean dirt'll never hurt anyone.

"Seems to me Emily that we are getting' all kinds of interference these days, the kind of attention we don't really want or 'spect out here in Procter. Just a couple days ago, I got a warnin' from the Food 'spections people, came in the mail, bout sellin' farm products, illegal farm products they call it. 'Parently you and I is makin' some kind of dangerous deal right now… eggs and milk, what am I 'sposed to think?"

"Now, why would they be sending you a warning, I wonder, Pearl. How can they know you sell anything unless someone has said something to them? It's not like you've got a sign up or anything?" she says.

"Exactly what I thought, Emily. Must be one of them new families moved in last year, from the city, but who knows for sure. Someone tryin' to keep us all in order, in their kinda order. I guess it's my job to find out who."

It was only 'bout two weeks later that them Ministry of Health people showed up. They actually find my house, not sure how, come stumblin' in to my property, tryin' to look all official. I'm down below my house, outside when they get out of their truck. It's a shiny, white truck and it's got an official lookin' logo on it, says: CFIA. There's two of 'em, one with a white lab coat on and a clipboard in his hand. The other one is a woman in a office suit with a brief case, all pressed and proper. Neither one of 'em fittin' in too good with my wild weeds and bent fencin'. I'm tryin' to trim down some raspberry bushes that's growin' just outside the chicken coop, watchin' them as they carefully step along the path toward my front steps, dodgin' the chicken shit, swattin' at flies. I walk over, callin' out, "Hey there, can I help you'se?"

They stop at the bottom of my step while I come' round from the side to meet 'em. I'm wearin' a stained skirt, wet at the bottom from dew in the tall grass, an apron over top with the tails of a checkered wool shirt stickin' out from underneath, the sleeves rolled up. My long, grey hair is tied off with some twine. Guess I'm probably lookin' a little akin to one of them gypsy refugees that's showed up crossin' the border somewhere. My rooster, Melvin, starts crowin' from the ditch below the driveway. They look over toward the sound but he's deep in under the ferns so's you can't see him. It's a warm mornin'. The flies are buzzing about the screen door behind me, tryin' to get out while other ones are tryin' to get in. I recognize what these two are up to, so I just step up on to the porch and set down on the wooden bench there by the door as if I'm all tuckered out after a long day's work. I look down at the two of 'em there on the walk way, stopped, waitin' for me to say somethin'. They's just lookin' round, as though they've never seen a farm yard before. "You folks just come out from Nelson then?" I asks 'em.

"Yes. Mrs, Masson is it? We're from the Canadian Food Inspections Agency. We're just following up on some site inspections in the area."

"Yeah, I'm Mrs. Masson. Followin' up you say? What is it yer followin' up on? Why here in Procter?"

The one with the clipboard, red haired guy, all tall and lanky, sniffling like he's got allergies, makes a note on his chart. Looks up, and says, "We've got a few addresses to inspect, yours being one, facilities that we've heard have meat or dairy products for sale. We've sent out notices. You did receive yours did you not Mrs. Masson?" He says, lookin' up at me, pushing his glasses further up on his nose as if he needs to inspect me too. His partner there just shuffles around a bit, lookin' in past me to the house as if she is expectin' to be invited in for a cup of tea or somethin'. "Yep, got the notice, but never thought you'd be showin' up here 'cause I don't sell things." I put down the pruners I'd been using on the bench beside me and press my back up against the back wall behind me to straighten it out some.

"Routine inspections mam, that's all. And these are the standards." The red haired one says, handing me some kinda brochure, all enthusiastic like he's just told me I've won one of them cruise trips on some fancy boat.

"Guess you guys got the wrong address is all I can think. Not sure why you're here but I'm plenty busy, so if you have somethin' I can help you with while yer here, let's have a look see." I say, lookin' down at the clipboard in his other hand, like I'm ready to fill in the blanks. Maybe it's like one of the multiple choice tests where the right answer is always there, you just have to choose it, or maybe it'll be one of them true or false ones where you have a good chance of getting' it right…least half the time.

"Right. We understand that you must have things to do," says the lady in the suit. She's got short, black, orderly hair that don't move too much when the breeze blows. She sets her brief case down on the bottom step and folds her arms in front. "But because we've heard claims that you could be selling milk products and possibly meat products, we must first establish that all the milk products you are selling are first pasteurized and packaged according to Canada heath regulations and that any meat products also meet health Canada regulation. Did you know Mrs. Masson that slaughtering, butchering and processing all need to meet required Health Canada guide lines?" She nods toward the pamphlet that is layin' on the bench where I dropped it. "We are just trying to be sure people are not buying hazardous, potentially contaminated consumable products. We don't mean to create any problem or difficulty for you. Our job is to help keep the local diet and food chain safe for all consumers." She stops her shpiel as she swipes at a fly that's landed on her forehead.

"Seems to me," I say, "we should all be able to choose whatever it is we want to eat. Don't need no one to tell us. Me, for example, I don't like any of them fancy diets, no carbs, all carbs, no meat, all meat, vegan, raw. I seen one where they was only eatin' cheezies and drinkin' vinegar….vinegar, can you believe that?" They's just staring at me 'siff I was one of them panhandlers and they don't know whether to give me some change or jus' keep on walkin'. So I jus' carry on "There's so many diets out there these days. I've got my own diet now real simple: if I like it, I eat it. If I really like it, I eat lots of it. You should try it out, makes you feel better."

"Mam, we're just here to test and record, not to discuss diets," says the red-haired guy with the binder, clearin' his throat, "we're looking for bio security infractions, CFIA distribution infractions, nothing more."

And the lady inspector adds, "Mrs. Masson, do you ever have anything for sale here, now or in the past? Milk or milk products, anything, and if so, may we have a quick look at what you have available at this time? Any meats as well, fresh or frozen?"

"As I told you when you just got here, I'm not sellin'. Once in a while, someone'll drop by to borrow some milk, or pick up some eggs if I have a few extras. I'm just being neighbourly. Folks round here would do the same for me if I was short."

My youngest goat kid, Calvin, I call him, runs full tilt round the house just then, turnin' and prancin' like he's puttin' on a performance, his voice all shrill and squeeky. He races by the lady with the briefcase, spinnin' up dirt, then stops, getting' distracted by a sunflower that's growin' all bent over by the path. He starts pullin' at the leafy petals along the stock and watchin' the flower head bob back and forth. Their eyes follow him a moment nervously, then come back to me.

"Sure, I've got some frozen meat, some eggs from my chickens here and milk in the fridge from my Momma goat, but I ain't got nothin' for sale, so I'm afraid I've got nothin' to show you. 'Sides, my freezer and milk fridge is out back under the back porch roof where I've got my gander locked up right now. He's been actin' ornery. I don't think you'll be wantin' to meet him right now if you value all yer fingers."

The two of them inspectors look at each other a moment, then the red-haired man says, "Well ma'am, we need to continue the follow up on this claim so long as we have information about food sales persisting. We will be looking further into the claims and if necessary, we will be back to take samples of any meats and or dairy products for testing. We will be testing for salmonella, listeria and ecoli among other things if claims can be substantiated. We have only your best interests at heart, but we must warn you that selling any of these food products we have been discussing, without proper permitting, and inspection, is considered an infraction of the Canada Food and Drug act and can be met with severe penalties. We hope that you will cooperate fully with any concerns."

"'Course I would cooperate," I say, "got nothin' to hide. Sounds to me like the only problem I got is some kinda nosy neighbor that's stickin' his nose into my business, getting' folks like you riled up all 'bout nuthin. See now, people like that just wastes everyone's time and energy, don't they? Can't say as we really want them kind livin' out here. We was doin' just fine without 'em. You people heard 'bout lotsa folks getting' poisoned in the area?"

"Well, no Mam. We have not been notified of any kind of outbreak recently."

"No, I figured not. Now, how bout we all just get back to what we was all doin' before then?"

The lady bends over to pick up her briefcase then, and the red-haired man scratches down a couple more real important notes in his binder, then he looks up closin' it and says. "Alright for now, Mrs. Masson. We will let you know if we need to drop back to see you."

"Okay, you call first next time, ya hear? You two have a good day now."

They turn and walk back up to their shiny white truck, hop in just as Gabe pulls up in his truck, right in front of 'em. He jumps out and starts comin' round before he notices that there's people in the white truck wantin' to get by. He walks up, and they roll down the window. I'm too far to hear, but he stops and leans up against the door talkin' to 'em. A couple minutes later he walks back to his truck and backs it out a bit so's they can pass, then he pulls back in and parks again.

"Just wanted to measure up that vent in the attic, Pearl," he says. He's got his tape measure clipped to his front pocket. "What's with these inspections people everywhere eh Pearl? First, we get the CP cops, the RCMP, and now, we've got Health Canada too? What the hell." He says, holding his arms up to the sky.

"Yeah, I s'pose we all been inspected just bout enough by now." I say, "….so what was it they got to askin' you bout anyhow?" I ask him, curious.

He walks down the path a little further and stops by me. He's already lookin' up above the veranda roof to see if he can get up there to measure for the attic vent that needs to be put on. All them swallows and a squirrel too, is getting' in there and makin' nests so we gotta stop 'em. "Yeah, they were asking me if I ever bought dairy products or meat here. Of course, I told 'em, yeah sure, the place is a regular supermarket…" he says smilin' at me, chucklin'.

"Mighty neighbourly of you." I say.

"Nah, I saw that logo on their truck before I even pulled in here Pearl," he says, "Heard they've been around. Graham told me they'd already dropped in to inspect the kitchen at the Bakery earlier." He says, carryin' on, "… told 'em that I've tried some of your jerky and that you've given me eggs sometimes, 'specially when I'm helping her out, like today, asked them if that was allowed, giving eggs, or do we need a permit for that?' Asked them if we should get a permit too if we go to the neighbors place for dinner one night or should we report the neighbour so's they can get their kitchen inspected before we go." His eye catchin' mine with one of them lit up sideways glances that end in a crooked smile.

"And what did they say to that?" I asks, shaking my head and chucklin so's the rolls on my neck quiver.

"They just asked me to move my truck. Guess they were in a hurry." He turns and climbs up on the old wooden box against the house that used to be a hatch for a coal chute. It's kinda rickety, but not as likely to fall over as the railing is, so he steps from there up onto the window sill above the kitchen sink, avoidin' the rail, then heaves himself up onto the veranda roof from there. "Forgot the ladder," he says, glancin' back down at me.

I'm happy to have Gabe drop by and I'm not sorry to see them inspectors go. Meddlers, always needin' to stir things up when stirrin' ain't necessary. This is just my little farm yard, not some kinda laboratory. Why do these paranoid city folks and the government food people have to get so riled up bout bacteria and listeria and things? People are so scared of bacteria now that if one even looks at 'em sideways they spray it with some kinda chemical to kill it fore it looks at 'em again. Folks are so sterilized they might's well have got up and boiled themselves in a beaker before they brush their teeth in the mornin'. When a bacteria gets into their system it can just run around their whole body like a starvin' student at a smorgasbord. It'll take over like them rabbits did in Australia, I was readin' 'bout. Saw it in the Enquirer, that they got rabbits there now bigger'n kangaroos. I think folks' bodies is better off carryin' a little bit of everything round inside all the time, like a full shelf at the dollar store, just a bit of this bacteria and a bit of that bacteria, all mixed up but meant to be there. Eat off the floor sometime; get a little clean dirt in yer system. When you have the right balance of them bacterias already growin' in you, seems like you have some kinda defense against 'em takin over, then you don't need them chemicals that they use- them antibiotics. People eat those like they was a bag full of Smarties these days. They always think they can solve a problem by wipin' things out stead of lettin' em grow. Spray, disinfect, sterilize, clean and scrub and do it all again till you take the skin right off, put the inside out in the open. It don't make any sense.

Gabe climbs down from the roof and heads back up the path, shoutin' back over his shoulder at me where I'm untanglin' that crazy Calvin kid goat from a wild rose bush, "got it Pearl. I'll be back tomorrow. Gotta run."

I just wave back at him, then mosy on up to set back down on the porch, starin' out as the dust rises then falls again behind his truck. Thinkin' bout how I don't like that them Inspections people havin me on their list now. I gotta find a way to get off a it; find out who it is soundin' off the alarm.

CHAPTER 8

Hailey

The neighbors are close but not that close, so I inch the volume up a bit more to get into the Norah Jones groove. Anyway, it's just as well that they know I'm home. They've had too much peace the last couple of months that I've been away, more than two; I think I left near the beginning of April so it's been closer to three months now. I've only lived here in Procter a little over a year, but I've already gotten to know lots of the locals. I'm right in the middle of town. There's only three streets and I'm living on the one in the middle. I've heard from others that it can take a long time to break into the community here, but me, didn't take me that long really; guess I kind of tumble out and spread myself around, so I'm hard to avoid. I guess it's easier when you're single. Can't stay home alone all the time.

Procter is great that way; the neighbours keep to themselves for the most part but are friendly at the same time- country in the city is just a saying. Of course, Procter is no city, there's only a few hundred people if you threw them all in a pile, together, everyone from all the nooks and crannies included. When I really want to make some noise, like at a couple of the big parties I've had, the solution is to invite everyone, all the neighbours too, not just my friends, that way, even if they don't come, I feel like I'm off the hook on the noise issue. That's how I was told to handle it by a table full of people sitting around at the bakery one morning. There's always lots of free advice available in there. They were right though, that strategy has worked well so far.

I love having that bakery right there. It's just a block away, a constant source of entertainment, coffee and baking. News too, real and imagined. They even have food sometimes, if you're lucky, and don't mind waiting. I'm kind of downtown in Procter, if you can call it that, as Procter is only made up of three streets, a store, and the old school house where the bakery, hair salon, chiropractor and the Harrop/Procter Community Forest office are located, but still, even though I'm downtown, I've got my privacy. What more could I want? Maybe a spill protection kit, a ventilator?

That's the big news right now, well, the big news for the past five or six weeks anyway; the train derailment. Heard all about it before I got home, a month back, when the reports first came out – twelve rail cars had crashed right outside Procter. It's been quite a spectacular event, the derailment, and controversial as well. There has been a lot of controversy over the months, even years apparently, leading up to it. There's been opposition heating up over the transportation of various toxic chemicals. I heard they move Cyanide, Hydrochloric acid, all kinds of chemicals I can't even pronounce, through the area and those people who have been vocal about it have warned that rolling that stuff by rail through our backyards day after day, could one day lead to a derailment and if that were to happen, that the air and waterways will be affected. Well, now it has happened.

The Harrop/Procter area has a deep-seated history of what some deem subversive behaviour, and that seems to have added fuel to speculation of intentional tampering in this case, so the local rumor mill has been busy and interesting lately - more action than we're used to around here, that's for sure, not all positive either. There's been a lot of fear and worry about the state of our air and water supply and general safety, especially for those living close to the tracks.

I had been two days into a five-day shift, tree planting high up in the White Swan area of the Top of the World Provincial park, the first week of May. Ingrid, our cook, had heard the news on CBC radio that day: a big derailment in Procter, a chemical spill. I was shocked, couldn't believe that a disaster like that, that big, could be happening in my little village. I was worried sick because I couldn't call from there- no cell service, but we did hear a couple more news bulletin updates through CBC radio, one of them confirming that no one had been killed, which was a relief. I had been picturing a locomotive toppled over into someone's living room, or worse. Still, the reports swirled nationwide. This was a big event, dangerous too, poisonous. All the stuff leaking out. How could this happen in Procter? What if people had been breathing these fumes? The next morning, the Ministry of Forests tree checker, Frank, brought up a local newspaper with an article on the spill. He knew that we had people from Procter on the crew, so he dropped it off first thing. I was grateful to get some news, Mel and Darren were reading over my shoulder in the back seat as the crummy sped off toward the planting block. The column on the first page read:

Questions remain over cause of catastrophic derailment

Procter, British Columbia. Early Tuesday, May 5, in the morning, on the Nelson subdivision line of the Canadian Pacific Limited rail line., between 2:20 and 2:45 a.m. pacific standard time, a C.P. R. Train derailed near Procter, B.C. Nelson Daily News has learned that a total of twelve cars including two locomotives have overturned, some carrying volatile chemicals. CP officials have confirmed that some of the twelve cars have been compromised and that fumes and seepage have been witnessed flowing from some of the damaged tanker cars. CP officials said they are: "taking this incident extremely seriously."

"Holy crap, I guess they're taking it seriously." I mumble, reading on.

"…we have mobilized teams to the site and are in touch with local emergency responders to coordinate a response. Safety is the priority. CP crews, contractors and equipment are on site and are already working to coordinate appropriate action. Environmental monitoring is taking place. All regulatory agencies have been notified. Some forty-five residents have been evacuated in the immediate area as a precaution."

"Forty-five residents evacuated," I say, glancing up.

"Jesus Hailey, isn't that like half the population of Procter?" Darren asks.

"Close," I add, scanning ahead in the article. "Listen to this." I read the lines aloud, haltingly, as the crummy bumps through a series of pot holes.

"Exact quantities from the chemical spill or their composition and potential impact have yet to be disclosed but there have been preliminary reports from witnesses who saw fumes and a white cloud rise from the area. The witness, Mike again, lives up the hill, outside the village, I add, glancing up, "… reported to an NDN source, that he saw a yellowish fluid leaching into a nearby stream from one of the cars."

Mel interjects, "Sounds like some nasty shit leaching out. What the fuck."

"Yeah, sounds like Mike got an eye full, probably a lung full too." I note, anxiously, "says here, Mike had been walking at first light along the tracks to his fishing spot when he came up on the crash site."

"Crazy action in Procter eh Hailey?" Maurice pipes up from the driver's seat.

"Yeah," I mumble, and read on silently to see what else Mike had to say about it.

> *"There were already two CP emergency response vehicles on site with personal wearing respirators."* He went on to say: *"They told me to evacuate the area. That it wasn't safe, but I wanted to see what had happened so I turned back and went down the bank and came up from below to have a quick look," he said. "I didn't stick around 'cause I could smell the fumes and thought it could be dangerous or explosive, but I did see that yellow liquid spilling into a little stream. What a mess, and that was probably three hours or so after the crash so imagine how poisonous that water is by the time I got there. And how long did it take them to stop it after that? That stream goes straight into the lake just below you know. I don't think the fish will be looking to eat that stuff." He commented.*

"Twelve cars, what a mess." I say to no one in particular as the crummy pulls up to the block and everyone piles out. They all start bagging up bundles of trees, ready to begin their day while I sit on the tailgate for a few more minutes, scanning through the rest of the paper. I can picture Mike Ratcliffe getting all riled up with a reporter. He is one of these quiet introspective fishermen, retired now, must be in his late sixties, and excitable, doesn't see people often; lives on a twenty-acre forested property up Alexander road, alone now, very isolated, especially now after his wife left him. I've walked through his land with him a couple of times, gathering mushrooms in the fall. It's mostly real shady and dark in there, dense. He hasn't even cleared around his own cabin, so it's kinda like a cave in there.

I don't know him well, doesn't say much, but seems like a straight shooter. I flip through to where the rest of the article continued:

"In this case, circumstances were such that there was no time for a warning to be issued by the pilot truck that routinely scouts ahead,", reported the CP spokesman, Dennis Feller. "The water had built up some 25 feet over the course of time to the level of the tracks which allowed wood debris, brush and wind fall to rise and flood over, partially covering the tracks, 'The pilot truck came around the corner, just past the 116 mile marker, heading west, and with only a short sight line, in the dark of night, was not able to stop before it was derailed by the debris, plunging the rail truck down a very steep embankment onto a rock out crop below on the lake side of the tracks."

I can kind of visualize the area, the 116-mile area. Walked out there a lot. Steep on both sides.

"… Fortunately, the vehicle stopped before dropping into the lake below, pinned between a huge rock slab and a large tree, however the impact was severe and the driver and his assistant were both seriously injured. The driver was knocked unconscious and his coworker was pinned between the door and dashboard with multiple injuries. They were incapacitated and so not capable of warning the train of the impending danger."

I feel relieved. In spite of the chaos, nobody had been killed. I can see planters from the corner of my eye, pounding in their first trees on the side of the skid road so I scan the summary of the article quickly. Have to catch up.

"Further investigations by the NDN investigative team, show that, due to the mounting water volume, rising along the tracks, the ground below had become saturated and unstable over many hours, that saturation, coupled with the fact that loose debris from the flood was blocking the rails, led to a catastrophic track failure. Furthermore, what has been described by an eye witness who had been walking along that part of the tracks earlier in the day… "poor maintenance in the form of several rotten ties and a loose stabilizer bar, probably contributed to the

derailment." CPR claims that maintenance levels had been 'up to standard.' And that, 'a full inquiry will show that work place safety is prioritized in all situations.'

NDN research indicate that the substantial weight, coupled with the velocity, and other underlying factors resulted in the locomotives plunging over into the softened substrate of the upper side of the right of way. Early reports show that the engineer had no opportunity to reduce speed substantively. The momentum forced 12 more cars to topple over. Some becoming partially submerged in the pool, including the two locomotives. Fortunately, both the engineer and conductor were able to escape the wreck with non-life-threatening injuries.

The conductor, Franz Peterson, in a hospital interview days later, reported, "the engine had turned into the pool of water, flipping over on to its side, throwing me and Darcy, (the engineer), onto the side wall of the compartment. We were banged up pretty bad but still mobile enough to climb out the open window of the other side which was still above the water level. Water had already filled up most the compartment by the time we climbed up on to the side of the engine. There were jets of steam blowing up around us… powerful blasts, from the heat of the submersed engine and so we had to escape back away from the engine to avoid being burned. We climbed up onto the next car behind until we were clear of the heat. Still, we both ended up with steam burns and my vision is still blurry. Darcy has three broken ribs and a minor concussion, but otherwise we came out pretty lucky."

"Damn lucky", I say under my breath. I fold over the paper to see the final clip.

"Despite their injuries, reports state, that the two, made their way back onto the tracks and walked west toward the nearby village of Procter until they' d reached the first road crossing where they had been able to find a nearby house, wake the inhabitants, and ask for help. The incident was then reported and emergency crews dispatched. Both men are now recovering from their injuries in hospital. The report went on to say: *"The*

two men, who had been trapped in the pilot car, whose names have not yet been released, are in critical, but stable condition. Further reports will be forthcoming, however the Transportation Safety Board of Canada (TSB) is investigating this incident to ensure all safety and maintenance requirements have been met by CP and for the purpose of improving transportation safety in general. The Board, however, does not assign fault or determine civil or criminal liability. Further investigations are pending."

"Investigations. Hmm, I wonder what that means?" I say, tossing the paper on the dash and grabbing my gear. I had lots of food for thought on my planting line today. End up with more questions cycling through my head than answers though. I want to hear from folks at home, but who to call and how?

I checked with Maurice on the state of the radio phone reception after work. He said that it was pretty good especially if you drive the crummy just up on the rise above the river. So, after dinner, I decided to drive up there and call the Village bakery. It was Friday, pizza night, so I knew it would be full of people. Graham, the owner answered, "get it while it's hot," he said, before he'd heard my voice. I responded to him with, "Hey Graham, it's Hailey, just checkin' in from my planting crew at camp. I'd order a pizza but I doubt you'll deliver." I said, "I'm on a radio phone so I can only talk when the button is down, then listen when it's not, just so you know." I cautioned. "Anyway, just wanted to hear your take on the spill, wanted to know how things are going, thought the bakery would be the best place to check in, the pulse of the community, right? How is everyone doing?"

Graham sounded uncharacteristically serious, yet still animated. He took the phone into the back so he could hear, and explained that there are "rumours milling about the village, claims and counter claims about sections of track that were poorly maintained, to cut costs, that CP emergency response plans were inadequate or nonexistent. That's what people are saying in here anyways Hailey," he said, "I'm hearing all kinds. Keeps the conversation lively, makes it hard to get my work done," he carries on after pausing and not hearing me say, "Whoa, heavy", "folks are saying that CP had no right to jeopardize the safety and health of people just to maintain a healthy profit margin for them and Tech. Tech Resources, turns out, is owned by CP" he hollered, raising his voice above clattering dish sounds in the background. "I didn't know that." I said, waiting for him to continue.

He talked about the giant smelter over by Trail, West of Nelson, which is serviced by the rail system. It's a massive plant that looms over the city, the big employer, spewing fumes over the town below. It consumes all these chemicals in its processing and production of metals and fertilizers and stuff. Graham went on to say it was too early to tell how bad the chemical spill was going to be, but he said that there were emergency response teams all over the place. "The village is crowded all of a sudden, never seen it like this. Looks like they are taking it pretty seriously now, and there is talk of an investigation. Seems they think someone sent that train over the bank on purpose, aren't taking any blame for it. But who knows, those folks are always suspicious of people out here. I guess I shouldn't complain about them being suspicious so long as they're still coming in for Cinnamon buns. Business has been great lately."

I thanked him for the report and hung up the receiver, had to get back to camp.

Even though Harrop/Procter area does have a history of what some deem subversive behaviour, it does keep the place interesting, right? There have been ferry protests, anti-logging campaigns, blockades for water protection, anti-chemical transport issues, several movements to create new protected areas, protests against private, public power installations…on and on, that, it seems has added fuel to speculation of intentional tampering in this case.

Before I hung up, letting Graham get back to his final pizza orders, he promised to keep me informed if I could call for updates, "just so long as you don't call when I'm rolling out my cinnamon buns," he said, "can't upset the flow". So, I called at various times, a couple of times on the way to the block in the morning when I knew he would be there serving coffee and listening in on the banter. Two days later when I called back, he said, "The CPR is trying to link the 'hold up' of the train three years ago, to the derailment now. Well that's the rumour anyway, seems like a bit of a stretch to me, but guess you never know. "You weren't living round here then were you Hailey?" he'd asked me, a bit of tongue in cheek suspicion in his voice. "No, well, saying I wasn't anyway," I had replied, "but I've heard about it." This, 'hold up', as they called it, was an event that had happened on two different occasions, took place in protest to a Provincial government announcement to limit hours of access to the local ferry and to install a toll booth on the Harrop side of the ferry landing.

I remember the reports of the time. One had linked the hold up to the ferry issue when they reported that the letter passed to the engineer had stated, in part, 'due to planned Provincial government disruption of the Harrop ferry, that the people of Procter/Harrop would "no longer allow trains to pass through the Procter Harrop area unimpeded."

"They've re-printed parts of those articles now and are asking people for any possible leads in connecting the two incidents." Graham said, almost shouting into the phone now as the din of the bakery in the background rises. "Listen to this," and I heard him straighten out the newspaper before he read: 'A CPR spokesperson, Donny Park, told the Daily News Monday, that, "This is an unprecedented attack, and we are taking this very seriously. Not only was this person trespassing on private property, but he or she was also putting themselves and others in danger by interfering with a moving train."

There was a pause and then Graham added: "The CPR Police have the same arrest powers as the RCMP in situation where crimes have been committed on railway property." He read, pausing again. I pressed the talk button and asked him, "So, sounds like they are actually merging the stories. Where does one end and the other begin?"

"I know. It sounds leading, doesn't it? I'm not sure where they're going with this, but time will tell. Gotta go now Hailey. Signing off with today's tree planter report," he said, sounding like some kinda foreign correspondent, before hanging up. "Hope to see you back here soon." I thanked him again for keeping me informed and turned the truck around to go back down the hill to camp. It was tiring to keep following up on the news that way, especially after work when my energy level was so low. A full day on the slopes leaves very little energy for anything else, but I continued to find the time to check in. It was intriguing and the crew was getting into it, asking me for follow up installments.

Yeah that whole, 'hold up' situation had been one of the most sensational I'd read about in the Procter history books. It's no wonder the news team is trying to rehash that one. When I got back home, I reread all the old articles. Some of them were posted on the Bakery bulletin board, a place which became a flash point for speculation over the course of the next few weeks.

People were pinning up all kinds of information, anything they thought was pertinent to the current situation. It was like the print version of the community email, preferable really, I thought, cause at least the bulletin board has some space limitation. It is a useful tool, the community email, for selling things or letting people know you have free fruit to pick, or a lawn that needs mowing, but at this point, I started blocking it from my inbox because it has gotten out of hand, overwhelming in number. You don't want to spend half your day pressing the delete button, right? Besides, the bulletin board is more colourful. Every day, there is some new addition. Someone has pinned up a cutout of a bright red train from a kid's book which winds its way across the board. Someone has burned part of one of the cars and pinned it back up, upside down. Random articles are attached at odd angles, a strand of orange flagging tape hangs down one side and there are two rail way spikes resting along the top of the frame looking like they could fall off if someone slammed the door too hard. It's starting to look more like a shrine than a bulletin. There's a newspaper photo of the flooded culvert with the boulder stuck in it right in the middle of the board, like a centerfold.

I nibble on a rhubarb square as I read the articles: *'In the first incident RCMP said the culprit lit a fire beside the tracks to get the attention of the engineer. "The fire forced them to slow the train, then halt, which is when this individual with a flashlight or a torch of some type stepped forward and waved them down," said RCMP Sgt. Jim Raeburn. "The balaclava-clad individual then handed the note to the conductor using a long pole. Once the note was in the hands of the CPR the individual scampered off. Despite calling in the RCMP dog unit the persons responsible could not be tracked."*

Two nights later the train was stopped again when somebody put a lighted flare attached to a board and propped it up between the tracks. On the board was a similar note to the first one, except this time it was handwritten.

"Though no further action has taken place this week," Raeburn said, *"this mischief is a serious concern for police. This*

creates a fear and safety factor because they [CPR] don't know if there has been any further tampering."

Then the article went on to quote the local government representative, *"This attempt to force the hand of the provincial Liberals by taking action on the rail line is unlikely to work,"* claimed local Nelson-Creston MLA, Blair Suffredine.

Graham shuffles up behind me a moment while I'm reading, looking over my shoulder, "Yeah, unlikely to work alright… but it did," he says, scanning. "You know Hailey, lots of us locals doubted that bullshit. Remember the gossip? It was swirlin' 'round this place for weeks.

"No. Remember, I hadn't moved here yet." I say. "But it makes for pretty interesting reading."

Graham turns back to the kitchen wiping his fingers on his stained apron then pulls some toast out from the toaster and butters it. I stand by the counter and watch. "Yeah, lots of folks speculated that the CP blockade by the two bandits could have been one of the key factors in the Government policy reversal," he says. "According to the rumours and reports, the plan by those two, had been pretty simple, but I think it worked. They must have waited alongside the tracks for the night train to come, knowing that the pilot car would be passing by in advance of the train by five or ten minutes. That's what the pilot car always does so it would have been easy to track it. The scheduled train usually passes by Procter around 2:00 am. You've heard that whistle blow many nights around then." He says, glancing over at me as he reloads the toaster and passes me two plates of toast and eggs. "Will you just drop these off to Shelly and Jake for me?" he says, tilting his head in the direction of the couple sitting at the table by the door.

"Yeah, sometimes it wakes me up, that train." I say grabbing the plates. "I'm just glad I don't live any closer to the tracks. Who needs that kind of racket running through your bedroom in the middle of the night?"

"Yeah right, well, reports went on to infer that they had prepared a sizable fire, those two guys, ready to light, right beside the tracks and waited there beside it for the pilot car to pass. Once it had gone by, sounds like they'd poured some gas on it and lit it up. Their fire was down there near the derailment, ya know, just a couple of hundred meters from the nearest turn on that one straight stretch?"

"Yeah, I know where you mean." I say.

Graham wipes up some egg spill off the counter, then tosses the rag into the sink beside me. "I went down there to check it out a few days later. Guess they'd built it there so that the engineer of the train could see it in advance and stop. The engineer told the papers that by the time he could stop the train, the fire was blazing pretty high, so he backed the train away another 20 meters to be sure before stopping altogether." He glances through the opening as two bicyclists come in in bright blue and red spandex and sit down at the table by the cash, eying up a tray of cinnamon buns on the counter.

He goes in to see what they want and plates them up with a cinnamon bun each, then nodding toward the coffee earn, he says to them, "Forks, knives and napkins in the middle, coffee in the urn over there, creamo in the fridge, help yourselves."

Then he comes back past me, adjusts his cotton skull cap so that the renegade hair tufts don't escape, goes to the counter and starts tossing peeled carrots into the food processor, but he doesn't miss a beat, carryin' on as if there'd been no interruption, "at this point, the two masked men strode out of the bush by the tracks. One stood in front of the train, holding and swinging a flashlight, while the other, who carried a long narrow pole with a paper wrapped around the end, moved forward toward the locomotive, passing the pole up toward the open window beside the engineer. The engineer reached down for it and tore it off the pole. Then those two guys ran off into the forest. Disappeared."

"How do you know they were guys, Graham? Maybe it was a couple of ladies?" I smile at him.

He grins up at me. "Coulda been," he says, "coulda been… still don't know… just what I read."

"So, what happened after it stopped then?" I ask him. "Well, after, the engineer called it in to the head office at CP and they ordered him to keep the train where it was till the area could be secured, till they could be sure that there weren't any more threats ahead, I guess. They kept it there, idling the whole time, for two days, people who lived nearby couldn't sleep it was making such a racket, and sending out all kinds of diesel fumes,".

He mutters, passing me again to go to the cash counter. "Everyone has an opinion on that one and I've heard plenty of 'em. I know it sounds like a controversial tactic, but that aside, the local position to counter the government initiative to toll inland ferries seemed to continue with an unusual level of community unity. Lots of people still talk about it, in kind of a proud way. Most folks I've talked to have seemed united against the changes and many were very adamant that limiting service to and charging for, the only accessible route to schools and hospitals was not a topic open to discussion. Can't say I disagree with 'em, and though maybe holding up a train is taking it a bit far, I would have been right in there, waving signs around too if I'd been living here then. Why not?"

That protest hadn't ended then either. More threats had been reported. Some saying they'd blow up the toll machine if it were installed. Protests and letter campaigns continued, locals created a temporary blockade of the Harrop ferry, complete with media cameras, politicians and placards. To top it off, Gabe, one of the local subversives, as he was often labeled, with the support of the local 'ferry protection society', a quickly formed group which had organized in opposition to the announced government cutbacks, had chartered a forty passenger Greyhound bus, filled it with local volunteers and had it chauffeured to Vancouver where the group set up a raucous spectacle of banners and props one day at the north end of the Lion's gate bridge and another day at the east end of the Port Mann bridge.

There were some great photos posted with the articles. I'd later had a chance to check them all out online. The Vancouver protests had managed to snarl traffic which created more media attention on TV news networks and local radio stations. At one point there was even a threat of arrest as this Gabe guy tried to move one of the banners onto the freeway. The article had gone on to say that, according to RCMP spokesperson, Sandra Anderson, 'A member of the group had been, jeopardizing highway safety'. "This kind of police interference is always good for added publicity." Gabe had been quoted after the incident. That quote was published in the paper under the photo of him and the officer who was threatening to remove him from the location. He had backed off in the end and so was not arrested. Ultimately though, when the dust had settled on all the commotion around that controversial government decision, they, the government, continued to state in the media that they would not back down, that the service cuts and tolls would move ahead as planned, that is, until later, after the 'hold up' which, the Provincial Government later contended: "had nothing to do with the reversal in policy." They went on to claim: "Neither this disruption or local protests had anything to do with the decision to look at alternatives to the planned changes to Harrop ferry services."

Though neither the government spokes people, or local pro- ferry organizers who were lobbying government, publicly endorsed that there was any link between the train hold up and policy change, the decision to install ferry tolls and limit service hours was overturned within two weeks. Local villagers still sound like they are rejoicing when they talk about the win three years later. No one in the village seems to care that the 'bandits' got away. Sounds like no one had been very forthcoming during that investigation. No big surprise if you know the locals. As Drake Blanchard, a local hunter, skidder operator, described to a few of us last year at the checkout counter at the Procter Store one morning: "when them RCMP officers came to my door to ask about the hold up, I just told 'em; 'what did you think was going to happen when you threaten to take away ferry service? Didya think everyone was just gonna roll over and say kick me again? Can't say as I'm surprised, told 'em, nope, don't have any idea who it could be, but seems to me there's lots of folks who might have wanted to hold up that train. Why not? Could be some shift worker, right? Some guy that was about to lose his job 'cause he wouldn't be able to get to work once they shut the ferry service down at night, ya know, ya ever think of that?' I asked 'em, or someone worried about not being able to get to the hospital?' Those cops didn't even know about the Government plans to totally cut all nighttime service. Buggers didn't seem interested," he'd said, pickin' up steam now that he had an audience. "Yeah and when they was leaving, I reminded 'em that we're the ones paying their wages."

Round the Bakery bulletin board this morning, Pat was pinning up a cut-out. He'd been hunched over a magazine with a pair of scissors mumbling then cursing, "son of a bitch, can never cut straight… fuckin thing…" then pausing, says, "there." He'd already pasted a giant mushroom cloud just above the turned over, half burned train car and now he was pinning up this cut- out of a group of torpedo shaped bombs with shark-like grins painted on them, dropping into the cloud. "There, just cleaning up the evidence," he says, grinning over at me as I watch over his shoulder. Raving Amy is just standing by the fridge watching, holding one of those crooked smirking looks she can keep in place so well, only adjusting it to tilt her tea cup in for a sip once in a while. She said, "Should pin a picture of that crazy yahoo Framer hanging onto one of them bombs. He held up that train back then, blew this one right off the tracks this time too, and is probably scheming up the next attack right now. Could be working with those Taliban for all we know."

"Yeah!" chirps Pat, frickin' Pakkies, or, maybe I'll pin up a shot of you up there Amy. Seems to me, you're the one I've seen wandering around the village in the dark lately." Amy manages to smile curving both sides up after that, but quickly recovers and glances back sideways at Pat with suspicion on her way out the door.

Thinking about it now, seems to me that with this kind of '*cooperation*', the RCMP and CP will have plenty of trouble making any case now or ever. I wonder if they will do any better with this case than the last one. Sure, I s'pose there could be a connection between the hold up and this derailment, but all kinds of misguided suspicion seems to be in the air, and I doubt it's going to make it any easier to navigate. 'Course, a new wave of interviews are happening now that could uncover some real evidence. I wouldn't be surprised if those guys end up on my door step too one day soon, but hey, what can I tell them?

Even though most folks don't take Pat or Amy's comments too seriously, I do think that the investigation will likely gain traction around Gabe Framer. It's been common knowledge that he's been battling this issue, opposing chemical transport. Fact is, I kind of wonder about him too. Never did get along with him that well, especially after that encounter up in the bush last spring left me wondering.

I'd been up at the top of Victor road, helping a friend pack a bunch of soil and water line up the hill to her secret garden. We had run into him on foot while he was scouting out firewood above the last switch back, in the woods. He'd been just standing there silent, surprised us, just kind of rooted to the ground, leaning on an axe handle, stringy hair parted and pressed either side of his face by his tuque. He's a sturdy one, comfortable in the woods, a little intimidating, but not threatening. From his tone, he'd made it sound like we had no business up there 'planting dope on public land.' "You guys better not be clear cutting out healthy wood up there and leaving your plastic bags and poly pipe laying around after." He'd warned, all grumpy like he owned the place, "seen all kinds of that crap around on these hills round here and I think that's bullshit."

With that, he'd turned and left us there, kind of wide eyed and wondering what to do next. But we had carried on anyhow, figuring he didn't really seem interested in helping himself to the crop or for that matter, in turning us in. I'll have to order some wood from him before winter, see if he brings it up again. I've seen him in passing lots of times since then, but he hasn't mentioned anything, not so far, just kind of looks at me funny. Sometimes I'm just not sure what is running through his mind; I guess that women's intuition isn't failsafe.

Now that all this talk and suspicion is on the table about the derailment, and Gabe, I've reflected on the last time I saw him. It was early this spring before I'd left to go to tree camp. I had been on one of my walks out on the tracks. I do like the view from the tracks. It is the only real decent trail that side of Procter, heading south, past the end of the road, where you can actually walk along above the shore line, so even though it's a little uneven for walking from tie to tie, and it smells of creosote, I still head out that way pretty often, just to clear my head and look out over Kootenay lake.

Sometimes I walk all the way out to Irvine Creek beach, about three kilometers, just to go for a swim, naked and alone. I hadn't gone that far that day or swam either. The water in March is pretty much almost like ice; I don't have the constitution for that, unless maybe I was stuck without a shower for a month in a tree-planting camp. I'm more of a fair-weather swimmer. On my way back, I'd seen a movement up on the bank, high above the tracks, where the cleared right-of-way meets the forest. It was Gabe alright. Only got a glimpse of him, but I knew it was him and I'm pretty sure he knew I'd seen him before he'd turned into the woods real quick and disappeared. I never thought much of it till now. Now I know that he had been in about the same place as where this derailment had occurred, up above that gully they've been talking about, where all the water had built up.

Now, this had been months before the disaster, so of course he couldn't have been doing anything to do with what happened, could he? But it does seem like a strange coincidence doesn't it? What if he'd been looking for a way to block the track and had found what he was looking for? What else was he doing there and why did he seem to hide when he saw me?

Sounds like CP and the RCMP do have some leads in their investigation, if you believe the rumours anyway. I'll be around the village now, most of the time, the next couple of months anyway, so I guess I'll be finding out who, if anyone, they try and nail for this. I have my suspicions, but I suppose I'll just be keeping those to myself. The latest article, the one that the picture on the bulletin board came from, has some more detail. It was in yesterday's paper that I just picked up from the bin on my way home. I scan down the front page to the body of the article:

> *"…after diverting the21c5lean creek water from entering the contaminated pool on the upper side of the tracks and pumping all the contaminated water from the area, investigators found that the source of the blockage was a boulder which had been lodged into the culvert. This boulder, almost 36" in circumference, had almost totally blocked the flow of water, immediately causing a rapid rise in water level, saturating the ground along the tracks. Upon inspection of the immediate area, a site was located some 50 meters above, on the bank, which appeared to be where the boulder had originated. Inspectors could find no sign of erosion around the site or any other mitigating factor as to what had caused the rock to dislodge from 'what appeared to be a secure location. The soil to the lower end of the depression seemed to be excavated, or undermined to some extent', according to investigators, 'however nothing conclusive has been determined.' they say. The investigation continues."*

I'm just relieved to be back home, whether I'm living next door to an eco-terrorist or not. I just want to air out my place, enjoy the property, relax, try to leave the CP spill at the back of my mind for a bit. There will be lots of time to follow the news as it unfolds. After all, I've got the bakery just down the block, the Procter central shrine; it's like a living newspaper in there, or maybe more like a tabloid. I'm just happy to be home now, to settle in again, makes me think that I should be seriously considering the 'rent to own', option I have on this place- still got a year to act on that.

At this point though, I just want to sink in and let the music flow from my blue tooth blaster that's perched up on the counter waiting for me as I come in the door. I turn up the song, 'Don't

Rush,' by Tegan and Sara and let my hips move me across the floor in rhythm, let the sound drown out the rumbling of locomotives as they continue to pass back and forth from the spill to the containment staging site by the village- that noise, a constant reminder that it's time to distract from for a bit.

CHAPTER 9

Ariel

I often avoided hanging for too long in the hallway between periods. I try to have less interaction with the crowds streaming by, but I find myself once again mid-stream, well, more of a back eddy really, leaning against the hallway wall while everyone slips by. I'm waiting for Carlie to turn up.

I spot Fin and Mick first. We call Fin, Trout, but it's not because he's a good swimmer. Probably could be a good swimmer though, he's got that kind of frame. The guys' like too long for his own body seems like, probably six feet but skinny so he looks smaller. He used to be into boxing but now if he's not hanging out in the hall selling Vape flavours, you can usually find him hunched over his laptop playing Mortal Kombat online against guys from Poland or Namibia. He combs his straight brown hair down over his eyes with his fingers as he walks down the hallway, then shrugs it back revealing some zits that are scattered over his forehead.

"Hey Trout, Mick whassup?" I say as they pull up to lean on the wall beside me.

"Just heading out to the parking lot for a smoke. Comin Wifi?" Trout says.

Between classes, the smokers can usually be found out between parked cars in the parking lot, especially now that the school's ban on smoking, vaping too, near the buildings, had been initiated. These days there are fewer smokers than before but still lots of kids go out there just to chill, vape, or find out what's being planned for the upcoming weekend. Some of us just pass a J around.

"Yeah, I'll be out in a sec." I tell them. They push off and head through the entrance doors, the giant letters of the acronym of our school name bolted on above: 'LVR.' We all call it LV. I don't even know what it stands for. Someone pounds on my shoulder from the other direction. I turn to see who.

"Hey fuck wad, holdin up the wall again?" It's one of the gym Jocks, Markus, one of the ones that come in the clean cut, oversized package, always impressively wrapped and usually linked to one of the cookie cutter girls who are dropped off in the same delivery. They move by.

I just grunt, not wanting to provoke the easily provoked. In reality, I'm usually kind of intimidated by the 'guerrilla faction'. I hate that I am, that I avoid that kind of confrontation all the time but seems that is how it is. I always seem to find a fast way out or diffuse a situation with distraction instead of facing it full on, so I weasel out of getting punched in the face. I wish that just once I could tell a guy to piss off, hold my ground, even punch *him* in the face if necessary, but I don't. I admire guys that can do that, especially if they aren't the bully types who really, I have nothing but contempt for. I don't get hassled that much anyway but I am always aware of those that are. See it all the time. The bullies don't target me much because of the confusion that ensues. Like the other day when Bruno told me I was the worst loser on the bus. He was like yellin' it right in my face. Outwardly, somehow, I was calm and asked him,

"If I'm the worst loser then no one else is worse than me, right?"

"Yeah… obviously, fuck face."

"Which means that really, I'm the best at being a loser, so really, in definition you are saying that I am the best. I am going to take credit for that."

He just walked away repeating, "loser, loser, loser", shaking his head, "loser, loser, loser…."

I hate being at school most of the time. I can't wait to just get out and hit the road. Not sure if I really think it's worth it to complete all these classes. Why carry on when I'm just killing time to attend? It's not like I'm gaining anything here. I'm just taking up space. What am I gonna get, some kind of scholarship to a university? Right! Maybe they've started up a new university that only accepts scholarship applications from under achievers… students with a D average and a sixty-two percent attendance record or worse. Maybe I'll get a bonus bursary for having achieved a record number of late slips. Yeah, I bet this could be a new trend, kind of like the musical movement toward 'unplugged'; or a new diet where you only eat sugar and trans fats. It will be 'post-secondary basics', where everyone starts at the bottom. Yeah, I'm pretty sure this could be the next big thing, the latest in low-average acceptance. Or, I could just quit school now and grow a lot of weed, sell it all, and go to Mexico for the winter. That's what Fran did a couple of years ago… seemed to work for him.

A balled up silky scarf lands on the side of my head and rolls down. I catch it and toss it back at her as she walks up.

"Hey Carlie, what's up, where ya been. The break is almost over."

"Oh, hey Wifi, just wrapping things up with social studies, had homework to sort out with Fisher. You? What's up?"

"Might be too late, but you want to head out for a puff in the parking lot; something's getting passed around out there."

"No, too late, let's just hang on the grass for a bit. Anyway, I've got to focus. If I'm all buzzed out for math I'll be screwed." "Yeah, you'd end up like me in math. When I'm straight, not a good thing. Keep it together okay?"

We sit on the grass on the slope that overlooks the neighbourhood and ball field below, and the street leading up to the parking lot. Few cars are moving by; the afternoon doldrums have set in. Lots of students are strewn around the grassy hill, soaking up some rays and relaxing between classes. Lately, I find, whenever I glance down the grassy hill beside the school, I've been getting flashbacks of the scene here a few weeks ago when there was a rock concert up in the school auditorium and hundreds of kids were hanging out here between sets, a few of us were smoking weed, pretty much out in the open. There were maybe eight of us passing one around when someone says, "Hey, cops, comin'." We drop the J, crush it, crotch the bag of weed and just chill. The cops are walking up fast, approaching us, when Petrov, a kind of hard-core friend of ours, starts walking away kind of too fast. Before we know what's going on, the cops pick up a bit of speed and then Petrov starts darting away along the asphalt entry to the school toward the grassy bank. The lead cop calls out for him to stop, and then they both start running after him. Everyone moves back. Petrov jumps over the concrete barrier, lands on the grass below and starts running down the bank. The cops get to the barrier, hop over and one of them pulls a gun and yells stop now! Get down! At this point everyone is totally freaked, watching the scene play out, wary but curiosity winning.

Petrov swings around and glances back as he runs; I guess he must have seen the gun. We were all shocked that they would pull a gun at all. He had dropped to the ground, face down. They cuffed him and took him to their car. Later, I was thinking, he could have gotten away, right? Like they never would have shot a kid in the back, right? I think it was kind of a strategic move on the cop's part to kind of showcase their power to the youth. As for Petrov, well, he must have had some other issue that they were after him for; we never did find out what- he never came back to school, and the news doesn't print anything on underage offenders. At any rate, we didn't have to worry too much about hiding our weed after that; those cops were occupied.

Carlie's voice brings me back around. "Two more weeks till freedom. I'm not going to screw things up now" she says, lying back, stretching her arms over her head, chest out, fingers woven into the lawn. I watch the thin silk of her scarf rise and fall over the curve of her breasts as she takes a deep breath. The tight tee shirt beneath tight then slack. "So, what's going on this weekend? Anything exciting?" she asks, glancing over, following my eyes.

"Well, yeah, for me and the boys anyhow," I say, trying to stay relaxed, releasing my clenched fist and grinding teeth. I'm never sure if anyone notices when I do that thing, tightening and releasing like that, must look kinda spastic. "Wish you could come with us to the Slim concert in Spokane." I add.

"Oh, yeah, I forgot that that was this coming weekend. You guys are going to have a blast. Can't believe you talked your parents into letting you all go."

"Yeah, I'm stoked." I say stretching back alongside her, our fingers touching a moment in the grass, both staring at the clouds moving across the gap between cottonwood trees. "It's gonna be great. We're only staying the one night you know, not such a big deal. But, hey, I'm in, should be cool; just the four of us, free in Yankee land."

"Guess you're taking Fin's car?"

"Yep, the Stang cruiser. Guess we're going to have to clean that thing up to get it across the border. Who knows what's fallen down between the seats lately?" I say, with a smile leaning up now on one elbow, facing her, watching the curve of her chest rise on the inhale. "We'll take her off to the car wash and use the industrial strength vacuum, suck all the goodies out of old Stang cracks before those border boys get their hands on it." I laugh, "… yeah, wish you and Jen were coming too. We'll have to plan another trip one day where we all get to go. A Procter to the city tour."

"Yeah, I'd love that. Once my parents loosen up a bit. I'm hoping to have my own car next year too. I've just got to keep up with working the store part time and more weekends at the pool when I can get 'em, then I'll have enough."

"Yeah, you keep it up, someone's got to save all those kids from sinking in the pool, especially the little round ones that float like an anchor," I laugh, as she pushes my shoulder to try and get me rolling down the grass bank.

"No, really, you gotta go for it, girl. You've got it all goin' on. The job, the marks. You're like the poster child for the new student movement, well not the movement I'm in maybe, but a better one. You're going to nail this thing." I say, stretching out again, arms in the air.

"Hallelujah!" She quickly darts her tickly fingers under my arms to shut me down, works well. She's laughing her cute little chuckly laugh. It's contagious.

"Yeah, they're going to be putting my posters all over the place. My face will be everywhere like pasted up, like the politicians do during elections. Maybe they can paint me onto the side of the school bus too so that everyone can be inspired each morning," she laughs, pushing herself up, looking ready to go.

"Yeah, and we could throw eggs and tomatoes at you if we're not, 'inspired', I say. The bell rings and we gather up our things and amble on inside again.

"I'll see ya on the bus Carlie."

"'Kay, catch ya later Wifi. Have a good one in Gym."

"Oh yeah, a blast." I say, but I have no intention of wasting my time in the gym with the muscle heads. I can head down to the Java Cup and see who's there, then pop back up in time to catch the bus home later. Gym is rarely any fun and besides, the moron that teaches it, 'Bernie', usually marks me absent even if I'm there because he doesn't approve of my gym strip: says that 'you can't' wear tee shirts with 'marijuana insignia' on them and not only that; he doesn't like my socks, 'non wicking,' or some bloody thing. So, whatever. If I'm absent when I'm there, I might as well be absent and not there.

I'm meeting up with Trout and the guys after school, so I've got to be back in the parking lot by 3:45 pm. We're going to ride home together, figure out the plan for the weekend. I downloaded the tickets last night, Mick's got the room reservation, so all we've got to do is figure out how to get our weed and maybe a few hits of Acid across the border and make sure everyone's going to have enough US, cash to have a good time. I don't want to get stuck bailing anyone out if I can help it. You never knew if Fin would have enough, and Freddie, well, you just never know what might happen with Freddie, in general. We'll just keep our eye on him and try to make sure he doesn't get us all arrested.

We have all been to Spokane before. It is the closest major city to where we live; a lot closer than Vancouver or Calgary, but we have never been there together before, only with family. The Slim Twig band is not like some kind of super group, but they are getting pretty big and we are all into their music. The trip itself, just the four of us heading off across the border is maybe the best part though. 'Procter Boys Do the City', my kind of headline.

"I think we can fit all that shit just inside the door panels no problem," Trout says. We're all together now, on the way home in the Stang. Trout pulls it out and swings right onto the main highway down the street from LV.

"Yeah, but that's probably the first place they look," says Mick, "why not drop a pouch into the gas tank on a fishing line and then tape it off and pull it out later? Seen it on a cop show once." "A fishing line," I say, "it'll probably melt and then the bag will just be floating away in the gas tank forever. And besides, if you tape it off, all they have to do is open the lid and they will be able to see it."

"I know." says Freddie, with a wry smile, "Why don't we each swallow a condom with all the drugs before we go and then hopefully crap them out in time. Like in Narcos."

"Nasty," says Mick. "I'm not diggin' through shit."

Freddie carries on, "Or if it doesn't come out quick enough, we can eat a bunch of ex-lax right after we get across the border, or better yet, let's just bring Lexie, Trout's lab, and feed him all the drugs in a Ziploc inside some burger and then we can follow him around Spokane until he shits it out." He laughs.

"Yeah, or we cut him open and sew him back up after." I say, "we'll bring a bunch of medical supplies, syringes, needle and thread, a scalpel, won't be suspicious at all." Trout pulls us into the Husky station. "Okay boys, let's just put a few bucks into the tank now, just enough to get us across the border. Gas is cheaper on the other side."

"Yeah, five each should do." I say, tossing a five onto the front seat. Trout hops out to pump some gas, leaving the door open so he can hear. Freddie says, "Look, the car'll be spic and span. We'll have concert tickets with us, everything'll be cool; they won't bother us at the border. I'm tellin' ya… no sweat. They search the car as much as they want and see nothing, that's the key. We just stuff the extras down our crotch; they're not going to search us, just the car."

"Yeah, Freddie could be right about that." I say, "We could even empty our pockets and get a pat down and they still wouldn't find it, well, that is unless they have a dog." Trout hops back in and pulls the car back out onto the highway.

"No, they never have dogs there at Nelway," Trout says, "been through there a dozen times with my Dad when I've gone along on his sales trips. It's just a backwater border with a couple of hick guards that can barely spell."

"You gave them a spelling test last time you were through Trout? I ask him.

"Just sayin', these guys aren't rocket scientists okay, we'll be fine." Mick says, "Main thing is not to worry about it. I've been through there with the soccer team too, a couple times, going to tournaments. It's just routine if you don't push your luck."

Mick's a pretty talented soccer player. I always forget that he still plays. The rest of us don't, not anymore anyhow, so we lose touch. Mick's one of those players that makes it look easy, scores almost every game, moves through players like they're posts in a slalom course. He's fast, short, stocky and full of muscle. His hair is tight and curly, and he keeps it short, so it sticks to his head without moving when he runs. I tell ya, if he didn't show up, you never knew if Procter would win. When he did, we usually would. I tried for a couple of seasons on the team, a couple of years ago, never really made enough of a difference to be called a good player. I could handle the ball pretty well, could even deak through the other team sometimes, but as soon as it came to shooting on the goal, man, my body would just take on this kind of super natural geekness and I'd miss even a wide-open net. So,

I dropped the team sports. Now, I hang out more with guys that aren't into sports so much.

"Just gotta be cool." Freddie carries on, "Don't say much, just let them do the talking, especially if we get that dick head, Mono- brow guy. He likes to be the boss, so we let him, even if we feel like punchin' his face in." Freddie says, sounding as though he is trying to convince himself more than anyone else, not to punch the guy's face in, I mean.

"Okay, boys, so it's settled, we just crotch the stuff, bring enough US, cash, and get the car good and clean first." Trout says, "Let's just leave a bit earlier on Saturday and drop by the car wash on the way. Hey, what about fake I.D. Anyone got any? The age is twenty-one down there. I know I won't pass, but we need to be picking up some beers along the way."

We cross the bridge, following traffic. The radio cranked up so that we can barely hear each other. The road is wet from the rain earlier in the day, puddles spit up spray as passing cars splatter the windshield and the broken wiper on the passenger side passes back and forth like a wet noodle, just spreading the drops around. Trout's got the window open a couple of inches to keep the car from foggin' up. It's almost summer but the air is still cool blowing in. I zip up my hoody.

"Yeah, I think I can use my brother's old driver's license," says Freddie, "he's twenty-four and has the same mustache so it might work. Problem is it's expired, and he won't give me his new one, I already asked him but he's bein' a dick. I'll take the old one."

"Okay, sounds like a plan, then," I say. Freddie is the best one to try to buy the beer anyway, 'cause he already looks a lot older somehow, kind of weathered and lots of facial hair and being over six feet tall and heavy doesn't hurt. Anyway, he has that calm about him, that kind of self-assurance where, whoever it was on the other side of the counter doin' the inspection, doesn't matter to him. That attitude seems key in influencing the split-second decision made by the one behind the counter.

"Okay," Fin says, "So I'll have enough fuel to get us across to the other side and then it's on you guys to fill it up eh? I'm supplying the car, so you guys can buy the gas, right? Anyways, gas is cheap in the states, cheaper than here, even after the exchange." "Yeah, we got it," Freddie says, "split it three ways boys." "Oh yeah, and don't forget to change your cash before we go, 'cause they don't like changing Canadian in the states. They barely even know where Canada is." Fin says. "Last time I was down there a girl at the Arby's asked me where I was from and I said, British Columbia, and she said, 'whoa, I've never been to South America. Is it really dangerous down there?" Unbelievable. "And don't bring any weed unless you've got it vacuum sealed,"

Mick says, "smells too strong,"

We wind our way home along the lake, heading toward the ferry, following the familiar road, always part of the routine. We're all hyped up for this trip, so it doesn't seem boring, Mick echoes my thoughts: "Wish we were already heading off. Too bad it's only Wednesday, but hey, gives me a couple more days to make some extra cash for the road." He has a part time job at the local garage in Balfour, doing oil changes and brake jobs some days after school.

Thursday and Friday drag by, so by Saturday morning we are all like pumped to hit the road early. Our place is the nearest to the end of the road, so Fin picks me up first. He pulls into the yard just after 9:00 am, not a bad start for a weekend. None of us usually get up till after 10:00 am, on the weekends anyways. I have a few things thrown together in a gym bag, a to go cup of coffee in the other hand. I give my mom a quick squeeze and wave to my Dad and the geeks as I turn out, pushing the door open with my back. "You boys drive carefully. Make sure you stay together, especially at that concert," my Mom instructs, "can you use your cell phones down there at least for text in case you get separated?" she asks.

"Yeah mom, don't worry, we've got the text going." I say, not for calls though, costs too much… the roaming. "We'll be careful, just going to the concert, then coming home tomorrow, don't worry."

Leif, my little brother, says: "I should be going along to make sure they don't go berserk down there in the states. Maybe the Americans will shoot them. I heard they all have handguns and they wear 'em on a belt like in the western movies."

"Yeah, right Leif, you'd be a real asset down there, catch ya later dude." I say.

"And make sure Fin's car doesn't have any pot or empties in it, son," my dad yells over his shoulder from the hallway, "They don't take kindly to that kind of thing at the border. I don't want to be bailing you guys out later."

Now that my parents are having hassles between them, my mom sometimes stays in Nelson at her cousin's place with Luna and sometimes Leif too. Leif likes to be in town to hang at the skate park and stuff, and so with only me and my dad at home, it's easy for me to kind of create my own schedule. They were all here last night though, so I have to make the rounds before I go. I like it best now when the house is empty, and I can just leave without discussing it. It's easier now that I have my own exit from the upstairs loft that my Dad and I renovated last year. I don't think he even knows if I'm up there or not half the time, seems kind of preoccupied in his own world most of the time, which is great.

Fin is just poking his head in the back porch as I come out. "Excellent", he says, "let's roll."

The sky is clear, the cool air promising to warm up soon. Our shoes already damp with morning dew as we walk through the grass to the car, spring in our step.

"Next stop, Mick's," Fin says, "lets hit it."

"Yeah man, finally we hit the trail. Right on, blue sky, sunshine and an open road. I've even got a few extra bucks. Gotta go to one of those all you can eat buffets later, clean 'em out." I toss my bag on the floor between us. The Mustang spins up some gravel as we take off down Higgins to the highway.

Mick's place is less than a kilometer down the road. We pull into his driveway and hop out, walk around the house through the carport and along the back walk to the kitchen door. Their lawn is always cut just right and the flowers in the flower bed along the walk are in order like little soldiers, all lined up. His mom is in the kitchen sitting at the counter on a bar stool sipping tea in her bath robe as we bang on the door. "Come on in boys," she says, "Mick's on his way. Don't forget your toothbrush," she shouts down the hallway. 'You boys have some lunch packed or are you planning on just eating all that American fast food?" she smiles knowingly.

"How 'bout those cherry donuts at Dunkin", she asks, "bring me back some of those okay guys?" Mick comes in, his curls still wet from the shower; he's carrying a leather hand bag.

"Yeah, sure mom, we'll bring back a bag full," he says, as he scouts around for his shoes. "Hey guys, all geared up for the ride, everything cool?"

"Yeah," I say, "great, tuned up and ready to go." We say our good byes to Margaret, his mom, and file out the kitchen door. Mick comes out last after soaking his mom for some extra cash. She's such a push over. We are all jealous of how easy he's got it. He doesn't even do dishes. Not like I have too many restrictions either I guess, but I do have lots of chores so it's a matter of getting them out of the way in time to have it my way, something I usually pull off, and even though my folks don't give me much money, I usually find a way to have enough. Mick's dad is always away, up north near the Yukon border, a Hydrologist working on some drilling project. He must make big bucks, cause Mick's never short on cash and doesn't have much in the way of chores or any real kind of restrictions, plus, they have all the toys, the latest snow board gear, a quad, snowmobile, even have a pool table in the back room. They have a ski boat too, so sometimes in the summer we get to go out wake boarding.

"Yeah! On the road!" Mick yells, slamming the back door. "Burn 'em Trout."

We pull out. I text Freddie to let him know we're minutes away. He always asks us to give him the five-minute warning 'cause he doesn't like anyone coming in. His old man is really uptight, so we don't mind avoiding the friction anyway. Don't really want to see him get cuffed on the side of the head again. His family's place is always kind of a shambles, lots to see. We pull up and turn around below the house. Freddie is already sauntering down the driveway, a couple of chickens scamper out of his way as he walks straight through them, and a goat stares at him from the porch, watching him walk away with a keen interest, like a concerned grandparent. I can never figure out how they keep track of all their animals when they don't have them fenced in. There's a milk cow up on the bank above the house grazing on long grass that's growing up around a rusty car wreck. She's swishing her tail, eyes following the scruffy mutt that's racing back and forth out-front chasing the ravens overhead as if they're trolling and he's on the hook. They caw and swoop, as Freddie skids up to the car.

"Hey guys. Great day for a ride, eh? Let's go see what the Yankees are up to today." He swings into the back seat with Mick and tosses his bag in, a plastic Ainsworth bag, the one's they give you at the hot spring to put your clothes in when you change. "Got myself some shorts in case we go for a swim," he says.

"Listen man," I say, "We ain't gonna be swimming at our hotel. It's some dive in the downtown, a one star on Priceline, cheapest thing going."

"Yeah, well maybe I'll swim at someone else's hotel then," Freddie says, "Or in the river. I'm swimming somewhere. When you go on a trip, you're supposed to go swimming, right? Anyway, what's a one star? How can a hotel have only one star? Does it get a star for having a bathroom, or blankets or what? Will we be pissing out the windows?"

Mick says, "not sure but I saw a picture and it has four brick walls and an elevator. I think they get one star for having an elevator. I don't think we'll be doing much sleeping anyways boys so who cares?"

"I just hope there's no cockroaches and hairy rats running around," says Mick. We're cruising into Nelson, along the lake, winding around corners. There's not a lot of traffic on Saturday morning. The sun is rising behind us and the lake is calm, reflecting it, only fish rising ripple the surface. Seems like a good day for an adventure, but what day isn't? Got the tunes cranking.

We pull into the car wash, and everyone gathers their loonies so we can stuff them into the vacuum and car wash. We pull all our stuff out and throw it on the sidewalk and then Fin cleans out all the crevices with the vacuum nozzle, even the trunk, glove box and side pockets. Who knows what kinda stuff got sucked into that thing, but whatever it was, it's better to have it land in the vacuum tank than in the hands of a border patrol, after all, that car is really kind of a party house these days, not just a ride, and we'd been hearing that even though laws were being softened up these days, you could still get locked up or at least refused entry for just having a seed in your car.

"Hairy rats", says Freddie, "what the hell other kind are there? I want to see a really hairy rat, like a rasta rat, with dreads down to his waist. Ya think they have those down there?"

"Probably have to go to Jamaica for that rat Freddie," I say. We've pulled out of Nelson and are heading to Salmo and the border, winding along through the tight valley corridor; the thick forest tight to both sides of the road. Lots of yellow leaves are scattered over the highway and dropping when wind catches the last ones that cling to the high branches of cotton wood trees above.

"I was thinking of working on some dreads," Mick says, "but then changed my mind and got it all cut off yesterday,"

"Yeah, quite the pig shave," Freddie says, "Now you look like a dork… more 'n usual."

"You should have seen how much came off. Like, the hair cutter guy was wading around in the stuff up to his waist." Says Mick. Mick is kind of prone to exaggeration, likes to colour things in a little brighter than they appear.

"Uh, huh," says Freddie, "You're delusional Mick, like you ever had enough hair to dread in the first place, and anyway, how do you dread an afro like that? You'd end up looking like a mangy mutt. Now your head just looks like one of them scrubbies we use on cast iron pots."

Mick just smiles back at Freddie, running his fingers through his hair and says, "Yeah, you're right Freddie, we'll have to use your hair for the dreads instead. Once all the nits die off and the bald spots grow back, you'll make a real Reggae star."

"I wouldn't mind going to see a reggae concert one day," Fin says, getting in on the action. "Maybe we should check out the music guide and come back to Spokane when the next show is on… or just get tickets to Jamaica?"

"Yeah, cool idea, just us, hanging in Jamiaca, starting every day off with a big spliff and a can of Red stripe," says Fin.

"Yeah, I could get into some Reggae." says Freddie, "Just mellow out on a beach chillin' to the tunes with a fat spliff every mornin'. Probably be better than this punk Slim Twig that we're goin to hear."

"Yeah, he's kinda punky, but they've got some good tunes too, like that one, 'jackin' box'."

"Yeah, or, 'Turbo', "I say, "gotta love that base line. Those guys have big energy. It'll be a blast."

"Yeah, I know," says Freddie, "but what a name. Where'd they come up with that dumb ass name Slim Twig," he says, in his weird back woods accent, like he's been living in the Ozark mountains all his life or something.

What is it with the Ozark mountains anyway? Where are they? Why do we always hear that they have the most backward hicks? I wonder if our hicks are just the same? "Maybe we can come up with a new name for the band as a gift. Like Swim Rig, or Dim Fig or something, eh boys?" Fin says, adding, "We could post it on their Facebook page. Maybe we can come up with a rap tune about Twig?" We're all putting rhymes together when our attention is diverted by the warning signs to slow for the border area ahead. We wind through the turns, pass the Canadian border building, then see the American customs just ahead.

We're pulling in, nice, slow, relaxed and Freddie says, "So, guys, got all your goods crotched nice and deep?"

"Yeah, yeah," Mick says, "don't even talk about it, okay? Just be cool."

"I'm cool Mick, what's your problem?" says Freddie, "You worried they're gonna go for your balls? Sure hope they don't grab mine and set off my handgun. Probably shouldn't have kept it loaded."

Freddie always has a way of creating unnerving situations; kind of likes to make a habit of it. Fin flashes a questioning glance in his direction as we pull up to the stop line, says, "Okay, now just shut up Freddie." Then we wait for just a few seconds before the red light turns green and we pull slowly up to the office window. Fin rolls his window down. We all look across and sure enough, it's Mono Brow leaning out from his post staring us down, like specimens in a petri dish.

"Passports," he says, holding out his hand. Fin hands the stack over to him after we collect them all. "Where you boys off to today?"

"Heading to Spokane to see a concert, just staying one night," says Fin.

"I didn't ask how long you were staying. Just answer the questions," says Mono Brow, glancing up from the passports in disapproval. "Where are you all from?"

"Procter," says Fin.

"Each of you. And speak up." He says, staring grim faced into the car.

"Procter," I say, "Procter," says Mick.

"Me too," says Freddie, staring right at the guy, "you know… Procter."

Mono Brow studies the passports for a few minutes, makes a few notes on his computer, clicking away, then says, "Okay boys, you just pull over up ahead and get out of the car."

"Is there a problem," Fin asks?

"Not yet, just pull over and get out." He says. "Like I said, I'll be asking the questions."

Fin pulls ahead. We all look at each other nervously. "What the hell," says Fin.

"Don't worry about it," says Freddie smiling, "we've got nothing to hide."

We hop out as the guy approaches and stand there waiting. Freddie walks around to the back as Mono Brow opens the driver's side door. "Get away from the vehicle," he says, turning to Freddie. You either stand in front or go into the office to wait. Keep your hands by your sides."

We watch him as he feels under the seats, his hands all sealed up nice in white rubber gloves. He roots through the glove box, bangs on the door panels and feels between the seats, examining every inch. "Looking pretty clean in here boys. Maybe a little too clean." He says with a smirk. He pulls out a little round mirror on the end of a rod and angles it under the car to examine the undercarriage, walking around the whole car. Then he opens the gas tank, peers in, feels under the wheel wells and lifts the hood to have a look in the air filter. He even unscrews it and pulls off the cover plate to see if there is an air filter in there or not, I guess, finds one and puts it back together again.

Fifteen minutes later he closes the hood and says, "Okay boys, follow me inside."

We all file in to the office and from behind the counter he says, "Okay, now just put the contents of your pockets on the counter, one at a time. You first," he says, pointing to Freddie.

"Yeah sure officer," Freddie says with his backwater accent, and piles up some coins and keys and bits of paper, a pocket knife and a half a hand full of sunflower seed shells; his wallet flops open next to the pile showing some Canadian and US, cash in it.

"How much money you got in there?" says Mono.

"Oh, about eighty bucks US, and just a bit of Canadian," says Freddie. "And pull your jacket pockets inside out," he says.

Freddie does it, adding a few crinkled-up bills and a hand full of coins and a lighter to the pile on the counter, then stands back and spins around like a ballerina.

"I didn't say to spin," Says Mono, now put that stuff back in your pockets and get out of here." And hands Freddie back his passport.

The rest of us follow suit, turning out pockets, counting money, until it seems like Mono Brow is finally satisfied. We all get back in the car, ready to get the hell out of there.

Fin starts it up. We make sure to buckle up as Mono Brow continues to watch us leave. We pull out slowly and put some space between us and that hulking, hairy browed bully before Freddie says,

"Told you that Mono Brow guy is a real dick, didn't I?" "Yeah, what a prick," says Mick, "can't believe he can just pick on us for being young."

"Well he picked on us, but didn't find my weed or my shrooms," I say, "so that's cool."

"Yeah, or my E," says Mick, smiling.

"Or my acid," says Freddie, "what a dork. Wish I knew where he lives. I'd like to drop by and take a dump in his mail box."

Fin says, "You don't really have a gun, Freddie, do you?" "Yeah right," says Freddie, "what do you think I am, stupid?

I was just getting you boys a little excited before the interrogation Finny boy. All in fun. Told ya they wouldn't search our bodies." "All right guys, into the wild blue yonder," Fin says. Let's do some damage!" And he floors it. We lean back into our seats and shout out in a kind of spontaneous relief.

Within two hours we're cruising into the city. It's always exciting heading from a small town into the city but doing it with a car load of friends is even better. We are soaking up the city sites from one red light to the next as we make our way to Spokane city center along the Division street strip. I'm reading a map, giving Mick directions 'cause we have no cell service to use GPS. We all disconnected to save on roaming charges. "Good thing your mom gave us this map," I say, looking at Mick, "We'd have been lost forever without it."

"Yeah, lost in the slums," says Freddie, "we must be almost to the hotel, I'm seeing more and more homeless people and prostitutes. Look at that guy's shopping cart boys, fuller than a hay truck." He says, pointing to the side.

And sure enough, Freddie was right, we are getting close. Within ten minutes we're pulling up to the address on the print out from Priceline. "I guess that's what makes a one star," I say, staring up at the stained brick walls of the hotel across the street from us. "Guess they lose one star for every homeless guy out front."

"Okay, beautiful," says Freddie, "where's the valet parking? I want the guys in little white suits to park our car."

"Yeah, well, we'll be lucky to even come back to a car, parking it out here," I say as we hop out. Plug that meter eh Mick. Home sweet home." We hop out, lock up and head on in to the check in counter. We get keys from some seedy looking clerk with greasy hair and a stubbed-out cigar in his mouth. He's eying us over like we are a bunch of ex-cons. The elevator works but it smells of cigarettes and spilled beer. As we open the door to the room, it's pretty musty, with high ceilings marked only by the single bare bulb and a web of cracked plaster lines, but it's clean enough. There're two lousy double beds with sunken in the middle mattresses, and a stained porcelain sink hangs off the wall. The shared bathroom is down the hall. We toss our stuff on the beds, kind of reserving a spot. Freddie lights up a cig and we just lounge around, checking out the crack-heads in the alley below. "Look", says Mick pressing buttons on a remote, "this TV doesn't even work." The old school TV perched up on one of those metal wall brackets sits precariously, looking down over us, that and the dusty iron radiator by the window are the only furnishings in the room. "Classy." Fin says.

"I'm hungry," says Mick, "let's get outta this dump and grab some Dicks' burgers."

"Burgers by the bag-full, at Dicks," says Freddie, through exhaled smoke in his southern drawl "Can see the sign from here, over there on the strip," he points out through the cracked glass to a high revolving sign a couple blocks away. "It's almost 3:00 am, man, let's just grab a burger now and then go for the big buffet later. We'll line up at one of them all-you-can-eat places and jamb our heads deep into the trough just like our hogs back home." He says, snorting like a pig, and pivoting his neck.

"Okay boys, sounds like a plan." I say, "let's just grab what we need then, might not be back before the show," I add, "everyone got their ticket and some cash?"

"Let's move. Grab that key 'eh Trout." Says Mick.

We meander around the downtown core for hours, just kind of soaking up the city, popping into head shops, music stores, and eyeing up the best bars and the girls going into them, longingly, knowing there is no way we're going to get served in one of them, not all of us anyway. We end up at one of these famous buffet diners where there are several aisles lined with endless platters and stainless-steel steam tables just waiting for our assault. There's even a soft ice cream machine where you can pump a stream of the stuff into a cone. Freddie tops up his mashed potatoes with it. Huge people sit in booths and line up with plates, piling stacks of ham, scalloped potatoes and fried chicken in layers as if they can never go back. We line up too, the four of us, making mooing sounds and snorting like hogs. We know how to entertain ourselves.

⁓

Slim Twig leaps from the podium and announces, "I'll never be fat." and the audience roars its approval. He dives into their out-stretched hands which suspend him as his body surfs through the throng. "I'm Slim", he keeps shouting and the crowd below shouts back, "you're Slim, you're Slim! You're Slim!" Now, well into the first set, the crowd seems like they are getting what they came for. The momentum is building. I started shouting back, "I'm fat!" And then Fin and Mick join in "I'm fat! I'm fat! I'm fat!" We got a few odd looks, but people are too wrapped up in their own euphoria to pay attention to us. Slim's surf journey lasts about maybe 100 meters in a wide arc that U turns him back toward the stage and kind of spews him back onto the platform in a tangle of limbs and hair, lubricated by sweat and greasy palms.

"Lomito! Lomito! Lomito! We want Lomito!" The crowd carries on and begins stomping their feet and rocking the light towers to the rhythm of their demands. Slim sorts himself out, picks up a nearby tambourine and signals the drummer to start the three count. Soon, the full band erupts again in a wave of sound that spills out over the crowd; the first few familiar notes of the song, 'Lomito', instantly recognized. Slim's voice is almost drowned out by the overwhelming vocal power of the collective crowd as they sing the familiar lyrics. Slim trades his tambourine quickly for a white rhythm guitar. In response to the gyrating movement of the frantic fans, brings the other two guitar players together until they form a triangle of pivoting legs, guitars and tangled hair, tossing themselves forward and back.

Freddie yells out to us, "Hey, isn't Lomito just some kind of sandwich?" His eyes are all wide and glassy and he's wearing a goofy grin. As the pitch rises, they crouch together, guitars screeching feedback and high notes, then at the crescendo, they leap back away from each other, then stride in unison to the deep base beat, step by step, straight across the platform to the pier like point of the stage. This action spurs the already frantic crowd into a rabid frenzy.

Spontaneously the crowd surges forward about two steps, which squeeze those in front into a paste of humanity where bodies merge and feet are lifted from the floor, the pressure and flow kind of eject those in front onto the stage like toothpaste being pressed up a tube, spewing out. Some are gasping for breath. We watch, dazed but energized, as those ones stage-side eject onto it and realize that they are part of a wild opportunity. An anarchistic energy overtakes the scene; pulsing, an unstoppable tide has risen; we all feel it. Dozens, then hundreds of rabid fans storm the stage. We move forward too, with the flow. Must be within fifty feet of the stage now, screaming along with the crowd at this point, caught up in the chaos. The three guitarists are still rocking hard together but now are engulfed by the crowd, so we can't even see them. Then the beat becomes more rhythmic, a little mesmerizing, maybe a defense response by the band to bring down the collective crowd energy a notch. The rhythm is defined and repetitive and all the fans on stage are bouncing together, arms above their heads, some jumping so high their heads rise above the sea of people like buoys on a stormy sea.

To the rear of the stage, up on his elevated platform, the drummer is smiling and shouting to the wild fans around his kit. He keeps the beat. The crowd, as seemingly chaotic and out of control as they are, are surprisingly careful not to knock into stuff. There is some kind of organized chaos in play, but then, just as a mellowing of the music and crowd begin the security forces in back begin to organize and react. Their orders, 'to clear the stage,' we read the next day in the local paper.

Arm in arm they come out from back stage and form a line in front of the drum kit, then slowly begin moving forward. I guess there are maybe twenty-five of them, all in uniforms, armed with batons and pepper spray cannisters. Surprisingly, the music continues. Slim calls out over the mic for people to move back a bit, to make room for those on stage to drop back onto the floor, but he says it over the continuous beat of the music. Security keeps moving, inching forward, forcing those in front to drop off, some kids dive in and try to surf the crowd, others try to get through the guards and stay on stage, but are forced back until the stage is cleared of fans.

"Crazy carpet ride 'eh boys?" Freddie yells over the din, his eyes all glassy and wide. He is leaning back into the pressing crowd, kind of rolling with the tide. He looks like he is an observer more than a participant, in awe of all around him. He has an amused, almost maniacal expression on his face. We're all pretty blasted at this point, all kinds of substances coursing through our blood stream; the effects seem to be elevated by the crowd energy. I look up into the rafters high above and for a moment I am floating over us looking down at the throbbing mass of humanity writhing below like a huge serpent. From this perspective I can relate to Freddie's 'crazy carpet ride,' and there we are, the four of us, riding along on a sound wave, just floating and bobbing along without a care, the brothers on a raft going nowhere and everywhere. "Yeah, let's ride," I yell.

After two encores, the stadium lights are finally turned on. The stage empties out and we file out too, out the exits, spilling onto the streets amid the crush, our ears humming, the crowd still energized, some singing, others screaming, flooding the sidewalks in all directions. Mick and Fin are talking and laughing with another group alongside. "Let's follow these guys," Mick says, "that guy says there's an afterhours electro club not far down the line." "That's the plan then," Fin says, and we move off with the others to soak up the aftermath. None of us ready yet to let the night go.

The afterhours club seems kinda lame after the craziness of the concert so we only last long enough to drain a couple of beers there before we decide to find our way back to the hotel. Each of us thought the hotel was in a different direction so we circle the block a couple times stumbling along, laughing, yelling, "I'm fat, I'm fat, I'm fat," not really paying attention to where we were going. Finally, Fin bangs on a taxi drivers window and asks him for some info and he helps straighten us out. By the time we finally spot the hotel in the distance, we can see the flashing lights of several fire trucks out front. "Wow, quite a show up near our shit hole," Mick says, "let's check it out."

As we near, we see that there are two fire trucks and an ambulance right out front of our hotel. There is a ribbon tied up keeping passersby away and a few hotel employees are standing on the other side of it watching the action. One of the trucks has a ladder extended way high up the building but it's being retracted now. We see a couple of firefighters emerge from the hotel with a coiled-up hose between them. "Looks like we missed the show," Freddie says. "Hey, isn't that ladder coming back down from up by our room? What the hell. Do we even have a room?" He echoes our thoughts. We're all kind of feeling a little worse for wear, foggy, comin' down, and ready to crash into any kind of bed regardless of its condition. We near the ribbon, and the hotel manager from the check in desk, with a name tag on his collar, 'Alan,' spots us. "Hey, you're the guys from room 503, aren't ya?" he says. "Yeah'" I say, "what's up? What's going on up there?"

"You a smoker?" he asks.

"Uh, no." I say, thoughts immediately streaming through my mind. "What's happened? Was there a fire? I don't see any smoke." "Oh, yeah, there was a fire, mostly smoke but some flame too, got put out a while ago. Looks like it started up in your room." He glares at us accusingly. "I think the chief there wants to speak with you," he nods over to one of the firefighters nearby. He looks us over and says, "Hey what's that in your pocket?" Pointing to Freddie's chest pocket in his windbreaker, the perfect outline of a pack of smokes pressing along the seams. "Not mine," says Freddie looking directly at the guy, without any hesitation, "some kid at the club stuck 'em in there, wanted to quit. Like he said, we don't smoke. What happened to our room?" he pauses, then adds "Can we go up there?" I stare at Freddie, wondering how he can come up with that line so quick at a time like this.

"You'll have to go talk to the chief about that," he says, glaring again at Freddie's pocket in an accusatory way, "I know there's lots of water damage."

"Holy shit man," I whisper to Fin, and the others, "we've got to get our stuff out of there and ditch this place." We're all a little more alert now, jarred by events, even though it's 3:30 in the morning and our heads are clouded with fatigue and chemicals. Freddie turns from the clerk, and in one fluid motion palms the pack of smokes and stuffs them into his crotch, then walks directly over to the fire chief. We move along behind. "Hey Chief," he says, "Alan there tells us that that fire could have started up in our room. Can we get up there and get our stuff out?"

"Oh, so it's you boys that were staying there. When were you last in the room? Who was smoking?"

"Oh, we haven't been there since this afternoon. Been out at a concert. None of us smoke. That fire must have started some other way." Freddie says. "The place is a dump. Crazy electrical crap everywhere."

"Well we're still investigating, but the source seems to be from near the radiator in your room, probably a cigarette or some other smoldering material dropped down behind the radiator." He says, looking us over carefully. "We will have to take names and identification, follow up on this. For now, the building is safe, just wet and smoky. The rooms are unlocked, and your stuff is still up there so you can go and grab it and bring it down. There are two firefighters up there that are securing the area. Just check in with them. We'll sort this out later. You'll have to use the stairs - no elevators." He turns away to answer to a firefighter.

We move in toward the entrance, duck under the tape line and head into the lobby. There's still water dripping from stains on the ceiling, some running down the wall too. We find the stairs and run up as quick as we can; the whole scene feeling kind of surreal. "Jesus," Mick says, "this is fucking crazy man, what if they charge us? That was you, wasn't it, Freddie? You dropped your butt down there probably. Fuck we're all in shit now."

"Yeah, I know, must have blown back in when I flicked it out the window and got caught behind the radiator. They can't pin that shit on us guys. Let's get our crap and get the fuck outta here." He says, out of breath as we rise up the five flights, the hollow echo of our footsteps bouncing off the musty, dark concrete walls of the winding stairwell. We get to the fifth. There's a firefighter in the hall outside our room throwing some dripping wet blankets in a pile. He looks up at us.

"Move it guys. Pick up your stuff and head back down to the trucks. It's a hell of a mess up here." He wades through puddles in his heavy rubber boots. We move in, relieved that no one is escorting us on the site. We quickly pick up the things we have there, stuffing them into bags, wet or dry and leave, turning back into the stairwell trying not to bring any more attention to ourselves. Once the stairwell door swings closed behind us, Freddie says, "Guys, let's head out the back when we get down to the first floor before we get pulled over by the fire department or the cops. I saw an exit that probably goes into the alley. Fin can just come back on his own and grab the car from the other direction after and pick us up from a few blocks away."

No one seems to have a better idea; there's just nods and murmurs of approval as we file back down the stairwell following Freddie. Near the bottom is a back exit like he said. I pull the door open to peek out. The alley behind the hotel seems pretty quiet, just dumpsters and hissing pipes.

"Let's try this." I say, and we make our way slowly out into the alley, scanning for uniforms. A couple of homeless people are laying amid piles of dirty blankets in doorways but otherwise the route seems clear. When we get to the street entrance and peer around the corner, we can see the tail end of one of the fire trucks, lights still cycling and bouncing off the brick walls, illuminating in strobe all the graffiti painted on the dumpsters. No one seems interested in us, so we just walk away, leaving the scene behind us. We find a Denny's all-night diner, and order plates of breakfast and coffee while we wait for Fin to pick up the car and come back. It doesn't take him long to pull up out front. Plates of ham, eggs and toast are steaming away in front of us now, rousing us from our stupor momentarily, foggy minds toss swirling memories back and forth, as we digest food and the nights events.

"They can't pin that on us." Freddie says sounding like he's trying to talk himself into it, mouth full of toast, "Sure they have Mick's name on file, but what can they do with that? There's no proof, and anyways, that hotel needs to burn down."

"Anyway, they don't have my name," says Mick, "They have my dad's name on the reservation and no credit card 'cause we paid cash at the counter, so we should be good. Anyways, that desk in the lobby looked like it had been pretty washed out from the fire hoses; probably lost any records that they had.

"Cleansed by fire," I say, "kinda biblical. We're just doing our part, I guess. Hopefully they don't find some record and call your dad though," I say, glancing over at Mick doubtfully.

"I'm just glad we got out of there and I got my car back," says Fin. "I'm wiped boys, need a bit of sleep. Guess we're all crashin' in the Stang." The breakfast is quickly settling in, mellowing the intensity of the night to a more stable state. We pay, hop into the car out in the parking lot and stretch out on the seats as much as we can. I throw one of the tee shirts from my bag over my head to block the street light and I'm out till the sun starts beating through the windshield at 9:00 am.

Sealed windows and locked doors have us coughing on the smell of, sweat, stale beer, and smoky clothes rising in heat waves to greet our senses. As we wake, squinting eyes protest, doors are flung open, gaping. We rise, hair tousled, shirts balled up, stretching, emerging from the Stang like a boat load of vagrants who've washed up on shore. We look around at the now bustling parking lot full of breakfast goers surrounding us. The light of day and blinding sunlight feel pretty harsh. I wish it were still dark. A family has pulled up beside our spot and they are unstrapping their kids from car seats as they watch us sideways, avoiding eye contact. A middle-aged couple walks by the back of the car, the guy, big, burly in a leather jacket, stares an accusatory glare our way. I watch out of the corner of my eye as his wife glances around the lot, probably to see if there might be a cop close by to help out just in case.

Freddie grins at them, says: "Morning folks. Nice day for a picnic." Then he shuffles over toward the light post behind the car, pulling down his fly as he goes.

"Jesus Freddie," Fin says in a loud whisper, "not here for Christ sakes. Just wait."

But Freddie ignores him. The couple pretends not to see, moving into the restaurant as Freddie pisses on the pole and a pool forms and spills along the curb into the gutter.

"For fuck sakes Freddie… a picnic?" I say, after they're gone. "What the hell Freddie," Mick says, tossing a dirty tee shirt at him. We all laugh, looking around from one to the other, laughing harder, uncontrollably now, as we see our own comical state and the memory of the preceding twenty-four hours reflects back from one to another through wet, smiling eyes. We clutch ourselves, bent over, banging on the car and howling. Mick throws his little leather bag in the air and it rains wet tee shirts and underwear down on us. After throwing the clothes back and forth at each other, we toss them in the trunk and hop in the car. "Let's burn," Mick says, "'fore the cops show up."

"Cruising the strip," I say, as we head up Division street, red light to red light, our blurry eyes checking out the multitude of stores, billboards and junk food outlets as we pass. A guy in a giant panda bear outfit dances on the sidewalk swinging a banner with 'fast wax,' on it and a thirty-foot-high inflatable elephant bends in the breeze outside a sports shop.

"Man, seems like everyone still shops on Sunday'" Fin says, staring at the endless stream of traffic. "Let's join 'em!"

"Okay, I'm in," says Freddie,

"Could use some new jeans," says Mick, "maybe pull into the Ross Dress for Less or the General Store or something eh Trout? What do you say guys?"

"Yeah, and I could check out some fishing gear too. Heard lures are way cheaper down here." I say,

"Whoa! Hang on boys!" Freddie yells from the back, his head hanging out the side window looking back down the street. "I just saw an ad on a sandwich board. Hang on. Go back! I'm pretty sure it said, whole keg, fifty bucks."

"What. No way, can't be," Mick says, "A whole keg of beer? A two-four costs almost that much at home. Let's take a look. Come on Trout, swing round."

Fin veers sharp right into a parking lot and stops. "Let's just walk back. It's only a block. I don't want to turn left back into the traffic."

We hop out, happy to move, ready to let some wrinkles unravel from slept-in clothes. The sun is beaming down, cool but strong. the stream of traffic relentless as we make our way back past a shoe-outlet store and a car stereo center. There is a four-foot-high sandwich board sign just ahead on the other side of the street. "Just like I said," Freddie says, gesturing with his head, "whole keg, fifty."

"Shit man." Says Mick.

"We've got to have a look at that man," I say, "I wonder if it's a full size. Don't they hold like ten or twelve dozen beer, those things? You have to use some kind of tap to get the beer out, eh?"

"Yeah, they hold a shit-ton of beer. Remember last year at the Grad party? Those guys had two of them. Lasted most the night for the whole grad class." Fin says.

We cross and walk up toward the shop ahead. They have all kinds of beer insignia all over the front, and cases stacked up inside in front of the windows. "It's like a giant beer outlet store," Mick says, "probably got every kind of beer on the planet in there, frickin' truckloads. Freddie, go in and check it out. See if that's really the deal. If we all go in, we'll just get kicked out and that will be the end of it."

We know he's right. Freddie nods and steps in as we kind of back away toward the sidewalk to wait. It only takes him about five minutes to emerge again, smiling at us as he walks over. "Yeah boys, no bullshit, a full keg of Ranier. The full metal keg for only fifty bucks, unbelievable. Only catch is you gotta pay a ten-dollar deposit on the keg and another ten on the pump, but you get it back later when you return them."

"Shit man, we've got to get one," I say, "but how are we gonna get it across the border? It's huge."

"Well… we've got that split seat in the front that's loose." Fin says, pausing, considering,

"Maybe we can take the whole middle section out, that console, and put it in the trunk and then put the keg in the gap and cover it with the blanket or some clothes and stuff."

"Yeah, and we can bring back the empty later cause an empty one can't be illegal, right?" Says Mick. "We're going to have a kegger boys!"

"Yeah, we'll probably have no trouble. They're never that uptight at the border when you're going back home." Says Freddie. "Let's do this. What do you say boys?"

"Let's go see about taking the front seat apart first," says Fin.

We head back to the car already planning the next party, "the house shaking kegger," as Mick says.

Fin finds a Philips head screw driver and crescent wrench in the trunk and I shine a cell phone light under the seat from the back while he manages to remove the cushion console, which leaves a nice sized gap between the front seats with just a couple of metal rail brackets left near the floor.

"Perfect," says Freddie, "It'll just rest in there nice with a bit of padding along those rails to keep it from rocking, then we can cover it with our extra crap."

"I guess," said Fin, "but remember guys, if this thing goes sideways at the border, we're all in this together. You guys gotta help pay my way out of the mess. I've heard they can seize your car."

"It'll be fine," says Mick, "She's gonna totally disappear in there… just like magic."

We pull round and head across the street through Division avenue traffic and turn into the alley, parking in behind the beer store. Freddie goes in with our pooled cash and his fake ID. We're all in awe as he comes out in less than ten minutes rolling a keg of beer out the door. We all cheer and hop out. "Nice work man." I say to Freddie, the other guys crowding round too. "How'd they like that ID. No problem?" I ask.

"Had my thumb over the expiry date when I passed it over… didn't seem to notice." Freddie says, smiling. Freddie and Fin each grab a side and heave the thing onto the front passenger side seat and Mick and I slowly lower it into the gap, padding it from the brackets with a hoody from Mick's bag so that it won't rub. We all peer at it in its final resting place. It's sticking up at least four inches above the height of the seats.

"Hmmm," I say, "Seems we have a bit of a protrusion there my friends, a growth" I say, fingers on my chin, "possibly a tumour. How about a little disguise?" I toss a folded blanket on top and Mick throws a jacket and Freddie's Ainsworth bag in as well. The whole mess looks pretty weird though, suspicious for sure, as if we are trying to hide something under a pile of stuff.

"Well guys, good enough for now, but I don't think this is gonna fly," says Fin. "Let's just head up the strip and see what we see."

"We got ourselves a keg boy, that's the main thing, can't wait to cool it off and hook up this pump. "Freddie says, messing with the valve and hose in his hand, playing like he's already draining the thing into his mouth.

We're making our way North up Division feeling pretty accomplished and a little short on cash. "How about swinging into the Sally Ann there 'eh Trout?" I say, pointing off to the right, "I wouldn't mind going home with something to show for myself and I'm running low on cash."

"Sure," Says Fin, I wouldn't mind scoping that out a bit myself. This one is huge, look at it."

We head in there and start rooting through aisles of clothes. Freddie goes over to the hardware area, and Mick starts fooling around with an old foozeball game by the change rooms, then joins Fin and me, flicking through hangers of jeans.

"There's some decent stuff in here," he says, "check this out, *Gap 69 straight legs* for twenty-two bucks," Mick says, "Cool. I'm going to see if these fit." Mick knows his brands. I just go for whatever fits right in the ten-buck range. I stack up a few things. So, does Fin and we head for the cash out line, looking around for the other guys. Freddie runs up behind us tossing a giant pillow in the air. "Guys, I've got the answer!" he says, all excited- well as excited as Freddie gets anyway, which means just speeding up his usually slow drawl to some kind of normal pace.

"Yeah man, check it out," We look. It's a giant overstuffed, kind of off-green, corduroy pillow, with a couple of stains on one side.

"Yeah, Freddie. You've got a pillow. We see it." Says Mick. "This is the answer to what?"

"The keg, dick head! Check it out. It's got this zipper on the back, so we just take out the stuffing and zip the keg right in, or at least cover it to the floor. And it even almost matches the colour of the car seat! I was thinking… Trout, didn't you have one of those flexible cup holders before you ripped out the console?"

"Yeah," Fin says.

"Yeah, right, so, perfect, we just put that on top and the keg is like part of the car boys." Freddie says, like all proud like he's just invented a new kinda light bulb or something.

"I'm liking this plan Freddie," I say, "I knew we brought you along for something…cool idea. Let's try this."

Out in the parking lot we find a garbage can and dump the guts of the pillow into it and slide it over the keg, then rethink when we see how hard the 'pillow' is. We grab a bit of the stuffing back out of the garbage and put a thin layer of it back in so that the top of the keg softens up a bit, "more like upholstery", says Mick. We put it all together and carefully lower it back into the slot. The cover fits right to the floor, pretty tight too.

"Damn, that does work well, "Fin says and puts the cup holder on top with the flexible rubber flaps hanging over both sides. Mick jams his to-go cup into one of the two slots, and there we are surveying our custom car with built in keg, all set for international transport. "Nice work boys. Good shopping Freddie." He says, "man, we're good."

"Okay guys, lets pull out. Time to gas up and grab a bite." We continue on up the drive, looking for the 'highway 2' turnoff to Canada. A half hour later we turn left onto the secondary road and relax into the return trip, leaving most the traffic behind. I grab a drum stick from the pail of chicken and pass it along to Mick in the back. "Toss me a can of beer, eh Wifi." He says, "gotta wash that shit down with something.

Fin leans back, spinning the wheel through corners with two fingers, turning the radio dial with the other hand. He finds a rock channel and turns up a Tom Petty tune. There's a lull in the mood as we just cruise along lost in our own thoughts as forest and fields blur by alongside.

In awhile we pass by Ione, a tiny run-down town that consists of a one block downtown surrounded by a few houses and a gas station. It's not just the sky that's gray, it's the whole town. Another gas station sits at the far side, boarded up. Train tracks parallel the road and remind me of the ongoing chaos back in Procter. A row of box cars sit still along a siding, look like they've been there a long time. "Whoa, check that one out." I say to whoever might be listening. I'm pointing at the third car in. It stands out against the drab back drop cause of what looks like a fresh paint job… graffiti, covering the whole side, save one gap where the sliding side door is partially open. It's intricate… loud text, with blended figures. "Hey, hold on a minute Fin."

"Yeah, pretty cool." Fin says, glancing over, slowing. "Shit yeah, check that out Freddie," Mick says.

"Fin, can you just pull off a sec." I say, "I wanna have a closer look. Check out the local style." He pulls off on a gravel shoulder to stop.

"Gonna pick up some tips there Wifi?" Fin asks, "What's that say anyhow? Can't really make out the second line."

"Yeah," I say, getting out and stepping around the car to have a better look. "Probably cause it's not in English. Looks like Spanish to me, Racion de…" I'm sounding out the words, but one overlaps the next and they're not familiar so it's harder… "think, the next word is, 'hongos.'"

Freddie hops out too, lights a smoke and leans against the hood. "All looks like Chinese to me." He says, "But check out the teeth on that guy eh? … sharp."

There's a crazy looking head, probably two-meters tall, with a spindly neck, sticking out from the lower corner of the side wall, bending around on an angle, sharp teeth and huge blood shot eyes staring out at us. He's got mushrooms sprouting out of his skin and there's more mushrooms overlapping in behind him… behind the text, in 3D, like they're growing off the box-car walls. "I think that's the word for 'mushroom.' Mick says, "Hongos.

Hey, who'd have thought a little shit hole town like that could produce good art? Pretty cool."

I pull my phone out of my bag, leaning through the open window and turn it on to take some pictures. Then I walk down the line a bit cause there's a couple more good ones up ahead. There's a tanker car that's painted to look like a guy's hands that are breaking through a space in the steel so that his face can stick out through the side-wall, eyes and tongue bulging out. On another car, between the vertical ridges are some horn players led by a guy in a gas mask, each painted into his own slot. Neither of these cars has any text added. I take some shots, stroll back to the car. Freddie and I hop back in. Fin pulls out again. "Yeah man, they did a great job on those," I say, "great detail, and texture… see those eye brows? Reminds me of Mono Brow," I add, smiling. "Yeah, it's true," says Fin, "… we'll have to wave at him on the way back through… mother fucker. Say g-bye."

"Right, here we go." I say, running my hand over the disguised hump between the two bucket seats.

"Think I'll moon Mono on the way by past the Yankee side." Freddie says. "Almost there, boys."

"Yeah, it's still a ways," I say, "past Metallaine. Remember Trout, gotta stop for a minute there to pick up the package." I'd told him a couple days ago about stopping there at the post office. Gabe Framer had called me a week or so ago and asked me if I could. My Dad had told him we were going, and he had some parts or something to pick up there that they won't ship across the border. "Just a couple of parts for my winch and some kind of supplement. Got 'em on Ebay." He'd said. "Stuff made in the US, so no duties at the border. Won't be a problem, just show 'em the receipt if they ask." He'd said. "Saves me some driving… really appreciate it Ariel… buy you a beer. Thanks."

"A case," I'd said, but I was just kidding. Anyway, we've got plenty of beer now.

We pass over the long steel bridge before Metallaine and take the turn into town. "Shit, this one looks just like the last one." Mick says, looking up the street.

"Yeah, cookie cutter isn't it," Fin says as we cruise slowly along the block, 'look they've even got one of them boarded up gas stations. Maybe it's a chain meant to look retro." The buildings are scattered in clumps, empty lots between, mostly built of brick, old red chipped brick. There's maybe two people on the street, otherwise looks more like a ghost town. A rusty sign hangs off two chains up ahead on the left marking the 'US,

Postal Service', an eagle logo below it. A dirty American flag is drooping down off a bent flagpole on the other side of the door. We pull in and all hop out to stretch as I walk over and swing the single glass door open; hinges squeak and a chime rings as I do. The floor boards move as I walk to the back. The place feels like a movie set in the wild west, could have been an old saloon or maybe even a tea house. It's not just a post office, that part is at a side counter at the back; the rest of the store is full of cheesy cards for sale, wrapping paper, ribbon, doilies. I pass a stack of weird hats made of old beer cans, a real shopping Mecca. I get to the counter and an older woman in a faded dress shuffles herself over, arms and chin all jiggly, asks, "What can I do ya for dear?"

"Just here to pick up a package please." I say. "It's for Gabe Framer. Said it would be sent general delivery."

The lady looks at me, nods and turns to the wall behind that's full of little square shelves, divided into a grid like they have up at the ski hill, to put your boots in for the day. She scans the wall, then pulls some packages out from one of the squares and puts them on the counter. "Gabe Framer. Right. Got three of 'em actually, for Framer," he says, double checking the print on each. She glances up, eye cocked at me.

"Right, okay. Thanks." I say, reaching for them as she pushes them over.

"Sign right here then." She says, pushing a form and pen over my way. "Right down here, once for each."

I sign and pick up the packages. They're pretty small, but the one shaped like a cannister is heavy, the other two, flat, narrow boxes. I walk back out across the creaky floor and get out of there as she and the other woman who's sitting behind a glass counter knitting, both stop what they're doing to stare at me leave.

"Fin, will ya open the trunk for me? I'll throw this stuff in the back." He's leaning up against the brick wall outside staring down the street. Mick and Freddie are strolling back across toward us from the other side.

"Fucking in-bred back woods place eh?" yells Freddie from the middle of the street. "Probably full of Meth labs and guys who fuck donkeys. Look around," he says, arms up in the air, "reminds me of that movie, 'Fargo'. We'll probably get thrown in a chipper if we hang out here too long." He slaps the hood. "Hop in boys, times up."

"Yeah, lets burn." Says Mick, looking around to see who's listening to Freddie's latest insight.

I unwrap the packages like Gabe had said to do. "Can't be bringing concealed packages across the border," he'd told me. I toss the two winch parts and the can of whatever powder that is in the cannister, in the trunk then throw the wrapping in the trash can that's on the street corner and stuff the paperwork in my pocket. We all pile back in, turn back down the block and hang a right back onto the highway, north.

In just a few kilometers the signs are already warning to slow for the border. We're all pretty quiet as we pull up, a nervous tension keeping a damper on the mood as we approach. Fortunately, Freddie doesn't drop his pants on the way by the US, customs building as we pull around to the Canadian side.

The customs officer slides the window open and says, "Afternoon boys. How 'bout passing all the ID's over to me." He's looking in, scanning the group, then takes the stack that Fin puts in his hand. We tell him where we're from and how long we've been away, then he slides the window closed and turns his back.

"Guess we're good." Says Freddie. "Anyhow, we already ate all the drugs." He adds, grinning.

"For fuck sake Freddie, just shut it man," says Mick, whispering, "who the hell knows if they listen in."

"Just sayin,'" he carries on, "we got nothing left, even cleaned out the beer cans at Metallaine." He leans forward, stroking the material over the keg, smiling ear to ear, the glint in his eye sparking nerves, like static electricity, through the car. I shoot a serious glance his way, catching his eye, trying to silently dampen any potential flare-up. Problem is, you never really know with Freddie, if he'll see your disapproval as pro or con in his calculations on how to react next.

The window slides open again and instead of the officer handing us the I.D.s like we'd hoped, he says, "Okay guys, just pull it on over ahead to the left. Just a random pass." Then he motions for the car behind us in line to pull ahead as Fin brings us up to the pullout fifty-meters on.

"Shit," I whisper, "thought we were through with this bullshit." A second officer is waiting for us as we park again, a short, solid guy with a crew cut, muscles bulging tight against his navy- blue button up shirt. "Alright, everyone please step out and away from the vehicle," He commands as we open the doors. "Just behind the barrier there, or inside. I'll just be a few minutes."

We wait just behind the line, watching. He bends into the front on the passenger side, opening the glove box and even pops the cap off the fuse box. He seems satisfied with that and to our relief, moves to the back door to check under the front seats from the back. He pulls out some socks, a wet sweater and some underwear, stuffs them back under. Freddie snickers under his breath, "Damn, I hope he didn't get shit stains on his hand from that pair." Mick just scowls at him. Then the officer slides his hands in between the back seat and the trunk before standing up. We relax a bit, shuffle our feet, ready to move, thinking it's done, but he just walks around the car, past the rear door on the other side and hops into the driver's seat. He pulls a small flashlight out from his belt and clicks it on. We're all watching intently, too intently for sure. He can probably feel our eyes trying to move him along. I don't think any of us are even breathing as he taps on the door panel then slides his fingers under the dash, leaning low to shine the light under, before moving his attention to the hump between the seats. He runs his hand along the material, then lifts the magnetic cup holder that's sitting on top, off, bends it, dropping a couple of coins that were stuck in the bottom out onto the seat, and then puts it back. He's reaching under, toward the floor, toward the base of the keg, when Freddie whistles, while looking over at a huge semi chip truck that's just pulled up next to the bay where we're parked, the air brakes letting off pressure with a whoosh as he stops.

The officer glances up at Freddie, distracted. Freddie says to Fin, next to him, who looks paralyzed, eyes averted, "You've heard eh? Those guys move kilos in those trucks man, bury 'em in the chips, probably put people in there too, fuckin' terrorists with weapons."

The officer looks up then, sits up straight and looks Freddie in the eye. "You've been watching too many border-cop reality shows son."

"Maybe." Says Freddie, looking closely over at the semi, "Gotta love some of the methods though. You guys must see it all."

The officer gets up, clips the flashlight back into his belt and asks Fin to open the trunk, ignoring Freddie. He finds the keg pump in there and picks it up, looks at more closely, then drops it and picks up the winch part I'd unpacked in Mettalaine and drops the shaft into some dirty clothes. He looks over at Fin and says, "What's with these parts and this pump… buy them in the US?" Trout just mumbles something about his brother leaving a sump pump and some parts from the wrecker in there before

I can tell him I'd picked them up in Mettalaine, "Been in there for weeks." He says. The border guy seems to lose interest, doesn't bother with the plastic can of powder. After another quick scan, he shuts the trunk and says, "You boys had better be on your way. I'll get you your passports."

We don't waste any time pulling out. Once we're around the first corner, there's a spontaneous release, as we all seem to take a deep breath at the same time. "Right on!" Mick yells, "nothing to it, bringing a keg across eh boys? Freddie man, you piss me off sometimes but I gotta say, I think you're the reason we made it this time." Mick punches Freddie's shoulder, who throws his head back, grinning.

"Yee haw!" Fin shouts, "Keg party next weekend! Yeah, nice work Freddie… terrorists in a chip truck 'eh? I swear, he'd have been pulling that keg outta there in another second."

"Just came to me." says Freddie, smiling nonchalant, "Figured he was getting a little too close there."

"And we even forgot to stash the pump," I say, "but it didn't really matter."

We pick up speed, heading home, feeling elevated like a winning team as we pass by the Welcome to Canada sign.

CHAPTER 10

Gabe

If there is going to be a disagreement about something it will often begin in the bakery. There are only four tables and they are very close together so it isn't a place you can, or would go, for that matter to sit alone and ponder or expect to concentrate on something other than your coffee or a neighbour at the next table. I make a point of dropping in at least a couple of times a week, even if it's for only a few minutes, but often, I'll just go at night for a slice of pizza. I'll pick up a few cold ones down the block at the store on the way to share with whoever happens along, which usually helps pick up a lively discussion. There are few people I don't enjoy sharing some time and banter with, Hector is one of them. Points of view at the bakery are many and widely varied, something I enjoy, but if Hector is there, I'll just say hi and move on to another table. There is only so much you can discuss with a guy that is usually bent on being angry about something. If someone is for something, you can count on Hector to be against it.

Tonight, there are several people scattered through the place already, Hector is sitting with his neighbour, Sam. He is stabbing his finger into the table making a point. Sam listens, nodding. I'm relieved that it won't be on me to have to engage him. Hector glances up at me with a bemused glance as I pass the table, stops mid-sentence from whatever he'd been lecturing Sam about and says, "Heard you up cutting on the hill behind our place yesterday Framer, doing some clear-cuttin' up there eh?"

"Yeah, clearing off the whole mountain Hector. I'm going to clear it then pave it so you can park your RV up there." I say, trying to sound more friendly than sarcastic to keep his hackles down.

"Well, yeah, sounded like it. I could use some clear-cutting up there. Makes for easier hunting." He says, both elbows leaning on the table, shirt sleeves rolled up, staring over at me.

"Anyway, how do you know it was me cutting?" I ask him. "Can you tell from the sound of my saw or have you got laser vision or what?"

"Oh, I know more than you think. I've been up there myself on the west wing of the new logging road. Went up there with the forest service when they were out too. Told them that I think we should clear off the whole goddamn area right down to the creek. Lots of beetle kill in there anyways."

"Got that right." Sam says shaking his head. "…Yep, lotsa that beetle kill up there alright."

"Yeah, well cutting away a bit of beetle kill is one thing," I say, "clear cutting the whole area down to the creek is another." "Well, I figure that's the way to go. That way you get the beetle kill patches and in between you get to take out all the cedar for a real payload so that bloody mill can actually make some cash, instead of just lolly-gagging about paying lip service to the huggers." He sneers, looking over for approval from Sam on the other side of table.

"Mmmhmm," says Sam. "Yep, got that right."

"Hector, that's steep in there," I say, rising to the bait, ignoring Sam. "Bad for erosion and anyway, there is no support for clear- cutting anymore around here."

"Got lots of support for clearing that area out," he argues. "Better than just watching as it lights up and burns in the next heat wave eh? I think it would look great all opened up, nothing left for miles and I could just sit up there in my pick-up next October and pick off white tail as they head to the creek for water, maybe even get some elk in there with all the extra grazing. Perfect, a win-win, meat in the freezer and money in the bank."

I just shake my head and move on toward the counter. Hector just snickers as he cradles his coffee, watching the door, waiting for his next victim, mumbling something back to Sam under his breath.

I say a quick hello to Katie who's behind the counter, pour myself a coffee in my to-go cup. I add a bit of cream from the jug in the fridge, leave a few coins on the counter and leave without another word. I hop into my truck and slam the door. It's getting late and I still have two loads to cut and deliver, no time to waste. I head back up to my most recent cut, Hector's proposed clear cut. I've already cut and split a mixed load of fir and larch and have the pile waiting there, ready for me to pick up. I get it stacked to the top of the side wall panels on my truck bed and with my saw sticking out of the pile, I pull up to the landing nearby to turn around.

As I'm turning, I notice a pile of cigarette butts in the road where someone has dumped their overflowing ashtray. "Friggin' slob" I say to myself. "Morons, dropping stinking garbage in our watershed." Probably Hector, hanging around up there waiting for something to shoot. One day he'll set the whole place on fire himself. That train of thought gets me going so as I head back down the mountain, I'm mulling over the argument I'd had with him. I hate it when the appropriate responses only come to me in the minutes and hours following an argument. During any kind of verbal confrontation or disagreement, unless I'm prepared for it, I usually find myself struggling for the right words, or missing the mark and leaving the dispute feeling weak and lacking. I'm not sure if that is how it's perceived by others, but it's often how I feel coming away. I try to respect the opinions of others, whether I'm totally opposed or not, but I have little forgiveness for myself when I feel I've missed a good opportunity to expose an adversary to an alternative view. I've had many such altercations, usually pretty level-headed dialogue I guess, but when voices rise and velocity increases, I often stumble, getting lost in the emotion and lose my way.

"Guess I'll never make the debate team Em," I say, walking into the kitchen after deciding to head home for a few minutes before dropping off the next load. She is in the kitchen chopping onions on the butcher block counter. I sit on the wooden flip top trunk by the entry and unlace my boots. "Just had a bit of a run in with Hector again, down at the bakery." He's trying to convince the forest service that they should expand the beetle kill cut blocks and clearcut everything in block C up the west wing of the new logging road. Figures that we should clear all the way down to the creek because there's lots of valuable cedar down there. And he thinks that if it's opened up by the creek, he'll have a better vantage point for hunting."

"You know Hector, honey. He loves to get you going. Loves to get anyone going."

"It's all about personal gain with these guys," I continue, "but what about water quality, erosion issues, natural regeneration?" I flip off my boots and walk into the kitchen, kiss Emily and have a look in at the pot that's starting to bubble on the stove. "Well, I guess everyone will get a chance to have their say at the annual general meeting Gabe. I just saw a notice about it for next week." "Yeah, I know; saw that message too. Just wish I could have come up with some quick response to get Hector thinking," I say,

"but when I get all heated up like that seems like all the facts and data in my head just start steaming and boiling together like that tomato sauce you got on the stove there and I just can't get it to simmer down long enough to put the words together."

"Oh well Gabe, Hector won't have much pull with that line of thought anyway hon." She says. "Can't see many people being interested in increased harvest levels, especially now, with the value of wood being in the tank."

Prices lately have dropped off because of the state of the economy and so it's been hard to turn a profit in the forest sector. "Probably he'll forget to even go to the annual general meeting anyway. Half those guys never show up so how much do they really care anyhow? I think Hector is just trying to get you going

Gabe."

"Yeah, I know, but still…."

"And I guess he's done a pretty good job of it." she says, chopping onions vigorously. "Maybe time now to settle down a bit. Have some lunch with me?" she says, tossing the chopped onions into the pot. "I'm going to grill us up a couple of sandwich melts."

I'm still leaning over the counter trying to find reasoning in the patterns of the wood grain for why we have to share the planet with cantankerous neighbours. "Let's have a beer with lunch and just take it easy this aft," she winks. "Auntie Sandy took the boys out." She quickly slices some fresh bread, tomatoes and Edam cheese and is buttering up the slabs as the cast iron pan heats on the stove beside her.

"But what about my deliveries?" I say. I'm not much for taking it easy in the afternoon. I always feel that I should accomplish as much as possible during daylight hours each day and save the relaxing for later. But I can hear a soft tone in her voice, a slight inflection that can only be detected by partners in a long-time relationship, something in the tone that says, there could be more involved in this relaxation than just relaxation. I know that the kids won't be back for several hours. I know my wood delivery can wait. It is early in the season. No one really cares about wood delivery timing right now. I saddle up behind her, link my fingers around her waist and nestle my face into the long wavy hair along the nape of her neck.

"Okay, lets." I say, "and maybe we'll even have time to practice a song after, so we can play something together next weekend when the family comes over, without forgetting how it goes.

"After what?" She says smiling seductively, "what you got in mind?"

We don't often take time, just the two of us, not when we're at home anyway. It feels good to break up the routine, especially when, breaking up the routine, means tossing around in bed in the afternoon with no kids in sight. We even managed to practice that song later on, 'Angel of Montgomery,' the old John Prine tune that I'd wanted to remember. Emily sings it real well when she can read the words, and now I think I've got the chords down on my guitar.

Later, late in the afternoon, she heads into town to pick up the kids and have dinner with her sister Sandy and her Mom, so I decide to head back to the bakery to cap off the day on my own, pick up some pizza and beer. I like to catch up with whoever is milling around the village when I can. It's light late these early summer days so the last direct sunbeams are just dropping behind the mountain, temperature dropping with them, as I walk through the door just after seven. Heat wafts from the kitchen where pizzas for tonight and baking for the next morning are being prepared; it spills over those seated in front, a comforting heat/aroma combination, especially on an unusually cool summer evening.

The windows are steamed over. Music plays from some sketchy little speakers connected to an old laptop on the corner table over by the cash counter. The art on the walls looks fresh and bright in contrast to the stained paint and dusty surfaces around the shop; looks like it just got changed. Graham, the owner, has alternating local art on the walls which changes every month or so. I haven't noticed this set before; it's a series of pieces, similar to each other, all featuring storms, lightning bolts and flash fires. I like it. The forties retro chrome-legged tables and chairs are scattered, regrouped in no particular order, most now occupied. I pull up one of the few spare chairs and sit with Sarah and Phil, a couple from just across the street – regulars.

"Hey folks, what's on tonight, anything good?" I ask. "Went for the Thai basil tonight." Phil says, "Ordered it about half an hour ago so I figure it should be ready in about two and a half hours," he smiles. The bakery is well known for its slow service. Sometimes I think people go there because of it.

"My beer will be gone by then and I'll have lost my appetite and my memory, which is what always bring me back." Phil carries on. "How's it goin' Gabe?"

"Yes, haven't seen you in a while Gabe," Sarah cuts in. "Been around... just wandering down a different passage in the maze than you guys." I say.

"Yeah, the maze. Well at least you're not lost and stranded... or are you... where's Emily tonight?" Phil asks. "You escaping?"

"No, well, kinda... they were out earlier, in town, her and the boys, be back soon, so thought I'd come and check out the local action. Guess this is it," I say, popping the cap off a bottle of Kootenay Ale with the heel of my Bic lighter. Graham doesn't mind people bringing beer and wine into the bakery. He doesn't have a liquor license and so this BYOB is a good compromise he figures. No one is really sure if it's really legal but often, in Procter, if it feels fair, and safe enough, people don't pay too much attention to rules and regulations.

"Hey Graham." I say, standing and walking over a few paces to make myself heard over the music and chatter, "How's it goin'? What's cooking over here? I just want a slice or two of whatever you've got."

"Hey Gabe, good to see you." Graham says. He's slicing up a pizza on the bake table, slips a giant paddle under it and slides it into a pizza box to-go.

"Got a couple of Hawaiian left and a fresh veggie just out and up for grabs. What's new, what kind of trouble you been in this week?"

"Ah, the usual, you know I came up with a new pyramid scheme: you work an extra fifteen minutes a day so you can make more money every day than the one before."

"Hey, sounds like my life," he answers, glancing up, "I'm working toward freedom eight-five, can't wait until I reach twenty-four hours a day so that I can get really rich," Graham says, always ready with a comment.

"Hey Gabe, what about that Jumbo decision?" he asks, glancing up a moment, more serious now. He knows that I would be well aware of the decision that most in the community were against- the most recent announcement, the one the Provincial Liberal government just released, explaining how they have created a totally new, fictitious municipal government, complete with councilors and a mayor, of a 'city', in this case, the Jumbo Valley Municipality. They've created this 'city' so that the new council can approve building a Resort complex in a Regional District jurisdiction where the people are totally against it. "Are you thinking of running for mayor up there in the next election?" he asks, a sly smile on his face.

"Yeah, what a bizarre fantasy this has become eh Graham? Like some kind of political wonderland. If it weren't so corrupt and destructive, it would be funny, or at least amusing. Even I could never have imagined that they would be so imaginative." I continue, pacing behind him. "Guess I should give them more credit. Where do they come up with this stuff, like kids playing SimTown, creating a city council for a town that doesn't exist, a city with no people? It sounds more like satire, like some Hollywood film plot, than simple Provincial politics, eh? Fuckers." I am getting louder now, realizing it, pausing when I notice Sarah and Phil looking up. "But hey, for now, guess I'll just eat pizza. Pass me a couple of those veggie ones, okay?" I grab my beer and drain almost half in one tilt.

Graham slips the paddle under two slices, deposits them onto a chipped white plate and passes it over. "I love the government." he says, smiling sardonically, as he turns back to start topping up the next pizza in line. "They are like the weather forecast, always giving you something to talk about but never anything really defined, always ambiguous. Like, we will have some grey periods followed by some darker grey periods followed by some lighter grey periods."

He's right; politics is all about speaking in grey, saying a lot, but saying nothing. I've had it with that kind of politics. Gets me all riled up when I think of how they try to play both sides of an issue, hoping to gain votes, not only on the Jumbo Resort proposal. It's been their same tactic for fracking proposals or the pipe line proposals that Enbridge, Keystone and Kinder Morgan have come up with, where they plan to move tens of thousands of barrels of dirty tar-sands oil through sensitive habitat every day, dissecting animal migration routes and threatening the land and water with future spills. This government pretends to play both sides on these issues, but we all know that as long as Enbridge,

Kinder Morgan and the rest are funding government elections, that they will get their way in the end. Seems to me, that more opposition than a simple vote against, needs to take place. Action, not words.

I take my two slices and find a seat as Graham picks up the next pizza, he's finished dressing, sprinkles it with a shaker of Parmesan and turns around to open the oven door to slide it in. A wave of hot air and the rich aroma of melted cheese floods over us once again as he slams it shut, wipes his hands on his stained apron, and announces to no one in particular, "Large meat lover's comin' up."

I can hear the boys are back and still playing outside as I pull the truck into our yard. It's around 9:00 pm, and still not completely dark. Their eyes have adapted better to the grey light than mine 'cause I can't see what it is they're both chucking rocks up at. I walk through the yard behind the wood shed to get a better look. They don't seem to be noticing the cool dusk air both still in tee shirts. They don't see me; the corner of the wood shed is between us. "I think I got that one in," screeches Noah, in his high pitched voice. "Nah, didn't." Gavin says, "now watch this." I pause a moment to watch silently from behind. They are trying to throw rocks into a wood pecker hole about four meters up the cedar tree by the shed. Emily is up on the back porch folding some laundry that she had brought in off the clothes line. She waves to me and smiles. It's just a few meters to the wood shed where I drop off the tool bag from my truck.

"Emily shouts over, "You boys… it's time to head in now… getting dark. Come on now." She grabs the stack of folded laundry and takes it inside. I come back out of the shed to nudge the boys in but stop in the shadows a moment when I hear Gavin telling Noah, "The glacier burros, yeah, just like I said, they're like little donkeys, only with really, really long hair. They come down at night, from the mountains sometimes looking for ice. They need ice to survive you know; they eat it," He says, knowingly. They've both stopped throwing rocks now. Noah is looking around, up the hill into the dark forest behind the house.

"Yeah, sure," he says hesitantly.

"Tellin ya," Gavin carries on, looking up into the darkness too, following Noah's gaze for a moment before looking back to him. "They are a lost species left over from the last ice age, you know, like alligators and sharks, and now they're just looking around for the next ice age, right, trying to find it, but they can't so they get real mad. Gotta watch it, 'cause they'll come up behind you and kick your ass."

I can't help but chuckle to myself, at this, but they don't notice.

"Yeah, right. Like you've seen one." Noah challenges.

"No, haven't seen one," Gavin says, all stern like, "but I've heard about how one kicked a kid right into next week."

Noah, gazing up at the sky now, mind wandering off to the ice age, watches his brother quizzically, churning through the possibilities.

"Hey boys, lets head in now." I say, striding up behind them. They both turn and say, "Hey dad," at almost the same time. Gavin says, "We were filling the wood pecker holes up with rocks." The three of us walk through the back doorway, letting the screen door slam behind. I close the door to block the cool evening downdraft from the hill behind as the night settles in. The boys run up the stairs noisily, Gavin chasing the cat, Noah protesting in defense of the tortured creature. I glance out over our backyard as Emily comes back into the kitchen. "What'cha see out there?" she asks.

"Just trying to spot one of those glacier burros." I tell her with a grin as I walk by. I drop myself into the chair in front of my office desk and sit reflecting again on another introspective dialogue I'd had with Noah early last year. Emily and I were planning a day hike with the kids; a full day up to Drinnon Pass in the Valhallas. I asked Noah, "Do you think you're big enough to handle a hike like that now so long as you don't have to carry much weight?"

"Weight?" He asked, peering up at me suspiciously.

"Well yeah, you've got to carry your own stuff at least, like your rain jacket and a sweater in case the weather changes."

"Oh yeah, 'kay. I don't mind that... but you mean the climate might change?"

"No Noah, the weather of the day; its unpredictable, not the climate. Why do you ask?"

"I've heard stuff 'bout the climate change, on the radio and from you and mom talking, what happens if the climate changes when we're on top of the mountain? Will we have to run for it? Maybe we should hide in a cave." His eyes are all bright with concern but at the same time you can see the gears of his imagination working.

"Then we could just live there up in the mountains in a cave, just like you did dad, on that trip you were talking to mom about, from before I was even born, right?"

"Oh, so you remember that eh, hearing about that?" I ask him, a little surprise in my voice. He hears more than I think he hears. "Yeah dad, it would be fun. We could build a tree house too in case it floods, or we could dig a deep ditch to hide all our food and keep it from getting burned by a forest fire."

I spent a lot of time reflecting on that conversation in coming months, pondering that if a four-year-old was considering consequences of global climate change, flooding and fire, my own four-year-old, worried about the state of the future, what will I do about it. How can I help ensure his future? How far am I willing to go? I don't remember being worried about things like that at his age.

The next morning, I am on my way back home after picking up one load of wood. It's Saturday; I figure one load is enough. The bag of ice I'd picked up at the store on the way home is dripping onto the seat beside me as I drive back toward our place. Emily had called me to stop and pick up a bag so she would have enough to mix up a couple of batches of Margaritas later for the gathering she has planned. She's been pressing limes to get ready. She is the social coordinator of the family for the most part.

It must be her warmth and energy bring people to the dinner table pretty often 'cause I don't invite people over that much. It's a good release to let loose with friends in the easy atmosphere that our home offers, and a great way to find out what everyone's up to. People often comment that they feel at ease at our place, that it feels comfortable, like home. Maybe it's the soft wood finishes or maybe the wine and memories. The place is dated and scarred with use. The irregularity of the upright log construction of the old original structure, and the pots and pans hanging from the sloped ceiling off the wrought iron hook rack add texture to a square room. The chipped brick chimney and rustic, plank flooring accent the mix. People don't seem to feel self-conscious or reserved when they're sitting in a place where they don't have to worry about spilling something or scratching the floor, lends itself to free expression I figure.

When Tammy, the new cash counter girl at the store swings the bag of ice across the counter, I have this flash memory of the girl I'd been infatuated with when I'd been working on a fire fighting crew a long time ago. I'd been just out of high school years before. Funny how vivid a memory like that can be after all those years - flashbacks - another form of self-persecution. I've always regretted my inaction on what I've known since, had been a missed romantic opportunity. She'd been waiting for me, Alice, I think her name was, to make the first move, and I'd been paralyzed with the awkward shyness of a late blooming teen. Not long after, I would often reflect on how obvious her intentions had been and how oblivious I'd been at the time, to her advances. "Damn, she was hot too." I mumble to myself. "What a body.

Bloody moron." I say to the rear-view mirror, as I pull back out on the road away from the store. I know that regret is kind of a useless sentiment, yet I catch myself wrapped up in it momentarily from time to time. I often find myself wondering just how things would have worked out if... but hey, life is interesting, not always that rewarding, but not dull, not routine. I have no patience for routine or regret for that matter. I've usually opted for self-employment, irregular hours and an overwhelming drive to have some control over my own destiny. 'Course, you sacrifice a predictable pay cheque and the security of a pension plan that way, but it's too late now- just can't see following orders at this point. Hopefully I'll never have to.

I slam the door of my muddy, 79 Ford 4x4 pickup, tuck the ice under my arm and pack my tool box in the other hand to head around back of the house where the chest freezer sits under the overhang of the roof. Space is a little tight in the house these days now that there are two kids and it seems that accumulation is leading to overflow. I know I've got to finish the upstairs addition soon or we'll be spilling out onto the road.

Emily is standing at the sink when I enter, one-foot resting on the inside of the other knee, like a stork, a familiar sight. That stance has always reminded me of the painting of an African woman by a river in a batik my parents have hanging on the wall in their house. She looks so natural and content somehow, perched like that while she does the dishes or rolls out some pastry on the butcher block. "Hey Gabe," she says. I stride over and hold her a moment, kissing her on the neck.

Hey babe, what's up? Been following the news at all today? "I ask.

"No, what's goin' on?" she asks, "anything wild and crazy?" "Yeah, well I guess, if you call creating a municipality in an uninhabited, remote wilderness, wild and crazy, and then after creating the municipality actually appointing an unelected Mayor and council to operate the fictitious city."

"Oh, so they actually followed through with that absurdity?" She asks.

"Yep, just announced it early yesterday, unbelievable."

Emily is familiar as well with the tensions that have been building lately around these government maneuvers, not only here in Procter, but all over the east and west Kootenays; this manipulative action, promoted by the Jumbo Resort development lobby. It's something that most had considered too far-fetched and desperate to actually be implemented. Now here it was, and all those opposed to the development have been left reeling once again from what we all consider an elaborate, deceitful, dictatorial maneuver by a government so bent on appeasing big business that it flagrantly disregards the will of the vast majority of those it will affect most: the local population, wildlife, waterways and wilderness.

"Yeah, and now, their installed mayor will run the *municipality*," I mock, "up at the Jumbo glacier. I wonder if he'll have a desk looking out over the giant uninhabited wilderness of his city limits? I ask, moving past her to the fridge. "They even have a budget paid for by taxpayers. They've already outlined the first agenda; it's to discuss the approval of building permits so that the developer can begin construction of the resort asap… bloody bullshit." I say, popping the cap off a cold beer and kicking the fridge door closed, Emily's eyes following me, silently, as she works the dough. "All this, possible due to the bureaucratic shuffle of an unelected council who govern a city with no people." I grumble to Emily as her fingers deftly enclose pastry triangles over spoon-fulls of spinach and feta filling.

"I guess it shows that when you are so single minded about a certain issue, nothing can block the way. They have found a loop hole to control the Jumbo area." Emily says, stating the obvious, as is often her way, something I often find myself waiting for now, or annoyed by, depending on my mood, like watching a storm cloud move in, knowing it's going to rain, but just sitting there waiting to get wet.

"Yeah, well I think it's time that we become just as single minded in our response. I've had enough of these guys bullying us into submission. I don't want to be a passive protester anymore. It's gotten us nowhere. I'm not sure I can live with the knowledge that there has been new construction started up there. I don't know if I'll be able to sleep much knowing that they'll be pouring concrete at the foot of a glacier that people have been fighting to protect for going on twenty years." I find myself speaking in spurts, haltingly, spitting the words out, as if I'm mad at her, not the government. I bend over to pick up the files and axes I've left in the corner earlier, set them down on the bench beside my beer and hold the first axe blade up to have a closer look at the condition.

"Well fair enough," she says, ignoring my angry tone, as she tends to, "but be mindful of your intentions and who you share them with. Remember how they're trying to link you to that CPR derailment. This could be the same, if anything happens up there." she drops it, echoing my thoughts once more. She places all the triangular pockets on a baking sheet covered in parchment paper, covers them with a clean damp cloth and sets them aside. "I was up there, you know," I pause, sitting down with the axe blade laid flat on my leg, the blade just clear of my knee so I have room to file. "Before the announcement - I knew it was coming down the..." Emily interrupts, "up there? What? When? I don't remember you going up there recently"

"Yeah, I know. I didn't want to worry you. I got all worked up. It was last Thursday night, after work, remember when I came home at 4 am? You barely woke up, thought I'd been at Randy's place, well I was up there doin' reconnaissance."

"Reconnaissance? Worry me?" she blurts, "what are you, Batman now? Are you putting together some mission that I don't know about, that you don't want me to know about?" She asks, as she continues to put dishes away from the drain rack, shoving them into place.

"No Em, look, if I didn't want you to know, I wouldn't be talking about it would I? It's just come to a head lately. These guys are moving forward at breakneck speed with their planning, all of a sudden, regardless of overwhelming opposition and local discontent. Why should we all just roll over and play dead?" I add emphasis to the word 'dead' as I press the file hard against the axe blade held between my knees, the fluid motion and pressure sending a dusting of steel to the floor with each stroke. There's a pause. Her eyes settle on me, waiting.

"It was a full moon, night mission." I tell her, my voice calmer now, "the sky was clear; the place lit by the moon. If you just looked off beyond the mess, it was just like it always was…. just ice and rock, meadows and water. You can hear the melt of summer, even at night. It was still cold enough though, cold enough that I could walk right on top of the snow where it hadn't melted yet."

"What mess, Gabe?" she asks, "Have they already started? You should have told me..." she starts, then lets it fade off, "I thought they couldn't start until after this phony municipality gave them permits." She adds.

"Yeah, true, but they have cleared a bunch, just haven't built anything yet. They have bulldozers up there already a container too, probably full of tools and materials, as if they already knew about the approval in advance, ready to start construction at a moment's notice. There's tangled piles of uprooted stumps, mud and rock - it's a mess. No bloody accountability."

She slides the tray along the counter, pausing, looking over at me again, says: "Let's talk about this some more later, Gabe. We need to talk this through, but right now, we need to prep some stuff for the dinner. These pockets are just an appetizer." She nods toward the covered baking sheet. "And I'm running out of time; we're doing Indian tonight, a couple different curries with prawns and toasted seeds, maybe a belly dancer or two."

"Right on, I'll be the judge," I say, smiling back at her. "Let's do it. I'll come back in and help in a bit. Just gotta head out back a minute, put these blades away." I say, rising.

She says to my back as I'm walking out, "and don't be doing anything about this without letting me know...no more *reconnaissance*. You've had enough attention from the CP investigations lately. Don't give them any more reason to be poking around here."

I carry on toward the back shed carrying my tool bag, reply over my shoulder, "Just going to put a few things away before people show up," but what I want to say is that I have to get back up there, that I need to see what they have done now. I need more detail so I can deal with these bastards. Maybe she's right, that I shouldn't go too far, especially now, but what is too far? Shouldn't I fight for what I think is best, for the planet, my kids?

The dinner gathering lasts to almost midnight. They usually do, these things, especially when the food is so good and the wine flows without reservation. Emily and I haven't hosted one of these dinners in a long time, seems like. We both enjoy having people over though, miss it when it's been a while. It's the answer to socialization when, going to town, just takes too much money and driving time, plus, if you go out in town you always have to worry about how many drinks you have before going back. So, often, here at the house, or at someone's house, we'll gather for the evening dinner with other families, friends who have kids of their own preferably. That way, everyone is occupied, not just us. The kids usually go upstairs to the boy's room after a while, or they'll go outside on warmer summer nights and we'll have a campfire. Some nights I'll light the sauna and the kids will sit in there, soaking up the heat before jumping in the pond. I like to go in the sauna too, later on after everyone has left, stoke it up hot, so hot that when you drop water on the rocks it spits back at you and the steam rushes up so fast that it takes your breath away. I'll just sit in there sweating, watching the orange flashing light of the fire bounce around on the cedar wall across from the open vent in the wood stove door.

I woke up early the next day with a little too much wine from last night and a turmoil of ideas tumbling around in my head keeping me from a typical Saturday morning sleep in. As is often the case, I need some time alone, usually with my axe, to clear the mind. It's a good way to sort out tension from whatever source. I rise quietly and without disturbing Emily, go downstairs and out. I walk across the dewy grass to the woodshed, the cool air bringing goosebumps up on my forearms. I haul in a few big butt-end cedar logs, left-overs from the mill, stuff I'd picked up a couple of weeks earlier when I'd dropped by to see the guys there. I'd been picking up a few pieces of rough-cut cedar that I'd needed to patch the garden fence. Cedar logs are the best source for kindling. They are the easiest to split, and fast to burn, so I always pick up a few whenever they're available. I like to use my hands when I have ideas swirling round in my head, whether we need kindling or not. I find that the motion and rhythmic repetitive action of splitting is a good remedy for sorting the swirl. I'd been lying awake for a while last night, with the words, 'single minded', running through my head. Was I being single minded? If so, how *can't* I be? I have to react to this latest assault by the Jumbo developers and their government cronies, don't I? Someone has to. I can't just keep passively helping with the organization of the Jumbo Wild lobby while all their efforts fall on deaf ears, can I? We have been fighting this thing for almost twenty years and yes, there has been some success, otherwise the thing would have been built by now. Still, here we are, having to continue repeating the same arguments, years later, carry the same signs at rally after rally, repeating the same old tired slogans, sticking the same bumper stickers on our cars… for what?

My hands move automatically, the axe rising and falling in a whirl of motion, grasped by the right hand while my left holds the cedar chunk in place, my axe inching closer to the fingers with each stroke, schlit, schlit, schlit, the thin cedar strips peel off and spring away from the chopping block to land in a scattered pile, like pick up sticks settling from a drop. Tension builds and drains and leaves space for ideas to form as kindling piles up around me. I organize the mess of sticks into the stack already started in the bin by the entrance to the wood shed. Split, collect, stack, split, collect, stack, split, split, split; they shear off faster and faster; schlit, schlit, schlit, as my focus is intent and purposeful, my movement automated.

Emily made a good point about attention from the CPR. It's not only that. There are all kinds of issues I have been linked to: I was arrested in the case of the anti-logging campaign, been investigated in two different CP Railway issues now, had publicity during the 'Save our Ferry' campaign. By being vocal in the past, I've been cast in a somewhat suspicious light. If anything 'happened' up at the Jumbo development, I would need to lay low, in advance, and later, be cautious in my approach… never be linked. Being anonymous can't be that hard can it? Can't risk turning any heads.

There's been too much action in and around Procter… can't afford to be aloof. When the CP rail train derailed back in 2001, some fourteen years ago, when the two trainmen were killed, there had been an investigation, which had shown that the land slide that had occurred was caused by natural erosion. Since then they have had all these other problems. There was the 'hold up', just three years ago, and now, this huge derailment and spill. There have been suspicions. And even though investigations by CP police have been inconclusive to date, they're still working on it, still convinced 'that culvert blockage is consistent with an intentionally placed diversion,' causing the derailment this time.

"…placed diversion." I say to myself as my eyes glance over the rising pile of kindling. "Heard that line enough in the past couple of months. Time to move on." I haven't been paying attention to accumulation, only thought. Then the rhythm, my train of thought is broken by Emily's voice. "Gabe, coffee's on!" she shouts from the back door. I stop. I'm breathing hard, beads of sweat on my brow have formed into rolling droplets despite the brisk morning air. The pile has risen up around the chopping block again. I raise the axe with one hand and swing it hard into the block. 'Gonna make some changes; I say to myself, under my breath. I feel energized and spin around, ignoring the scattered mess of kindling and walk back to the house to a waiting cup of coffee steaming on the table.

The kitchen is empty. Emily must be back upstairs in the bedroom. I pull out a chair and sit, cradle the coffee and sip slowly as I consider the many forms of protest, each with its own individual validity - one method can strengthen and support another, can't it? Just because one is deemed more extreme than another, by some, doesn't make it wrong does it? If anything, more radical action can make the more moderate responses that much more credible, can't it? I will be doing them a favour, the moderates. I'll help to create the perception that the passive protester, the eloquent environmental negotiator, is the moderate, the diplomatic preference - the credible choice for the government to negotiate with, to listen to, especially when what they consider a more sinister, extreme force is at play. The aroma of the coffee rising from my mug is as intoxicating as untested ideas, fresh air and a new day.

Emily walks in, holding her cup and an armful of folded towels. She kisses me on the cheek as she moves into the kitchen. "Morning Gabe, you're hot, were you splitting out there?"

"Yeah, you know, just sorting stuff out. Nice day. Good to get the heart pumping, clear the head…coffee's great …helps lift the fog of last night's wine, oh and that Margarita."

"That was a good night, wasn't it?" she says, dropping the towels on the kitchen counter.

"Yeah, great. And we almost nailed 'Angels from Montgomery,' eh Em? sounded good, 'specially with Seth pickin' up the harp." She sings softly: *"How the hell can a person go to work in the morning and come home in the evening and have nothing to say.* Think I got those lyrics wrong last night, but I like 'em."

"But hon, after a few glasses of wine, it all sounds pretty good," she smiles, then slowly starts putting dishes away from the drainer. She glances over at me sitting, contemplating my cup.

"You've been thinking." She pauses, "it's the Jumbo thing isn't it?"

"Don't worry Em, yeah, …just thinking… still no crime last I looked." I say.

I have definite thoughts on the next direction to follow but at the same time I realize that I will have another opinion to consider - Emily's. I'll have to keep her informed this time to some extent. I know my habits: to plunge headlong into new projects and challenges, on my own, sharing little till it's nearly done, but some previous experiences have been reminding me to hear other points of view these days prior to, not after, deciding on a given train of thought. These current ideas are consuming me, growing, like a root system, branching out in a myriad of directions. It's exciting to think about, but who can I tell? There are very few people I feel inclined to burden with the responsibility of knowing what I'm considering, someone who will be both helpful, knowledgeable and supportive of the cause, but will at the same time, remain quiet about it? I've usually avoided asking for help in the past, opting instead to try to work through problems on my own, but in this case, I may be left with no choice. This just seems too big, too complicated to tackle on my own. One step at a time. Right now, I only know that I've become resolved to move ahead. First, I'll need a map, some kind of direction to follow, don't want to be lost.

As Emily carries on with her tasks, moving purposefully around the house, I refill my coffee cup. 'Yes, just need to follow direction,' I mumble; something I can usually do is find my own way. I head to the desk where my computer is. I want to see a topographical map of the Jumbo area. I suddenly find myself reflecting on the visit I'd had with my cousin in Toronto earlier in the year, being lost, on foot, without a map, losing track of direction, something I pride myself in not doing- but I tell ya, cities are much harder to navigate than forests and mountains, for me anyway.

I'd been walking along Dundas street, in the Kensington area, gotten turned around while being distracted by vendors, colourful characters, eyes following beautiful women, not street signs. There are people from all over the world there. I'd become totally disoriented but kept walking toward where I'd thought the condo of my cousin was located, over on Delisle Avenue. I walked on for an hour and a half, always thinking I was just about to find the right cross street, but too proud or too withdrawn to actually ask anyone where I was. I don't like asking for direction. I rarely will instigate a conversation, I mean like in a bank line up or dentist office waiting room, or something. This was no different. Even though I know these kinds of interactions are often helpful, or at least interesting, I still generally fall into the old habit of avoidance, sit, tight lipped and try to figure things out on my own. Be in control. I have this guarded independence that is not always such a helpful trait.

I need to ask someone I know for help. I begin running various friends and neighbours' names through my heads as ideas form and solidify. My resolve is growing. This news of this government initiating the municipality act has now unleashed the beast. I just hope that whatever progress the developers are hoping to attain this summer is at least slowed down by the Jumbo Wild opposition. I need time to plan and I don't want to see a whole resort built up there by the time I'm ready. Should I take action now? If not, when?

The early heat we'd had in June has now succumbed to an uncharacteristically cool July, this week anyway. Kids are out of school now, so our schedules have been modified lately. Emily's dropped one of her shifts at the store for a couple weeks until we can adapt, and I sometimes start work a little later. We'll get it sorted out soon. Today I'm heading back to finish up a little fencing job at Pearl's place. I don't do the work for free anymore like I first did right after we sold the place to her years ago, but I do give her a better rate than most.

Emily and I had moved to Procter just a couple years before Pearl had shown up. The property prices at the time were really depressed but had begun to rise the following year, so, not long after we had bought our own place, and had a little equity in it, we managed to borrow enough on a second mortgage, to put a down payment on a cheap, run down, modified mobile, just down the road. It had a little land around it, quite a nice setting really and I'd spent time fixing it up to make it rentable. I found a young American couple that wanted to 'live close to nature.' I rented it to them. He was studying at the Oriental Sciences school in Nelson and she mostly stayed at home with their two young boys. They had paid their rent on time each month, and had stayed almost a full two years, but they were a constant source of irritation. While he was off studying each day, she seemed to have plenty of time to call me, two or three times a week, to complain about a draft, a dripping tap, or a loose door hinge... always something. When it started to get cold out, they wanted more insulation in the place, a better wood stove and new steps, 'that weren't so slippery.' They wanted to renegotiate the rent, 'due to the higher than expected heating bills' and they wanted me to install motion detector lights on each side of the house to keep bears and intruders away. I'd had about enough of them by the time they were ready to move on. There were few words of farewell as they loaded their almost new Toyota Land Cruiser up to the roof with belongings, placed the two boys in their car seats and pulled out, their New Hampshire license plates bumping along the gravel road one last time, inviting us to 'Live Free or Die,' before fading off down the highway.

"They wanted to pay less rent, but they drive a car that's worth more than the house they're living in," I'd complained to Emily, after returning from their final exit from the place that day. Instead of looking around to find better tenants, after the Americans left, I decided I'd rather just sell the place, take whatever gain had been made over the past couple years of prices rising, and maybe put it into a rental place in Nelson instead. I advertised it to sell in the local online classifieds and posted it on the community email forum; that's how Pearl had found it I think or did she just hear about it in the bakery? Can't remember. She'd been coming in to Procter a lot; hanging around the bakery those days, chatting with folks and decided to make a go of finding a home here. She was single at the time, still is, guess she was in her late fifties then, a confident, no nonsense woman, sure on her feet. She hasn't changed much over the years, just gotten a little heavier. She'd explained that she'd had enough money to buy a simple place after selling hers in Asbestos, back East. Our little place had just over an acre around it, all she needed, she figured, so she'd bought it, just spur of the moment it seemed like.

I had helped her out with some upgrades as part of the deal; putting in a smoke cabinet for her meats and fish and later when she was more settled in, a small chicken coop out back, an extension of the wood shed. I'd learned a lot from her about smoking meat and fish to make jerky. I found out over time that she had acquired an amazing amount of practical knowledge, a rare quality these days. She's got some Metis blood and seems to have learned a lot from that side of her family; the ones she'd grown up with back in Ontario. Sometimes, her voice will meander and fade when her mind has travelled down that path, the one her ancestors have followed. Her eyes get glassy and distant and she seems to take on a kind of mystical presence as though, for a moment, she's elsewhere and my being there beside her, is immaterial.

Other times, we would end up discussing her ancestral methods, treatments, recipes, mostly for smoking and brining meats, but sometimes she'll veer off and reflect on the bend of a light beam, or the pattern on a fern bough. Something to make you wonder about, make you think twice.

While I was there on various jobs, I even learned how to make corned moose meat. One time she steamed up a pack of that stuff for lunch while I was working there. Once it was steaming hot in the pot, she showed me how she'd just peel off strings of meat to layer on hot slices of rye bread with mustard and sauerkraut. The result was this rich, juicy, Moose Reuben sandwich, that spurted drippings all over the plate when you bit into it. The aroma from the melded flavours rose up in the steam, flooding the room, making you hungry for more, even when you were full.

I haven't seen much of Pearl lately. Stopped by to drop off some cedar 1X4 and some fence posts a while back, but didn't have time till now, to get over there and put the rest of the fence together. Still have to dig a few more post holes. I'll try to fit that in today. Maybe I can pick up some of that candied salmon she smokes or some of that jerky; she is usually game for a little barter. Maybe I can talk her into making up some of those Tourtière pies she's famous for, trade her for extra firewood or something, except usually, she only makes those up for Christmas Eve.

It's always interesting dropping in on Pearl, but really, haven't spent much time with her since back when we were blockading the road into the Lasca area together years ago. That's where we really had time to get to know each other better. There wasn't much to do there at the protest tent except wait and take up space in the road, keep the road builders out.

Summer is too short. Seems like the kids just got out of school but it's already the end of July, summer half over. The bloody Provincial government has already 'elected' and approved the full city council and mayor for their new Jumbo Resort municipality. Despite opposing arguments by environmental groups and the NDP who are the official opposition, the phony council moves ahead unimpeded. And so, aside from a few minor delays, they are able to issue road building and bridge construction permits by early August. The proponents have moved ahead quickly to begin road building. They don't want to lose any chance to alter the landscape. They know that any progress they make now, will make it harder and harder for those of us opposed to reverse that progress. In a flurry of activity, they've installed a new pre-fab bridge, built an equipment compound encircled by an eight-foot-high chain link fence, then erected hundreds of feet of rebar-grid within a maze of plywood forms. By the first week of September, regardless of protester opposition efforts and regional government delay tactics, the first cement trucks already begin pouring concrete on site, all of this proudly documented in photos and captions on the Jumbo Resort website.

Toward the end of September, there is little left we can do to stop these fuckers as dozens of cement trucks dump hundreds of square yards of concrete at the resort's future lodge location and chair lift sites high up in the formerly pristine wilderness of the Jumbo valley. All we can do is read progress reports, watch media footage and listen as the Resort promoters let us know what a great job, they are doing investing in our future. I'm reflecting on the Bruce Cockburn lyrics: 'If I had a rocket launcher, some son of a bitch would die,' as I click page by page through their online status updates.

Finally, a few weeks later, work is slowed, then halted due to heavy rains, which are causing erosion and rutting in the access road, so they lock down the project for the short term, with plans to continue in late spring, once they can plow out the road again. It's been hard to watch the fast-forward momentum of this project over the course of the summer. The only thing that keeps me from losing my cool every time I hear the news and see the pictures, is the realization that now I've gained some certainty about my intention to create some *real opposition*. My resolve has hardened like the concrete that has set in those forms. They have shut down operations for the winter and that'll give me start-up time, time to figure out how to deal with them. I can see now. It's clear. There's no other choice. They've pushed me over the line. I'll need to get back up there as early as possible in the spring or early summer when the snow melts off and assess the situation. Until then, I've got research to do.

CHAPTER 11

Pearl

Last fall, we'd seen the last of them full time CP clean-up crews on the tracks. They'd spent months there and seems they were able to sop up the mess pretty good, so now that it's warm again, and clean, I can walk along by the rails like I used to without all that racket. Winter has a way of coverin' everythin' up and givin' you a fresh start in the spring. Bracken fern and fireweed compete for top spot after pokin' their way through the compost of the last generation along the banks, all fresh and crisp like a felt pen on a blank sheet. It's all greened up now round them monitorin' stations they built alongside the tracks. They put in three of 'em, little metal huts, 'bout 200 meters apart, each with a circle of chain link fence around 'em. Sometimes when I'm walkin' by I can see CP workers, or government people workin' inside them, takin' samples and readin' monitors and such. They's nice and quiet, not like all them machines that was workin' all last summer out there on the clean-up.

Can't say as I'm missin' all that action. I like it just like this, all peaceful again. Well, less you count them investigators. They still come 'round doing what they calls, 'follow up.' To me, sounds like they jus' couldn't find the answers they wanted to the questions they was askin' and so they jus' keep askin' the same ones over'n over. When I'd walked in the bakery on Saturday mornin' Sam'd been sayin' to Hector, loud enough for all to hear: "Yeah, they shoulda just locked Framer up first thing last spring, put some pressure on him. Now the trail is stale."

Those two can fill ears with drama and hearsay even better'n a talk show host.

"Sure seems like that's what they wanted to do," I said to 'em, kinda buttin' in to their space on the way by to the sink with my cup, "but seems to me, they couldn't do it cause of what they call, lack of evidence."

"Yeah, well that could be," Hector says, "but I ran into them yesterday and they haven't given up yet. I had a few things to tell 'em too. They were taking notes, let me tell ya." He adds, soundin' all 'portant like. I stopped for a second to look him in the eye, then back to my tea cup circling. Tell him, "If swirlin' rumours runnin' round these tables was close to as accurate as them tea leaves reads in the bottom of my cup, we'd of had all of this figured out a long time back."

He jus' mumbled somethin' toward Sam, quiet like, probably figured I'd put a hex on 'em or some darn thing - maybe I shoulda.

Now, it's late in July already and while the days are still long enough and mornin' light early, I like to get up some days and try my luck castin' off the point for a Rainbow or a Kokanee. Sometimes I catch a Dolly Varden. Even if I don't catch any, it's just a nice time to be on the shore listenin' to the waves lappin' at the rocks, the osprey or an eagle fishin' alongside.

It's only a fifteen-minute walk down there from my place if I go along the road, then out the tracks that leads to the point at the mouth of the lake; I have a small old aluminum boat too, so I don't have to walk if I don't want to. It's parked down at Drake's boathouse. Stark, I call him. He's got a 7.9 Mercury outboard on 'em, runs real good. Drake lets me dock him down there during the summer alongside his boat house so's I don't have to trailer him back and forth whenever I take 'em out. Today, I just don't feel like takin' him out and hearing the noise of his motor, so I decides to just walk to the water and cast off the rocks. Water and air is calm today. Cottonwood seed is floatin' by, risin' and fallin' along air currents. If I were a cottonwood seed, I reckon I'd love that time of free floatin', just followin' the summer air currents, ridin' by trees' 'n water, fields n rocks until I finally found my place to take root. Fish are risin'. Just saw one, looks like a Rainbow, jumps clear out, must of been a ten pounder, at least, a beauty, but none of 'em are bitin' at my line so I decide not to stay too long. 'Sides, I want to get up the hill this morning fore it warms up too much and cut some willow for weavin'. There's a good spot up the trail behind where me and my neighbours live, up near the third switch back off Higgins road.

It's all wet in there and so the younger willow that grows out of the marsh, stays softer even though it's not early spring, which is when it is best to harvest it if you want to use it for weavin'. I take one last cast out into the current and while I'm reelin' in, a Mallard duck comes skiddin' in for a landing nearby, on both feet, leanin' back, like a water skier before comin' to a stop, then he dives right under when he sees me; they's funny, them ducks, acts like they own the place. I bring my lure up and hook it on my pole 'n head back home.

Today, I only need an armful of thin switches, maybe a half inch thick or so, to finish weavin' the arms of a chair. I like weavin' with willow. I'm more of a cotton weaver most the time, or wool, but workin' with the thick switches of willow makes for a nice change. All you need is a pile of switches and your fingers, nothin' more. It's simple and satisfin'- watchin' a form take shape from the movement of your fingers, turnin' switches into seats or a basket. My lungs are beggin' for more air, makin' me wheeze some while I'm meanderin' slow up that path.

I come up to the willow thicket through the wetland, there's moss growin', thick and lush alongside the trail. Lichen grows on all the rotten wood; mushrooms have popped up too, mostly gooey and rottin' from the heat - maggots eatin' 'em up. In the fall, a day or two after a rain, I often come up here to pick fresh mushrooms. I usually find the Boletus or Morels, but my favorite is the Pine. When I find the Pine mushrooms, I pick 'em all, all the fresh white ones anyhow, bring 'em home and fry some up with garlic and butter to have alongside my dinner. Then I slice up the rest and dry 'em so I have 'em to use later on, add 'em to soups and stews, or maybe a pasta sauce, in the winter.

I've already got enough willow switches cut down and stacked in less than an hour; my pruners workin' quick on the thicket. I stack 'em up neat and tie a bit of twine round the bundle so to keep it together for the walk back down. I'm pickin' it up to go when I hear a chainsaw start up, not too far off. The sound of the saw is quickly drowned out by a huge blast. I drop the bundle when I hear it, kind of shocked, and look up quick but can't see anythin' from the direction that the sound came from- too many trees between. I know I can't be far from Higgins road on my path. I'm curious to what is goin' on over there but I don't really want to get much closer, so I pick up my bundle and head back down the trail, thinkin': that sound wasn't a shotgun or a rifle, not a backfire either, too loud and too much vibration for that, so what? Why so powerful? Why with a chainsaw alongside?

I get back home in about twenty minutes and put the willow in the shade, covered with some wet burlap to keep it supple. Don't want it crackin' and splittin' later on. Got enough there now so's I can finish up my project one day soon, soon as I can get Hailey back over to work with me. She's been askin' for willow weavin' lessons, so now, before I work on one of my projects, I call her to let her know it's time for a lesson. I'm about to go back in the house when I hear a vehicle comin' up our road. I stop to look. It's Gabe alright, a partial load of wood in the back, saw stickin' out the top with the blade down in the pile to keep it from fallin' out. He doesn't look over as he passes my place, but I wave anyhow. He heads on up the road to their place, a trail of dust rising along behind the truck. It's only a few hundred meters further up, at the dead end where they live. Seems to me, it was probably him up Higgins that I heard. Not too many others do any cuttin' up there.

❧ ❧ ❧

A few days later I get a chance to ask 'im what that was about, still wondering. I'm pullin' up to the bakery for a mornin' coffee and cake, turnin' my truck round so's it's pointed back down the hill, when Gabe pulls up and parks just inside the parkin' lot on the flat. It's around 8:30 am, which is the best time to find people passin' through, seems to me, so that's when I likes to go. I park and amble on over as he's getting' out, sidle up to his tailgate. "Hey Gabe" I asks him, "how's my firewood guy doing today, still haulin' in this weather?"

It's a warm mornin' for the Kootenays, probably already eithteen or twenty degrees, the sky is open, the kind of blue that promises not to get in the way of the oncomin' heat.

"Yep, you bet Pearl. I like to stay steady. You are about due for a delivery yourself pretty soon aren't you? How many cords are you going to need this season? Still got some left from last year?" "It was a pretty mild winter eh?" He's still got the door of his truck open, peerin' over at me.

"I've probably got almost a cord left, Gabe, but I'll be takin' another three sometime before fall. No hurry, 'corse." I pause a minute, considerin'. "Think I heard you comin' down Higgins with a load on Tuesday mornin'."

He turns in his seat to finish findin' whatever it is he is lookin' for behind the back seat of his truck. He's rustlin' through some tangled rope and wrenches, brings out a roll of orange flagging and stuffs it in his pocket, puts the seat back up and slams the truck door. Some dried mud falls out from the wheel well and lands by my feet.

"Oh, yeah?" he says, "Yeah, was just hauling some dead fall out of there. Found some nice, dry larch up around the third switch back, musta come down in the last wind storm." he says, leanin' up, his elbow resting on the truck box now.

"Yeah, good," I says. "Reason I mention it is, I was up there too, on one of my trails that goes up behind the properties, not that far from the third switch back when I heard a loud 'splosion. I figured it was you up there, after I seen you come down. Sounded like some kinda blast, and there was a chainsaw runnin' at the same time. What was all that about you reckon?"

Gabe kinda looks real quick down at his boots when I say that, turns back toward his truck cab, as if he'd just remembered the thing he'd forgot. "Yeah," he mumbles under his breath, openin' the truck door again, rummagin' through papers on his passenger seat. He picks one up and glances at it a moment, readin' it as if he needs to read the answer to my question but is just checkin' to get it right, then he looks up, looks me straight in the eye and says, "Well Pearl, it's probably not legal, so I don't really like people to know so much, but I was messing around with a small explosive device to see if I can use small charges to help me knock trees down in the opposite direction that they naturally want to fall." He seemed a little anxious at first, kind of rattlin' off the words too fast, but is now loosenin' up z'iff he'd just remembered the answer he'd forgot. "You know, like when a perfectly good dead snag, say a giant Doug fir or larch, not far off the road, is there ready for me to take it out, but is leaning hard down the slope so's if I cut it, it ends up falling the wrong way, too far down the bank to haul it out, you know? So then, I figured I would try to blast out some soil on the high side at the base of the tree. Idea being that when the soil blows out and leaves a hole under the roots there, the tree will collapse into it and fall up the hill without even cutting it down."

He's looking over at me, leaning back on the truck, lookin' a little, I think quizzical, yep, that's the word. I like that word, quizzical, sounds like a bee buzzin' round a flower head.

"All sounds like a lotta trouble to go to get you some firewood Gabe. "Seems to me that lots of men, in general, likes to play with things that esplode anyhow. Ain't that the case?"

"Well, gotta say, Pearl, it didn't really work out that great first time 'round, but it was kinda interesting, fun to watch, to experiment." He says, smilin' a little now, lookin' more relaxed. "Sorry if it made you worry at all. Hope no one else paid any attention. Guess I shouldn't really be doing stuff like that near where people can hear it."

"Oh, I doubt that anyone heard but me, Gabe, 'cept maybe across the lake over in Balfour. Sound carries over across the water better than nearby. No, I think you was safe up there in yer back wood's playground. Safe with me anyhow, but you know, them investigators sure askin' a lot of questions 'bout you last year, and I've heard tell that they are still round from time to time now, so I'd say, yer pushin' yer luck with them shenanigans. Don't think they'd take kindly to the idea of you blowin' things up on the mountain, ya hear."

"Yeah, you got that right Pearl," he says, his voice harder, "But hey I don't believe much in luck and those guys got nothing on me. They're just moving through the motions, putting on a show for the media. This is probably the first time in years any of those CP cops ever got any public attention and so they don't want to miss out on the opportunity - can't blame 'em really." He says, chucklin', but ya can see the tension in his neck; the vein over his temple is throbbin'.

"Well Gabe, you comin' in with me for a cup of coffee and a snack then?"

"You bet," he says, relaxin' some again, "I can smell those rhubarb squares baking off from here."

We walk over the parking area to the bakery door which is wide open today, lettin' all the baking smells out with the heat. The screen door squeaks as usual when Gabe swings it open and we go in. Some folks are lined up at the till waitin' to pay, others are sittin' round two of the four tables stirrin' their coffee and nibblin' on crumble cake and toast, talkin' bout the flow of the creeks in the area and the snow pack, how it's meltin' off this year. Graham is back at the pastry table, where he often is, rollin' out some kinda dough. A puff of flour dust is still in the air from him tossin' a hand full across the surface. The stainless-steel bake oven behind him is throwin off lots of heat- addin' to the risin' temperature of the summer air.

Graham's forehead is all beaded up, sweatin', as he leans into the dough with the rollin' pin. Some banjo, bluegrass music is playin' from the laptop computer that is plugged into a little sound box on the table in front of the cash counter.

"Howdy Graham, Maggie." I say as I trudge over to pick a coffee cup off the top of the espresso machine and toss in a tea bag. Something sticky on the floor is pullin' at my sandals. Shammy, one of the village dogs, brushes by my leg and starts lickin' at the spot. I pass a cup to Gabe and we both fill 'em up, him from the coffee carafe, me from the hot water thermos.

"Hey, how'd Shammy get in? No room for dogs right now." Graham says, as if there was some kinda capacity limit that has jus' been passed. "Put him out will ya Gabe?" Or maybe he's worried 'bout them health inspectors catchin' him with a dog in the kitchen. He's told me that they drop in on him too. I'm not the only one they're after.

Gabe opens the screen and calls him out but Shammy doesn't go, so Gabe just takes a seat at the table by the door, starts talkin' to Alec, a guy who's sittin' at the table alongside. He's complainin', sounds like, 'bout the latest, 'dating disaster.' "Tellin ya, that Plenty of Fish site's got all kinds of women on it, but once you get one off the site and have 'em sitting there across from you, they're just not the same as you thought. You know. They don't look or act like the profile led you to believe, usually older and fatter." He says, shakin' his head. "Think I'll just stand off for a bit and wait for a new batch. Seems like, unless you're willing to travel way out, the picking is pretty limited around here."

"Yeah, well I'm sure that the women on that site are saying the same things about you and the other men, eh Alec?" Gabe says.

"Yeah Alec," Graham pipes up, overhearing the conversation from the back, "does your profile shot give a full-frontal view or just a shot from above the belly?" he laughs.

"Yeah Alec, and do you have a cig hanging out of your mouth in the photo?" Gabe asks, smiling.

Alec just smiles and shakes his head, runnin' his hand down over his belly, happy enough to be the target today, seems like. I sit down across from Gabe and Alec, at the table besides, with one of them rhubarb squares Gabe's always talkin' bout. I asks him, "Gabe, I was thinkin', if you do have a load next week, I could get started early stackin' it into my shed. I'll clear out some room in there just in case. If you come with bigger logs again, maybe I'll get Ariel over to do some splittin' for me too. He still workin' for you sometimes eh?"

"Yeah, pretty soon he'll be, mostly in the fall I'll get him when I can, when I've got lots of orders for split and delivered."

He nods, carryin on, "I get him splitting and loading my flat deck while I'm delivering a load with my truck and then I just fill the truck up again, hook up the trailer and deliver two, every second trip- works out good. He's a good worker," he says through a mouth full of rhubarb square, holding onto his coffee cup with the other hand, "sure, I'll try to bring you an early load Pearl, maybe more if you want. It's always better to beat the rush. No one's thinking about wood while it's still July. It was eighteen-inch for that stove, right?"

"Yes sir, eighteen-inch. Anyhow, time for me to get the goat milked 'fore she bursts." I say, pushin' myself up from the table. I take a last sip from my tea cup and drop it by the back sink. I pull some coins out of my change purse and leave them off by the cash register and make my way through the tables, sayin': "We'll see all you folks next time."

"See ya Pearl, next week." Gabe says, joinin' a couple of other 'see ya's', from behind, as the screen door squeaks open and bangs closed behind me again. Warm, summer sun pours onto the asphalt outside, already risin' in visible waves, like heat from the bake oven. The tall grass along the roadside by my truck is wilted over a little, like it's lookin' down for some water. We've only had a few hot, dry days in a row, maybe a week, yet the ground already feels like drought.

Been down to the bakery the last two mornin's so I guess I'll have to miss goin' tomorrow. What I find is that when I do a thing two days in a row, it's just doin' it twice, but when I've done it three days in a row, seems like a habit or ritual, pending on what kinda thing it is. Makin' habits is a bad habit, I figure, so I try not to make too many of 'em. 'Corse I do have to have the habit of milkin' my nanny goat. She don't feel too comfortable if I forgit. I rope her off to a fence post and pull up the milkin' stool. For a while there after them inspectors was here, I found myself lookin' over my shoulder when I'd be milkin' her, zzif I was doin' somthin' wrong. They got no use for a simple farmer, no sympathy, not for one like me anyhow. They need to find some sympathy, or is it empathy? I always get them two mixed up… then there's other ones… I looked 'em up…. telepathy and apathy, so many pathys, all leading different ways. I'm never sure which one to take. Anyhow, them inspectors just don't seem inclined to be offerin' any of it either way. They got me all jittery, rootin' through my things, lookin' round. They don't seem to have any kind of rule that can stop me doin' what I'm doin', but I'd rather they'd see us country folks is just tryin' to find balance with things; if they could see that what they are doin' is upsettin' the balance, they'd understand or least try to.

They need to understan' better about the balance, the world around us, even in my yard. The chickens eat bugs and weeds, my cat eats mice, my goat cuts the grass and when there's too many deer in the yard, I eat them. That's the kind of balance I like. 'Course I'm not supposed to be shootin' deer in my yard either, 'specially out of season, so I'm pretty careful 'bout that. Last time I shot one, he was eatin' my pole beans. It was late in summer when the beans are so high that he had to reach up to eat 'em. I let him eat for a while, then he moved on to the basil and tomato plants. I had already fetched my rifle by then. I keep it in the back shed, hidden behind the freezer. I keep the shells inside the freezer, all lined up in a box by the frozen peas. I knew that my closest neighbours, the Krokers, was away at the time 'cause I saw 'em load up their car and go out earlier, so I figured no one else would pay any heed to a single shot off in the distance.

I walked up close to him, near the garden gate. 'Corse the gate hadn't kept him out even though it's closed; that fence is all bent down in places and some of them deer know better than to let that keep 'em out; they just hop right on over and help themselves. I'd do the same myself if I was a deer, but if I was, I hope I'd know that I should run when a human comes out carryin' a gun. He jus' looked up at me, had a good look, then jus' kept right on chewin' on a mouthful a tomato leaves. When he puts his head down again to get another mouthful, not really too interested in me being over at the gate, I rest my rifle on a rail, sight him in real slow and easy and shoot him through the heart just behind the shoulder. He looked up at me all surprised, like a stranger when you ask him his name, kind of confused, then he had the good sense to take two or three steps out of the tomato patch and onto the path before fallin' over into the grass, so's not to flatten all my plants when he laid down to bleed out.

He's all wrapped up neat in small brown paper packs now, in the bottom of my freezer, most of him anyhow. Parts, I like to smoke into jerky.

The tougher bits and some of the organs and blood, I throw in the blender and mix up with stale bread and old milk for cat food or as a treat for one of them friendly dogs that drops by. I freeze it up in cubes, then thaw a few every week. The cats like the fresh meat, so when they smell more of it comin' their way, they usually stop by and wait for a sample. Sammy, my big ol' tom cat was more interested in the process than Shreddie, she don't have a long enough attention span, just pounces from one thing to the next 'ziff somethin' is always chasin' her, crazy Siamese. Sammy just comes by all casual when I'd been cuttin' that deer up. He waits all patient like, as if his plan'd always been to just while away the day waitin' up on top of the kitchen cabinet with no interest at all 'bout the deer meat.

But when I'd skinned the carcass out by the woodshed earlier in the day, it had been hanging from a crossbar just off the ground and he'd been below it lickin' blood from the dirt, so he already had a taste for it.

Inside, later on, he just sat there watchin' my hands work the knife through the meat and bone, waitin' his turn. I like to watch cats watch me. They are a peculiar beast; all independent and thoughtful, always lookin' like they're really figurin' things out, but they're doin' it for themselves, not for you, all that figurin'. Not like a dog does. A dog is always there for you, always tryin' to help and be supportive and obedient. Me, I have more respect for cats I guess, even though they ain't much use. Cat's won't come less they want to, won't be told what to do. You have to respect that. Have you ever seen a organized cat fight, or a cat race or even a drug sniffing cat? No, course not, 'cause they just don't care to help out. They're like me; got their own concerns to tend to.

CHAPTER 12

Hailey

I scan the land around my house, from the veranda, like the captain of a ship: grass needs cutting, branches have fallen in a previous wind storm and lie poking up in the yard, deer have pruned back my Azalea reducing it to a stubby nub…not so bad. These are problems I can deal with. It feels right to be back here again after three months away, much like it did last year on my return, only more peaceful. It strikes me now, that I was met by the opposite last year when I pulled up to the noisy, chaotic sounds of the CP Rail disaster relief crews working round the clock. Now I get to come back to what seems so much more like a sanctuary. Maybe this is the place I need to always return to? One tree planting season merge into the next; the aching joints and tired muscles beg once more for the promised break from daily exertion; the psyche begs for calm and solitude, and the poor bedraggled marigolds, dahlias and rose bush by the front path beg for water. I need to nourish these needs.

The property I'm on in Procter is only about an acre and a half, but it has lots of trees, those, and the high row of lilacs out front, shield it from prying eyes. I've been renting it now for more than two years, but I've got a contract that gives me a buyout option with part of the rent from the first two years to go toward the purchase. I have another six months to decide if I'm going to seal the deal or not. If so, I have to come up with another twelve thousand bucks as down payment in order to meet the bank requirements. I'm still thinking about it. Am I too young to own my own place, to settle down? Guess I could still rent it out and leave if I needed to.

Anyway, twenty-eight's not that young is it? I can hear my Father's voice, with his clipped words and heavy Russian accent, saying, "No, no too young. Need land, need man, cow, growing beets in garden, making kids." But he pronounces it: keeds. "Making lotsa keeds". Used to be, in his day anyway, a girl my age would be married and have a bunch of kids by now, "just like all Belikov's been, seence old country," yet, here I am, still single, well, usually single anyway. Investing in a home base could be a good thing though, I figure. Be self-sufficient. Still, I've got six months to figure it out, raise some funds. Hmmm, buy a house, or a trip across South America?

Right now, all I've really got to consider is what to make for dinner.

The house smelled a little stale when I first unlocked the door, but it's getting aired out pretty quick now with all the windows and doors open. The fridge hums along, flies buzz in the windows and I sing along to Alabama Shakes singing 'hold on… you got to…', nice and mellow from my Bose speaker.

Moving hips to the music, I unpack some groceries that I picked up on the way through Creston earlier. I had stopped there to kill a little extra time because I knew I was at least an hour early for catching the next ferry across Kootenay lake to Balfour. Long as you time it right, the ferry is the best way to go; it saves on gas and it's a way nicer drive than going over the pass 'cause you get to drive the winding number two highway along the lake shore. If it's warm and summery out like it is now, and you have extra time at the ferry landing, you can always hang on the beach and go for a swim too, like I did. From the beach you can see Procter in the distance on the other side of the lake, so it feels like you're almost home.

I'd been grateful to dig my bare feet into the warm stone pebbles of the beach, to feel their heat, to survey the surface of the lake in front of me. Then, I'd heard a heavy gait approaching, clomping through the loose stones, closer.

"Searching for a sign?" a familiar voice said. It was Ron. "Hey honey," I'd said, where'd you come from?" I sat up and hopped to my feet. "Just pulled up and spotted your truck in line." He says, moving closer. We'd hugged, his sweat stained tee shirt quickly engulfed me in its musky odour and flashing memories. "Nice warm body; been here awhile?" he asked, looking over my bikini clad body in a glance before dropping down to sit on the beach to pull at the laces on his short top hiking boots.

"Haven't seen you for weeks," he said, "Lookin' good, just come from 'Top of the World?" He's referring to the name of the park where I'd been planting the last few seasons, up near Invermere. We'd worked, and played together there, not only earlier in this season but also part of last one. I guess you could call us a casual couple, more off than on, without commitment, but always some promise. I'd missed him when he'd left to work with another crew a few weeks ago. I figured I wouldn't see him again till mid-summer.

"Yeah, just finished up two days ago and broke down camp yesterday." I said, stretching out again on my side, elbow propping head on hand, watching him as he pulled his tee shirt over his head, tossing it on the beach. "This is my first day off and man, it feels good. Can't wait to get home and spread out again…sleep in."

"Yeah, got that right," he said.

"Hey, thought you were going to be working another couple of weeks. What happened with that?" I'd asked him. "Or are you just on a break?"

"No. Plans have changed… contract got cut short. Would have shut 'er down anyhow…. getting too dry, so they've postponed planting the last blocks till the fall… probably October sometime. Looks like I'm on free time, just like you girl." He pushed himself to his feet and grabbed the tee shirt.

Now he's down to just a pair of shorts, but he's still got his socks on. "Gotta rinse this mess out. He strode off down the beach right into the lake, tossing the shirt in first before submerging himself too. He popped back up smiling, "Yes! …that's what I needed. Come on in Hailey! Feels great," he yelled back at me, then started swishing the shirt around, pulling the socks off and tossing them all up on the beach before doing a quick hand-scrub on himself.

"I was goin' in but not now that the whole area's been polluted with your b.o." I'd said, smiling as I walked toward the water. "I can see the swampy cloud around you from here." We lounged and swam in the calm Kootenay water for fifteen minutes or so, chatting, catching up on planting news, making summer plans. "Hey," I said, "Time to dry off, ferry's getting close."

We spread out on the beach for a few more minutes as the ferry unloaded its traffic, then sauntered back to the vehicles to drive on. On the boat, we carried on the conversation on an upper deck bench overlooking the lake, watching the opposite shores of Procter and Balfour near. As we parted ways to drive off, we kissed, lingering, and promised to meet the following weekend. "If there's a good live show at the Aurora in town, do dinner too." He promised.

My mind turns back to Ron as I pull the duvet off my bed to hang it on the line to air out. Each time we meet again, I'm reminded of how easy it is to be with him, to easily reconnect and disconnect each time. Sometimes I wonder if maybe we shouldn't always be doing the disconnecting part. I push the window of my bedroom open wide. The warm afternoon breeze flows in. I stand there a moment letting it wash over me, reveling for an instant in the realization that I have no agenda. I lie back on the cool sheets of my bed and lose myself in the freedom, breathing deep, blossoms and abundance.

When I wake up an hour later, a little chilled, in only my bra and panties, wondering for a moment where I am, grateful when I realize I'm not waking up in my tent. The sun has begun to set, the air temp begun to drop off. My toes are cold. Goosebumps climb up my arms. I dress, shower and decide that unloading my truck can wait till tomorrow. Right now, I'll just focus on making some dinner and looking through my mail; I've got quite a stack. I'd left the mail key with my neighbour, Molly, who'd agreed to pick it up once in awhile. I dropped the stack inside my door.

Maybe I'll go on vacuum patrol, I'm thinking, scanning the room, and suck up all those cob webs in the corners. Instead, I brew up some Earl Grey tea and settle down to the pile of mail, leafing through quickly to sort out the most interesting stuff, like birthday cards and cheques. It's always fun to add up the cheques at the end of the season.

The pay I'd be receiving from my planting season will be pretty substantial this year. I had started out with a bit of cash left from last year already too, plus I had been getting employment insurance for part of the winter, so I really hadn't needed to draw from my pay with advances this time. I figure I could invest the extra for a while in some kind of fund until I figured out this house purchase. I know I'll need at least twenty thousand to cover the down payment, closing costs, and some improvements on the place that are needed, like replacing the flat part of the roof that overhangs the entrance way. It leaked sometimes. I start jotting down the figures on a scrap paper, adding, totaling, estimating, making imagined plans as I simultaneously throw together a salad for dinner. I top it off with some braised chicken strips marinated in Tamari and wine, sprinkle a few cashews on top and sit down to enjoy a meal for one for a change.

As I review my notes, and columns of figures, seems to look like I could come up with most of the twenty grand I would need, maybe eighteen of it anyway, from this season's planting, then live off EI for awhile, and at the same time, start up some indoor plants to cover the rest.

I've seen lots of grow rooms over the years. It's the underground industry of the Kootenays, but I've never run one myself. I've grown plenty of outdoor crops though. Nothing too substantial but enough to have a good understanding of the process, the timing and plant maintenance and stuff. I used to grow just enough so that I would have my own personal smoke over the winter to save on buying it, but each season, depending on my living situation, I would add a few more plants to the crop if I could, get them all ready and strong, then plant them in as wet an area as I could find before leaving for the tree-planting season. Sometimes I would get a couple of days off during the season when we were changing locations and I could drop by to have a quick look at the crop, clear out weeds, fertilize and water, but otherwise I would just hope for the best; hope they wouldn't dry out or get grazed by deer, and usually I would end up with some kind of crop.

Last year I grew two and a half pounds of bud, which was pretty good, way more than I smoke and share with friends, that's for sure, so I ended up keeping about a pound and selling the rest. 'Of course outdoor bud is not as valuable as indoor and the market for bud has been dropping off lately due to some states legalizing, including Washington, next door, which has dried up a lot of the demand for BC bud, so my extra production wasn't worth that much. Now, with Canada too working through the legalization process, who knows what will happen? Guess I'll just take it as it comes.

As the summer flows by, I start to warm up to the idea of subsidizing my income this way, using this as the lever to push me into a position to own, rather than rent. I've crunched the numbers over and over and started figuring out how to put together a nice simple indoor grow op. I figure that would be more reliable than the outdoor. I'll try to produce and sell five or six pounds per cycle. If I could do that, I would then have enough cash combined with my planting pay to cover all the costs of the purchase, the home improvements *and* to repay the startup costs of the grow room itself.

I've run the idea by a couple of local growers over the past year, checked out different growing techniques. There are lots of varying systems and equipment for growing inside. Some people have pipe systems where they grow all the plants small in kind of a pyramid shaped set up where there are three or four tiers staggered up on each side forming a central valley, starting at about waist height. You can walk down the middle of each valley and see all the plants neatly lined up in rows along each side. They just sit in long six-inch, PVC pipes, with holes drilled out every foot or so and you drop the plant into the hole which is the same size as the plastic net pot that the plant is growing in. The lights are suspended down the center of the aisle giving equal light to both sides. The roots just dangle down into the pipe and tiny sprayers mist the roots every half hour or so from a central reservoir where the pump timer controls this powerful jet pump. They call it an 'Aeroponic System'. It doesn't require any soil so it's all clean and tidy and very efficient, but it's also very mechanized, which is kind of intimidating. There are lots of plumbing parts, pumps, timers and precision. I'm not sure I'm up for it. I don't really like the idea of learning all about that stuff, or, relying on someone else to fix it. Some people just plant the old school way, right into plastic pots with a soil mix that you make up at home in a wheelbarrow or on a tarp. They just plant, hand water them till the water runs through the bottom and that's that. It's kind of dirty and labour intensive but simple. The plants can just sit on the floor if you are going to grow tall ones, or you can grow lots of shorter ones in staggered rows if you build up some steps for them to sit on so they don't shade each other. With this method you have to be there all the time to water because nothing is automated. They will dry out in just a couple of days.

I was in Nelson at a small house party at my friend Helen's place late last winter when I got a tour of their little grow-op. She and her boyfriend have a little place in the uphill area of town. They have two little kids too, and she works part time as a landscaper for about half the year. Daniel, her partner works for the ski hill. If they can fit a grow op into their busy life, I figure it'll be a piece of cake for me to pull it off. How do people do all these things, and have kids too? Helen showed me her system before people showed up to the party that night. It was taking up about a third of their basement. Daniel had built a frame wall with an entry door in it to divide it so that they could separate it from the rest of the basement where the hot water tank and furnace were, and also so they could lock it up away from curious eyes. Helen told me earlier that they had originally had the whole basement full of plants and equipment, "back when the kids were just babies. But later," she adds, "as they got older, we just kind of got used to having it there - didn't think much of it, you know? Till last year, when Katie started going to grade one. Know what she did?" I shake my head in response. "I find her on the couch with her little notebook, drawing a sketch, looking all concentrated one day after school. I ask her what she's up to and she tells me, while she's drawing these long leafy plants with a green crayon, that she is, 'just getting ready for show and tell tomorrow'." Helen says, eyes wide, smiling, her arms held high, open wide emulating her daughter's message to the class.

"I ask her what she is going to talk about, and she explains that she's going to tell the class about the 'jungle in the basement, cause it's so beautiful and bright and warm.' We had a little family talk after that. Even though pot is technically legal now, growing more than four plants still has all kinds of rules and regulation around it and a lot of us just haven't met the requirements. The next week, Daniel reduced the size of the grow room enough to seal it up all tight with a door and lock. Man, that was a close one," she says, smiling, "so we turned the, 'show and tell jungle', into a workshop full of 'dangerous tools'." Helen gestures, quotation marks in the air. "Katie showed the class pictures of our tent trailer journey to Quebec instead. Whew." She smiles, turning into the hallway.

"Yeah, sounds like a safer topic." I say.

"Yeah. Okay, just follow me now." Helen says, walking down the stairs while Daniel and the kids cut up veggies in the kitchen. At the bottom of the stairs she says, "Here's some shades to put on. Makes it easier to look around at things without getting blasted by the light." She hands me a grubby pair of old sunglasses and puts a pair on herself. She has a shelf outside the grow room door with sunglasses, gloves, a respirator and some hose clamps on it. Below are shelves of plastic bottles with concentrated plant nutrients and additives, empty net pots, jars, bottles, plant markers, pruners and plumbing parts. On the other side of the door up on another shelf she points out a row of ballasts. "We keep the light ballasts outside the room so that they don't heat it up in there any more than necessary. These are the old school ones. You can get better ones these days."

The ballasts are buzzing away, each with an electrical cord trailing out behind, which are coiled together and bound with zip ties before going through a hole in the wall. There are six all together. Helen opens the door and steps in. "Okay, just step in and close the door behind so we can keep the vacuum," she explains. "The exhaust fan needs to always be sucking air through the charcoal air filter or the bud will stink up the whole house - the whole frickin' neighbourhood."

The lights are on and are kind of overwhelming for an instant as we step into the flood of lumens produced by six one-thousand- watt sodium bulbs. "Yeah, I can see why you use the shades in here." I say after wiping down the lenses and putting them on, "This is brighter than a white sand beach in Mexico."

"Yeah, not a bad place to work in the winter months." Helen nods. "It's all kind of warm, bright and tropical in here eh? I kind of like it when it's cold and wet out. It does get a little much in the summer though. That's why we have the lights in the off cycle during the day time. They just came on about an hour ago so It will be hotter in here in another hour or so."

She putters about a bit, absently pulling yellowing leaves off a plant and looking closely at the leaves on the undersides. "I used to have a bug problem in here, so I keep checking to see if they have returned. You usually find them on the underside of a leaf, spider mites or thrips," she says, studying a leaf before tossing it in a pail. "Hard to see, tiny little buggers. They can be a real problem, something you want to avoid. Damn it, I shouldn't have even touched a plant... just habit. That aroma, even though the plants haven't budded out much yet, still sticks to you. I'll scrub up before more people show up." She throws the leaves into a pail on the floor. "So, this is the flood table you were telling me about eh?" I ask her, pointing to the rigid, plastic table top full of plants by our side. She had been telling me that it was a good compromise. 'Easier than soil but not as complicated as a pipe system.' It does look pretty straight forward. Just a bunch of plants all about two feet tall, all grouped together on four-by-eight-foot tables with two lights dangling over each one. There are three tables, up around waist height, in the room, separated by about a two-foot gap so you can walk between to take care of things. "How many plants are on each table?" I ask. "Looks like a lot." They're so close together. These look really healthy." I motion toward the group. "Are they very old?" Helen ignores me a moment as she peers at a digital screen that is hanging on the wall above a huge plastic reservoir full of water. The little screen has wires coming out the bottom that trail their way into the reservoir full of water below. "There are about twenty per table." she says, "and they have been under the twelve-hour cycle for about two weeks already, so they are just starting to bud out." "Nice." I nod.

"Yeah, first they go through quite a growth spurt when you reduce the hours from the vegetative timing which is eighteen hours of light, to the bud timing, which is twelve. These are doing great. Should be a good crop. What do you think?"

"Yeah these look vibrant." I say, "all pumped up like they're ready to take off. Are these a Kush or some other strain?"

"Yeah, this is a purple Kush cross, a hybrid. Not as heavy as some strains but potent and sticky, easy to sell. Looks real nice in the bag, all shiny and dense." Just then a pump comes on with a whir and gurgle and starts dumping water onto each table from a black plastic pipe that's clamped to the top edge. The tables are actually shallow plastic bins about eight inches deep, sitting up on what looks like a 2x4 frame. All the plants are in rock wool cubes about four inches square, sitting on the floor of the bin side by side so that the the whole four-foot by eight-foot surface is a sea of green plants, branches intertwined, growing toward the lights above.

"The pump comes on for just a couple of minutes every half hour and floods the table tops with nutrient water from the reservoir. You can see that the tables are off level so that the water flows from the top, across the plants and roots systems to the bottom and out the drain back into the reservoir. Simple eh?" She says.

"Well, I'm not so sure it's that simple. Looks to me like lots to remember." I say.

"Once it's running it's simple, just pumps and gravity. The plants absorb a little bit of the nutrient water each time it's pumped over."

"Mmhmm" I say, taking note.

"Just hang on a sec, I'm going to grab the jugs and top up the nutes." She says, opening the door and stepping out. She brings three-gallon jugs into the room from the shelf outside and puts them on the floor by the reservoir. "The Trimeter, tells you your nutrient level, water temperature and ph balance." She tells me, pointing at the digital screen.

"And those jugs are the nutes?" I point.

"Right, … now, the nutrients are down to 580 ppm you see?" she says, nodding to the numbers on the screen. "That means parts per million. You want to bump them up to around 900 ppm, then let them deplete for a couple days. You also have to adjust the ph level so it stays around six and make sure the water's not too warm or cold. Only takes a few minutes once it's routine." She adds a little measuring cup of each from the three jugs, stirs it up with a stick and puts the lids back on. She has everything all in order and there are notes and what looks like a shopping list on a dry erase board beside the Trimeter. Helen is a very precise person, shows a lot of attention to detail, and it strikes me that I would like to pick up on some of those details if I am to succeed in this. Once she's finished stirring and adjusting, she grabs the jugs and opens the door. "You've got to change the nutrient, like flush it out once a week or so, trim the plants up, you know, lots of little things to learn, but the basic maintenance is pretty easy.

Come on, let's head upstairs before more people show up." She lets me pass so she can lock the door behind me.

Then she stops as I turn to wait, her eyes serious for a moment, catching mine. "You do need to learn to trouble shoot if you're going to do this. That is the key, to be able to go into the room and just listen, look and smell for a moment. Usually, when something is amiss, you notice right away if you're tuned in." She turns and climbs the stairs.

"Thanks for the tour there, girl. I'm stoked to get something like this happening one day." I say, trailing behind. "Just me and my little home-based business, hanging out in my own tropical basement next winter could be a plan. I would miss the real tropics, but hey, some extra cash could be a close second, 'specially if it means I can buy my own place."

"Yeah, sister," she says over her shoulder, pausing before the top of the stairs, "just let me know if I can give you a hand with it. If you choose this type of system, Daniel and I can point you in the right direction. Maybe work together a bit on cutting clones and getting you fired up."

"Oh, yeah, clones. I've never tried using them. I've only started from seeds before. Should be fun. A new learning curve." I whisper the last words to her as I hear other voices above in the kitchen.

After that, I had returned a couple of times, intrigued by the methods she'd shown me. I had helped them with their next harvest before I'd gone out planting this spring. We had chopped down all the plants with pruners, stacked them up on the floor in the basement and four of us, Daniel, Helen, me and their friend Bart, sat there, around the pile, grabbing one plant at a time, trimming them up, branch by branch bud by bud, till we ended up with buckets full of nicely trimmed buds. All the residue, piles of loose leaf, stems and branches, were left littering the floor. We listened to music and chatted away, our hands all busy, clip, clip, clipping, like a bunch of knitters making socks.

Then Helen carefully spread all the bud out on-screen shelves when we were done, slid the shelves into slots in a wall cabinet, turned on a fan under it to blow moisture off, and left it to dry. "Can't have curious neighbours or teens looking for some free bud, now can we?" She said. "The smell of bud is a powerful thing and very distinctive, 'specially at harvest time. When that resin is all ripe and sticky, you better be sure your air filter is doing the job." Then adds, "either that or get a license."

"Yeah, I've heard about those charcoal filters," I said, "work pretty good eh?"

Helen had warned me to bring an extra set of clothes to the job too so that "when we're done the harvest. You won't be leaving the house all covered in skunkiness," she'd said, adding, "if you get pulled over for a speeding ticket or even stop to talk to someone on the ferry or whatever they will know right away what you've been up to. That aroma sticks to you like glue."

"Yeah. Or stigma," I note. She nods, thoughtfully.

We wore latex gloves and long sleeve shirts. When we were done, we scrubbed off the excess resin from our wrists and fingers with vegetable oil. I even washed my hair. I came away from that visit convinced that I could do this thing. It felt like the right direction, something I could handle on my own for a while to make me more self-sufficient. Growers are saying that there will still be an underground market for years to come, despite all the efforts of government to gain a monopoly.

The next day, I gave her bank a call to see what the time line was like for getting approval if I was to have the down payment ready before December when my lease was up. They said I would first have to provide a property appraisal. The appraisal was only valid for a maximum of six months and it cost 450 dollars. I'm going to go for it now because if the appraiser comes after I've built my grow room, once I've got all those beautiful plants in there, well, that just wouldn't do, would it? If I call them now, I will have time to quickly get my room installed, get the plants growing and do the harvest all before December, then close the deal, and it will all be mine. After that I would have time to put in another crop and if it goes well, I could keep going with more and more crops, one every 3 or 4 months or, I could just harvest the next one in the early spring, then shut it down and go planting again for one more season. I'll decide that in the new year. For now, it's time to get an appraisal and start shopping for grow- op supplies. I saw an ad on Craigslist with used equipment the other day, lights, ballasts, shades and reservoirs, but it seems weird to buy stuff like that from some random guy online, so even though it will cost more, I guess I'll just go to the local hydroponics shop and pick up what I need in a few days, all new and shiny.

The day I drive in to check it out, I awake to sunshine streaming in my bedroom window. I usually don't sleep in long enough for that to happen. It feels real luxurious. I stretch out, still ironing out the kinks of the tree planting season from my joints. After a quick coffee I sip my smoothie breakfast and scan my 'town list', which has a second sheet attached, with, 'Grow Show,' written on top. Not very stealthy, I think as I toss my things in the truck and head toward Nelson. I decide to drop into the grow supply store first, but I park down the street a ways in case someone passing by recognizes my truck and wonders why I'm shopping in there. 'Course, you always run the risk of actually running into someone you know while you are in there too, which could be a real problem, but hey, what are you going to do? Just gotta go with it. I could go to a city nearby, maybe Castlegar or Cranbrook or something, and buy my stuff there where I can be anonymous, but then I figure, what's the point, cause I'm going to have to get used to shopping for all my regular maintenance supplies here in Nelson anyway.

Turns out the guys in there are cool anyhow. They never ask questions and they always bag up your stuff in generic black bags, no logos. If you want, they will even load up your car out back in the alley, like, if you are getting a bunch of stuff and don't want to go out the front door. I figured I would copy the same system Helen and Daniel have, just for simplicity's sake. I have plenty of room in my basement, so I know it's all gonna fit. I hand the guy at the hydro shop the list I've made. Daniel helped me write up the details and measurements, so it is pretty detailed.

"Sure," says the young guy at the counter. He's only about twenty-one I figure, has green hair and lots of piercings, covered in bling like a Christmas tree. "Not a problem. We'll get started on this right away, won't take long, but if you want to go and come back, feel free to just pull up out back and we'll load you in about half an hour. Otherwise you can just browse - up to you." So, I wander around looking through all the latest paraphernalia that they are selling. They've got automatic trimming machines, expandable drying racks hanging from the ceiling, complex extraction devices for breaking down bud and leaf into concentrates like hash oil, honey, and shatter, which are all different forms of more powerful THC concentrated products that you can smoke in these new vaporizers and other gadgets. I read through some of the pamphlets alongside, where different brands make all kinds of fantastical promises for their products to produce: 'massive buds, faster,' or to 'double your yield in just one crop.' The place looks more like a lab supply store than a head shop. There are aisles with multiple shelves overflowing with plastic jugs and beakers of all sizes. Colourful logos, with names like, 'Bush Doctor Kangaroots, Jungle Juice, Bloom Boom, Liquid

Karma and Massive, all promising 'faster growth', a 'sea of green.'

There are enzyme formulas, mineral additives, humic acid and ph balancers. An overwhelming number of options and additives. How do you sort through all these options?

On the back wall they have stacks of different sized net pots, rock wool cubes, tanks, tables and racks of plumbing parts, sprayers and electrical fittings. Seems to me that nothing is gathering much dust either. These guys are moving stuff out the door as fast as they can restock shelves. I guess the pot industry's not doing so bad after all. I'm reading the instructions on a bottle of rooting hormone, when buddy there, pops by to check in. "Yeah, that's a solid product for getting your cuttings rooted, but we have another new one, made by a local guy, an organic version that is real popular right now too." He says, pulling a small plastic bottle from a shelf behind me.

"Hey, you guys have too many options here," I smile, "how's a girl supposed to decide on anything.?"

He nods in agreement. "Yes, it can be confusing. Just keep it simple, is what I say. I know we sell a lot of additives, but if you are just starting up, I would advise you to just get going with the basics and see how it works."

"Sounds good to me. I'm not looking for a way to be more confused," I say, and we move to the counter to check out my stack that's piling up there. Other folks are wandering around the store shopping, looking out of the corner of their eyes to see who else is in there, or just avoiding eye contact altogether, pretending they are alone. "A couple of choices here though," he says. "In the 100-liter reservoirs we have this type." He's pointing over at a rack displaying half a dozen different plastic tanks. "That one is low and wide so it can fit under a table or whatever, and then we have this taller one that's squarer, takes up less floor space, either one works fine depends on your space and configuration really. Either way, the same pump and supply kit will work."

I look through all the options, choose what seems best and pay my tab, in cash. Buddy loads up my truck in the alley, turns out, everyone in this industry is named Buddy. I just learned that last year. Doesn't matter if it's a bunch of trimmers clipping bud, your friend's friend with the grow room, your friend's friend's dog, or the guy behind the bar selling you a half ounce… Buddy is the name.

As Buddy loads me up, he is giving me some useful tips on the installation process, such helpful guys there at the shop. Sometimes it pays to be a woman; I think we get better help and advice than guys do, or maybe we just listen better? I tarp the pile and weigh it down with some loose firewood chunks and a lug wrench, stuff that I have lying around in my truck bed, then I'm off. It feels good to have an exciting new project underway, specially a potentially profitable one. I can't wait to fill 'er up with my own personal 'sea of green.'

After loading up, I make a couple more downtown stops; the usual, Save-On Foods and BC liquor store, then on to the post office, Kootenay Co-op, and the drug store. I take it easy on the way home, feeling a little wary about my load. I don't really want anyone seeing the stuff or even asking me what's under the tarp, but hey, why would they? People aren't really all that nosy round here, well, except when we are all gathering gossip down at the bakery maybe. Some of the stories that get swapped around down there could definitely be classified as nosy, or even invasive, but I prefer to call them creative.

At any rate, my new grow room project won't be getting tangled into that grapevine, not if I can help it anyway. Once you've got a story rolling in the bakery, it's fair game to wheel it right out of there, add a little weight to it and let the momentum take it away. Take Pat's story for instance, like how believable is that, someone actually hijacking the

Harrop Ferry? Crazy right?

Hard to believe, but it does make for great ferry talk during the five-minute crossings. I turn off the highway at the ferry exit and park. The boat is heading the other way, so I've got a few minutes. Maggie's car is two ahead of me in the line, so I hop out to say hi.

"Hey Mags, how's things?" I say into her open window. She looks up, pulls off her sunglasses and smiles that lopsided grin of hers. "Hailey girl! Looking hot!" she says, looking me over. "Leggings in the summer? Looking like we should head to the bay and take a dip to cool down."

"Yeah, guess it was a lot cooler when I left home this morning." I say. "Heading to work?"

"Yep, if I can get across without getting hijacked, I am," she smiles. "Heard they locked some Meth head up for that. Guess Pat wasn't making it up after all. Some guy from Surrey. Heard he's related to the Orbisons. Probably out trying to steal their quad or something, sell it for drugs. Great story though eh?" she adds, smoothing her thick, dark hair back and slipping it through an elastic, then propping her sunglasses back on.

She's talking about when Pat had come storming in, late, right before Procter store closing time. "Yeah, I was trying to close up and end my shift, but before I had a chance to ask how he was, he was already chattering on faster than an auctioneer" she says, trying to mimic Pat's voice: "He came up the stairs of the ferry with a tire iron in his hand held high, threatening me as I was coming down from the bloody control cabin. He musta thought I was the operator, but I was just up there visiting Randy on the way across. Guy says to me, get the hell back up there and turn the ferry upstream, take me to the BBI or I'll cave yer head in," Her arms are flailing around the steering wheel as she talks, trying to emphasize Pat's excitement. "Damn straight," she says, that's what he told me. Imagine… cave yer head in. P3a2t5said the guy was slurring his words too, spitting, his eyes all over the place. Kept raising the iron, threatening him. Quite the story."

"Yeah, so I've heard." I say.

"Gotta stretch," she says, swinging her door open and hopping out now as the ferry inches closer. "Looks like we're in for just another regular ferry crossing, nothing exciting." Then we both move back to our driver's seats as we see the ramp starting to drop. I'd heard more on the story at the bakery just a few days ago.

Pat had been in there, railing on, repeating it to anyone who would listen: "I was backing up a step or two. Fucking shit-stain had me worried." He looked like he'd been at it a while, had the attention of everyone in there. He carried on, "'Course the guy is out of it, like how does he think the ferry is getting us across the lake if I'm the operator and I'm standing on the stairs?" he says, arms up in the air. "Then he'd start losing it and the tire iron would drop down to his side again and he'd look like he didn't know where he was. He'd get this crazed look in his eyes - they'd be rolling around in his head like a bag of marbles." Pat's eyes were rolling around, whites showing, trying to look crazed and doing a pretty good job of it. "Then he'd get ready to swing at me again. That's when I told the ass wipe that it was a cable ferry. He stops, says to me, "Cable… what the fuck. You shittin' me? Mother fucker! Un hook the mother fucker!" That's what he says, no shit, 'unhook the mother fucker!'"

"Then he turns around and looks at the water where the head light was shining, and I guess he could see the cable coming toward us as we moved along."

"Mother fucker," he says, and starts to go down the steps again, but course at this point I kick him in the back of the head so he stumbles down the stairs real quick and drops the iron." Graham interrupted him at this point, with "What… seriously? "Didn't come after you?"

"He was alone?" A hijacker in Procter?" I asked.

Pat ignored us. "By this time, we're getting to shore and the ramp is going down. He picks up the iron again, looks up at me, and smashes the engine room door with it on his way by. Pat's hand smacks the bakery wall. "Then fuckface jumps into some piece of shit old Ford wagon. He fires that thing up and does a burn out on the deck. I'm just staying clear. Dumb fuck guns it off the ramp before it's down all the way and smashes the bumper into the pavement so hard it falls off. 'Of corse, then it gets caught under his car in the frame and gets dragged along, sparks flying everywhere like a fucking shit storm. Looked like the little puke musta knocked himself silly in there when he hit the pavement, 'cause his car kind of jerked its way up the hill there for a few seconds before he guns it again and fishtails up the loading area spraying the cars behind him with loose gravel."

His teeth are clenched, and he sweeps his arm around just missing the top of Terry's head who is sitting at a table sipping coffee and listening. "Cops came out real quick when Randy called them," he said, "but I s'pose he was parked and hidden by then. Don't think they caught that waste of space tonight, but I gave them the license number so I'm sure they'll catch up to the piece of puke soon enough. Besides, how's he gonna get back across now without getting caught?"

Sounds like they did too, catch him I mean. I do miss these stories when I'm away from home. You couldn't make up this kind of stuff, could you?

I've only been back a couple of weeks now, but it already feels like I've been here for months; I've gotten so much done in such a short time. Guess the energy level and long hours of the tree planting regimen have spilled over into my home life. I've been really getting into just being here, in my own space, with the comfort and privacy, such a contrast to camp life.

I take my steaming to-go cup of coffee from the counter and stroll out to greet the morning on the front deck in my bare feet. The cool air rolls down from the north faced slopes above, always dropping the temperature a little lower than for those on the other side of the valley. The sky is clear, and the sun is just now landing on leaves and petals to dry the dew of the night, resting on all surfaces. I pick up the compost pail in the other hand and head up the path.

Always got to dodge the slugs these days. It's nasty to have one of those squishes up between your toes. Skunks have been rooting through the compost in the bin by the garden, ravens too, so the pile doesn't seem to grow much; it gets scattered around, but I don't mind. I don't have much of a garden anyway, just the bit that was dug up by a previous tenant. I just like to keep a compost so that I don't have to take more stuff to the dump. The little critters seem to clean it out fast enough that I never have anything much in there to attract the bears. Sometimes when I'm sitting out on my lawn, I see a raven taking off with a stale piece of bread or with some old noodles hanging out of his beak, looking like a shopper in a hurry who didn't take the time to pack his grocery bag very well.

I dump the pail onto the pile and quickly duck back so as not to get sprayed by the sprinkler that I left on in the garden all night. I wait for it to pass its rotation before darting up the garden path to shut the valve off. Everything is dripping, mist rising where the dark soil absorbs the sun's rays. Robins are singing and crickets chirp to the world. The hum of bees pollinating the raspberry bushes plays background vocals to the rest, and the lush green audience seems to grow before your eyes. It's hard to believe that we live in such a crazy world when in this tiny, vibrant space there is no room for anything other than vigor, beauty and abundance. Sometimes it's great to live in your own little bubble; if only I could stay in there.

I've got nothing on but a thin satin robe loosely wound around and tied at the waist. My hair is wild and loose. I'm not sure why I went through the whole season with such long hair, but here it is, getting longer, split and frayed. I am starting to look like a bit of a bush woman, all tough with calloused hands, gnarly cracked toe nails, weathered skin, and unruly hair. I think it's time for a little indulgence, girly time, maybe some exfoliation and a peel, maybe a little laser bikini treatment to tune up for the beach, 'specially now that I'm all toned. Can't have all that hard work go unnoticed, can I? I'll have the split ends trimmed, keep the length but maybe add a wave and some hairstreaks to blend in with my sun-bleached tangles. Can't say I don't want to retain a certain amount of that 'bush woman' image though. Hard not to. I know now that my female curves coupled with my tough girl image, are no handicap in the find-a-guy department.

My dad always liked my boyish antics. He used to say, "Do like you mean, it's no come easy, when she don't come, get mad, then she come." He had grown up in a Doukabour household where the boys and girls had different roles, traditional in that sense. They are a very hard working and practical bunch, very self-sufficient. My sister and I learned a lot of those ways when we were younger, whether we liked it or not. I guess I am more of a tomboy; I liked to learn all the things that mostly the boys were supposed to learn, handling a chainsaw, swinging a hammer or changing the oil on my truck. Dad never tried to pressure me not to. I never told my dad that, actually. I can do some of these things better than a lot of guys now.

I wipe the dew and grass cuttings from my feet on the front porch and go back in to fry up a couple of eggs for breaky. Time to get started on another productive day. The personal grooming will have to wait. I've got plans. Unfortunately, the plan entails working in a dark basement, regardless of the fact that another gorgeous Kootenay day promises to beckon me elsewhere.

I have all the goods I bought at the grow store stashed away under a tarp by where I park my truck. I'm just going to clean out the basement at this point and get ready to frame in a dividing wall to enclose the future grow room. Daniel agreed to come and put in a day's work with me later in the week once I'm ready and the bank appraiser has come and gone. Together we'll do the framing and hang the gyp rock and door. I'm pretty handy with tools but can't say as I have much experience with framework so I'm sure it will go a lot quicker with him along.

Once that work is done, I'll wrap the whole inside with black and white plastic and tape off all the seams to make it air tight, just like they did. "The white plastic gives you a nice finished look that is cleanable, keeps the humidity from getting into your house, and helps reflect light back onto the plants," Daniel told me. I figure I might as well put it on the floor too to cover up the musty old concrete. Once that stuff is done, I'll build three frame tables from 2X4s and put the plastic flood table tops on them. Guess I'll have to get some help with the wiring too. Gotta make sure that is done just right so as not to be a fire hazard. Those lights burn hot and the ballasts give off a lot of heat too unless you buy the newer, more expensive digital ones, but I opted for the economy model, so I figure I will just find a way to keep them cool with a little fan or something.

I'm excited about having my own personal grow space to drop into whenever I want. It'll be all rich with growth, warm and humid like the tropics and once it's been up and running a while, it'll be buying me a new roof, house insurance and paying my taxes… that's the hope anyhow. I decide to roll one up from my personal outdoor stash from last season. It's getting a little stale but still packs enough of a punch to put me into that zone for a couple hours. I kind of like that mellow feeling to sink in over me while I'm working on something simple, something mindless like cleaning out a basement. It can make the mundane seem a little more interesting, or at least assist the mind in wandering off somewhere interesting while you get it done.

❧⸻❧

I've got my place pretty organized and cleaned up on Wednesday morning when the appraiser guy shows. He's got a reel tape under his arm and a ten-inch iPad in his grip. He's an office guy, all neat and organized. "Jack Brogan, Kringle Appraisals," he says, reaching out his free hand, letting his eyes drop too quickly into the cleavage at the open top two buttons of my blouse. I straighten my back. "How's it going? You want to show me around a bit? Nice and private here," he says, scanning the yard now instead.

"Yeah, well I've got an acre and a half round me so keeps the neighbours at bay." I say, "hoping that one day soon it'll be mine so I can start making it look like my own."

"Okay, I guess that will kind of depend on how high the value is on the appraisal, eh? He says, "Let's see how this goes. Why don't we start upstairs? After you."

I can feel his eyes on me as I climb the stairs ahead of him, buttoning my top up tight as I go. I stand back to let him by at the top. "There you have it. Go ahead and check it out, bathroom's over there."

"And this? The master bedroom with ensuite?"

"Yeah, it's just this bedroom up here, eh. You can call it the master."

"I sure will." he says, looking me up and down slowly, deliberately.

"I don't come with the room there, dude, let's try to focus on the job okay?"

"Oh, a little testy on the uptake here aren't we? I'm just scanning the territory, nothing more." He pulls out his tape and quickly measures the rooms, then says, "'Course, sometimes it takes a little longer to get the right numbers on a place, you know?"

"Okay, well you've probably seen enough of this floor. Let's move on down." I know that if I kick him out now, I may not get a real appraiser back for weeks, so maybe I should put up with his bullshit for a few minutes, try to get this done. I go downstairs hoping he'll follow. He takes a few more minutes, probably rifling through my top drawer or something…fucking pervert. He comes back down, snaps a couple of more photos and measures up the kitchen and dining room. He leans in over me to hand me the end of the tape, his arm brushing my breast, takes my hand and presses the tape in. Could you please just take this to the other end for me?"

"Yeah, sure." I say, moving away. He finishes up on the main floor, jotting down a few figures in his binder, then we go into the basement. "Okay, just the one open space down here then." He says, poking away at his iPad again. He takes another couple of photos with his phone and says, "Okay, maybe we should just take a bit more time upstairs then, try to get this right. What do you say?"

"Oh, I'm sure you'll get it right," I say. "Want to have a quick look at the property before you go?" He quickly walks the perimeter of the house, measuring the outside walls as he goes, then when we're back up in the kitchen, he takes more interior shots with his phone, one of them, I notice is of me while I'm bending over the counter to pick up a dust pan that is leaning against the wall. He comes over closer to stand beside me, looking at his phone. "Hey, good shot on that bend. Check it out. You fill those jeans out real nice. What do ya say we just finish this up upstairs once more, get the numbers just right before I go." He moves his arm around me and moves his face in toward my mouth, but I dodge out and head to the door, pushing him back a step.

"Listen buddy, I'm not sure what kind of appraisal you think you're going to get here but as far as I'm concerned it's over. Now, you'll just head back out to your car and back to your shitty little office and your shitty little desk and you'll write this thing up just right and on time, all nice and pretty." I open the door and pick up the bat leaning just inside the cabinet by the hot water tank. My voice is shaky, cracking, with anger and emotion. "You should be moving off now, not later, 'fore I kick your ass, and believe me I wouldn't need this bat to make that happen either." I swing it up over my shoulder.

"Whoa, easy girl. No need for…" but I cut him off as he backs up a step or two.

"And I could toss you around like the waste of space you are with just these two hands, but I don't want to get polluted by the stink of touching you, so move it before the bat does the work for me." At this point, he sees my eyes mean it and he's moving out past me, eyes on the bat. He moves down the steps to the path.

"I have no idea what you were thinking," he says, "I was just trying to get the job done right and now you're hurrying it up." He's heading to the car, turning back. "I'm not sure how I'll be able to deal with this now."

I pull out my phone and press a couple of keys, lift it up and face it at him: "I'm not sure how I'll be able to deal with this now." It parrots, playing his voice back. "Yeah, I say, "I've got all your nasty little insinuations recorded right here on my phone, fuck head, right from the get-go, so you will go back and get herdone just the way I want, maybe with the value just about 10 grand higher than what you might have thought it would come in at. If not, you won't mind if I go over this recording with your boss before the end of the week eh? I'm sure he'd like to see how you handle your appraisals."

"Listen miss Belikov, I'm sure you got the wrong idea about this. The appraisal will all be in order just as was intended. Don't go getting all riled up on me now,' he says, in retreat, closing his door and starting up the car as I continue to approach, swinging the bat from two fingers like the pendulum of a grandfather clock, tick ticking away, kind of surprising myself at my outward calm. He pulls out onto the main road. I bend over and pick up a cone that has fallen from the tree overhead, toss it in the air and bat it across the yard.

"What an asshole." I say, but despite my bravado, I am feeling shook up; I set the bat back in its resting spot and walk to the bathroom, my fingers nervously picking at my nails as I sit to pee. I wipe a bead of sweat from my brow, take a deep breath, rise and move on. Could have been worse, I think. Still, I'm shaking.... not sure if it's from the anger or from the fear... that scenario could have taken another turn.

I often wonder if all the situations I have had to deal with in my world travels help me in situations like these, to act fast, not think, just deal with it. Or maybe it's just an innate knowledge that has been ingrained from being raised by such overly practical parents who always promoted independence over indulgence. Either way, cowards like that can't do much damage unless they drug a girl or come across those that are predisposed victims, right? Like women who question their own worthiness you know? I've known a few of those. I always want to take them under my wing and cradle them, guard them from the next assault, but I know I can't. I'm a little surprised he had mistaken me for one of those, but not a lot surprises me anymore. Maybe it's time to brush up on my Tae Kwon do; it's been a while since I tossed anyone over my shoulder but who knows when maybe I'll need to?

I'm in no big hurry to push the paperwork through on the house deal, but I am curious as to what my prospects are, so I arrange a meeting at the bank a couple of weeks later. The banker looks through my income statement which outlines my last two years of work, checks through my bank statements and credit card history and the appraisal. "Seems to me things are looking pretty positive here miss Belikov," he says, "Turns out your appraisal is coming in higher than your purchase price too which is beneficial to your loan application. According to these numbers you are getting a good deal on this one. I hope we can work something out with you."

"Great," I say, "that's a nice surprise, it's a special private deal with the vendor. I'm glad that you think the numbers are solid. I'll be back just as soon as I have the full down payment in order. Should only be a couple of more months. He said that would work, but not to push it much further because the pre-approval was only good for three months.

The next week, Daniel and I get those basement division walls up in record time. The door he hangs in the newly framed space latches shut with a smoothly satisfying click. I guess it pays to use a square and level when you're putting things together. I've learned a thing or two working with him. I know it will be easier now to build my own frames for the flood tables that I'll be installing in the coming days. I'm excited knowing that I'll be planting my first rooted clones already. I've got them patiently waiting for me in a plastic tray in the sunny window ledge above my kitchen sink. Once they see their new home, all bright, shiny and warm, they will shoot up like a magic bean-stalk.

CHAPTER 13

Ariel

I don't mind riding the school bus sometimes, 'cause it usually gives me a chance to hang out with Carlie. We haven't been back at school long, just a couple of weeks, so the ride hasn't got that tiresome yet. I get on the bus before her stop, so I'll often take the outside seat and hold the inside one till she gets on in Harrop. That's what I do today, and as we near the Harrop bus stop, just past the tracks, I see her standing there, waiting. She spots me and walks down the aisle. I move my knees around so she can squeeze by and take the window seat, her fragrance following her, flooding over me.

"Hey Wifi," she says, "how's things?" She's looking all soft in a velvety sweater that clings to her curves; her jeans hug her hips and stretch as she slips down in the seat to rest her knees on the seat back in front. She tosses her hair behind her shoulder and looks over at me, smiling, settled in. "I'm good," I say, "for a Monday. Can't say I'm too stoked at going to school, but here we go."

"Good weekend?" she asks.

"Nothing special, pretty chill really. Called you yesterday to see if you wanted to watch a movie, but your brother said you were out at the border or something."

"Oh yeah, I went out with my Mom to Waneta. Had to bring an extra I.D. to my little sister. She was on a swim team trip to Colville and lost hers so they wouldn't let them through."

"Sucks. So, they were on their way home?" "Yeah, yesterday afternoon."

"Bloody border, she's just a kid. Should have let her through. What do they think… that the swim team was kidnapping a twelve-year-old girl? Maybe selling her off as a sex slave?"

"Yeah, right, fundraising for the team, right?" She smiles. "They wouldn't have got much for her, kind of a runt." She slips down in her seat and pulls her brush out of her hand bag, starts brushing her hair back, coiling and clipping it in place with some kind of pin. The bus pulls off the ramp of the ferry on the other side.

"Tell ya, those guys at the border can be brutal. When we came back through from Spokane that time, me and the guys, took us more than an hour."

"Oh yeah, that sounded sketchy," she says. "That's when you had that keg, last spring, right?"

"Yeah, we'd taken out the center console between the seats in the front and replaced it with the keg. But we had the keg inside this old cushion that Frankie had found in the Sally Ann. It was brilliant."

"Yeah, so what did those border guys do anyway?"

"Oh, he took his time on us, feeling around, was just about to uncover the keg when Freddie distracted him. Had us shaking." I say, catching her eye as she glances up from checking text on her phone. "Then he goes to the trunk and pulls out the keg pump," I say smiling, dangling my lunch bag above my head like he had with the pump, inspecting it.

"What'd ya say?"

"Trout told 'em it was a sump pump. Good thing too, cause the rest of us were scrambling for something to say. He told 'em it just got left in the trunk, that it was from home. The console we'd ripped out of the front seat was back there too."

"And?" Carlie says, "did you tell 'em it was for the dwarf you keep in the trunk?"

"Never thought of that. Good one though, maybe we'll bring you along next time." I say. "No, Trout just told 'em that it was a part for his brother's car, that it came from the wrecker, with the parts. I had some parts in there that I picked up for Gabe, … Gabe Framer. You know, stuff from that weird little post office on the other side, at Metallaine."

"Oh yeah, and they bought that bullshit?" she says, "What did Gabe have you pick up over there anyways, some dynamite or something? Or was that after the train went off?"

"Yeah, yeah, it was after," I say, pausing, thinking back, what was that stuff anyway? Didn't look like any kind of supplement. "Not sure what he… oh yeah," I add, turning to Carlie again, "and the guy even picked up the cup holder that was on top of the keg cushion and put it back down again. None of us were even breathing. Figured we were going to get locked up or have the car impounded or something. But then, the guy just gets out, after Freddie distracts him with the semi-truck that's pulled up, and says, "'Looks okay boys, why don't you guys get going home.'" And he passes us our passports. We pulled out of there just a howling."

"Yeah, you guys are nuts. Can't believe you pulled that off. That was a great party you guys had with the keg that weekend. You going to get another one for our grad this year?" She asks, laughing. "Now that you're pro smugglers."

"Maybe." I say, "but I figure I've had enough border stress for the year. Seemed like a good idea at the time."

⸙

The next weekend comes, and I'm stuck around the house. Been working on some graffiti designs in my spare time, but today the sun is flooding in the window and makes me want to head outside after a while. Was thinking I should head to the lake and try to catch a Kokanee or two, but then I remember that someone in the store the other day was going on about how good the huckleberrying is just right now. I'm a bit of a huckleberry fanatic, so I figure now is the time, and because there's been plenty of sun lately, berries should be good and ripe higher up. I head down the trail and walk over toward Pearl's place. Nobody knows huckleberries like old Pearl.

I walk up the four wooden stairs to her old trailer. They are slippery with dew, soft with rot in places, the rail broken and leaning out at an awkward angle. The door is open, the breeze of the afternoon flowing through the house, bending the cob webs at the corner of the doorway. I can see her just inside, sitting on the arm rest of the old stained, overstuffed sofa. She's carving a short stick as I walk in, the shavings dropping onto the floor; a cigarette smolders from the ashtray beside her.

"Whatcha carvin' Pearl?", I asked her. She doesn't look up, knows it's me.

"Oh, I just lost the damn cap for my gas can spout so I'm carvin' a plug to put in it, nothing really. What are you up to little one?" She smiles, looking up a moment, her nicotine stained teeth the colour of the wood in her hand.

Her old bent body seems shorter, like gravity is working too hard. Is it her getting older, or me taller? I guess it seems weird because I still remember looking up to her when I was a little kid. "I'm just out hoping to find some huckleberries and decided to drop by and see if you knew the best spot to go this year," I say, sitting on the couch watching the wood chips fall.

Pearl always knows the best spots for huckleberrying or getting firewood, or mushrooms or even a part for your truck for that matter. She seems to have all the inventory of the area sorted into little slots in her head like files, just ready to choose from and open when you need one.

"Well I'd say, now that it's getting later in the season you should go up Higgins, up to around the four-K and look to the high side of the road where there are more openings that get sun."

"Oh yeah, around the four-K eh?" I say, glancing over her as she clenches the stick in her grip.

"Guess I could drive you up there and pick a few myself if you want to go right away. I've got people comin' over later but still should be plenty of time if we go now. I guess there will be plenty of berries left up there, less the bears got 'em all."

"Sure, sounds great Pearl. Let's do it then." I say.

I had hoped she'd offer to join me 'cause she knows her way better than me and besides she always has something up her sleeve which makes everything more interesting, especially when you're bored. No one seems to be around today to hang with. Carlie's not back yet either- went off to Calgary for the weekend with her family. Sundays are usually pretty quiet around Procter anyway. If I could, I'd just head into town to catch up with some of the guys in Nelson, but I've got no wheels.

Pearl picks up the gas can, pushes the wooden plug into it, but it doesn't quite go so she carves off some more shavings then tries again to plug it back in, forces it in, and sets the jerry can down again. I follow her out to the outside cabinet on the porch where there are some tools stored. A few old, stiff looking furs are hanging on pegs on the outside of it, maybe weasel or squirrel. I don't know what she does with those, but they look like they've been there a while.

We find some small pails and neck hooks in there- she has these hooks, rigged up, made from old coat hangers that she uses to hang around your neck while you're picking so that your pail is held which frees up both your hands. Also keeps you from spilling your pail over if you set it down on uneven ground. We gather them up, with the pails and lids. Pearl grabs a couple of cans of orange crush and a bag of chips and we toss everything on the bench seat of the truck and hop in. She turns the key and puts in the clutch, letting the truck roll down the hill, then pops the clutch lurching us forward down the slope till the motor catches.

"What are you wantin' berries for anyway little one", she asks, once we're up and running.

"Oh, I don't know, just something to do I guess, and anyway, I love 'em on my cereal in the morning. I throw 'em onfrozen." I say, "or Mom'll put 'em in pancakes. Heard it was good picking right now." I add as we wind up through the gravel switch-backs, bumping over washboard, Pearl keeps glancing over at me as if just to see if I am okay, or still there or something, I'm not sure. We pull off and park a few kilometers up with barely enough room for another truck to get by on the narrow road. There is a small spur road nearby, so she can turn around to have us facing down the hill so we can roll start it later. We climb out. I block the wheels with rocks, like she asks, 'cause her e-brake doesn't work. We pick our pails and hooks out of the back and scramble up the hill into the berry bushes. I can see from the road that they are all thick and pretty heavily laden just as she'd said they'd be. Pearl is more nimble getting up there than I expect she'd be, seems strong, even though her breathing sounds like there's a rattle in her throat. I thought she was kinda old for this, seems old, but she moves like a weasel, a chubby one mind you, darting off then poking her head up to look around. She settles into a good patch and starts picking. I'm not far off. Picking is good, lots of big juicy berries. "Seems like we've found the spot alright," I say. "I knew you were the one to ask." Pearl comes up with all sorts of things that you never would expect. I guess that's why so many people drop by her place. It's not just to pick up some milk or eggs; it's 'cause they're curious too, or have a question.

We settle in to picking berries. "So Pearl, what have you got goin' on these days?" I ask her. "What are you going to do with those skins you had pegged out back there?" People know Pearl as a healer, a weaver, gardener, forager, explorer and trader amongst other things, depends on your connection. She knows how to trap and smoke fish, do all kinds of things that most people don't do anymore, stuff you read about early settlers doing, and most of all she has a simple way of explaining things that I would usually not understand or even ask about. She gathers wild plants that they use to make tinctures down at the old school house. If she were living back in the day, they'd have labeled her a witch and burned her at the stake.

She says, "Oh, them skins is no good. Didn't tan 'em in time to keep 'em soft, so now I'll just use 'em for patches. Like everybody, I learn by mistake, at first," she says, pausing, inspecting a berry then throwing it out, "doin' things once, you know, doin' 'em wrong and then doin 'em again, just like everyone. 'Corse," she says, glancing over at me, "I had some good teachers when I was young, not school teachers, mind, mostly my parents and grandparents; my aunt too. They knew the land and my grandmother knew the spirits. I used to want to be like her."

"Mmmhm," I mumble, listening, picking, making sure my berries drop into the pail instead of on the ground. Pearl continues: "She was a spiritual healer who knew the Cree ways. She also studied the ways of transference. I followed her, wanted to help folks like she did till it got overwhelm'n." She shifts to another bush. I shift the same way.

"What's transference?" I ask. She goes on, "Well, when I was a lot younger, but a little older than you are now, I thought I could help others heal."

"And you still do, right?" I said. "Like with your remedies and stuff?" We are both plunking berries into our pails, shifting around to find the best spots. I keep finding bushes that look better than the one I'm on, so I keep moving.

"Yes, but not the same way. Its true folks do drop by my place, bringin' me their troubles, 'corse, we're only talking mostly 'bout emotional troubles, not physical. No one wants advice from an old woman who smokes and eats Cheezies, 'bout their physical health." She chuckles, before continuing, "I thought at that time that the best way to heal someone was to take on their pain, not take it away from them, but experience it, to help them understand it better. There was a lot of folks had a lot of pain, a lot of mixed up people."

She looks up at me to see if I'm listening. I glance up to meet her eyes. "My grandmother understood the method but didn't use it much. I think she understood the danger. Didn't really want me to practice the method." She moves over the slope a bit. "But I did anyways. I learned to experience the pain people felt, transferring it to myself, for a moment. It took me years of practice and meditation and healing ceremonies to learn. I had many visions, sometimes from a semi-conscious state. I studied ancient and modern methods and combined them. I was able to create my own unique methods, makin' the transfer possible just by being near the person, silent and focused. I could direct the energy and it would gather and bounce back to me from the other one, the one I was working with. Hard to understand I s'pose," she says.

"Yeah… weird," I say.

"In this way, I'd experience what they were experiencin' and at the same time, they'd get a moment of relief, which would remind them that things aren't always that bad. I thought this would be the most effective way to find a solution to help heal others."

"Must have worked if they kept coming back to you." I say. "Well yeah, it was effective, and I learned plenty in a few short years, but it cost me." She pauses a moment to move up the hill a bit, to another bush. I move along too. "I became all drained and tired out, weak." She shifts again, checks her pail and moves up the slope to straddle a nearby log, which makes a comfortable perch to pick from.

I look down at my pail. Only the bottom is just covered with berries, hers probably double deep in comparison. "I had three or four people comin' to the house every week once they'd heard 'bout how people was being helped. And after that, there were more and more of 'em. Amazin' how many people need help once they think you can help 'em," she says. "When I think about it now, seems to me, they was expectin' too much from someone as young as I was, but I was always willin'. I had a passion for it." "You were like one of those witches in Salem that we were reading about in school, eh Pearl? Good thing they didn't hang you."

The sun is finding its way through the trees now. I can hear a chainsaw off in the distance and not far off, the sound of the nesting Blue herons that have been there for a couple years now. Man, do they make a racket.

"Yeah', she chuckles, "good thing those days are over. Back then they would've hung me for sure. But there's lots of ways to learn and heal. You don't have to be a witch like me. You are learnin' every day. There are lots of different dimensions to learnin' and teachin' and healin'. If you let 'em, the spirits will speed up the process. Sometimes it's better to just relax and wait, let things follow the way they will stead of trying too hard, stead of studyin' all the time. The knowledge is all out there, but you got to meet it at the right time, when you've got room for it."

"Guess that's my problem in Math class… got no room left in my head." I say.

She climbs further up the hill to get into a better clump of bushes and I move up nearby, trying to get into a spot where the sun is shining through the gap in the trees created by the road below, to warm up a bit. "Now don't get me wrong, nothin' wrong with studyin', I'm jus' sayin' that it ain't the only way to learn." She pops a few more berries into her mouth with a satisfying smack. "What do you mean that there are lots of dimensions to learning anyway, Pearl? I just learn stuff in school, not much mind you," I grin, "or sometimes from guys *at* school or from the internet, mostly You Tube. Last week I figured out how to make traps and trip wires." I thought she would be interested in hearing about my trap cause I kind of got the idea from one of the ones she had shown me at her place last summer. "I figured out how to catch and release a skunk in a live trap without getting sprayed. Me and Fin let it go on the school bus in the night so that sour Steve got a surprise in the morning, the bugger. You know; he left me behind twice last week, even though he could see me running toward the bus in his rear-view mirror?

"Pearl chuckles, then laughs her raspy laugh that usually ends in a coughing spasm like now. She hawks and spits phlegm on the ground then keeps picking away, dropping more berries in the pail, shaking' her head, smiling, doesn't comment. She looks up, switches position again and looks over at me until she catches my eye, then she begins to explain, more serious now, as if she has decided something, or that I'm ready or at least listening.

"I'm talking about sometimes seein' and learnin' from other dimensons that we don't always notice are there. Maybe the other dimension is in your mind's eye. Maybe it's in another place in the intervals of time. You have to listen to your own breath and the space between footfalls when you are walkin'. You have to notice the movement of a tree, or just the aura around that tree." She's talking slowly, like she's thinking about each word, picking words, not berries. "The main thing is to look for it, to be open to the other dimension, the one most ignore, recognize, not be clouded by the endless cycle of thought all the time, then, when the opportunity to enter is in front of you, you will see it."

I'm sure I'm looking kind of perplexed when I glance up at her questioningly, between berry drops. She sees my confusion. "See what?" I say.

She tries to explain: "So, say you are walking along a trail and there is a shallow pond ahead. I'm talkin' about a place I know. I know it well. The trail is a little steep and you see the pond just above, maybe ten meters ahead in the forest." She holds her arm out straight for a second, like it's the still of the water ahead. "It's all calm and shady, quiet and dripping wet. The flat surface reflects branches, ferns and light when you look at it which is what most people do, look at it, I mean. Or they might step to the edge and scoop out a drink with cupped hands and disturb the surface. But if you come to a stop, below, along the trail, because you've recognized a potential, because you've felt the depths that are there, then you'll move ever so slowly toward the pool. While it is ahead and uphill from you; you'll be even with its surface; you and the pool will be at eye level; and you will peer carefully toward its edge, calmly, breathing deeply, aware of the water."

I'm watching her now. Her eyes are steady and calm, her voice clear; uncharacteristically so, she's looking out over the sky as if the pond were there. "You'll be barely moving forward now; you may see into a crack at its edge…be aware of that, of the soft, moist soil, roots, needles and cones… the water. Stay focused, breathe… follow your breath, as you inch forward, lowering to a crouch, seeing through the space above your eyes, then lower yourself onto your knees, always remaining eye level with the surface."

I am mesmerized by her voice at this point. She continues, calm and slow, eyes on the sky. I can't pick, just listen. Her speech is puzzling, different somehow. Her words are more articulate. I just stop and watch her, her voice a soothing breeze washing over me. I don't want to interrupt even though I have questions, even though I don't understand.

She starts picking but her eyes are not seeing her fingers pick the berries. "You keep your focus on the edge, on the space between shadow and reflection. Move forward, slow but sure, lower, until you are slithering like a salamander on your belly. As you approach the pond, the gap at the edge will part; you know it will; the opening between shadow and reflection will create a bigger gap, it will beckon you and you will enter the space, without moving any further – that is the fourth dimension. You will be on the other side. You will be there; you will learn from being there." She stops.

I sit back on the ground for a moment. She keeps picking, eyes back on the bush. I'm not sure what she has said or why she has told me this. "But where is that place?" I ask, "why would you go there and how could you get back? If you've been there, what did you see?"

She stops a moment, looks around, as if to find another bush, but really, she seems to be, coming back from somewhere else. "That story is for another day little one," she says, picking faster now, trying to top off her pail. "That's what my grandmother always told me at the end of every story: 'that story is for another day', she'd say. She could go on and on 'bout things, grandmother. A pure blood Cree, she was." Her words and tone changed, breaking the spell, "sometimes she would mix up Cree words with her English and get all confused," she chuckles and picking up her almost full pail she carefully makes her way down the bank toward the truck. I follow. "Maybe I'll be doin' that too, pretty soon little one. Then you'll have to just leave me up here on the mountain all covered in huckleberries so that the bears will come and finish me off.

"You already sound pretty confusing" I laugh, as I too try to fill my pail fuller before we go. "so, I guess we'll have to bury you pretty soon then, eh?"

"Nah," she snorts, "just stick me up in a tree. Don't want to be buried in one of those crazy cemeteries. I been thinking what a waste of land it is to take up all that area with a bunch of graves. They don't let you just put the body up on a platform in a tree anymore like the Indians used to do."

"Yeah, I read about that once in a class at school," I said, "seems like a strange custom."

"Well, this cemetery thing is even stranger." she says, "Guess we'll have to go with the cremation then. Least that don't take up a bunch of space, just some firewood. Maybe we could reuse the ashes even, so's not to waste 'em. Maybe add them to a soil mix, or feed 'em to a house plant, or we could put them into some peanut butter, and stir it in a little at a time." She glances over at me, her crooked smile asking me if I believe. We bump along the gravel road.

"Peanut butter?" I said.

"You'd go downstairs one morning and say to yourself, 'hey, I feel like a peanut butter and grandma sandwich, you know, or better yet, a peanut butter and Pearl sandwich, with jam, yep, right, with jam, and you would probably feel really good 'bout it. Be like keepin' the family unit together. Don'tcha think?" she says, the questioning glint in her eye lighting the green streak that runs across her otherwise calm, dark brown eyes.

"Yeah, sure Pearl," I smile back, "a peanut butter and Pearl sandwich. Nasty."

"Anyway, all this talk 'bout peanut butter is makin' me hungry, for somethin' more than berries. Think maybe I ate more than I put in my pail. Let's load 'er up," she says, smiling over at me, exposing bits of chewed berries on stained teeth behind purple lips.

"You still got more than I did." I say, glancing in her pail. We make our way back down the rest of the slope, walk down the gravel road to the truck and throw our stuff in behind the seat so it doesn't roll around in the back and spill out. Pearl swings herself up into the truck cab and plunks down on the seat grasping the steering wheel with both arms, out of breath, wheezing a bit. She waits a minute to catch her breath then leans back, presses the clutch in and turns the key to the on position and gets it rolling in second gear before popping the clutch. The motor rumbles to life as we maneuver back down the hill, dodging potholes as we go.

CHAPTER 14

Gabe

Over the winter I'd had plenty of time to become familiar with the details of my plan. With few firewood deliveries, and minimal funds to invest in furthering renovations, and having the kids in school, I've had the time to be pretty focused. I'd studied methods and explosives, reviewed online forums and blogs. There have been fewer distractions since the CP investigation scaled back last fall. Even though I'd had another run in with Blevin the inspector guy, a few months ago, he still didn't seem too hungry to bring me in. Lots of threats, no action. Didn't bring anyone else in either, far as I know.

Their evidence is just too circumstantial to stick to anyone. Some of their guesses were right but turns out they were just guessing. Those Crime Stoppers posters didn't reel anything in for them either. If they would've, I'd have heard about it by now. I know they are all still poking around, but I've got other things on my mind now. Now that summer is here again, it's time to get back up into the Jumbo valley. Can't afford to give them any more time to gain ground on construction.

"It's easy for them, the developers." I'm telling Emily who's listening from the couch, as I fry us up some eggs and sausages. The kids are still asleep, and we are having a slow morning.

"They have only the weather to slow them down, not the law or government. I've got to get up there and help put the brakes on this thing." She's flipping through a magazine, absently, not really listening. "The Jumbo Resort proponents don't have to worry too much about finding friends in the BC Government." I flipped a sausage as they spit grease from the pan all over the stove.

"It's easy for them, especially now that the right has formed this coalition that's been in power. They've tossed all those radical right wingers in with the moderate conservatives, along with the long defunct Social Credit party and all those other pro corporate lackies, thrown them all into a meat grinder and churned out this generic neo-conservative sausage, just like these," I say, poking the sausage with a fork to let the juices flow out. "That they've labeled, 'Liberal.' They've gone through a whole string of 'em now," I say. Emily just mumbles, hhmm, flipping another page. I carry on, "of these Liberal leaders, but they all cook up about the same. Least, this sausage they're serving now, the Premier Cristy Clark version, has each end turned up just a bit so that it's served with a smile- guess they figure it sells better like that." I smile at her as I drop a bent sausage on her plate wrapped around a couple of runny eggs for eyes to make it look like a happy face, a slice of toast for a hat.

"Great," she says, moving over to a bar stool at the counter, pulling her plate closer, she pokes at the meal, "Now you're trying to give me heartburn." She stabs the sausage with her fork and tosses it over on to my plate.

"Aw come on, try some," I say, with a chuckle, "be open minded, local bratwurst."

"Think I'll just let you or the kids be open minded with this sausage." She says. She often opts out of the meat in a meal, no matter how good.

After breakfast, I get a few chores done around the place before starting to organize my trip. I know that my old '79 Ford truck is going to be too recognizable so at first, I'd been thinking I'd bring my Suzuki Enduro up to the trail head when I go, but now after sharing the plan with Emily, she's convinced me that taking her more generic Toyota Corolla might be a better idea.

"Everybody's got one of these", she says, "I don't want you getting noticed. I would rather that you just got dropped over there by a beam of light or a drone or something, but I guess they don't make drones in your size yet."

"Yeah, maybe you could have me delivered like a package from Amazon, then later, when I'm done, you can send me back as a returned item?" I say.

"Not that funny Gabe," she says, "It's starting to sound a little more serious than that. I have some idea of your intentions on this, Gabe, and believe me, I'm understanding of the emotion behind it, but I'm a little concerned that I don't know exactly what you have in mind or how I can help. I need to know that you're not at risk."

"You're already helping Em," I say, more seriously now, "just being calm and quiet about this. I'm just going to go up there and have a look around for now, make some notes, take a few photos. That's it, but I don't want anyone to know I've gone in case I do decide to take further action later, that's all." I can hear myself sounding confident about my plan of action, but at the same time, her word: 'emotion', is eating at me. She's right; I can't let emotion disrupt.

"Okay, and so, if you decide ' *further action*', is the next step, what will that entail?" she says breaking my train of thought.

"Let's chew on that one later okay Em? It's too early to say, and besides, wouldn't you rather…let me rephrase that…wouldn't it be better if, later on, if, say, there were questions about what happened, wouldn't it be better that you could answer, in part, truthfully, that you have no idea?"

"Well maybe, but because I will know who, I'm not sure that, not knowing exactly *what*, will make much difference." She's at the counter now slowly painting a pink glaze onto her finger nails; she glances up at me with a knowing gaze, kind of inspecting the serious concentration I must have on my face. I face her gaze and for that passing moment at least, we have found a mutual understanding. Under more normal circumstances she would have pushed the issue further but in this instance, she seems to recognize an uncharacteristic intensity in me, her husband, already known for intensity, raising pressure to another level. She leaves it at that for the moment, blows on her nails, puts the polish away, and grabs her purse, ready to head out the door. She has a short shift to cover at the store. I think she can see that with my intent, there is an accompanying calm, not just some kind of maniacal carelessness. I hope she can anyway. I hate for her to worry.

⁓⌖⁓

After she leaves, the boys get up and I feed them breakfast. Gavin snatches the portable game console from Noah's hand as they sit. Noah shoots him a sideways glance and puts on his phony smile. When they don't have friends over, they make do playing together, even though Noah is three years younger. Gavin is in charge but usually tolerates the younger one so long as he stays in line… and doesn't use his portable game screen.

Today, neither of us will be home, so nobody is coming over. We've arranged for their Grandma to pick them up. "Don't forget your beach bag," I yell at them when they hear her car pull up. They grab it, yell good-bye and run out to meet her. Once they're gone, I can settle down with the computer and start to plan my route on Google maps. I outline a rough trail line to give me a closer idea of how much distance is involved between sites, and how long it will take me to cover the ground on foot. After mapping it out, I print it and then transfer the route onto my hand-held GPS I decide I'll bring along a paper copy too, a compass and a topographic map in case the GPS fails. There are lots of things to research in order to pull this thing off in an effective and safe manner so it's time to head up there for some more reconnaissance. This time, I'll be able to actually see firsthand, the newly poured concrete construction that to date, I've only seen a few photos of. Being there is the only way to create a real plan. I need to see it, record the details. I brew up another coffee and sit down at the office desk which is jammed in under the rise of the stairway to the upstairs bedrooms, my study cave.

I've compiled a list of research to tackle in there. I start looking into some of the items, searching online for detail to print but then I realize that some items are just too sensitive to have linked to my personal computer, so I jump in the truck and drive into town to spend a bit of time at the Nelson municipal library where I can search away on their computers more anonymously.

There, I'm able to pull up some sites and systematically set about gathering, printing and compiling. I know that it will be impossible to purchase certain restricted products that I'll need to complete these plans without being traced, so I'll need to find alternatives that will work using materials that are more readily available. I begin, making notes, scrolling through lists and instructions, recording recipes and methods I find online. I gain momentum, start losing track of time.

"Excuse me, sir."

It's a librarian. She's standing behind my shoulder. I minimize the screen and glance up.

"It's just that we have a limited number of computers, so when they are all in use, we ask that users stop after one hour."

"Right," I say, "Gotcha, moving out."

I doubt she spotted anything I was looking at. Why would she care? I pack up my things and clear out.

On the way home, I'm thinking about what I've learned. In some cases, there are two or three different alternatives to attain similar results. It's confusing but I decide to move on, keeping all possibilities in the file. I'll have time to define the best methods later.

Now that I've gathered small amounts of some of the basic supplies and made a small prototype, I have some idea how to proceed. First thing is to get up the mountain and try it out.

It'll be easy enough to pick up a bunch more instant cold packs at a drug store to use as the ammonium nitrate component for the next test, but to play it safe, because I'll need so many, I'll have to buy them in several different stores so as not to draw attention. Aluminum powder, the other key ingredient, is not so easily found though, but with a little research I did find a Marine shop that sells atomized aluminum powder, a perfect fit for this application. Problem is, it's in the States so I had to order it online and use a U.S. address to receive. Fortunately, I kind of lucked out on the timing of that because Ariel was able to pick it up for me on his way back from Spokane. When I put it all together, the theory is, I'll have a larger prototype Tannerite bomb, a bigger boom. It should be good to learn from but still only a test size version. I'm hoping that Farley will guide me further along on this. If he'll share his experience with me, it'll be a big boost. He'll understand the volumes necessary, ratios, impact.

Once I'm up there, on site, I'll have to confirm what I've seen photos of: various potential targets, machinery, fuel caches, structures. I need to find out exactly what they have up there that can be useful to me too. Why bring it with me if it's already up there? Save me some carrying capacity in my pack. Wish I had the explosives ready now so I could get on with it. I want to do some damage. Don't want to wait, but I should, shouldn't I? Take time, study, be methodical? Or is surprise a better tactic, surprise and spontaneity?

The following morning, I wake up early and unfold myself as stealthily as possible from Emily's arms so as not to awaken her. I go outside right away as I so often do, especially in the spring and summer, to feel the fresh morning air wash over me. I enjoy feeling the air and seeing the sky, to gather the days forecast, a much better, more accurate diagnosis than the one provided by the weather network I figure. Thimbleberry and fern are dynamic and almost super natural in their vibrancy this time of year, the rich green growth adding inches each day. Sparrows and robins sing, dew sits sparkling on leaves and the aspen flutter in the soft breeze, like a thousand butterflies taking off at once. Some jagged bits of leaf from the mountain ash tree that leans outover our house, are being cut and carried by ants parading along from one end of the porch to the other like a line of placard waving protesters.

I step over them figuring I shouldn't interrupt their busy schedule as I walk down the two wooden steps to the path below, resisting the urge to disrupt their flow, stifling the anger and impatience that keeps rising to the surface. If I let that kind of emotion take root, I'll be stomping the life out of those poor unsuspecting ants and what purpose will that serve? Got to keep Jumbo at bay. Got to keep those that choose to destruct our wild Jumbo, to tame it, in the recesses of my mind, not at the forefront. Emily has gotten up and showered by the time I'm back inside. "Got a full shift today," she says as I come in. She kisses me and hands me a full cup of coffee. We each prepare for our day.

Emily often walks to work at the store. It's only a twenty- minute walk but it gives her a chance to be on her own, "to breath," she says and absorb the always changing foliage and weather patterns. She says that she likes to look out over the tracks to the surface of the lake, check it out, "to get a feel for the day." I glance out to the lake as I pull her car out onto the main road. Ducks dot the surface in the distance, diving and bobbing, gulls float in the breeze and a Bald eagle inspects the surface below from the high bough of a cottonwood tree along the shore, searching for the silvery shimmer of a rising Kokanee or Rainbow trout. Emily is almost to the store when I drive by, so I pull over and wait for her.

I glance at my watch; It's early still, only 7:45 am. We'd managed to have both boys sleep over at friends' houses last night, so logistics are easy this morning. I just want to reassure her a bit before I take off. She understands and shares in many of my deep-seated beliefs, but I know she also worries about recklessness and unpredictability. Not sure why, but she sometimes looks at me as though I could spin off, out of control, it's not like

I have a history of hazardous activity and broken bones. Does she think I'm reckless? I jump out and give her a hug as she reaches in her purse for the key to unlock the store. She is the opening shift today. "I'll be fine, honey. Don't worry. At least I'm going in the light of day this time. It's just a hike. See you tonight okay?"

"Yeah, I know. Just don't be taking any uneducated risks Gabe. You had better be following the invisible guide today, the one that seems to take you in the right direction, okay? Remember, if I don't hear back from you by dark, I'll be coming up there after you. Me and the boys." She opens the door and props it ajar with a wedge as Margaret, Emily's friend from up the block, walks up to come in. "Hey Em, Gabe, how's things? Heading to work Gabe?"

"Well yeah, more or less. Checking the mail first, yesterday's mail. Maybe I'll find an ad for a new job to follow up on instead of hauling firewood. Join the circus or fill a position to be a flying squirrel or something. Have you seen those guys? They just put on that squirrel suit and then jump off a cliff or a fifty-story building and fly down." I grin, feeling energized all of a sudden.

"Emily," Margaret says, "I think you need to keep Gabe on the firewood. Could be problematic letting him get distracted, from the sounds of it," she smiles, as she walks by into the first aisle.

"You have no idea," Emily mumbles under her breath, smiles over at me.

"Anyway, Em, I don't think flying squirrel is a job." Marg says from down the aisle. I give Emily a quick kiss and turn to leave. As I leave, I hear Marg continue, "He sometimes reminds me of my brother's cat, Em. My brother used to throw him up in the air to do the triple flip and even though the poor thing always looked really disoriented, he would always land on his feet." Emily responds from the cash counter, "Yeah, similar, usually lands on his feet I guess, pretty unpredictable Marg, but hey, predictable guys are boring." I smile at that one, as the door closes behind me, but I don't think she sees me listening. Those are the best, or sometimes worst kind of comments: the ones you're not supposed to hear. Either way, the most telling.

I glance across the arm of the lake to the Kootenay Lake ferry as I pull out, the MMV Osprey is spinning round to dock in Balfour on the other side of the arm, white foamy water spewing up in its wake as I pull out on the highway and head toward Harrop.

I figure I'll make it to the trail head around 9:45 am, if I stop only once for fuel in Kaslo. I've cleaned my slate for the day and been quiet about my plans. I'm timing all intervals and documenting my route on GPS and on the topo map. I want to have a clear record of all the times and distances between waypoints. I drive up the ramp of the Harrop ferry as a fifth wheel vacation trailer gets pulled off.

Even though it's only a five-minute ride across on the cable ferry and you can easily see across to the other side, we still sometimes get tourists coming across asking for directions to Creston. They get confused after being told to ride the ferry across Kootenay lake and carry on to Highway 3A to Creston on the other side. The Kootenay Lake ferries dock just a few kilometers further up the road at Balfour, so they'll mistakenly turn down the side road that brings them to the Harrop ferry instead and end up driving to the dead end that is Procter before figuring out they have to go back where they came from and find the right ferry. There is no other route out of Procter/Harrop.

I usually hop out to see who's in the line up to catch up with if I have to wait for the boat, the social hub for a four-minute visit. For some it's the only chance to trade news and greetings with neighbours they rarely speak to. This time though I wait a few minutes up the road from the ferry so I can time it to drive right on just before it pulls out. In this way, I'm parked at the back of the line to minimize the odds of being approached by one of our friendly, often inquisitive neighbors. I don't really want to be noticed today. I pull up, park and focus on my map instead of looking around at the other cars like I usually do. Don't look and they won't see you, right?

I drive off without having to fabricate a story to avoid discussing my upcoming hike. It feels good to be driving north, up the lake. My energy is coursing as I drive, details of my surroundings seem more vivid than usual. Leaves shimmer back at me from the tree lined route and I form clouds into idea bubbles like I used to see in comic books as a kid. I lean into the corners as though I'm riding my motorbike, weaving through the rocky bluffs on the cliff side route high above the choppy water of Kootenay Lake. I fill in the bubbles with questions and answers. They evaporate. That's the problem with having good ideas on the fly, if you don't write 'em down right away, they just evaporate. I wish I could remember more. Sometimes

I feel like I'm a zoom lens on fast forward and I can focus on everything at once, in passing, without ever blurring the intensity or clarity of vision. If life was always like this no one would take drugs, or maybe, if it was always like this they still would, just to get to the next level, or to drop down a level. I wonder? I just feel super aware right now like I'm tuned in to absorb - it's a good feeling.

After gassing up in Kaslo at the Husky station, I pour a top up into my to-go cup of hot coffee from the thermos, pay cash, and pull out along the windy road, north, toward the head of the lake. The road narrows; it is less traveled further along, and its sharp turns keep me focused as I drive.

It's not quite 9:00 am. My timing is pretty good and with the rhythm of some old Tracey Chapman tunes strumming away from the CD player, I cruise along the highway not lacking for speed. Beyond the Duncan river bridge at the end of the lake, the road splits and turns to gravel; I keep left at the fork, toward Duncan lake. The dust rises behind and when I pass the oncoming logging truck it engulfs me momentarily in a dust cloud. I'm accustomed to rough gravel roads from years of hauling wood and back country exploration. This road is better than most, so my speed doesn't need to reduce much from highway speed except on sharper corners where inevitably, the potholes and wash board vibrate the car sideways in a bit of a drift. I have no problem recovering from those, kinda like doing the drift actually. It reminds me of those cold winter days when me and Sam, an old friend, were younger. We would wait till after a big snowfall when the banks were piled high from the snow plow clearing the road, then at night, when few cars were on the road, we'd pick up speed, jam on the e-brake and crank the wheel so that the car would spin down the middle of the road on the compact snow and ice. Usually the car would end up ramming into one of the banks and come to a stop or bounce off. We could usually just drive it out without a push. What a rush that was. No wonder we learned how to drive so well-off road, or at least, thought we could. Thinking you can is part of the recipe though, right?

I figure I'll make it to the Jumbo trail head in about a half hour barring any road problems. Maintenance on some of the back roads in the area has been pretty thin over the past few years, as government cutbacks on parks have been implemented, butso long as there are logging or mining activities in the area the roads remain accessible. Why are those the only values that count when it comes to keeping roads open?

I passed a couple of pickups, one of them Forest Service, but that was about it for traffic. Weekdays are pretty quiet up in the mountains this far, especially this early in the season. Most come out on the weekends to explore the back country, and mostly in the early fall, not early summer. Usually, you can't even access the higher elevations this time of year, but we have had an unusually light snow pack over the winter, that, coupled with early spring heat has led to an earlier than usual melt and run-off. People are already talking about the possibility of having a bad fire season. I swing the car into the tight turn of the Jumbo trail access road, drive carefully up the last couple of turns over drainage swales and pot holes, then decide to overshoot the parking lot a little way as there is a truck parked in there and I figure I might as well limit any recognition and conceal the car a bit. I pull into the shoulder 200 meters or so up, pull my day pack out of the back and lock it up. I check my watch and set the timer. It is only

10:20 am. I've made good time. I zip off the bottom of my convertible hiking pants, tighten up the laces on my boots, glance quickly at the settings and adjust my GPS to record the trip. I stride off, buoyant with a new levity of purpose. Feels good to be taking action, but I can feel my heart beating faster than it needs to.

In a while, I break a moment to take off a boot and remove a broken twig that's lodged inside it. It's almost 11:00 am, and I am over halfway to the pass already. I'm hungry but decide I won't have lunch till I've made it to the foundations, so I pull a power bar and a bit of venison jerky I'd picked up from Pearl one day and chew on those while moving on. Probably meat from one of those deer she's poached out her back door. Wonder how she's doin' dealing with those health inspectors poking around? Seems she and I have some things in common these days- being questioned and accused. At least she has a good sense of humour about it.

Last time I saw her she was cackling away, re-telling how she'd told them about her cross-breeding program: "Out in the back shed. Told 'em I was crossin' rats with Pit Bulls so I could have a guard animal that ate all my garbage," she'd said, "after that they didn't want to look in my shed anymore. Then ya shoulda seen 'em when the gander got out, I tell ya, talk 'bout a guard dog." I can still picture her face telling me, her cackle turning into one of those coughing fits where she's still smiling, showing off those brown, stained teeth, while at the same time, gasping for air, then spitting a phlegm ball onto the ground, before putting the cigarette back in her mouth. I'm just glad it was her that caught me up on the mountain with my Tannerite, not someone else.

The mosquitoes have hatched recently. They circle, whining around me in clouds as I swing the pack over my shoulder and carry on. Little fuckers. Easier to eat my jerky while on the move when the bugs are bad, so I don't stop. The sun is in behind clouds most of the time, the temperature warm but not hot and as the elevation increases, the shadows are a little cooler. Still, sweat beads along my brow as I push on at a pace that most would find manic. I am energized by the vigor, propelled by the possibilities. Various scenarios sweep through my consciousness, one vision replaced by another as I round switch backs, sweep past huckleberry bushes and bound over windfall that litter the trail. I always find a clarity of mind and a more productive creative process while hiking alone. Close, there is only the sound of my own step and breath – beyond, robins and sparrows sing, and the breeze blows through the aspen.

Sometimes I come up with some of my best ideas while lost in the rhythm of my own pace. Letting the imagination flow in all directions often results in time lapses. I like it when time lapses. Suddenly, the murmur of a voice strikes my attention. People.

Close by, coming my way. Must be whoever was driving that truck, just hikers? I quickly grab my ball cap from the side pocket of my day pack and pull it on low. There's no time to hide. They would hear me moving into the woods and be alarmed. I'll just pass them like any hiker would. Two people come round the next switch back carrying full packs, keeping a good pace. I carry on, keeping my pace, not slowing, "Hey guys." I say, eyes on the trail, moving past. They slow, step aside a bit and the woman says, "Hi. Heading up to the cabin eh? Beautiful up there this time of year." "Yep." I say, past them already, not looking back. "Have a good one."

Her voice trails off. "We had two ni…" as I turn the next bend. Guess she noticed that I'm not stopping to chat. Don't think they could really describe me and why would they have to anyway?

As I gain the height of land at the pass, I'm walking on snow. It's only patchy snow until now, but up top, as I hike over the last rise, there's still an almost solid blanket, all compressed from the warm days of melting, a thin film of gray dust lying over its surface. In another half hour I'm standing in the pass gazing out over the expanse of valleys and peaks, meadows and lakes. They engulf me - what a feeling - Jumbo pass stands at about 7600 feet, the divide between the east and west Kootenays, a majestic panorama to absorb. There's that overwhelming feeling again, the one that never seems to diminish, whether you've seen it before or not, flooding over you like a deep breath as the vast expanse unfolds.

The pass is just a few hundred meters south of the old cabin that had been built for wilderness adventurers about thirty years earlier. The forest has thinned to sub alpine fir and Engelmann spruce at this elevation, some larch too. Most of the Lodgepole pine mixed in are just dry, dead skeletons, wiped out by the beetle invasion over the past few years, some blackened by lightning strikes too. The landscape is mostly open, with meadows and rock fields between thinly forested pockets, allowing for unimpeded views. Lichen clings to wet rock faces. Patches of western anemone swing their mop top flower heads in the breeze wherever snow patches have receded enough to allow first growth; they bob around like sixties hippies at a rock concert.

Jumbo and Monument glaciers are both visible from this vantage point to the north east, and the white wave of Glacier Dome is off toward the west. Just below, in the Jumbo valley, Jumbo creek rushes along, all white and frothy. Jumbo creek road and the Toby creek forest service main road follow along the creek several kilometers below, winding its way through the dense forest, appearing and disappearing from view with each turn. My view of meadows and rock fields is soon distracted by the giant scar of interference, still too far off to see clearly, at the head of the valley, the mess that I know is there, created by the proponents of the Jumbo Resort developers, who have so recently altered the natural landscape. The only visible sign of human disturbance anywhere to be seen. The sight immediately triggers the anger that simmers in me. "Fuckers." I whisper, to myself.

I know there has been other human involvement in the valley in previous decades, exploitation of timber and mineral extraction has taken its toll up here, but those scars are only visible now to the eye of one who can recognize the subtle changes between what is and what could have been. In contrast, the geometric lines and ridged forms of poured concrete slabs, rebar, steel, fencing, the fresh construction I've seen up close in photos, all lies stark and vulgar. Foreign bodies in the familiar place below me, far off in the distance.

"Fucking invaders! I shout out loud: "I'll help show them out." With that thought I set off down the slope, the momentum of gravity and the force of conviction adding velocity to an already fast pace. I watch for new trails and survey lines as I hike, changes added by the developers, but haven't noticed much yet. I'm thinking that if I can find flag lines and layout stakes, I'll take them down, but the only evidence I see of visitors at this end of the valley is a couple of bear scat and multiple prints, bear and deer, mostly, along the trail, mainly at lower elevation as I drop into the valley bottom where huckleberries are already starting to ripen.

I breathe deeply, sucking in pure mountain air, tonic to my energy level. I try to aim foot falls on rock and soil to avoid the blooming dogwood, wild strawberry and paintbrush sprinkled through the meadows as I spring along, weaving through. I figure I can make it down to the first work site in just twenty or thirty minutes from here. It's probably a little over a kilometer away. I stop whenever there is a clear view of the site to see if I can note any movement of a vehicle approaching along the Jumbo creek road, the one and only access.

It seems the place is abandoned, for the moment at least, which suits me just fine. It's eerie, even from a distance, this huge angular disruption I'm seeing below. I move along. Now that I've dropped lower in the valley bottom, trees are dense in pockets. I circle around off trail, to get a better vantage point, make sure no one is about. There are still lots of soft, wet areas through the bush where the grassy surface beneath is spongy under foot, still retaining moisture from the late snow melt. I'm careful not to step into them and leave obvious prints.

As I near an opening directly above the site, a rocky outcrop, I see that I'm still several hundred meters away. I stop and focus on the area, searching for movement, any sign of people, but I notice nothing; a lone crow is the only sign of life, gliding over the area, scouting for eatable tidbits. I move lower, cautiously until I am within fifty meters or so, scan once more and then I'm out in the open on the construction site road. A movement alarms me for a moment, out the corner of my eye, but I see it's only a ground squirrel popping out of a hole. I see that tire tracks have churned through the mud in previous days and weeks. My mood immediately changes. The serenity of solitude and wilderness where I've been has gone, replaced by a horribly violated landscape. Sometimes I feel the anger boil up from beneath, though I've been through this valley before, and to the pass and Jumbo cabin many times, I've never seen firsthand the damage recently done by Jumbo Glacier Resort. I've seen the pictures and read reports, but this feels like a gut punch in comparison.

I stop. I reflect a moment on the scene in front of me, part of which I've seen previously in film. I recall the eloquent words of description by the film maker, Nick Waggoner and the Ktunaxa nation citizen and spokesman, Joe Pierre, from the film, 'Jumbo

Wild'. It was the Ktunaxa people, they explain in the film, whose territorial land this is, this land being violated:

"What's sacred for you?" Pierre asks in the film. "We have to prove the sacredness of a place to them? On the land we have lived for 400 generations? We should be able to tell them it is sacred, and they need to accept that. We should be able to say no, and our no should be heard." Those words are still imprinted in my mind. "Our no should be heard."

Seeing the destruction first hand and realizing that the impact I can see today is only a tiny fraction of what is planned is very disturbing. The rights of many, quashed by the single- minded architect, Oberto Oberti, and his self-absorbed partners and investors who so single-mindedly support his development plan. The rights of wildlife, water and wilderness trampled in the name of real estate investment, profit for a few. The voiceless confronted and crushed by those voices who have the ear of government and big business. The anger rises in me as I gaze out over the site, only the very first tiny step, relatively, in an ongoing massive development of a planned city Resort, which includes the construction of accommodation and infrastructure for some ten thousand beds. Twenty-two lifts and gondolas are planned, rising to over 11,000 feet in elevation, from condos and shops below to mountaintop restaurants above. "The ultimate mountain resort access in North America," says Oberti.

Somehow, I feel like an intruder even though this is crown land, First Peoples land. I keep looking around, expecting to be told I'm trespassing, fearful of confrontation. The Bastards even have me second guessing myself as I read the warning sign looming in front of me:

IMPORTANT NOTICE!

You are inside the Jumbo Glacier Resort
Controlled Recreation area (CRA)

MOTORIZED VEHICLES ARE PROHIBITED NO
FIREARMS- HUNTING IS PROHIBITED

Glacier Resorts Ltd. Holds a License of Occupation Under the
lands Act over the CRA. Entry is permitted for purposes of
Glacier Resort activities only.

ENTRY FOR OTHER PURPOSES PROHIBITED

The CRA contains many hazards. By entering you accept Any
liability including injury or death and you agree to release Glacier
Resorts and its employees and agents from all claims
Including claims of negligence.

If you do not accept these conditions, do not enter.

"God damn it." I curse, throwing a hand full of mud at the sign. "They don't even own this land... fuckers." I kick the post holding it up and it rocks back and forth before settling again, with a bit of a lean. A ground squirrel scurries out from behind rock, dodges down a hole. I bring my attention back to the construction.

A massive concrete slab spans a good 100 feet, at least 80 feet wide, over 8000 square feet of concrete, who knows how thick, with hundreds of rebar protruding up in lines from foundation walls that fan out in front of me. The cold face of construction lying flat and rigid, a stark contrast to the irregular rock outcrops, fields and pristine meadows just behind, like a giant landing pad dropped by an invading alien force. A landing pad which has reportedly had 10,000 tonnes of snow avalanching through it at 320 kilometers an hour, just this last winter. They have not only pressed forward with a plan that most are opposed to, they have built it in an avalanche path... incredible. Maybe an avalanche will help dispose and bury this mess once I help break it up. "Mother Fuckers," I say aloud, spitting out acrid phlegm on the slab as if it were corroding my teeth. I scan the slide chutes that scar the steep slopes above the area imagining the massively powerful flow blasting down from above.

I drop my pack and bend over it to find my camera. I pull the portable shovel from its strap as a giant horsefly buzzes my head. I swat at it, swearing. I quickly unwrap a sandwich and eat hungrily while assessing the location. I'd been distracted from my hunger, but now realize it's time to catch up on some badly needed caloric intake and get that bad taste out of my mouth. I have a lot to accomplish and not a lot of time to spare, I'm thinking, as I munch through most of what my food bag has to offer.

I get busy clicking off a series of shots from various angles, muttering away while I work: "fucking destructors. Bloody disaster, …fuck this and fuck that", clicking my way through the destruction surrounding me, then remind myself, 'it's time to focus on the tasks, not be distracted by the emotion. I have a job to do.' I step through the maze of rebar, forms and rigid concrete foundation walls, take the last couple of shots, put the camera away and pull out the shovel. If I am to finish digging here, reach the two lower sites and return before dark I'm going to have to move fast.

I work tirelessly, like the ground squirrels, excavating small exploratory holes to find weakness and vulnerable central targets within the structure - details that I'd researched which will be key for me to create the most impact from the least possible weight of explosive material.

I notice that some of the ground squirrels have burrowed right under parts of the foundation the way I have. Piles of loose gravely debris lie mounded here and there where they have churned it out. I find one little tunnel that's dug near the central core structure. "Started one for me eh guys?" I ask. "appreciate that, do need to get some idea on how thick that chunk is."

I stab my shovel into the tunnel and start pulling out loose gravel and sand, then as I burrow under, a larger rock blocks the way so I dig around it till I can roll it out… too heavy to lift. Now the side walls start to cave in a bit so there's more room. I inchworm my body in to the cavity and keep poking away at the back, following the underside of the concrete slab. It's thick, probably twelve inches or so. Once my shovel is in about three feet it hits another solid wall with a ping, the shock reverberating up my arm. "Fuck. More reinforcement." Probably part of a central footing. "That bitch'll be tough to crack." I scrape away at it for a bit, the salt of sweat combining with dust, dripping into my eyes. I crawl backward to reach for my pack. Need to grab the headlight to get a better look, but as I reach for it, I hear the distinct sound of squeaking brakes in the near distance. "Shit! People! A truck! Fuck!" My heart races. My eyes dart as I cautiously inch my head out and just above the concrete slab above the hole I've created.

Through some brush, I can see the outline of a pick-up. It's maybe sixty feet the other side of the construction, not two hundred feet from where I am. "Jesus!" Where to go? Can't run. Too late. They're too close. I see the both doors open at the same time. "Shit." I duck back down pulling my pack in with me, back into the hole. I start pulling gravel and sand back in to obscure the opening. It's not enough. Too slow. I eye the huge rock I'd dislodged earlier. Got to roll it back. Will they see me? Where are they? What are they doing? Can't let them see me. No way to explain. I poke my head out again, twisting so that now my legs are in the hole. There are two guys, one with a ball cap, the other a hard hat. The guy in the hard hat has an axe over his shoulder. They're strolling slowly, backs to me. Looks like they're heading around the structure. If so, they'll be turning around the corner toward me within twenty paces or so. I lunge forward and grip the rock. With all my weight and strength, I heave it over, up the bank onto the mouth of the hole. Once it's perched there, there's still enough room from inside my little excavation to reach around with one arm and scoop a little more gravel and debris up onto the rock.

I can barely move my limbs inside the tiny tomb, but by ramming my elbows into the bank and pushing with the heel of my hand, I can plow tiny mounds of sand into the remaining gap. Only fragments of light now filter through the gaps, illuminating the thick suspended dust that I'mbreathing. It makes me conscious of my breath. Too loud. Got to be calm. Settle. I close my eyes and try not to think of my claustrophobic tendency. A crow caws. I hear gravel crunching underfoot. Voices approaching, can't make out words. I breathe into the fabric of my pack. The steps get closer. Voices clearer. "Yeah, next set of forms just off there."

"That the main entrance then?" the other voice asks.

The smell of cigarette smoke blends into the dusty air. No crunching gravel! They've stopped?

"Why so much fresh digging round here?" 'Fucking picas I guess. Maybe a marmot?"

Gravel crunching. Steps closer. Voice clear now. Close. "Don't know. Look, tough to say. Hmm. More over here." "Yeah, fuckin' mess. Could destabilize if they keep it up." "Should I grab the shotgun?" Maybe do a little target practice?"

Steps passing now. "Na, not now man. Do the rounds. Keep going."

"Yeah, still got that report to write as…. "the voices fading. I breathe-realize I've been holding my breath. They're moving away, circling the perimeter.

A few minutes pass while I wait for the sound of the truck starting. Once I hear them pull out, I push the rock away, toss my pack and shovel out and worm my way out of the hole.

Damn close, that was. Wasn't expecting full on security dudes. Wonder if they are? That could have spoiled the whole future plan. Got to stay invisible. Think like a ground squirrel.

Once I calm down, I reflect on some of the critical points, online discussions, forums, try to extract every detail worth noting from the scene in front of me. I won't have a second chance; got to get this right.

I take more photos of the holes I've dug before re-filling them, take notes and begin formulating some new ideas as to how to help speed up the 'decline' of this concrete obstruction. Erosion and decay will, over time, eliminate all evidence of this structure; the natural cleansers of the earth; but why should the earth have to wait hundreds of years for that to happen? My ideas flow and congeal; having the site under foot adds a lot of clarity to the vague strategy I'd been planning. Yet still, I can see that the strength and solidity of the construction here won't be easy to tackle. I'm going to need some professional help.

Time to move out now. It'll probably only take me a half hour to hike down the road to site two, the machinery cache. I'll have to move even more carefully now, knowing those guys could still be around, yet I don't want to push this day into a retreat in darkness. It's already almost one o'clock. I gather up my things, pack quickly and stride out onto the Jumbo creek road, same direction that the white pickup had gone.

The terrain along the gravel road is mostly jagged rock faces and loose rock debris that have been blasted to accommodate entry. Gravel is loose underfoot, pockets of dense trees line the road side and a Jumbo creek subsidiary gurgles along, bending round each turn. Because I'm now walking down the middle of a road, cover is almost nonexistent, this open terrain makes me feel exposed. I'm jittery, ready to dive into the ditch at the first sign of sound or movement. I round the next turn and I can see below. The machinery and storage shed I'd known were there are clearly visible now. It's less than a kilometer away, I figure.

I stand behind a rock outcrop, drop my pack and take some time to scan the area for movement. There, is a white pickup parked alongside the metal shed near a loader and skid steer. Could be the same one. An excavator and bull dozer are parked nearby. Nothing is moving. It makes no sense to me that a pick up would be left behind so probably it's them or someone else there doing maintenance. I watch for a few more minutes but see nothing change.

I decide to move closer, but not along the road… too exposed… makes me nervous. There's more foliage, some trees and bushes below the road at the base of a rock slide, so I decide to approach along that green band, get a closer hidden vantage point to search from.

I pull the pack on again but as I dart out from behind the rock, a flash of light catches my eye. I stop and step back behind the granite slab again and peer out once more. The pickup door has opened and is now closing. It's the side mirror, reflecting sunlight. I doubt they see me, but I stay still to be sure. It's the passenger door that I've seen close, so I know there are two of them as the truck backs away from the shed and pulls out. I'm sure it's the same two. Must be a security, or maintenance team. Hopefully they'll be done for the day and heading out. The truck pulls out and begins to make its way back up the hill toward me, not down as I'd hoped. "Damn it, gotta move."

They are heading directly toward my position, back toward the construction site. They round the first turn and are momentarily out of sight behind a rock outcrop, so I run to the next boulders, which lie between my location and the trees below, gives me a few more meters of distance from the road. I'm not sure if I've made it behind in time as I dive behind the first one. I peer out cautiously and can see the truck slowly gaining elevation, moving along. The road is very rough and jagged; the truck lurches. My position is about twenty-five meters below the skid road now, and though I feel I have pretty good coverage, I'm not sure if I've been spotted. If I have been, the guys will probably come after me to ask why I'm here, which at this point, would be difficult to answer. After all, it's pretty apparent that I'm trying to conceal myself, plus I'm so covered in dirt and scrapes now they could easily put two and two together. Can't simply walk along the road innocently as a hiker looking like this. Anyway, I don't want anyone to be able to identify me now or in the future.

I wish they were moving faster. They're barely driving faster than walking. The rigidity and irregularity of the blasted rock surface of the road causes the truck to lurch, jarring back and forth. It crawls around the curve near the bend, below where I'm hidden, then stops. I don't look out. Don't dare to. My breath is shallow, too fast. I hold it in for a moment, listen. Can't smack the horsefly that is biting my neck. Can't move. I can hear a truck door open, then the other one. One slams shut.

"Tellin ya, something right down there… big. Could have been a person. Wasn't a marmot."

"Bear maybe?"

I hear them move closer, stop. I silently swivel remaining in the shadow of my rock shelter. The bank below me is steep. There are scattered rocks between me and the forest, some big enough to hide behind, but there are gaps between them.

"I've got bear spray. You grab the shotgun, just in case." "Yeah, could at least give him a scare."

I wait for the sound of the truck door opening then toss a stone as far as I can away from my position. I quickly dart away as it lands, dropping to take cover behind the next big rock eight or ten meters away. I don't look back, just press my back into the rock and wait, listening, panting, ready to sprint.

"Over there.'

"Yeah I heard it too, sounded like a rock."

I'm coiled like a spring, ready, but it sounds like it worked, like they've turned, voices more directed toward the rock I'd tossed… for the moment anyway.

I yearn to be in the forest cover only a few meters away. Without thinking, I run for it. It's only a few steps before I'm obscured.

"There! Something, someone, ran in there!" "You sure! Oh yeah, I can hear it."

Those are the last words I can hear clearly before the voices are obscured by breaking twigs underfoot and the growing distance between us.

Blam! Blam! Two shots explode, shocking the airwaves. I can feel the hair on my neck rise, nerves electric. I hear the shotgun pellets spread out and thud well overhead, into trees and branches as I run, full speed. Branches scratch across my face and arms as I race through, not around them. I leap over rocks and windfall, movements fluid, gaining space between them and me. In a couple of hundred meters I allow myself to stop and look back… listen. Another two shots ring out, the sound coming from the same place, like they haven't moved much. I can hear distant voices, but they don't sound like they're getting closer.

I sink into the soft forest floor. Breathe. Listen. Wait.

Do they know it's a person? I try to review the landscape as they must have seen it from up there on the road. Could they have made me out? Certainly, couldn't have identified me. For sure they heard me running through the woods, but could have thought I was a bear or deer, maybe an elk?

I wait, still, a few more minutes, only the sound of flies and a gentle breeze fluttering nearby fern fronds unsettling the silence. Then I hear the distant sound of the truck doors slammingshut, one, then the other. Can't hear the truck start, so I cautiously move back the way I'd come, trying to find a safe vantage point from which to peer out. Finally, I can see through the remaining trees up to where the road is, where the truck is moving along now.

It slowly jostles along, squeaking and lurching in complaint of the rigid, rock surface of its path. They don't stop… thankfully. I wait until they are well beyond my sight line before I move out into the open, relieved, tension now replaced by renewed energy. I can get back to the task at hand now. Got to gain ground fast. I soon cross the creek over a temporary bridge they've set up and I am alongside the machinery cache, the chain link fence that encircles it is just ahead. It's eight feet tall and has one of those angled barb wire guards on top, sloping out, to make climbing over difficult. I circle it to have a quick look and end up at the gated entry. The two, eight by eight foot, entry gates have a thick chain wrapped round their center posts, secured by a heavy padlock. Above them there is a small gap between where the two barb wire guards meet, looks big enough to fit through if I just roll over the top as flat as possible.

I try to climb up the eight feet to the gap but it's too hard to get a toe hold in the chain link so I grab a couple of broken 2x10s from a burn pile they have nearby and lean them up on an angle onto the lock and chain, which is about half way up the gate. Then I take off my pack, pull out the rope I've brought and throw the coil over my shoulder. I leave the pack on the ground and take a run at the ramp. I'm able to reach the top of the fence, grab on with one hand and hang on with the toes of my boots jammed onto the makeshift ramp below. I grab the rope with my other hand and quickly tie one end on to the top of the gate and throw the other end over the fence into the compound.

I heave myself up till I'm facing down into the compound upside down, poking through the gap, still hanging on with my hands behind me. I can't seem to swing my knees over without catching on the barb wire guard above the gap, so I try to flip my legs straight over, or just slide down the rope forward, face-first. The landing doesn't look like it would be too forgiving if I slip, so I hang on tight, shaking now, losing strength as I strain. I swing my legs over, try to spin but I catch my left leg on the wire as I hurry. It cuts into my pants, tearing them and hangs on as the rest of me hangs down inside. I pull hard and it tears away as I drop down and land on my feet, panting, exhausted.

I have a quick look around and when I see nothing has changed, I check out the damage. The pants are ripped from the knee almost to the ankle and my leg is bleeding from a long gouge, but it's not deep. There is a bit of fabric on top of the fence that I'll have to pull off before I go. I catch my breath and move over to the bulldozer, can't waste any time. I have a look at the machinery, take some photos and make a few notes.

The skid steer seems pretty new. The Excavator looks like the one our neighbors used to build their driveway with. A pretty good size, a Cat 315 D. and the bulldozer is a Case 750. I take pictures of all the machinery, makes and models. Inspecting their tracks, I can see that they have been busy with these machines lately, look well used, caked in mud not yet dried. Now I turn my attention to the storage shed. It's locked up with thick padlocks behind steel doors. There are no windows. I need to find out what's in there. My heart is still pounding too hard, my breath shallow and fast. I feel like a burglar about to be caught, but I remind myself that there is no one around… well not now anyway, but who knows when those guys in that truck might come back? What if they forgot something? What if they have suspicions or just do a quick check on the site instead of just driving by? Fuck it. If I have to, I'll light a rag and drop it into one of the fuel tanks for a diversion then run for it again. Gotta keep on.

Shouldn't have left my pack on the ground like that, exposed. So stupid! They could probably see it from the road. Can't make mistakes like that. They did lock the place up though, so probably they are done for the day, right? Once they start down the Jumbo main road toward Panorama, they'll have to pass this point, but likely won't turn into the machinery cache entrance. If they do, I'm in shit. I'll have to think fast and do as much damage as I can right now 'cause I'll never be able to come back once they get wind of a potential threat. Got to remain calm. Breathe. Focus on the plan. Got to keep my eye on the target. Stop speculating. I circle the shed, looking for an opening of any kind but the only opening in it I can see is an air vent that is up in the eve about nine feet off the ground. There is an empty forty-five- gallon barrel behind the excavator, so I knock it over and quickly roll it to the side of the shed, flip it up and climb on. From this height I can reach the vent. I pull out my knife and unscrew the two screws holding it in and pull it off. Now I can see in, enough to see that they have left a lot of hand tools and equipment in there, along with a generator, a tidy tank with a hand pump, some jerry cans and some tool boxes stacked along the wall. Wonder what's in 'em? Wish I had time to get in and see.

I assess the room best I can, take a couple of flash photos into the vent hole, and screw the vent cover back on. Still, no sign of the truck returning. Feels like time is running out. The blood flow in my head is throbbing. I can hear my pulse in the silence when I'm still. My neck is stiff, jaw tight with tension. I roll the barrel back into place, scan the area to make sure I haven't altered anything, then climb up the rope to the top, and this time swing over to the ramp without catching my leg. I untie the rope, remove the torn pants material from the barb wire and drop back down, scan for movement. The distant hum of a plane high overhead snaps my head back involuntarily… no, not a truck. I take one last picture, put my things back in the pack and stop a moment just to take it all in. I wish I could just light this place up right now. I'm here; maybe I should? The urge to spill over one of those jerry cans and just let it rip is goading me. Mother fuckers deserve it!

I let the moment pass. The tension drops again like a downdraft from a hillside. Instead, I just move on down the road feeling grateful not to be trapped inside that compound anymore. I check my watch. It's just after two-thirty. I figure, it'll take me about an hour and a half to get down the valley to site three - the bridge crossing. Time to move.

Clouds are beginning to form overhead. The bugs seem to be increasing in number and intensity. Whenever I stop to add GPS way-points or to scan an area, deer-flies immediately begin burrowing into my hair and skin, the mosquitoes too are relentless and horseflies buzz bomb my head like Japanese fighter pilots in that war film on the attack on Pearl Harbour.

I swat at them sometimes, try to pick one out of the air, or wait a second for one to land so I can smack it, but soon realize that there is an endless supply so there's no point. I make note to be a little more prepared for these irritants on my return. Little bastards are driving me crazy. I'll need to maintain a high level of focus and concentration to achieve my intended goals in the required time and any distraction will impact that effectiveness. For now, I'll just try to stay on the move. I notice movement ahead and stop. It's only a deer dodging away with its young spotted fawn trailing behind. The occasional grouse too, has taken me by surprise, gotten my defenses up a few times along the path. That rapid signatory wing flap they have always alarms me at first. One flees now into flight without warning, breaking the silence again. I decide to stick to the road now to save time in getting to site three. I hope I'll be able to hear any oncoming vehicle in advance, enough to quickly duck into the brush at the roadside for cover. Anyway, that truck must have been on its way back up to the construction site so will take at least forty-five minutes to go up, turn around, and come down, maybe longer if they are waylaid or working on something, so I should be fine for a while.

I like multi-tasking. I usually feel more acutely tuned in to my surroundings when I know that my focus needs to be multi- directional. I'm running through various scenarios as I travel along. I remain wary to the sound of any approaching vehicles from either direction, and maintain a rapid, ground covering speed, simultaneously I'm trying to process these various plans of strategy. There has been a lot of stimulating input already presented today with more to come. I don't want to be overwhelmed by it. Have to keep it sorted in my mind.

The flow of water ahead catches my attention as it tumbles down the bank and funnels into the culvert beneath the road. Hmm, a nice spot for a pond maybe? A potential diversion?

The anger rises in me; the feeling of being powerless, impotent against the big machine. I have to keep that anger in check, focus on the possibilities of *not* being powerless, instead; focus on beginning to take some control *back* from this tyranny. "Fuckers", I say aloud. "What a bloody mess". If I were being monitored right now, I figure they would just lock me up for sounding unstable. I pull the water bottle from the side pocket of my pack and drain it, gulping thirstily before slipping it back into the pocket. I will soon be able to refill at the river. The bridge is just ahead. Still no sign of that truck.

The time is approaching four-fifteen. The sun is still high enough, but I can feel humidity rising with the settling of the day. I want to evaluate the site and head back to the car asap. Still no sound of approaching vehicles but I know that I will have a hard time hearing anything coming when most sounds are drowned out by the sound of the river running by in full force.

Now, as I approach the bridge on the flat gravel road, I can see that it's not much different than I expected. I drop down the bank to get a better look from underneath. It's a standard forest service bridge installation: two big steel 'I' beams span the gap, reinforced by diagonal cross members. Then, a series of creosote soaked wooden beams lie on top, perpendicular, those, covered in a thick layer of timbers above which form the surface of the bridge deck, a solid and simple design. I climb up the bank on the high side to get a bird's eye view and a couple of photos. I quickly descend out of view under the bridge again where I can inspect the framework more carefully without having to watch for an oncoming vehicle. I pull off my pack, post a way point on the GPS and pull out a bag of mixed nuts to munch on while I ponder what's in front of me.

Yes, the two main beams span the river- thick, steel, I-beams, probably forty feet long I figure, each resting on the foundation of, five by three foot, stacked concrete retaining blocks on top of one another at either end like Lego pieces. On top of the I-beams the timbers are probably about a foot thick, securely bolted onto the top plate of the steel beams. Those beams combined with the whole wooden layer of the bridges surface adds up to a whole lot of flammable material. It's only those two steel beams that will put up any resistance to flame.

I take more pictures, add some notes, check the height and width and note the flow, which is strong but not quite as high as it has been. I can see the high-water mark etched on the boulders along the bank. The river, 'Jumbo Creek', is about sixteen feet wide at this point but probably had been twenty-five or thirty feet during peak flow. You can see evidence of loose windfall and boulders that have been thrown around and become lodged at odd angles in and around its banks.

The cool river air flows over me in the shadows and sends a shiver up my spine as I try to relax a moment and study the area. I'm not one for waiting around long though, no need, so within fifteen minutes, I figure I've seen enough. Besides, everything is on film to study more carefully later. The afternoon is well upon me now. Time to make fast tracks back now or be caught wandering along the trail later in the dark, not an enviable position. Fortunately, this time of year the sun sinks later and gives light enough to make your way until almost nine. Barring any unforeseen problems, I should make it back well before that.

I sit down to tighten up my boots, then just lean back a moment more to watch the water rush by, the constant foaming force. The power of nature, a power that can't be stopped, but possibly harnessed, altered, just for a bit, I figure, just maybe- can this river momentum help me make this statement? Maybe with the right force.

I fill my water bottle, secure things in place in my pack, make sure I've left nothing behind and stride out into the fading sunlight, down the road. I want to get off the road as quickly as possible, head up the trail toward the pass. I keep glancing both ways for signs of movement on the road as I move away from the bridge. Within a few minutes I'm already closing in on the east end trail head parking area. There is an SUV parked in the pull out. Damn it, another hiker. I don't want to run into anyone, especially now that I'm kind of run down, my pants all torn, face scratched, covered in grime.

I'd spotted an open slide chute earlier where I think I can gain the height of land, parallel to the trail. Maybe I can follow that till I find my way back to the upper trail along the ridge. I like to rely on ridges when I can because they are generally pretty clear of windfall, so even though it won't be as fast as walking the trail, I'll be better off by not having to worry about dodging hikers, and with them off my radar, I'll have some time to consider what I've seen today, let the ideas percolate, try to focus on action, not anger. I turn off the trail and am soon rock hopping along the slide chute.

Those fuckers, … really, pushing to construct all this stuff with so much opposition in their midst. What the hell. They need to know that everyone can't be bought off or shut up. I wish I could just blow the whole fucking thing up right now. Okay… steady, no, got to think… head to the ridge.

A ridge isn't just a good vantage point. A ridge, especially one that has no trail, few, if any, human footprints, is a place of exhilaration, a temple of wilderness. Its where seemingly groomed pasture meets sky, where mossy alcoves and weather kissed rock faces allow narrow fissures for paintbrush or anemone to spring from and bloom, punctuating the path with colour. It's nature's scenic highway; a ridge, like a conveyor belt. Just have to get on and it takes you to there, almost effortlessly. I do find myself at odds when I hike a ridge though- in conflict between speed and observation. Sometimes I just want to stop and fully absorb what's in front of me, while contradictorily, pushing ahead to see what awaits just around the next bend, over the next rise.

No, today I won't be stopping. Today, I will reduce the beauty around me to a blur, a blur interspersed with blinding bursts of anger that rise and bubble to the surface as I reflect on what I've seen today.

My legs are automated pistons. I cover ground quickly - the priority - just getting back in time before dark. My muscles feel the exertion of the pace of the day adding up, but at the same time, my energy surges, propelled by this new-found confidence in the idea of finally fighting back. This newly forming plan is not out of my depth is it? This thing is realistic, right? A plan simple in its execution and potentially powerful in its impact. Given the right planning, some careful research and meticulous installation, this can be done, can't it? And if not soon, when?

The more I've been out in the open today though, the more exposed I've begun to feel, the more I'm leaning toward the idea of planning this whole undertaking, when the time comes… under the cover of darkness. On the one hand, yes, it will be slower and more difficult to maneuver, more challenging not to have clear, long range vision that daylight would provide, but on the other hand, my stress level will be much lower, not worrying about being constantly on the lookout for wandering hunters, hikers or maintenance people. The other advantage will be that I could probably put this whole plan in motion without being missed a full day at home, which will make it much easier to have an alibi for. Will I need a pair of those night vision goggles? Jesus. Night vision, alibi's, stealth and explosives… all sounding very much like terrorism. Am I a terrorist? A saboteur? Saboteur sounds better. Is this going too far? Should I go home and reconsider one more stab at good old negotiation instead?

Partake in that group effort? I'm distracted by the sound of an engine. I stop and listen, looking in the direction of the source. It's coming from38d5 own below. A vehicle must be winding along Jumbo road. A narrow gap in the trees below the slide chute allows for a split-second glimpse of the white of the truck as it turns a bend. Finally, they are on their way down the road, toward Panorama. Took 'em a while. A plume of dust trails off behind and rises through the trees before settling. I'm lucky this time. Don't have to worry about dodging them. In a moment they will be crossing the bridge that I'd been under just twenty minutes ago.

I take a swig of water, sling my pack back on and take off again. I feel calmer now. The only people I have to avoid now are hikers.

I need to go home now and figure out the best timing for the final attack. I will need the weather, the work schedule, the right day of the week. How can my absence be less noticed while I'll be away? Is it possible? I'll need time to research all the explosives, buy the necessary items without a trace, build prototypes and test them in a remote area. I've got to talk to Farley about this - he's the pro. Should I? I need to bank on him being a solid ally. Maybe I'll do some more testing up on the mountain when I'm cutting wood. I'll keep the chainsaw running to mask the sound like last time but move higher up the mountain out of view. Will it be too loud still? How far will debris fly? Will I even find an explosive strong enough to wreak the kind of havoc I have in mind? Will the components be available in those amounts? How can I buy everything in bulk like that and still remain anonymous?

These kinds of questions build pressure in me. They kind of creep up my neck, coiling, rising, in through the back of my head, pressing, contracting, like the grip a python must feel and inflict. But it's me gripping me, the pressure predictable because I'm applying it. I'm in control, feeling some pain, but allowing it to continue, almost craving it, the pressure building. That pressure seems to add power, strengthen conviction. Where does that come from?

I come out into a large meadow opening as I gain elevation once again. I stop when I hear the sharp sound of a motor turning over coming from far below. I freeze and listen. Yes, it's got to be the SUV that was at the east trail head. I didn't hear them hiking down the trail. Guess I've been far enough away, but they must have passed by. Makes sense. That time of day. Great, now I can head back to the trail, which should be just south of my position. I continue along the ridge as it curves in a horseshoe upward to lead me back to the pass near a notch; I remember crossing early in the day. I know that if I follow it a little further along to the south, I will come across the main trail. I soon do.

The sun has set, and the residual light brings a calm to the boughs above as I negotiate the turns of the trail. My legs ache but feel automated as I once again gain speed, now dropping down the side of the pass, quickly closing the final gap to the west trail head where I'd come from this morning. The forest echoes the warmth of the day and breathes in the fresh new cool and calm of sunset. Birds chatter to one another reassuringly, adding calm and normality to the scene. I coast along the familiar switchbacks, one after the other, until the gravel road and parking lot appear below. It seems to be empty as I'd hoped it would. The truck that had been there, now gone. It must have been theirs, that couple I'd passed by earlier, in the morning.

Emily's car is a welcome sight as the light begins to dim further and my legs become unsteady. They've been aching, getting that rubbery feeling. I've had missteps, ankles buckling over, twisting, but not all the way, just enough to warn me that the next one could be the one that sends me toppling down the bank with a sprain if I'm not careful.

It's almost 8:30 pm by the time I finally pull the door open and settle into the driver's seat. The cushion feels good. I take a deep breath, let it out, settle, eyes closed a moment, exhale.

I start her up and turn the little Corolla around, feeling like I've accomplished something. I've pulled this part off. I've learned what I need to know. I've not been identified. I'm going home.

Before picking up much speed at all, I notice the aroma of antifreeze. I stop and cut the engine - damn it! Not now.

I jump out after pulling the hood release. I walk to the front and can see the trail of fluid on the ground and the flow dripping down steadily as I lift the hood. I prop it open and then lay down to poke my head under the radiator for a closer look at the leak. I spot the offending rubber hose and see that it's been gnawed all around. Other lines too have marks but they aren't yet leaking. "Little bastards!"

I know that porcupines, notorious for being attracted to rubber, have been busy snacking on my car while I've been hiking. I lift myself up, open the trunk and rustle through the loosemix within to see what Emily has stored in there. There is a garbage bag with plastic plant trays, some planter pots and two trowels. There are a couple of toy cars, some baking pans and a bag of bungees and tie down straps. I move it all to look underneath - no tools of any sort, no hardware. "Damn it". I slam the trunk. I open the passenger door to check the glove box and notice in the door pocket, a black roll behind some loose papers

- electrical tape! "Yes", I exhale with relief. That may do it.

I pull it out, grab my headlight from my back pack and dive back under the front of the car. I dry the hose with the bottom of my tee shirt then start wrapping the rubber line with tape, working my way from the intact part over the gnawed part, across the hole and beyond, then I double and triple back over the weakest part. The dripping stops, but will it hold when it's under pressure? I add a couple of more layers to be sure, pulling tension on the tape. I scan the other lines, tape up another that looks like it too could fail… looks like a fuel line. Jesus.

Satisfied, I roll out from under there, brush off the gravel and weeds stuck to my jeans and hop back into the driver's seat. I start her up again, then hop out again to double check the patch while the engine is running. It holds, but I know the coolant level in the rad is really low now, so I drive slowly up the road to the first creek, keep the car idling and open up the radiator to top it up from my water bottle. I have to refill and pour in three more liters before it's full, adding them slowly so as not to shock the hot motor with the ice-cold water.

Hoping it will hold, I drive off as the last light of day fades to dusk. I'm mulling over this situation as the bumpy road fades into the dust behind me - be prepared - think through the possibilities - if a porcupine can potentially spoil my plans, what more could I have in store? A chicken wire wrap around my car will solve any future porcupine woes, but what else? What other threats have I not thought of? How can I think of them all? Maybe this whole idea is crazy.

I pull out onto the road once again, tires spinning up the loose gravel, the pillow of dust rising low with the weight of the first condensation of dusk dampening all surfaces. I've got a couple of hours of driving time to bounce ideas around; must add all the new input to my consciousness, stir and sort, but at the same time, keep eyes from slipping closed. I glance in the rear-view mirror, at my own reflection. Marks streak my face, scratches and sweat stains. I glance over my clothes: torn and worn, stained with blood, but I'm intact, feeling accomplished, like a war hero after a successful mission or, maybe more aptly, like a Viking returning after a raid.

It's almost 10:30 pm by the time I'm home. Emily hears the car approach and walks out to greet me, hugging me tighter than usual. "Been worried Gabe," she whispers, lips grazing my neck, voice muffled, "It's late…wish you would have carried a phone."

"I know babe, sorry, so tired."

"Jesus Gabe, you're a mess…" her voice fades as she pulls back, eyes glancing over me. "The boys were asking for you too, been in bed for a long time but I doubt they're asleep." We walk in toward the house, my arm over her shoulder, "They wanted to see you first and tell you about the crazy jump they made with Kyle and Ricky today." She smiles.

"Uh huh, I'll see 'em in a minute. I'm fine Em. Just got to clean up a bit first", I say, as I relax on the bench inside to unlace my boots.

"I think Noah is getting an ear infection. she says, as she pulls a loaded plate covered in foil from the oven. "We'll see by tomorrow."

Alright, I'll pop up there and see 'em… in a minute." I settle into the couch, Emily beside me, a foaming beer wet with condensation in my hand, a plate of reheated, barbecued chicken and a slice of bread in my lap, the intoxicating aroma rising in steam over my face. A Suzanne Vega disc plays, strumming softly in the background. Salivating, I take a deep pull from the beer, then dive into the plate to appease my hunger. The weariness abates for a moment, replaced by an overwhelming gratitude. Emily turns to me.

"Had a look at my car," she says, "a bit of a mess. What did you do to it? Looks like it got caught up in a dust tunnel."

"Yeah, a few dusty miles and some potholes took a bit of a toll but she's fine except for the porcupine damage. Think I'll take close up shots of tooth mark incisions like they do on CSI, so that I can track that little bastard down later and link him to the crime scene through his dental records."

"What? What happened? Did he wreck my tires?"

"No; took out a rad line. Made it home. Wondered if I would. Good thing you had some electrical tape in there, honey," I say through a mouth full of chicken.

"Well, you'd better be sure my car is fit to drive. I'm off to town in the morning, Gavin's got a dentist appointment. Anyways, how did it go out there today?" she asks, her curious glance catching my eye. Her knees are tucked up on the couch, feet nestled under my thigh.

"It's on Em," I say, looking directly into her eyes, "I covered a lot of ground, like, totally energized, did some investigation, took lots of notes and photos. The site is a mess, an invasion by the aliens. Looks so out of place you know, like men on the moon."

I take a long drink from the frosty bottle of Face Plant Ale by my side, set it down and finish off the remnants of meat on a drumstick, gnawing it clean. "How can they do this Em?"

"I can't believe you made it all that way, through the pass, down the other side and back again… all in one day."

She too had hiked the pass more than once and knew the distances involved. She also knows that I can hike faster than most and that now more than ever, I'm driven, driven by some inner force. I think she understands my conviction. Our eyes meet in an uncertain glance; mine prying, trying to decide if she has any intent of impeding this trajectory of mine, but I can't discern the answer. "Yeah, I made pretty good time today… felt good, like I was taking the first step. it's empowering."

"You must be exhausted," she says, sliding her arm around my shoulder and laying her head against me.

"Yes, I'm feeling it. The legs are going to be burning tomorrow. Got a couple deliveries to make too, a chord to the Jantzen's and another one over to the Balfour side, but I'll be fine Em. Just feels good to be back, curled up here, sinking into the couch with you. Beats the hell out of swattin' mosquitoes under a bridge," I say, rearranging arms and pulling her face into mine, her gentle lips and lingering kiss like a whispered promise.

"Getting late," I say, rising a moment later, "I'm going to make sure the little gorillas are asleep."

Each step burns my aching legs as I head up the stairs. I pass the doorless opening where the third bedroom will be. There are only two finished bedrooms upstairs, a bath room in between. One day, when it's all done, Emily and I will have our own ensuite bathroom and the boys will each have their own room, but for now, they share one, Gavin on the upper bunk, Noah down below. The window in their room is propped open a foot or so by a book, and the cool spring breeze flows in, filling the cotton curtain, billowing it out. I stand by the door in the dark of the hallway, light off behind me, so as not to let them know I'm here. I could already hear their hushed voices before I reached the top of the stairs. I often sneak up on them in this way to overhear their conversations as they lie in bed and talk at night. It can be good entertainment, revealing. A couple of weeks ago I overheard Gavin saying: "And I won't even tell you about the submarine bear right now cause you're such a chicken, you won't be able to sleep, then you'll just tell Mom and Dad." God knows what other story he'd come up with before that. They catch me listening sometimes and try to surprise me or tackle me in fits of giggles, but usually they are too engaged in their own chatter to notice, like now. "… always turn over 'cause it bugs me on that side," Noah is telling his brother.

"What bugs you anyway, your stupid ear again? Want me to come up there and fix it for ya?"

"No. I've just got an ear-*egg*, "he says, through a stuffed-up nose, "nothin' you can do."

Gavin hesitates a moment before answering, "Oh, an ear egg eh? Yeah, I had one of those before… no big deal. I could come up there and crack it open if you want."

"Not an ear egg, an ear *egg*, "he says, "just hurts for a while, mom said," his voice still stuffy.

" Yeah, it hurts cause of the ear egg inside." Gavin tells him. Then he pauses for a moment, gathering ammo… "You just heard wrong cause you can't hear. An ear egg is when a tiny bird, probably one of those ones that lives up in the roof of the woodshed, comes and lays an egg in your ear while you are asleep at night. You don't really notice when you wake up the next day because it's so tiny and the bird has already flown out," he hesitates a moment, adding "and the egg is at body temperature so it's not very noticeable."

"Yeah right, like a bird can just get in and sit on your head," says Noah, hesitantly, on his back now, looking toward his brother's upper bunk, "… without waking you up."

"Yeah, it's true. See? The screen is off."

He motions toward the open window, "and those little birds just fly in, lookin' for a warm place to nest. They can sense body heat, like a bat."

Noah ponders the idea of his older brother and pokes his finger into the sore ear cautiously.

"…and you shouldn't ever touch it because if you break the shell, the thing will rot in there and then your whole head will stink; and anyway, it will only bother you a bit until the egg hatches, probably in just a couple of weeks."

"What? How could it even fit in there?" Noah says, pulling his finger out. "I don't feel anything. Mom didn't say there was an egg."

"Yeah, well she doesn't want to freak you out, but it's no big deal. One night when you are asleep, it will just hatch, and the little chick will just fly out and then the broken bits of shell will just turn into ear wax. I've had lots of 'em, doesn't even hurt."

Noah considers this for a minute. I can see him staring off into the dark, a hint of moonlight glancing off his eyes, his thoughts seeming to drift through the room. He's probably visualizing a stream of freshly hatched chicks emerging from his ear, flying around the room.

"I'll ask Dad in the morning." Noah mumbles dreamily as his eyes settle slowly, fading.

"If he's home."

They must know I'm back, that I'll always be back, that I'm here for them. Isn't that why I'm doing all this in first place?

I decide I'll wait to see them first thing in the morning. I think we are all too tired to visit right now. I head off down the hallway, shaking my head, smiling, considering the wild imagination of my elder son… an ear egg? It could serve him well one day, this imagination, but I'm not sure how well it serves his brother.

I do a cursory body wipe-down with a face cloth before I fall into bed, depleted, satisfied, no energy for a shower, grateful to be horizontal, yet restless, too tired to sleep. I listen to the muffled noises of Emily, straightening things up downstairs, the solace of routine sounds, a comforting backdrop, like a boat bouncing through waves, sending my thoughts off in all directions: Those signs I'd seen today suddenly flash across my mind's eye: Entry prohibited! Keep Out. …Bullshit! They can't stop me now. I've got momentum, knowledge. Aluminum powder, ammonium… can I do this alone? I will; I will, won't I? Watch me! Fuckers! Tannerite, machinery, noise, smoke, media. So much, too much to consider; can't stop now can I? The images whirl and spin, ebb and flow, create tension then calm.

I don't remember Emily undressing to join me, only the warmth of her body against mine, her soft breasts pressed against my back through the thin film of her nightie, lulling, my moment of longing soon suppressed by the dark veil of an unsettled sleep.

Thank you so much for the attention to detail and encouragement of Claire Matze, of Mendoza, Argentina, who did a pre-edit and to Vivian Hansen, of Calgary Alberta, who added thoughtful and thought provoking feedback throughout the final editing process. Thanks to family and friends and insightful readers, Gabriella, John, Hans and Cecilia.

And to John for rescuing my deleted digital book. Those were a few tension filled days followed by intense relief.